THE HEART OF
MATTER

Text copyright © 2012 Evan Currie
All rights reserved.

Printed in the United States of America.

Published by 47North
P.O. Box 400818
Las Vegas, NV 89140

ISBN-13: 9781612182353
ISBN-10: 1612182356

THE HEART OF MATTER

odyssey / one

(Being the Second Voyage of the NACS *Odyssey*)

EVAN CURRIE

47N⬤RTH

DEDICATION

To Wynn Currie, my mother, who never doubted that I
would eventually succeed in my writing endeavors. Without
her support, I would never have made it as far as I have.
Thanks, Wynn.

PART I:

Once More Unto the Black

▼

LIBERTY STATION

Lagrange Four, Earth Orbit

▲

►CAPT. ERIC STANTON Weston walked along the gently curving corridor that circled the exterior of the immensity of Space Station Liberty. He had to admit that the sensation of generated artificial gravity felt quite different to him after the time he'd spent on the *Odyssey*, both within the Sol System and without. The larger curve of the station's outer wall felt more natural, but after spending so much time on the smaller, faster moving habitats of the *Odyssey*, he found that he preferred the sensation that had once nearly made him nauseous. They'd seen so much out there that he'd occasionally caught himself thinking of Earth as somewhat provincial compared to the huge megacity he'd seen on Ranquil.

The alien world—or perhaps not so alien, he supposed—had been the indisputable highlight of their last mission. Eric only wished it had been more of an accomplishment of note, but considering the horror and destruction they had witnessed across three star systems, it didn't take much to qualify as a "high point."

Rather than a simple shakedown cruise to confirm the viability of the *Odyssey*'s transition drive and other experimental systems, they'd found themselves on a charge across the galaxy right through the very middle of a war that they probably had no business involving themselves in. Eric was fully aware that was certainly the opinion of more than a handful of his superiors. He'd seen too much death in his career, however, to ignore genocide when it was danced in front of his face, so he had no regrets. For all the action they'd seen, and sacrifices made, he was proud and confident of the fact that his crew had none, either.

Still, coming back now jarred his sensibilities, to be able to look out on space through horizontally mounted ports, unlike the few sections of the *Odyssey* that allowed such a personal view of the expanse. He followed the lines that adorned the floor, mapping out the various areas of the station, watching the rainbow idiot guides drop off as he climbed through the security zones into officer country.

He had an appointment with Admiral Gracen, presumably concerning the new orders for the *Odyssey*. He hoped that the orders weren't more of the same, since he'd spent the last three weeks after completion of repairs working the crew up to an invisible standard that no one appeared willing to tell him. It was time for the *Odyssey* to be under way again, long past time. He could feel his crew getting antsy, sitting still in a ship that was the fastest thing ever built by man. Steph was checking in almost constantly to see if they had their orders yet, and Eric had been forced to order several of his junior officers to relax. They'd seen the universe, and now they all wanted more.

Whether that would happen, given his current status of "mixed" esteem within the military and political realities of the North American Confederation (NAC), he didn't know. He and much of the *Odyssey* crew, unfortunately, were currently what one might call "odd ducks." They were too valuable, both politically and experience-wise, to be tossed away. However, there was a growing movement within the political and military communities that harbored ill will toward them for bringing the Earth, at least marginally, into a larger universe that appeared quite willing to kill them all. Not only did they now have to deal with non-Terran humans, the Colonials, but also voracious and warlike aliens. Well, he supposed that if you were going to explore the universe, then that was the chance you took.

"Captain!"

Eric paused, glancing back, and saw a young man, Lt. Walter Daniels, approaching from his six. He held his step until the young man had caught up to him, then nodded politely.

"Lieutenant."

"Sir." The lieutenant came to a halt and saluted. "Commander Roberts sends his regards and wanted me to give you this, sir."

Eric returned the salute, then accepted the memory chip from the young man, wondering why Roberts had sent him on a gopher job. "Thank you, Lieutenant."

"Not a problem, sir," Daniels responded. "I was heading to the station lounge, anyway."

Eric smiled slightly, nodding. That explained why Daniels had been tapped for gopher duty—it gave the young man another excuse to visit with a certain young ensign assigned to the Liberty Communications Center. Eric supposed he didn't blame him; he'd done more for less in his day, and he was sure that his own commanding officers had given him a little latitude more than once. "Very good, then. As you were, Lieutenant."

"Thank you, sir."

Eric watched him leave for a moment, then pocketed the chip and turned and continued on his way. He still had an admiral to meet, after all.

▶▶▶

Amanda Gracen looked up as Weston was shown into the office, nodding curtly to her secretary. As the naval attaché retreated from the room, she eyed him for a moment before gesturing to a chair across from her. "Take a seat, Captain."

Eric stepped forward and slid into the comfortable chair that was situated across from the admiral. "Admiral."

Gracen looked down at the files displayed beneath the hard plastic surface of her desk, idly flipping through them with economical flickers of her fingers. Weston wondered what she was waiting for, or if she just didn't want him to feel comfortable. It was a tactic he'd used himself more than once when he wanted to stress a point with a subordinate, mostly because it was damnedably effective, even if you knew what was going on. After a moment, she looked up again, then leaned back in her high-backed chair. "Well, Captain, do you have a status report on your ship?"

Eric stiffened, just slightly, then nodded. "Aye, ma'am. The *Odyssey* is fully repaired, and her crew is fully integrated and as good a group of people as I've had the honor to serve with. We're ready for orders, Admiral."

A glint of something floated in the eyes of the admiral, but Eric couldn't quite identify it. Amusement, perhaps, but he just couldn't be sure. She nodded at his words, then flicked her finger along the display and opened another file. Eric wished he could tell what she was looking at, but the display in the admiral's desk was designed to be read from the admiral's position only.

"Have you followed the developments with the ambassador's dealings?" she asked after a moment.

The "ambassador," Elder Corusc, had been charged by his people with negotiating a treaty with Earth in the aftermath of the fierce battle the *Odyssey* had waged in their home system against the "Drasin," so named by the Colonials. The technology of the two human cultures had diverged heavily in direction, leaving the *Odyssey* with an advantage in weapons sophistication, though woefully underpowered in the area of pure brute force.

He had spent a great many nights since then imagining what the Earth technology base could do with all that pure energy. Many of the limitations the *Odyssey* suffered from were due largely to a lack of power, as opposed to a lack of technology.

Weston shook his head in response to the question, though; he hadn't had time with the make-work projects the *Odyssey* had been forced to endure. "I'm afraid not, ma'am. I've been a little busy."

The narrow smile on the admiral's face told Eric that she knew precisely what he had been busy doing, but that was another matter.

"Pity, you might have found it interesting," was all she said on the subject.

"I'm sure that I would have," Eric replied, keeping his tone neutral.

"Unfortunately," she went on, "much of the technology won't be of any use to us for several years at least..." She let her words drop off, then abruptly started speaking again. "Including, I'm afraid, their power systems."

Eric stiffened almost at once. That was the last thing he wanted to hear. "Pardon me, ma'am?"

"The Colonials—sorry, the Priminae, as they apparently call themselves," Gracen said, "use a power system entirely different from ours, and I'm afraid that we haven't figured out a way to generate electricity with it just yet. Not with any real efficiency, at least."

Eric grimaced. He should have thought of that, he supposed.

"We have some designers working on entirely new weapon and ship designs, but for the immediate future, we won't be tapping that particular resource," she told him.

Eric sighed and said, "Understood."

"Still, that's not to say that no good came of it." The admiral half smiled. "The medical technology, while still not compatible with our own systems, doesn't really have to be. We've already begun integrating a great many of the techniques into our own medical center here on *Liberty*, and so far, the results are promising."

Eric nodded absently, still in the back of his mind mourning the loss of all that power. It was only then that something about the conversation made him frown.

"Pardon, Admiral," he said after a moment's thought, "but have we reached an agreement with the Colonials' elder?"

Admiral Gracen smiled again, this time a little wider. "Yes, we have."

Eric nodded again, his mind working hard now. He knew that the elder, Corusc, had been a little frustrated with the pace of Earth-born politics, but by the same token, the Colonials all seemed to be fatalists in one way or another—or rather, most of them were.

He'd met a couple that were the same sort of struggle-unto-the-death types that Eric generally associated with human beings, but those were both military, more or less. Corusc was certainly a great deal more patient than he would have been, taking over three months from their arrival in the Sol System to patiently bounce from one state dinner to another in the hopes of recruiting some help, practically any help, for his people against the Drasin.

Three months was a long time in any war, but even more so in the type of genocidal struggle that the Colonials faced. So Eric understood the elder's frustrations quite easily.

He looked back at the admiral. "What kind of agreement?"

"We'll supply advisors for their ground forces in the form of Green Beret detachments," Gracen replied, "as well as providing them with the technical specifications on both our adaptive armor and laser systems. We won't be giving them either the technical specifications on the transition drive system, nor will we give away the coordinates of the Sol System."

Eric nodded, agreeing with both points.

The transition drive was certainly the ace in the hole for the Terran forces. It was a rather nerve-racking system that allowed effectively instantaneous travel across distances of up to thirty light-years. Even more if they could generate enough power to do it.

Likewise, the exact stellar location of the Sol System wasn't something to be traded away at any price in the current situation. Eric wasn't certain if the enemy had any way to learn it from the Colonials, but it was far, far better to remain under the radar, as it were. At least until a home fleet and system-wide defense system could be put into place.

However, in order to carry out even this agreement, it would mean sending the *Odyssey* on another mission. Eric's eyes narrowed as he considered that. Not that he was opposed to another mission, and he was reasonably confident that his crew would welcome it; however, at the moment, the *Odyssey* was the single-largest accumulation of firepower in the Sol System.

"When will we be returning to Ranquil, then?" he asked, as casually as he could.

"In two weeks," she replied. "Your crew will have that time for leave."

"Yes, ma'am, they'll appreciate that," Eric replied, but he was still thinking about local defenses. "Admiral...without the Odyssey stationed here, if the Drasin should arrive..."

"That's unlikely to happen, unless they managed to back-track your transition bursts," Gracen replied. "But if it does, we should be adequately prepared."

Eric didn't say anything, not because he agreed, but because he wasn't so sure.

Gracen went on. "The *Normandy* and the *Enterprise* are well under construction by our own crews, as you know, and they'll be approaching minimal operational status in the next two weeks, though they'll need another month to be completed. Additionally, the Soviet Alliance has begun construction on the *Gagarin*. She's a light destroyer the Soviets had originally planned to use as a test bed for some new ideas of theirs, as well as a matter of showing their 'flag' in the new space race."

The Soviet Alliance was still relatively weak, coming out of the Block War with a nasty pounding to their credit from the Chinese forces that invaded from the south. They'd done well enough, considering that their military had been badly outmatched by the newer and more modern Block forces during the war.

Ironically, though, it had done them a lot of good on the economic side of things. Since the end of the twentieth century, they'd been struggling to find their footing in a world that was jumping ahead by leaps and bounds and leaving them far behind. The war had forced the entire loose-knit agglomeration of nations to face a common enemy on even ground and to pour a lot of effort into a common goal.

Since the end of the Block War, the alliance had been making great strides in stepping back into the field of Premier powers on Earth, and the *Gagarin* would be an important prestige point to them.

"The Block, of course," Gracen said with a mild twist to her lip, "has the *Mao Tse Tung* under construction in addition to their in-system freighters and armed shuttles. So I believe that we're covered."

Eric supposed that was true enough, even though the *Mao* wouldn't have nearly the defenses it needed to withstand a strike from a Drasin laser. If they could outmaneuver it, though, they should have at least some measure of weapons parity, if you threw in the impact of existing orbital defenses. He didn't have the slightest clue what the *Gagarin* would boast in terms of defensive and offensive power, however.

Even so, a small handful of ships just didn't sit well with him as the main line of defense for the NAC and the planet as a whole. They needed fleets, and they needed energy systems to power them to parity with the Drasin, at least. A power parity, with the NAC's sophistication advantage, would let him sleep a lot better at night.

Of course, some basic intel on the enemy wouldn't hurt, either.

"Very well, Admiral," Eric said aloud, "I'll inform my crew and begin preparations."

Gracen nodded. "I hope you'll ensure that your own name appears on the leave list as well, Captain."

"Yes, ma'am," Eric replied, though he'd not really thought about it. Commanding his ship was something he rather enjoyed doing—when they weren't floating in geosync orbit over Washington, at least.

"Good. Dismissed."

▼

TEMPORARY COLONIAL EMBASSY

Washington, DC
North American Confederation

▲

▶ THE MAN KNOWN as Elder Corusc to the humans of Earth was both elated and frustrated as he looked out over the provincial city he and his people had been housed in.

This Washington place is interesting. Both so much simpler than a Priminae housing, but there is an age here, a feeling of history that I've only experienced in Mons Systema itself.

Comparing a city as seemingly small as this one to Mons Systema seemed downright absurd at first glance, but there was something about the atmosphere that spoke to him. For a place with only a few centuries' history, he found himself admiring the character.

Though, if they didn't fix the traffic issues, he wouldn't wonder if the whole place simply exploded one day. It was utterly inexcusable for a place of such limited population to be so crammed full with people only during certain times of the day.

He had been utterly unable to believe how few people actually lived in the city when it had been told to him during his first week on this world. Mons Systema held more than fifty times the number in a space not much more than twice the footprint, and one could quite easily go one's entire life without seeing another soul, if you were so antisocial as to desire it.

Washington was a curious mix of a planned environment, with a rather impressive artistic flair, and the organic growth one normally only saw in truly ancient ruins among the colonies. As if someone planned for only so many people and never took into account what might happen if more chose to move in.

Corusc sighed, setting down his drink as he considered the situation beyond the skies of this one small world.

They now had an agreement of sorts with the people here, one that would provide them with weapons and defensive technologies to help defend Ranquil and the other worlds that still existed within the colonies. Or concepts, if not actual technologies, he supposed. There was a bizarre nature to the technology of this "Earth," he had learned since arriving.

They'd tread a disparate path than the Priminae, developed technology and tricks that had never been conceived within the colonies, yet most of it was absurdly antiquated. They still split and fused the atom to generate power, a marginal source of power at best when applied to human-scale endeavors. Certainly, fusing atomic bonds was tremendously impressive at a stellar scale, but you simply couldn't pack much value into something that fit safely on a planet, to say nothing of a ship.

Still, they did more with what they had than he would have dreamed possible, and Corusc was well aware that his people needed precisely that.

He looked up to the skies, knowing that soon it would be time to return home.

The Priminae elder just hoped beyond hope that there was still a home left to return to.

▶▶▶

As Comdr. Stephen Michaels waited for Ithan Milla Chans in the office supplied for the elder and his two aides, he acknowledged it was nice enough. But it didn't fit how he had come to view Milla's people. Of course, a lot of his knowledge of them was largely secondhand, so he probably was at least as inaccurate as the office. He did know, though, that Milla, and to a lesser extent, the elder, had expressed surprise at how unplanned Washington, DC, seemed; their cities were planned down to the last detail. They had to be.

He wondered if the rumors were true, that they were shipping out again shortly. He hoped so, though he knew that if they were, then they'd probably be back in the fire before long. Milla's people were in a bad way, but Stephen had found that he liked the ones he'd met, and he didn't enjoy seeing people he liked get hurt.

The way he saw it, the only way they'd be shipping out was if the brass and the politicians had come to an agreement with the elder. He hoped that was the case.

"Stephen?"

Stephen shook his head clear of the random thoughts and smiled when Milla appeared from the doors that led to the back offices, and the living areas within. "Good afternoon, Ithan Chans."

She smiled, probably at his formality, given that they'd stopped using titles a long time ago in a star system fairly far away. But she also looked a little puzzled. "Why are you here?"

"Well, I told you that when I got leave I'd show you the city if you wanted," he replied, then shrugged. "I got leave."

▼

NACS ODYSSEY

Geosync Orbit, Earth

▲

▶ "WHOA! WHOA! WHOA!" S.Sgt. Max Greene yelled, waving his arms at the trundling loader that was hauling a massive crate into the maw of the *Odyssey*'s hold. "Hold it right there!"

The automated loader immediately rumbled to a halt, its lights still flashing as Greene looked up at the massive packing crate, then glared at the door the loader had been about to attempt to move it through.

"Awright, who screwed the pooch on the packing dimensions!" he demanded after eyeballing the offending material. "This ain't gonna fit in the fucking armory room!"

Same old Greene, Major Brinks thought, watching the scene play out. *Energetic and observant, and just slightly salty.* He walked over and said, "What's going on, Sergeant?"

Greene glanced over and stiffened. "Sir, some jackass must have slapped the wrong sticker on this sucker. The loader just tried to put it in the armory…And no way is it supposed to be in here."

Brinks eyed the crate curiously, then plucked a radio frequency identification (RFID) reader from the sergeant's hand and queried the crate.

"I already checked that, sir. It just says—"

"Powered Armor, EXO-Twelve." Brinks frowned.

"Yeah, that," Greene replied. "But look at the number of units."

Brinks glanced down, and his eyebrow went up. "One unit? In *that*?"

"Like I said, Major, someone screwed the pooch when they riffed this puppy." Greene shook his head. "We'll have to recheck the entire shipment now."

"That won't be necessary, Sergeant."

Brinks and Greene both turned to see a man with lieutenant's bars clomping over in their direction, looking distinctly uncomfortable in his Magboots.

"What do you know about this, Lieutenant?" Brinks frowned as he eyed the young man. The kid was wearing the dark-green uniform that identified him as a member of the ship's assault company, but he didn't recognize him.

"Crowley, sir," the lieutenant, who couldn't have been more than twenty years old, replied with an eager-puppy look on his face. "Jackson Crowley, Major."

"Lieutenant Crowley." Brinks nodded, then repeated his question. "What do you know about this?"

"This is a power suit, just like it says, Major," Jackson said with a grin.

"Bullshit," Greene snorted.

Brinks spared the sergeant a glare, then turned back to Crowley. "Lieutenant, that crate could pack twelve power suits."

The young man grinned with the air of a kid showing off his favorite toy. "Oh, I guess they haven't sent you the specs yet, sir…You're gonna love this…"

He walked over to the crate, then addressed the loader. "Lower the crate here, and pop the latches, please."

Brinks heard Greene snort again and knew that the sergeant found it amusing whenever anyone was polite to a machine, but ignored the man. He was curious to see what the hell was going on here.

The loader set the crate down, the magnetic clamps locking it down to the floor with a solid thump, then took a step back and pivoted its grasping forks to slide them into the latches built into the top of the crate. A simple twist and pull was all it took to open them, and Lieutenant Crowley was there to catch the front of the crate as it floated free. He swung it down, stepping out of its way, and let it attach itself to the floor on its own clamps.

Brinks stepped forward to look inside, Greene beside him.

"Shit on a stick," Greene muttered.

Inside was about the largest "power suit" Brinks had ever seen, and he'd seen pretty much everything they issued and then some. The "armor" was about twelve feet tall, built like the proverbial brick house, and looked like something out of a bad sci-fi flick.

"Lieutenant, I'm not in the mood for jokes," Brinks growled in annoyance.

He'd seen lots of similar units, though most were smaller than this, and had even tested a few in the past. They'd all failed miserably to pass minimum battlefield standards because they were too clumsy to be of serious use, which was why the smaller armored suits were used.

"No joke, Major," Jackson said, looking puzzled.

"Lieutenant, I know a little something about armor. And that will fall flat on its face the first firefight it gets in," Brinks said with certainty.

"Sir, no, sir," Jackson insisted, shaking his head. "It's based on the NICS system. Trust me, Major, it's battlefield ready."

"NICS?" Greene muttered. "What the hell is NICS?"

"Sorry, Sergeant," Crowley said. "That's still classified—"

"Son, tell us what the hell it is," Brinks growled in annoyance.

The lieutenant swallowed, then nodded. "Yes, sir. NICS stands for Neural Induction Command System. It's the same stuff they use in the Archangels and—"

"Bloody hell!" Greene exploded. "You want us to stick fuckin' needles in our goddamned necks? Are you out of your fucking mind? Do we look like those lunatics up on—"

"Sergeant." Brinks cut him off. He liked Greene, but the man had to know there were limits.

"But, *damn*, Major!"

"That's enough," Brinks told him, then eyed the suit. "We don't have anyone checked out on that system."

"You do now, sir." Crowley patted the crate. "This here is my baby. So the sarge there doesn't have to worry about needles jammed in his neck."

Brinks looked at the lieutenant, then RFIDed the man's dog tags with the reader still in his hand. A short perusal was all he needed to tell what he wanted to know. "Lieutenant, have you seen any action at all?"

"Well...No, sir. I enlisted after the war," Crowley admitted. "But I'm fully trained and certified..."

"Why didn't they just give us a couple tanks?" Greene asked. "We don't need this shit."

"Tanks are too high maintenance," Crowley responded instantly.

"And that thing ain't?"

"No, Sergeant, it isn't," Crowley replied evenly. "Most of the base technologies in this baby predate tanks by a couple thousand years. Simple hydraulics. Treat it right, it'll run a hundred years without fault. And those are the only major moving parts…The computer is top of the line, of course, and heavily shielded…"

"Yeah, right," Greene muttered, eyeing the brute and shaking his head. "Battlefield don't treat nothing right, kid."

Brinks eyed the unit with a weary eye, then shook his head. "It's your coffin, Crowley. Can you get that thing out of the crate and…Oh, hell, Sarge, find him a place to hide this thing, will ya?"

"Too right," Greene muttered. "Half the guys around here will laugh their asses off at this."

They might, Brinks thought wryly, *but they might laugh at you, too. Not to your face, of course.*

LIBERTY STATION

Lagrange Four, Earth Orbit

▶ERIC WESTON KEYED open the door to the conference room where he knew Comdr. Jason Alvarez Roberts had been sitting in on an informal discussion concerning military nomenclature in the modern era. The room itself was huge, its centerpiece a single-piece table that stretched over twenty feet from end to end. At the far end Eric saw, sitting alone, the commander.

"Commander."

Roberts looked up, nodding curtly. "Captain. Thanks for coming."

"Something wrong?" Weston tried not to appear too amused, but he had a good idea just what was bothering the commander. He had, of course, been invited to participate, but unlike Roberts, he had enough seniority and other business on his plate to successfully refuse.

The normally stern man shrugged and actually smiled a little ruefully. "Not really, sir. I just needed to talk with someone who wasn't clinically insane."

Eric chuckled softly, pulling a chair out and sitting down across from the well-built black man. "What's the problem?"

"You ever been cooped up in a room with thirty-five representatives of different military branches, all of them arguing that their branch should be the one whose name and traditions form the foundation of the new service branch?" Roberts asked disgustedly.

"Can't say that I have." Eric grinned. "And, if I do say so myself, better you than me."

"Har har," Roberts said sourly. "You know, it's insane. It's not supposed to be this complicated to just pick a damned *name* for a service branch."

"Can't be that bad…" Weston suggested, his smirk clearly making a liar of him even as he spoke.

"Captain, the Marines are arguing tradition; they want the shipboard troops to be named 'marines,' of course."

"Of course." Eric Weston, former Marine, smiled slightly.

"Well, the main army representative is arguing that spaceships have nothing to do with anything 'marine' and the tradition is null and void," Roberts replied. "His committee, however, is currently stymied by a two-way tie between 'soldiers' and 'troopers.' To be honest, that's probably the sanest of them, too."

"Oh?" Eric asked, still smiling as he leaned back.

"Yeah, there was one colonel in their group that wanted shipboard contingents named 'rangers,'" Roberts replied with a hint of disgust.

Eric raised an eyebrow. He happened to know that Roberts was a former US Ranger, so he found that reaction somewhat curious. "You disagree?"

"Me and whoever doctored that idiot's food," Roberts replied testily, then gave Eric a grim smile. "He came down with a mild case of food poisoning on the day he was to present his argument."

Eric blinked, frowning in confusion. "And you think some-one did it on purpose? Why?"

"Why? Because no self-respecting soldier who wears a tan beret wants to be known as a freaking 'space ranger,' thank you very much," Roberts growled.

Eric couldn't help it. It started with a snicker, but quickly grew into full, powerful laughs.

Commander Roberts waited, more or less patiently, as his commanding officer laughed at his expense, fingers tapping on the hard composite surface of the desk. When Eric had gotten himself back under control, Roberts just gave his cap-tain a cool look. "Are you done yet?"

"Yeah, I think so," Eric replied, snickering a couple more times. "But I have to say that I see your point."

"Thanks ever so much," Roberts told him dryly. "I don't suppose that the rest of the service is having these problems?"

Eric shrugged. "To some degree or another, of course. The Navy and the Air Force went head-to-head on a lot of things when they were ironing out the command structure of the *Odyssey*. For the most part, though, the Navy took the argu-ments on the simple fact that their procedures were easier to adapt."

Roberts nodded, but Eric had the sense that he'd heard some of that before, though probably had missed out on the details.

"So what we got was a bit of a hash, but not so much of what you seem to be dealing with," Eric admitted.

"Thankfully. Or we'd never have survived our first mis-sion," Roberts replied dryly.

Eric shrugged. "Maybe. But don't sweat the details is my advice, Commander. Things that don't work out, we'll hammer into place as we go along. We've got time to work out our traditions ourselves."

Roberts nodded. "I suppose. It's just rather frustrating that we can't even seem to get past the name." Eric hoped for Roberts's sake that they could get past it for now—there were a lot more important things coming down the pipe.

"That'll be the worst of it," Eric said. "Once you get past that, it'll just be the minor details of who obeys who to deal with."

Roberts glared at the smirk on his captain's face, but declined to comment. Instead, he just sighed and nodded. "I hope that's all I have to deal with, then. Thanks for coming by, Captain."

Eric smiled, this time a little less in amusement and more in tolerance. "Not a problem, Commander. I'm sure that you'll get it all figured out sooner or later."

Roberts nodded, standing up as Eric did likewise. "I know. It's just going to drive me to drinking in the meanwhile." Eric believed it already had.

He couldn't resist. "Buck up, Space Ranger," he said, "you'll do fine."

"Good day, sir," Roberts replied through gritted teeth.

As Eric was walking out, he received a signal over his induction set and took a moment to check his messages. A note from the admiral was waiting for his attention, requesting that he take a meeting with someone shortly. Without a name of whom he was supposed to meet, Weston was hardly pleased, but he wasn't going to turn down an admiral, either. He accepted the meeting and left Roberts to his own personal hell. The Lord knew, Eric had resided there more than once in the past, so now it was someone else's turn.

▼

WASHINGTON, DC

▲

▶ "HAVE YOU BEEN out much since you arrived?" Stephen Michaels asked conversationally as he and Milla Chans walked down the crowded street.

"No. Only very rarely," she replied, her own musical language sounding odd as the English echo sounded through the induction set he wore on his jaw. "At first, there was much security, and then there was even more things to do."

Stephen nodded, deftly avoiding bumping into a man who was talking on a civilian comm with video capabilities. The man didn't even notice the two of them as Stephen allowed the man to walk right through.

Milla's eyes followed him for a moment, but Stephen just shrugged.

"Some boys shouldn't have some toys," Stephen said in mild irritation. "If I zoned out like that in my fighter, I'd have been dead years ago."

He knew Milla didn't really understand the meaning behind the words, but found it endearing that she imitated his shrug as they continued walking. "This is a very...*busy* city."

Stephen smiled, noting the hesitance in her words. "It's pretty small compared to your cities, I know. But we like it—some of us, anyway."

"It seems to have so many people, but I was told that there are only a few million?"

"Yeah, something like that." Stephen shrugged, then frowned slightly. "I'm not really certain how many though—course, DC's not my hometown."

"Where are you from, then?" Milla asked.

"Small town down in West Virginia," Stephen replied with a slight smile. "Haven't been back there in…Well, I think it's been over a decade now."

The last time he'd been home, the town was on its last legs, most of the wartime income from the labs that built the Archangels had dried up, and what had been a bit of a boomtown for a few years was reduced to an almost ghostlike atmosphere. People still lived there, of course, a few like his own family who had been there for generations and likely would be there for generations more, but so many buildings and homes had been abandoned and shuttered that it felt empty all the same.

"You do not go home?" Milla's curiosity turned to puzzlement.

"Me and the folks don't get along much," he told her with a shrug. "And I've been pretty busy as well, so…"

"Ah," she replied in a tone that made it clear that she didn't understand but wasn't going to push.

Stephen "Stephanos" Michaels just smiled softly for a moment, then pointed out the Washington Monument in the distance and guided his charge through the throng of people toward it.

▼

NACS ODYSSEY

Earth Orbit

▲

▶CHIEF PETTY OFFICER Rachel Corrin snorted as she watched the next shipment of equipment destined for the *Odyssey*'s stores come trundling off the shuttle at the behest of one of the automated loaders. Whoever was signing off on this mission wasn't taking any chances with the stores. Where the *Odyssey* had left on her maiden voyage with a heavy inclination toward exploration, this time she was definitely packing heat.

She RFIDed the crate with her reader, identifying the package as yet another preloaded high-velocity missile (HVM) magazine, and made certain that the loader had scanned the right information. That done, she just stepped aside as the trundling loader stomped off across the deck toward the ship's magazines with its current payload.

It could be worse, she supposed. The fleet could use nukes or something equally insane.

The HVMs were lethal, certainly, but they packed all their killing power in pure kinetic energy, so they were as safe to store as anything else on board and a damn sight safer than some. She was on her way to RFID the rest of the cargo to make sure that it all matched her manifest when a call from across the zero-gravity deck turned her around.

"Chief!"

Corrin looked over her shoulder, frowning when she recognized one of her petty officers waving her over. "What's going on, Jeffrey?"

"Loader here don't know where to store these things." He pointed to a stack of crates a previous shuttle had offloaded.

Corrin grimaced, shaking her head. *This shit is ridiculous. I like that they're sending us all this stuff, but I'd like it better if they'd tag it with the right transmitters.*

"What's in it?" she asked, walking over.

"Looks like more HVMs," the petty officer replied. "But the staging numbers are all wrong, and I can't find them on the manifest."

"Great." Corrin sighed. "All right, we'll have to pop the case and eyeball the contents."

The petty officer nodded and ordered the loader to back off and do just that. When the big machine popped the seals on the can, Corrin stepped up and yanked the sides down.

"Those aren't HVMs," the petty officer said simply as they stared.

"No shit," Corrin replied, sighing. "Hang on, I'll put a call in to the duty officer. Maybe they've got the manifest code for these things up on the bridge."

It wasn't supposed to work that way, she knew, but mistakes happened even with the "miraculous" inventory management system and the most advanced computer networks.

"Bridge? This is Chief Corrin. I need a data check on an inventory serial," she said into her induction piece. "That's right. Just came aboard a couple hours ago. Serial number

alpha-niner-dash-twelve-four-bravo-sixteen-three-two-niner…
That's right…I'll hold."

She looked over the crate of munitions idly as she waited
for the check to come back, eyeing the slim rocket-shaped
items with only mild curiosity. "You know, PO, these look like
they might be for the Archangels."

The petty officer glanced at the weapons for a moment,
then scratched his head. "Well, they're sure in the wrong
place, if that's the case."

"No shit," Corrin snorted, then stiffened as the bridge
contacted her. "Yes, I'm here, Bridge."

She nodded, then shook her head. "That's fine, we'll
stock them aside until someone figures out what they're
for. You might want to check with the Archangels and see
if they're missing a shipment. These things might be for
them."

With that, she signed off and shook her head. "What a
cock-up. We've got shit being delivered here that even the
bridge don't recognize."

"What do we do with it?" the petty officer asked, eyeing
the twenty crates sitting there.

"Standard procedure," Corrin replied, a little harshly.
"Seal this one back up, and grab a couple Marines to stand
guard on the shit until we find out what it's for. If we don't get
an answer back before the last shuttle goes out, we ship it right
back to the brass and let them figure it out."

"Right."

Corrin eyed the munitions until the petty officer sealed
them back up, then went back to her job.

▶▶▶

Topside, in officer country, Ensign Lamont was stalking through the knee-knockers and door locks with her tablet in one hand and a computer's location report in the front of her mind. Her prey wasn't carrying his induction unit, and so she had to get ahold of her man face-to-face. Up ahead of her, she heard a familiar voice calling out and quickened her pace to catch up.

"Hey, Lieutenant, how come you're still on board?"

As she passed through a lock, she saw Lt. James Amherst pause in midstep as he finished throwing on his flight jacket and glanced around to the speaker. When he saw Chief Sittler, the Archangels' crew chief, approaching with a friendly smile, he returned it easily. "Just getting ready to take off. You?"

"I'm on duty until we finish loading for the mission," Sittler replied with a smile. "I'll be Earth-side in a couple days."

Amherst nodded. "Glad to hear it. You guys need the break."

Sittler laughed. "We do OK."

"Better you than me," Amherst replied, pulling the zipper up on his jacket, though it wasn't cold. He was about to say something more when Ensign Lamont made herself known.

"Chief Sittler, I've been looking for you," she said, sounding a little put off.

"Sorry, ma'am," the chief replied, coming a little straighter. "I was about to take a shower and hit the sack, so I tossed my induction set a while ago. What's wrong?"

"We've got a shipment on the parking deck that looks like it might be one of yours, but we can't identify it," she said, relaxing slightly, and handed him a data plaque.

"I can see that you're all busy, so I'm off." Amherst grinned, turning around and heading for the door while

Sittler frowned at the information. The chief never noticed him leave.

"I don't recognize these numbers, ma'am. Hang on a second while I check our manifest." Sittler sighed, grabbing another plaque from his thigh pouch and punching up another set of numbers.

"No...No, it's not...Hang on..."

"What is it, Chief?" Lamont frowned.

"I've got a blacklisted number here," Sittler told her. "Could be your mystery package. With all the new work and gear we've been getting, some of the clearances haven't passed through the computers yet. I'll just send a request—damn it." He sighed, shaking his head. "I'll have to get back to you on this, ma'am."

"I'm sorry to mess up your sack time, Chief," Lamont said, actually sounding sorry. "But you've only got two hours; then we ship those crates back where they came from."

"Got it, ma'am." Sittler nodded. "I'll figure it out."

"Very good, Chief. Carry on."

▼

LIBERTY STATION

Lagrange Four, Earth Orbit

▲

▶ ERIC ARRIVED IN the private conference room early, more than slightly curious about the nature of the meeting he'd been called to. The admiral hadn't had much more information than the location and the order for him to "be there."

After a few minutes, a nondescript man walked up. "Captain," the man said evenly as he sat across from Eric, "thank you for seeing me on such short notice."

"Did I have a choice, Mister…?"

"Call me Gordon, Captain." The man smiled. He could afford to smile, Weston supposed, as he was clearly with some ABC agency or another.

"Gordon, then," Eric replied evenly. "Now, I don't suppose we could get to whatever matter brings us here?"

"Certainly, Captain," the man replied, drawing a data plaque from his case and thumbing it on. "I've actually been meaning to have this conversation for some time; however, it always got put off. Since you'll be shipping out soon, I opened up some room in my schedule."

"I'm pleased for you," Eric said dryly. "However, that doesn't tell me much."

The man smiled slightly. "How much do you know about the Priminae?"

Eric blinked, taking a moment to process the term, then shrugged. "Apparently not enough to use that term for them."

The man smiled again. "Well, it's the closest we can translate what they call themselves. I suppose it doesn't have the ring of 'Colonials,' but it doesn't have the latent meaning, either."

"I suppose."

"We want more information about their central 'computer,' Captain."

Eric raised an eyebrow. "Then ask them."

"We have. A lot." Gordon smiled again, reminding Eric of a particularly sleazy shark.

Eric didn't.

Gordon cleared his throat. "Well...To be frank, we don't know if they're holding out on us or if the translations are simply missing something. In either case, we want someone to eyeball their computer and, if possible, figure out exactly how it fits into their society."

"Pardon?" Eric frowned.

"Captain, there are some indications from our conversations with Ambassador Corusc that the Priminae have an established technocracy," Gordon said, then smiled apologetically. "That is, we think that their central computer might be a little more than a repository of knowledge."

"I'm aware of the meaning of the word," Eric replied, thinking back to his conversations with Rael Tanner.

It was possible that there was some truth to the statement, he realized, though he wasn't certain what difference it made. In any case, what process a people used to rule themselves didn't really matter so much as how well they did so. Still, he had to admit that the central computer intrigued him.

"What we'd like to know is exactly how much influence this computer has and what are its capabilities."

"Influence?" Eric asked with a confused frown. "It's a computer—what influence could it have?"

"Quite a lot, actually. However, that's another issue. The fact is that we're really not certain that it is a computer. The refined translations aren't giving us much of a confidence level in this case, I'm afraid."

"What difference does it make?"

"Really, Captain, I'm surprised at you," Gordon replied, actually looking surprised. "Knowing how a potential ally is ruled is vital information. It goes to predicting how they'll react in given situations and can be of vital importance to our embassy people."

Eric blinked. "What embassy people?"

"Weren't you informed?"

"Informed of what?" he asked, beginning to become exasperated.

"Why, we're sending an embassy staff with you, of course."

▶▶▶

Eric took a seat in the comfortable lounge, trying to forget his meeting with Gordon while he waited for the next shuttle Earth-side. The view from the lounge was impressive, almost as good as what he routinely saw from the *Odyssey*. Outside Station Liberty, the lounge he had chosen looked almost directly on the nearly complete NACS *Enterprise*. That sight took his mind off of Gordon—quickly.

It was going to be a big ship, he could see, eyeing the changes that had been made from the original Odysseus Class plans. Some of those changes were only noticeable to his highly trained eye, but others would leap out at anyone.

He felt an almost sad pang as he noted that the *Odyssey* was going to be the only ship of her class to actually be built. The *Enterprise* was similar, of course, but enough changes had been made from the lessons learned during the *Odyssey*'s construction that the ship was a class of its own.

Her habitation drums were larger, for one, which was supposed to reduce the nausea one had to endure on occasion when shifting from one section to another in the *Odyssey*. The large rear "command tower" was gone, having been scrapped from the plans when the *Odyssey*'s power plant proved to be inadequate to the task of powering those sections with artificial gravity.

The *Enterprise* flight decks were three tiered as well, which Eric thought was mildly interesting, but that was normal since the *Enterprise* was destined to be a dedicated carrier, as opposed to the *Odyssey*'s multifunction stance.

He'd stolen a glance at the plans for the fighters that would make up the largest part of her complement and had to admit that he was impressed. The naval planning board had opted not to go with the original space-only design that had been proposed in favor of a more versatile multipurpose space-superiority fighter.

The space-only design would have been more effective in its element, of course, but the board hadn't really believed that there would be need enough for such a thing. The majority of conflicts in Earth space were still *on* Earth, or at least directly connected to some Earth-bound resources. Space-only fighters would have been superfluous in that case.

Was that decision a good thing or a bad thing? Eric wasn't sure.

Versatility was good, of course, but it was clear to him that the Block was the least of their worries now. The Drasin, whoever was guiding them, and whatever else existed out in the very large galaxy they lived in were a great deal more dangerous, and with the Drasin, at least, if they got into your atmosphere, then you'd already lost half the battle.

▶▶▶

He wondered what they would name the new class of ship but was interrupted in his musing by a booming voice from behind him.

"Eric! There you are, you little scut!"

An involuntary smile crossed Eric's face as he turned in his seat to see a familiar figure approaching him. He responded to the insult by rising crisply to his feet in an academy-straight stance and snapping off a perfect cadet salute at the man. "Commodore, sir!"

Cdre. Gregory Wolfe glared at him, then just chuckled ruefully as he returned the salute sloppily. "Put that away before you hurt yourself."

Eric Weston grinned, relaxing as the commodore stepped in and the two men embraced quickly, slapping each other on the backs.

"Damn, Wolfe, it's good to see you in person," Eric told his old friend. "I didn't know they let you off Demos."

The commodore nodded as they broke apart, and Eric realized that he actually did look good. Like the *Odyssey*, Demos Base most likely fell under the mandatory exercise rules that covered all microgravity workers. Either you worked out or you worked planet-side, no exceptions.

Not even for captains.

"I'll have you know that I'm the warden, not one of the inmates." Wolfe grinned back as they stepped apart. "And I have some leave time coming, so when I heard you were being ordered out, I decided I'd take it. You been briefed yet?"

Eric nodded, sobering up. "Yeah. A couple times."

"I can tell from that look that it's a mixed blessing." Wolfe grinned wryly. "Am I right in assuming that you're taking the next shuttle down?"

"That's the way things turned out," Eric confirmed.

"Excellent. I'm scheduled on that one myself," the commodore told him. "Though, I was afraid I was going to miss you."

"You almost did," Eric replied truthfully. "I was held up by another briefing with a suit by the name of Gordon."

"Gordon?" Wolfe frowned. "You mean Seamus Gordon?"

"I don't know." Eric shrugged. "He didn't give me another name."

"He wouldn't." Wolfe scowled. "He's a little intel pissant who doesn't like his first name. Brown hair and eyes, hook nose, and a stupid smile that never goes away?"

"Sounds like the guy," Eric confirmed.

"Watch that one, son," Wolfe told him. "He's trouble in a cheap suit."

"Might be," Eric said, "but I'm due to be a couple dozen light-years away from him. I don't care what ABC agency he's working for, he can't throw a spanner in my gears that far out."

"You have to come home someday," Wolfe countered with a grin.

NACS ODYSSEY

Earth Orbit

▶ CHIEF PETTY OFFICER Corrin grimaced when she heard a snap from a short distance away, and turned her attention to see just what was going on. Since the *Odyssey* began taking on stores in earnest, it had become clear that the crews charged with organizing the process were in need of more than a little polish.

Chief Sittler glared at the face on the other side of the transmission. "No, you listen to me. If I don't get clearance for those numbers in the next ten minutes, we're shipping it back to you. Is that clear enough?"

"Yes, Chief," the flustered young woman on the other side replied.

"Good. The clock's counting down," he snapped, then closed the connection.

"Trouble?" Chief Petty Officer Corrin asked, glancing over at him.

"Just the regular bureaucratic red tape." Sittler sighed. "Sorry for the distraction, Rachel."

"No problem, Sit." Rachel Corrin shrugged. "Just get that stuff out of here, OK?"

He smiled ruefully. "If it's mine, I'll have it stored twenty minutes after they finally tell me what it is."

"And if it's not, or they don't, I'll have it loaded on that shuttle in fifteen." Rachel grinned in return.

The two chuckled slightly at that, only to be interrupted by an insistent tone from Sittler's data plaque. He pulled it from the thigh pouch and glanced at it for a moment. "Well, I'll be..."

"What is it, Sit?" Rachel asked, glancing over.

"It's mine, all right. Prototypes for some new ship-killer rockets for the Angels. I guess they decided to let us test out all the new toys," Sittler replied, uncertain whether he should be happy about that or not.

Rachel Corrin snorted. "You think you got it bad? You should hear the cursing coming from Marine country."

"Oh? What happened there?"

"I guess some bureaucrat decided that we needed some heavier firepower..."

"Can't fault them there." Sittler grinned.

"No, I suppose not." Corrin smiled in return. "But they sent us this monster of an armor package, I guess. Twelve feet tall, walks on two big feet...both of 'em left, to hear Greene tell it, and a fresh-as-the-driven-snow butter-bar to pilot it."

Sittler winced. "Ouch."

"Gets better." Corrin smirked. "Apparently it's got a NICS-based control system. Looks like your guys aren't the only lunatics in town no more."

Sittler stiffened. "It's got a what? You're shitting me!"

"'Fraid not, Sit."

"Damn it!" Sittler cursed. "The captain is gonna have kittens!"

"What? Why?" Corrin frowned, puzzled.

"Don't you—no, of course you don't. Sorry, Rache," Sittler replied, waving his hand. "I forget that most people don't pay that close attention to the Angels. You know how we only have a single flight of 'em?"

"Yeah…Well, they're expensive planes."

"Sure, but not that expensive. It's harder to find pilots able to handle the NICS control system than it is to actually build the damn things," Sittler griped. "During the war, we never had enough pilots and always had too damned many planes. The captain and Steph aren't gonna take too well to competition stealing qualified people away from the Angels."

Corrin shrugged. "Hey, it's just a groundhog. It's not like he'd likely have applied to fly one of your babies, anyway."

Sittler sighed. "I suppose. Still, it's not gonna go over well at first."

"Shit happens," Corrin said, then smirked. "Now, get this shit out of my bay!"

CHEYENNE MOUNTAIN

NAC Military Command
Colorado

▲

▶DESIGNED TO WITHSTAND a near-nuclear strike in the mid-twentieth century, the Cheyenne Mountain facility housed NORAD, the North American Aerospace Defense Command, for over a century before the underground facility was refit to handle the joint operations command for the short-lived Allied Nations counteroffensive at the start of the Block War.

By the middle of the Block War, with missile threats looming on either side of the American continent, the joint chiefs were moved from the Pentagon, which was considered a soft target for the new ground-penetrating explosives despite the extensive underground bunker systems then in use, to the Cheyenne Mountain facility.

Since then, the Confederation had maintained and constantly upgraded the area's defenses against ballistic and energy threats, and the mountain stronghold had become the defacto primary command center for the entire NAC.

Admiral Gracen walked briskly through the stone tunnels with her aide, ignoring the few others moving about on their own business, and hooked a sharp right into a large conference room.

"Gentlemen." She nodded to the generals, admirals, and various high-ranking political figures waiting there. "Sorry to have kept you waiting, but I'm afraid something came up."

"That's all right, Admiral." A three-star general nodded as he motioned to a seat. "We all understand the vagaries of command. Have you conveyed the orders to Captain Weston?"

"I have, General. He's accepted them and will have the *Odyssey* prepared to leave the system within two weeks," Gracen said as she set up her things on the table and sat down smoothly.

"I still don't like the idea of letting that man have another chance to get us in even hotter water," a one-star general said, scowling. "It's only pure luck that things have turned out as well as they have."

"We can all appreciate your concerns, General McGivens," a man in a suit said calmly. "However, removing Captain Weston from command at this time would be ill-advised."

"Only because your damned PR department turned the man into a national hero!" the general growled back.

"Gentlemen!" the three-star said gravely. "Please. This is hardly the place, nor the time. Whatever else we might think, I believe that we can all agree that we need better intelligence on both the Priminae people and their enemies. And to get that, we need to send the *Odyssey*."

"A few more weeks and we can have the *Enterprise* fitted and ready for service," McGivens objected, but only by rote.

"That's a few weeks more than we can really afford, Larry," Gen. Howard Sullivan told his junior colleague. "The ambassador has been getting, understandably, concerned about the progress of the war and his people."

McGivens scowled. "I still think we should have made him wait. He came here with hat in hand; we don't need any of his toys."

"Perhaps," Gracen smoothly slid into the conversation. "However, we wanted a good many of them. You do realize that the medical advances alone will effectively eliminate death from 80 percent of cancer cases over the next three years? That's to say nothing of the rejuve treatments, which I believe you have scheduled for next month?"

"A few weeks won't change anything on the war front."

"No, but it would mean sending in an untested ship, an untested crew and captain, and expecting them to work themselves up in a potential war zone," Gracen replied. "Besides which, Captain Weston and his people enjoy a certain...*popularity* among the Priminae people, if Corusc and his aides are any example to judge by."

"Precisely," one of the politicians spoke up. "And that's a reputation that we can take advantage of. My god, General, Ambassador Corusc practically considers Eric Weston to be his people's savior! You can't buy that kind of influence, and it's priceless leverage."

Admiral Gracen and the two generals all rolled their eyes at that comment. Though they were often on different sides of arguments, they had much the same opinion of some of the civilian counterparts.

Of course, the civilian politicians had their own opinions of their military colleagues as well.

TEMPORARY COLONIAL EMBASSY

Washington, DC

▶ "ELDER?"

"Yes, Ithan?" Corusc said softly, looking up as Coar Sienthe spoke.

"Do…Do you believe that the colonies will have held the line against the Drasin in our absence?"

Corusc sighed, setting down the work he had been doing. He'd often wondered the same thing himself, but had never really been able to answer that question.

"I don't know," he told her, finally, shrugging slightly. "The Forge had eight more vessels nearly built before they threw all their available resources into finishing the *Cerekus*. The other central worlds will have been able to produce at least some warships of their own, though the Forge is the largest and best protected of our facilities."

He tilted his head, then extended his hands to either side with palms up. "Whether it was enough, I do not know. However, it doesn't matter so much as you might think, I'm afraid."

"What?" She looked up sharply, confused.

"Our presence could not have changed the tide of war, not if we had stayed home," he told her. "By coming here, perhaps we will have that chance. And a few weeks is meaningless in the scheme of the universe, even on the scale of these events."

She nodded, looking fairly miserable. "I understand. I just…"

"I know, Ithan," he told her, hiding his own pain behind a false formality. "I, too, wish I knew how the war went at home, but we have served here better than we could have hoped to at home."

He paused, considering his words. "These… *Terrans* have provided us with the concepts, if not the actual plans, for weapons that could easily turn the tide if we can get them integrated into our ships. The idea of a multifrequency laser is so simple it really should have been obvious to our designers. Their energy defense is also a brilliant concept, much simpler and less power intensive than our own energy shields, yet far more effective.

"If nothing else, Ithan," he said, "the ideas themselves may well save our worlds."

She nodded, then looked out the windows at the night sky. "I will be glad to see home again."

"As will I."

▼

NACS ODYSSEY

Sol System

▲

▶ CAPT. ERIC WESTON settled back behind his command console as the powerful ship hummed under power and made the long climb out of the gravity well of Sol. They were running a course toward Saturn, same as their first trip out of the system, and would rendezvous with the NACS *Indigo* for refueling before they made the last leg out to the heliopause.

Lieutenant Daniels had plotted their course through four hops, taking them across just over one hundred light-years of space before settling the *Odyssey* down in the Ranquil System, their ultimate goal, so there was little for Eric to do but wait. Even so, he found himself going over the ship's manifest again, eyeing all the stores they had taken on in preparation for the mission.

In addition to the prototype weapons, which Eric wasn't certain he was happy about, they had also picked up a number of new life detection software (LDS) modules, which were supposedly calibrated to detect the Drasin as living beings. That would be handy, he supposed, though, for the most part, it had been easy enough to detect them before, even if the computer software liked to insist that they weren't alive.

"*Indigo* is hailing, Captain."

Eric straightened, then nodded. "Put them through."

"Aye, sir."

The screen flickered and the captain of the tanker *Indigo* glanced up at them from the large screen. "Hello, Captain."

Weston smiled. "Good day."

"On time this time around, I see."

"We try on occasion," he returned. "Are you prepared for fueling?"

"It is what we do, *Odyssey*," the captain of the tanker replied. "Though, we don't usually have to come out this far to do it."

Eric made a motion to the helm. "We'll be matching your course in the next...eighteen minutes."

"We'll be waiting. *Indigo* out."

The screen flickered back to a starscape as Eric made a few notations on his panel, then pushed the computer interface away. "By the numbers, Mr. Daniels."

"Aye, aye, sir."

Weston relaxed back into his chair as he listened and felt the living ship rumble comfortingly under and around him. No matter what they found out there this time, it was good to be back where the *Odyssey* was built to exist. The black of space felt so bizarrely comforting when he compared it to dealing with the brass of the NAC.

▶▶▶

Rachel Corrin was in a good mood, too.

She loved being on a ship under way, though it had taken a little time to adapt to the significant differences between the *Odyssey* and the naval equivalents. Now, though, the nearly imperceptible charge that the CM (counter-mass) generators sent along her skin and the soft rumble of the ship's reactors through the deck felt good to her.

They felt like home.

The *Odyssey* had been something of a mess when she'd first come aboard, almost nine months earlier. Her crew had been the scattered sprinkling of individually great people, with none of the sense of family that existed in a truly great crew.

Egos and conflicting habits had made true integration difficult, but they'd lucked out with Captain Weston, she believed, and when the chips came down, they'd pulled together and sailed through real history in the making. Something to be proud of on every level, she supposed. A lot of captains would have called it quits after the first contact with the Drasin, and possibly with excellent justification.

Certainly, they wouldn't have stuck it out to the end while on the wrong side of the six-to-one odds for a people they didn't know and had no responsibility toward.

And they probably would have been right to leave.

However, it wouldn't have felt right.

Captain Weston had made a moral decision to override what was perhaps his legal responsibility. There were damn few men who would have made that stick, and even fewer who could come out of it with their career intact after making such a stand.

The chief petty officer felt pretty smug about it all.

A good captain was one thing, and important, to be sure, but a *lucky* captain, well, that was something every crew could get behind.

▶▶▶

"Hey, Jackson!"

Lt. Jackson Crowley paused in his work and glanced back around toward the voice. "Yes, Sergeant, what can I do for you?"

Sergeant Greene and three others were approaching in the distinctive walk of people wearing magnetic boots.

"Yeah, LT," another man wearing corporal's insignia spoke up, "we were hoping you'd show us your new toy."

Crowley eyed the group warily, trying to gauge their attitudes. He certainly didn't mind explaining how the EXO-12 armor would work as part of a combined arms team, but he didn't have the desire to put up with the kind of crap that Greene had laid on him earlier.

Finally, though, he sighed and nodded. "Sure. Come on over."

If there were any ground action on this trip, after all, they'd have to work together as a unit. And while the briefing he'd placed in the computer was available to all of them, it was better to get a jump on such things. It was bad enough that they'd not been able to properly train with the EXO-12 on board ship.

He stepped down from his perch on the deactivated armor and pulled the cables from his programmer. He'd had to physically jack into the armor in order to review its core programming and make a few adjustments, a security measure in a world of wireless connectivity, and was almost happy with the adjustments he'd made to the armor's sensor codes.

"The EXO-Twelve," he said, waving a hand at the imposing machine. "It's mostly the same package as your power suits, so don't get too intimidated by its size."

"It's almost twice the fucking size," someone said, looking up at the "head" on top of the armor. "It's a walking tank!"

"No, it's armor," Crowley corrected, "We don't have the control systems to make walking tanks feasible—yet."

"Yet?"

"You've got to be shitting me."

"What's the difference?"

Jackson focused on the last question. "The difference is that you pilot a tank. You wear the EXO-Twelve. That way, the operator can use his own sense of balance to supplement the onboard gyros, and it also makes operation more intuitive."

"What kind of tactical response are we talking about?"

Jackson looked surprised and looked around to find the speaker. It was another lieutenant whom he didn't recognize. "Good question…?"

"Bermont," Sean Bermont replied, pronouncing his name with the French habit of dropping the *t* at the end. "Sean Bermont."

"Well, Lieutenant Bermont"—Crowley nodded—"the EXO-Twelve has a state-of-the-art interface that's based on the fifth-gen power suit systems. I'm not sure if you've been issued those yet?"

They shook their heads.

"We're still using the fourth-generation interface and optics," Bermont replied.

"All right, then the differences aren't too hard to explain. Unlike the fourth-gen systems, the fifth-gen optics are processed by the onboard computer so that you get a full three-hundred-and-sixty-degree view at all times."

"Our suits do that," Greene objected.

"I mean at *all* times, Sergeant." Jackson smiled. "The operator can view the entire three-hundred-and-sixty-degree image at once instead of having the computer assign priorities to targets that are out of your immediate view."

Greene shook his head. "That's got to be a headache to control."

"It's not so bad once you get used to it, Sergeant." Jackson shrugged. "The forward ninety degrees is shown in real time slash real view, while the rest of the circle is displayed in an increasingly compressed peripheral vision mode. It feels a little like looking down a tunnel at first, until you get used to the system."

"Great. Permanent tunnel vision," Greene cracked with a wry smile. "And this is a good thing?"

"It increases response time by 28 percent in our studies," Crowley replied. "What I'm mainly worried about is how the sensors will handle nonhuman targets. They didn't exactly spend a long time worrying about that particular possibility when they coded the targeting software."

Bermont shrugged. "I wouldn't worry too much about that. But if you want to get a real good firsthand technical opinion of the Drasin, I'd talk to Savoy."

The other men nodded in agreement.

"Savoy?"

"Lieutenant Savoy. He and his geek squad handle a lot of our specialist missions," Greene replied. "He's the boy to talk to if you've got a question about those doggies and how they look on a computer screen."

Crowley nodded. "I'll do that."

▶▶▶

Weston was more than ready for the next step. Fueling had taken a couple of hours, since pumping the enormous reservoirs of the *Odyssey* full of liquid hydrogen was an incredibly long and involved process. It left the entire crew practically vibrating with anticipation, so he was thankful that the climb to the edge of the sun's influence had taken only a few more hours after that, and they were soon within the transition range.

"All systems report ready for transition, Captain."

"Very good, Helm. Are we aligned for the initial transition?" Eric asked as a matter of course.

"Aye, sir," Daniels responded with a curt nod. "The board is green."

The routine of it all felt so false, like window-dressing on something so much larger than he could comprehend. They were about to become the fastest-moving people in history, yet again, and somehow it had all been boiled down to a checklist. Weston almost felt like there was something…*sacrilegious* about that, but in the end, all he could think was that they were about to start out on something nobody else had ever done before.

He slowly nodded and reached down to access the ship-wide.

"All hands, this is the captain. We have reached our initial transition point and will be powering the tachyon generators momentarily. Please ensure that all preparations are complete for transit. That is all." Weston knew he had a good crew, a fire-tested crew, but he wondered what they were thinking now, knowing they were going back out for real. How many of them felt the same surge of excitement he did?

He closed the ship-wide and looked up. "Mr. Waters?"

"Aye, sir?" the young man asked without looking back.

"You may sound general quarter."

"Aye, sir. General quarters." Waters nodded, signaling the alert.

"Very well, Lieutenant," Weston said, glancing back at Daniels, "you may engage when ready."

"Aye, Captain. Beginning transition sequence...now," Daniels responded then, keying in a command.

At first, there was nothing to indicate that anything had changed; then the humming whine of the powerful capacitors pouring the energy into the tachyon generator pierced the veil. A moment later, the bridge lights dimmed slightly as the power draw was fed from their main taps as well, and then everything went silent.

"Spires have transitioned, Captain. The effect will overtake the bridge...now."

And then everything spun away into the void as the bridge crew gritted their teeth and held helplessly onto their seats as the black of space seemed to engulf them.

From the outside, the big ship just vanished in an instant, though sensors that were powerful enough would have registered a cloud appearing from the void and swallowing them like a ghost. To those inside the ship, the moment stretched out into an eternity, then ended as their bodies were swept away by the effect, and all that was left was the screaming.

▼

MILITARY COMMAND AND CONTROL

Planet Ranquil,

▲

▶ "ADMIRAL, WE JUST detected a tachyon event from the outer system."

Is the moment arriving sooner than even I expected? Adm. Rael Tanner asked himself. Perhaps it was just he had been hoping the moment would never come, that the people of Ranquil could expect some brief respite, some semblance of a normal life. The weight of all of those lives made him stooped sometimes, pressed down on his thoughts.

Tanner turned to examine the results of the sensor sweep, and frowned. "Direct the *Vulk* to identify."

"Yes, Admiral," the young woman replied diffidently, lightly pressing a series of commands into the projected control interface.

Far out in the outer system, the signal was received and a hulking mass of starship shifted its long orbit to intercept the center of the pulse they had recorded.

"*Vulk* reply, Admiral. They are changing orbit to locate and identify. Orders for Captain Maran?"

"Identify only at this time," Tanner replied, taking his seat as the display was updated. "It may be a Drasin; however, the pattern is not a bow wake."

"Yes, sir. Identify only."

Tanner watched the screens, waiting for the *Vulk* to arrive on-site, and hoped that it was who, and what, he thought. The intervening months since the Battle of Ranquil had not been easy on any of the colonies. They had lost a total of fourteen of the outer worlds, with a combined population of nearly thirteen billion people.

That was a relatively low number compared to the forty billion that the Battle of Ranquil had saved; however, it wasn't something that was easy to forget, just the same.

None of the central worlds had been lost, thanks be to the Maker. The initial attack on the central combine had been poised to pass through Ranquil, and when they had held them off, it had apparently thrown the Drasin battle plans out of order.

That was to the sole credit of Eric Weston and his crew, Tanner firmly believed, and he would very much like to see that man again.

He would like even more if Elder Corusc had managed to negotiate an arrangement for technology concepts, designs, and military aid from Weston's fellows. The Drasin were still out there, and their attacks had begun a battle of attrition against the fledgling fleet the colonies had managed to construct.

They had managed to achieve parity with the Drasin. Power for power, a Colonial ship was at least the equal of a Drasin cruiser; however, they had lost as many of their newly commissioned ships as they had killed Drasin ships in the two months of warfare that followed the Battle of Ranquil. In the past month, things had grown quiet, though, with no sightings of the alien ships at even the few surviving outer colonies.

The populace was now hoping that it was ending, the fear and despair having worn them down.

Celebrations were the norm within the habitats of the great cities now, but Tanner and his people didn't join in. Neither, for that matter, did Nero and his slowly forming ground force.

Nero had once explained why the quiet brought such a sensation of dread to Tanner's inner soul.

He had told Rael of a great storm that had once struck his farmstead as a child. For hours, the winds beat at the sturdy little home that Nero grew up in, ripping up pieces of the very ground around them and throwing it to the skies.

Then the silence came, and Nero thought it was over. His father refused to let him go out, told him to stay quiet and keep his head down.

That was when Nero learned of the heart of the storm, its very calmness the most lethal weapon in the storm's arsenal. It could draw the unwary out and suck them to their deaths.

Tanner thought that they were now in the heart of their own storm and the Drasin would soon try to take advantage of the peace. Neither Tanner nor any of his captains would allow that.

But, thankfully, the moment was not now. They had a reprieve.

A few moments later, the young woman in charge of signals relaxed in her chair and, turning around with a smile, said, "Admiral, we have an identification on the source of the tachyons. It's the *Odyssey*, sir."

NACS ODYSSEY

Outer Rim, Ranquil System

▶ "REPORT!" WESTON CROAKED, trying to get his voice back after the last transition.

"Systems check coming back, sir," Lamont said tiredly, sounding like her throat was constricting. She keyed into the damage-control net, calling for status reports. "All stations report. I say again, all stations report."

"Helm?"

"We're on target, Captain," Daniels replied, keying up his screens. "We came in just above the elliptic, within forty thousand klicks of our target."

"Outstanding, Lieutenant." Eric smiled, nodding slightly toward the navigation officer.

"All stations report clear, Captain." Ensign Lamont looked up. "We are showing a misalignment in the tachyon sensors, but they're working on fixing it now."

"Thank you, Ensign," Eric replied, keying the ship-wide open. "This is the captain speaking. Welcome to the Ranquil System. I'd like to congratulate everyone on a masterful execution of a very difficult series of transitions. You have my admiration. Weston out."

▶▶▶

People watched with mixed expressions of disgust and amusement as Lieutenant Crowley's guts hurled what few contents his stomach had left into the head, his body racked by the heaves. It was a common scene the veterans of the *Odyssey*'s first voyage remembered from the post-transition moments, but those who were new to the ship were all pulling as far away as they could, save those who were intent on joining the lieutenant on the floor.

"Damn, Lieutenant. You sound like you're in pain," Sergeant Greene said from the other side of the room, where those who weren't afflicted by what had fondly become known as "transition sickness" had congregated.

The lieutenant wasn't alone, either. He'd picked up three buddies in his moment of crisis, and they were all on their way to mutually stinking up the room with the pungent aroma of stomach acids.

"Christ, what the hell is going on in here?"

Greene glanced over to where Bermont was walking in. The former member of the Canadian Joint Task Force 2 Special Forces unit looked about as cocky as he did at any other time, walking with a half-swagger that summed up his personality just about perfectly. He was also one of the very few members of the *Odyssey* crew who actually enjoyed the moment of transition.

Most everyone else either hated his guts immediately before or after a transition, or envied him until they turned green and had to make a rush for the head.

"These boys just can't take a little fifteen-light-year hop." Greene grinned, trying to cover the sensation of his own stomach turning somersaults. They had Dr. Palin to help them through it, but if he ever solved all the symptoms, they'd have to find something else to complain about. Where was the fun in that?

Bermont snorted. "Here, I thought we had some real men on this trip."

▶▶▶

On the bridge, Weston was getting the reports from his subordinates.

"Captain, I'm getting a thermal bloom from about thirty degrees around the elliptic," Waters announced, frowning as he tapped in a command. "I'm reading out a ship, sir. It's turning…I lost the bloom. Either they've cut their engines or they're accelerating this way."

"Any sign of Drasin presence?"

"Negative, Captain. Ranquil appears to be in one piece, and I'm not reading anything that looks like a Drasin cruiser."

"Do we have a profile on the source of the bloom yet?"

"Negative. We'll have to wait a few more minutes for the passives to pick up a good silhouette."

Eric nodded. "Very well. Helm, give me a course to the planet. Tactical, prepare to paint the bogey."

"Aye, aye, sir," both stations replied just as Ensign Lamont half turned around.

"Captain," she said, "you have a call from the ambassador."

Eric thought about it a moment, then nodded. "Put him through."

She nodded and opened a channel directly to the captain.

"Ambassador, what can I do for you?" Eric asked genially. He was in a good mood and figured that it probably wasn't a Drasin coming at them. Even if it were, they had plenty of time to react.

"Captain," the ambassador's thin voice returned, "I have just been contacted by the vessel *Vulk*. They will rendezvous with us and escort us to the planet."

Eric blinked.

Since when does the ambassador have a commlink?

Aloud, he merely acknowledged the information. "Very well, Elder. We are laying in a course for the planet now. You should be home within half a day."

"Thank you, Captain."

Eric shut the channel down and made a note to have the ambassador scanned—unobtrusively, of course—before he was disembarked. It would be interesting to know where and how he had hidden what had to be an FTL comm.

▼

PRIMINAE VESSEL VULK

Outer Rim, Ranquil System

▲

▶ CAPT. JOHAN MARAN eyed the small ship on his screens as his pilot expertly brought the *Vulk* alongside it.

"So this is the infamous *Odyssey*," he said, his voice cool.

"Yes, sir," one of the young men manning the sensor stations replied.

Maran fixed him with a cold expression and he gulped, looking away.

The young fool should know when a comment is not a question and requires no answer, he thought as he maintained his stiff stance.

The ship wasn't impressive on the outside, that much was certain. It was smaller than the *Vulk* and its sister ships by probably four or five times at least. Maran had also been briefed on what the rotating drums were for, and he found it amusing that any space-faring people would resort to something so primitive when the basics of effective space travel were tied so tightly to field manipulations that could easily provide artificial gravity.

However, no matter what it looked like on the outside, this little vessel had a sting that perhaps even the *Vulk* could not match.

Maran would be very interested in learning how it managed that particular feat, especially with a power curve as apparently flat as was indicated on his scans. Still, he'd seen the records of the Battle of Ranquil, and as much as it pained him to admit it, he and his people owed a great deal to this single, small vessel.

"So this is the *Odyssey*," he repeated, his voice pitched lower this time, as he mused upon its design.

No one said anything this time, if they heard him in the first place.

▼

NACS ODYSSEY

Ranquil Planetary Orbit

▲

▶ERIC SWUNG EASILY into the parking deck just ahead of the elder and his two aides, angling his glide so that he connected with the floor about fifteen feet farther along, the boots clamping down instantly.

The *Odyssey* had just come to a smooth halt, relative to the planet, and the crews were now preparing both the planetary mission and the requisite combat space patrol that the NAC had instituted as standard procedure for a ship in orbit of an unsecured planet.

Eric wasn't certain how the Colonials would take the implication that their world wasn't secured, but having dealt with them before, he didn't think that they would object to a two-fighter wing flying a simple patrol. Though, to be honest, that was another thing that Eric figured had to be amended. A two-fighter patrol could actually work in many situations on Earth, where you generally knew what direction the enemy would come from. In space, it was going to require at least a sixteen-fighter patrol just to handle a close radius patrol.

That was a problem for another time, however, Eric decided as the Terran Embassy staff approached unsteadily from another lift door.

The embassy's Marine guards were in the lead and were the most composed of the group, marching almost at ease in their magnetic boots as the ambassador, his aides, and their secretaries followed.

Ambassador LaFontaine was an exceptionally tall woman in her mid- to late forties. She looked every bit as "aristocratic" as her name and position might indicate, though Eric's perusal of her file said that she actually came from a lower-class family in New Brunswick. She'd risen to prominence negotiating the cease-fire that had ended the Block War eight years earlier, and had been a powerful player in NAC politics ever since.

Eric wondered if this assignment was a sign of that power waxing or waning. Certainly, being the first ambassador to an extraterrestrial civilization was a coup that would guarantee her name's immortality; however, it would also effectively remove her from the workings of Confederation politics for several years at least.

At any rate, whichever of the two it was, Weston didn't think he had to worry about it. Politics were, thankfully, outside his purview.

The ambassador's two aides had similarly distinguished, though considerably thinner, files. Both of them had managed various negotiations quite capably over the past decade, so Eric was happy to leave that side of the affair in their capable hands.

"Madam Ambassador," he said, stepping forward, "nice to see you again. I'm sorry that we didn't have more time to talk during the trip."

"Quite understandable, Captain," LaFontaine told him easily with a casual smile. "It was a very...*interesting* voyage. I can't say that I would have been much good at conversation over a dinner table, even if I had been hungry."

Eric smiled slightly in return, nodding. "Believe me, I know the feeling. The transition drive isn't the easiest way to travel, just the fastest."

"Quite," she replied.

Eric gestured to the shuttle that was prepping as they spoke. "That's our ride down, Madam Ambassador. If you and your team want, you can board now and make yourselves comfortable. We'll be leaving within twenty minutes."

"Thank you, Captain." She nodded, then gestured to her entourage.

The Marines began moving a hairbreadth ahead of her and her aides, and the secretaries had to hurry to catch up. Eric watched them go, then glanced toward Elder Corusc and his considerably smaller group.

"Elder"—Eric inclined his head slightly—"you may board as well, if you wish. I'm just going to check a couple last-minute details, and then I'll be with you."

"Thank you, Captain," the elder replied. "I believe that we shall. Milla, Cora?"

The two young women nodded in unison and followed the elder as he walked, uncomfortable in the Magboots, onto the shuttle. Eric watched them step on and shook his head slightly, perhaps in amazement, perhaps in admiration, he wasn't sure. The elder hadn't even made a peep when the NAC had "requested" the "loan" of his orbiter.

Eric didn't think that many Confederation politicos would have acceded to such a demand with anywhere near the grace of Elder Corusc. Whether that was a good thing or not, however, Eric wasn't entirely certain.

No matter, he had other things to accomplish.

He clomped over to where the military portion of the landing contingent was prepping and found the leader of the motley group.

"Colonel Reed."

"Captain." The small, wiry man nodded as he packed his gear and secured it to one of the automated tractors that would carry it all to wherever they needed it. "We'll be ready to move out in five minutes."

"That'll be fine, Colonel. How did you and your men handle the trip?"

"We've had worse." The wry grin belied the remark as the colonel used his thumb to clear a layer of perspiration from his forehead without dislodging the green beret perched on his head.

"I'd doubt that, except that I've seen some of the places you people work," Eric replied with a matching smile, then turned serious. "You have everything you're going to need?"

"I hope so, Captain," Reed replied, shrugging. "The key to our work is to figure out what the locals have access to and give them the best training we can manage to incorporate it. Used to be that pretty much meant starting with bows and arrows and working up from there. I'm hoping it won't be that bad this time."

Eric shook his head. "I think that you'll find that they probably have the base to create a lot of very advanced gear, just not the concepts to use it the way we would."

"We can work with that," Reed replied. "I was assigned to Russia during the 'Mongrel Invasion.' Most of our duties then were digging out the military equipment the old USSR had buried almost a century earlier."

Eric snorted slightly, mostly at the soldier's informal nickname of the Block's push on Moscow. The remnants of the Soviet military at that time had been largely working counter-smuggling operations for the better part of three decades and didn't have the training, let alone the equipment, to match themselves against a serious invading force.

The cached equipment from twentieth and early twenty-first century military caches weren't the equal to the Block's modern technology, but a 125mm howitzer was still a force to be reckoned with in modern warfare.

Especially when the US Airforce was busy airdropping FAE, EMP, and micro-nuke shells for the antique weapon.

The Block learned pretty quickly that the method of delivery wasn't as important as the package arriving on your doorstep.

"All right"—Eric nodded—"get your team packed and gear stowed. We'll be leaving in fifteen."

"You got it, sir."

▶▶▶

Admiral Tanner stepped out onto the landing platform a little ahead of the estimated arrival time of the shuttle from the *Odyssey*. He'd taken time to change his uniform from the utilitarian one that they still used for most duties to the cleaner, more impressive black "dress" model he'd commissioned after his last meeting with Eric Weston several months earlier.

They'd discussed a great many things over the few days that they had had, and one of them was the drab utility coveralls that all members of the Colonial military wore. Weston had pointed out that, while utility was a primary concern for soldiers, there was a sense of morale and confidence that came from wearing a distinctive uniform that separated one from, say, an apprentice service specialist.

Rael had decided to implement Captain Weston's suggestion, and while it was still going into effect, he'd begun to actually see a certain difference among his own people.

The admiral was thinking about that when a rumbling roar from above him announced the arrival of his guests.

As last time, the Terran shuttle made an impressive sight as it came into sight, slowing to a sweeping glide that brought it to a halt about thirty feet above the platform. The immense lander swayed slightly from side to side on its thrusters as its pilot keyed down the counter-mass field that "hid" its weight from the normal universe, then settled into a slow descent as its landing braces extended.

There was a groan of metal on metal as its weight settled completely in, and the big shuttle came to a full stop, its engine whining as the pilot cut power to the thrusters, the cooling fans working at full force.

For a moment, it just sat there; then the belly of the beast opened up and dropped an extending plank down. Tanner watched for a moment, patiently waiting, until the first of the people stepped off.

"Elder"—he nodded to the first to disembark—"it is good to have you back. I've informed the Council of your return, they will assemble in two days to meet with you."

"Thank you, Admiral Tanner." Corusc nodded in return. "I have much to discuss. First, though, I must know...What of the Drasin?"

"They pressed their attacks for two months after you left, Elder. We lost eight ships and three more of the outlying colonies before the situation stabilized. In the past month, we have seen no sign of them." Tanner's face turned grim.

"The Council is of the opinion that they have retreated permanently."

"I judge from the look on your face that you do not share their opinion?"

"No, Elder, I do not." Tanner shook his head.

Corusc nodded. "I will discuss the situation with them. In either case, I do not believe that we can go wrong if we prepare on the assumption that they have not finished with us yet."

Tanner nodded, smiling in turn. "My thoughts exactly, Elder."

Elder Corusc nodded, then gestured slightly behind him, causing Tanner to look up and notice the group that had disembarked from the shuttle.

"This is Ambassador LaFontaine," Corusc said, gesturing to a tall woman in elegant clothes. "They are representatives of the Terran government. They will need appropriate premises to live and conduct business. Admiral, if you could spare some of your people...?"

"Immediately, sir." Tanner waved a young man forward. "Neril, please arrange for whatever the ambassador and her staff requires."

"Yes, Admiral."

"Excellent," Corusc said, turning around. "Now, unless I miss my guess, Miss LaFontaine, you and your people are as weary as I and mine. We shall retire for the moment and meet again tomorrow?"

"An excellent idea, Elder."

"Good," Corusc said. "Then we go."

The two groups moved off the platform, following the naval attaché Tanner had assigned them, while Tanner turned his attention to the striking figure in gleaming white who was approaching at the head of the next group.

"Captain Weston"—he grinned widely, clasping the man's hand as he'd done after the Battle of Ranquil—"it is good to see you again."

"And you, Admiral." Eric inclined his head, as he'd become accustomed to doing when dealing with the Colonials. "I take it from your comments to the elder that the war has stabilized to a degree?"

Tanner nodded, but sighed slightly. "Yes. Perhaps too much. Many of my superiors believe that it may be over."

Admiral though he was, Tanner was particularly pleased to have the *Odyssey* back in orbit for that very reason. It wasn't the ship's military prowess that he was pleased to have nearby—though, in the deep and dark part of his soul, he certainly didn't mind that—but rather, just the reminder that it had taken outside intervention to save them the last time. Tanner would certainly drive that point home every chance he got, and the physical presence of the *Odyssey* would give him yet another chance to ensure that no one forgot.

They had to stand on their own, if they were to survive this crisis. He was grateful for help, but he would not abide his people being reduced to beggars.

Weston considered that, then shrugged. "Let's hope that they're right, Admiral. However, in the meantime, let's assume that they're not and prepare accordingly."

Tanner smiled. "As I said to the elder, Captain, my thoughts precisely."

"And on that note"—Eric half turned—"let me introduce you to some people who are here to help you do just that."

Tanner switched his attention to the assembled people standing behind Captain Weston. Unlike the last time Eric Weston had set foot on his planet, Rael didn't see any of the heavily armored soldiers. Instead, it was a group of hard-looking men that he thought would fit in quite well with Nero Jehan and his people.

Or they would have, had Nero's world not been one of the casualties in the opening rounds of the war.

"This is Colonel Reed," Eric said, gesturing to a man who was scarcely any larger than Tanner's own slight build.

As the man approached, however, Tanner had to revise any thought that the man might not be capable of personal violence. There was something about the set of his stance and the look of him in general.

"Colonel," Tanner replied gravely.

"Admiral." Reed nodded. "I understand that your people might have need of training in ground warfare."

The words were not a question, they were a statement, and Tanner rather doubted that the man before him was in the habit of asking questions he had the answer to. Even so, however, Rael nodded in response. "Yes, Colonel. My...*colleague*, Commander Nero Jehan is in command of our ground forces here on Ranquil. I'm certain that he will be most receptive to any suggestions you might have."

The colonel smiled thinly, as if the words Rael had spoken were amusing in some way, but merely nodded. "I'm certain that we'll work something out. These are my main advisors, Admiral. Captain Scott..."

A man in a mottled uniform of sandy colors stepped forward and nodded. "Admiral."

"Scott is an expert on what we call 'combined arms,'" Reed went on. "He'll be in charge of liaising between your naval forces and the ground forces."

Rael almost frowned at that, but swallowed his questions until later and merely nodded.

"Major Carson"—Reed gestured to a rather large man in drab clothing—"he's a combat engineer and specialist in field expedient mayhem."

A few of the men chuckled while Tanner frowned, trying to decide if the translators had scrambled some of the words as they were wont to do. Again, he pushed his questions aside and nodded. "Major."

"Master Chief Wilson," Reed went on, gesturing to a barrel-chested man in Navy blues. "Unarmed combat trainer, demolitions, and one of the best commo men in the business."

Wilson stood about six feet six inches, and Rael Tanner had to crane his head to look up at the man, even from eight feet away. He didn't change his expression, however. In his days in the Colonial Exploration Fleet, he'd had to deal with a great many people who towered over him, and giving them the satisfaction of even the slightest intimidation would have placed him in a very poor position, indeed.

"Master Chief," he said evenly, then glanced over at Eric for the first time since Reed began speaking. "I understand most of these things, but what is the word…*commo?*"

"Communications specialist, Admiral, sir," Wilson spoke up for himself, holding his position very carefully as the alien admiral looked him over again. As the smaller man's eyes lighted on him, Wilson resisted the urge to look down at him and instead kept his eyes pinned right on a far wall.

"Thank you, Master Chief," Tanner said after a moment, running the odd title through his mind as he spoke it.

His own people had no ranks to measure it against, and he wondered where this "master" stood in the line with the others present.

Reed apparently decided that it was time to speak up again. "These are my advisory staff; the rest of my team is still on the *Odyssey*, Admiral, waiting for instructions. If I could be directed to this Commander Jehan?"

"Of course." Tanner nodded. "Cathan!"

"Sir?" A man stepped up quickly.

"Show these men to guest quarters and inform Nero that the Terrans have sent an advisor team."

"Of course, Admiral," the man replied, then looked diffidently at Reed. "If you would follow me?"

Reed and the others nodded and followed him off the platform, leaving only Tanner, Weston, and their own "entourages" standing out in the "cold."

Tanner smiled slightly, gesturing toward the closest tower. "Would you care to join me for a meal, Captain?"

"It would be my pleasure, Admiral."

▶▶▶

Nero Jehan roused himself slowly when the soft chime broke through his deliberations. He rose to his feet and walked over to the gently curved door, keying the access control.

"Yes?" he growled.

The man at the door, one of Tanner's boys, if Nero remembered correctly, flinched back in surprise from the mostly nude giant glaring out at him.

"A...Admiral Tanner sent me, sir."

"Why?" Nero asked gruffly.

"T...uh...the Terrans, Commander. They've arrived."

"I'm aware of that," Nero replied stonily. He didn't like dealing with the majority of the people here on Ranquil; they were too nervous and afraid of being forthright with one another.

"They...uh...brought advisors with them, Commander. Military advisors."

Nero curled up his lip and barely refrained from shaking his head. Of course they had brought military advisors. It was obvious even from the short time in which they had been on Ranquil that the ground forces here couldn't fight a stiff breeze.

"They wish to meet with you, Commander."

"Where? When?"

"Uh...at your leisure, sir. I'll have a conclave room cleared."

"Do so. Tell them I will be ready in one division."

"Y...Yes, sir."

Nero shut the door in the man's face.

▼

PLANET RANQUIL

▲

▶ "SO, CAPTAIN, TELL me of your world, now that we have more time," Rael Tanner said as he finished pouring a tall drink for Eric.

Eric considered the question as he picked up the drink, examining the dark-tinted liquid. He bought some time by lifting the drink to his mouth, breathing in the aroma, and finally taking a sip. It wasn't alcoholic, whatever it was, but its taste had a sharp bite he wasn't familiar with.

Not unpleasant, just unfamiliar.

He found that all the food was in a similar vein. Close enough to things he was familiar with, but just enough off that he often found himself taking second takes with every bite or sip.

"Well, Admiral," he said with a crooked smile, "I wish I knew where to start…"

"Come now," Tanner replied, "surely it's not that hard? You yourself said that your world was young. Can there be that many places to start that you can't choose between them?"

Eric stifled a laugh. "We're not old by your standards, I guess, but it's still got more than a few thousand years of history to deal with. Most of it not especially nice."

Rael considered that statement. "Ithan Chans believed you to be of the 'Others,' a splinter of the colonies from many thousands of years ago—so long that it's myth and legend now, scary stories for children to frighten one another with."

Eric nodded, remembering what Milla had said back then. "Yes. I remember. I'm afraid that a lot of the things she said then went right over our heads. What were the 'Others,' exactly?"

Rael frowned, unwrapping the meaning of the words as they came through the translator. It was an expression, he finally decided. "They are…a moral tale, yes?"

"I believe that we'd call it a fable, perhaps, or a morality play," Eric replied, thinking about smilar stories he'd grown up hearing, or reading, about. *Le Morte d'Artur* came to mind, among many others.

Rael nodded. "Yes. The second sounds correct. I'm not familiar with the first word you used. Still, no matter. The Others were, according to legend, a faction with the original colonies that did not believe in the power of the Oath."

Eric had to hold his hands up again, smiling apologetically. "Sorry to interrupt, but what's this Oath? Milla mentioned it as well, but wouldn't talk about it when I asked."

"No, she wouldn't." Rael managed to smile slightly, despite being a little uncomfortable. "Ithan Chans is an adherent of the Old Ways. Most people here are, probably as much as ninety-five out of a hundred or more. The Old Ways include the Oath; however, they hold it in extremely high regard and do not speak of it easily."

Eric nodded, thinking back to his first impressions. He'd been right to assume it was religious, then, and probably better left well alone.

"The Oath, in its simplest form, is 'Do No Harm,'" Tanner said after a moment. "Though, there are degrees and long sections describing guardianship and so forth."

"Sounds like what our doctors swear," Eric replied with a slight smile.

"Pardon?"

"Our doctors have to swear an oath before they are allowed to treat a patient," Eric said seriously. "I don't know exactly how it goes, but I think is starts with, 'First, do no harm,' meaning if you are going to treat a patient, your first responsibility is not to harm him any further."

Rael nodded. "That is remarkably close to the Oath sworn. Perhaps there is a connection between our people, after all."

Eric shrugged. "Maybe. Probably, in fact, but that oath isn't that old by your standards. Two, three thousand years, at most."

"Very young, indeed." Rael nodded. "Still, a connection, even if only in spirit."

NACS ODYSSEY

Ranquil Planetary Orbit

▶COMDR. STEPHEN "STEPHANOS" Michaels stood in the doorway to the Archangels' common room, eyeing the nine people sitting inside. Other than Paladin and his wingman, Lieutenant Samuels, who were out on the CSP, the entire group was here. With the losses to the flight, they'd gotten permission to recruit back up to strength, but as he'd found out the hard way, the current Congress wasn't interested in expanding the flight past its current size.

During the war, the Archangels had served as a Special Operations flight group, flying missions deeper into more dangerous territory than any other airborne group in the Allied Nations. In a world wired for sight and sound, their exploits had become legendary practically overnight, with major news networks running full-color, high-definition, and often holographic documentaries compiled from their onboard computers.

While even Stephanos, who was as huge a supporter of the Archangels as it was possible to be, wouldn't claim that the Archangels were anything more than another part of the framework that had eventually won the war, to the public, they were quickly turned into the symbol of victory.

Since the war, however, Steph had learned the hard way that symbols of victory were the first to be stashed safely out of sight. He didn't mind the assignment to the *Odyssey*, though it was largely just to get him and his team out of the Sol System and away from cameras. In fact, he had to admit that he reveled in it to a certain degree. The last time they'd come out they'd been able to prove that the Archangels could take on the neighborhood bully in a much bigger neighborhood, so he couldn't quite manage to regret the assignment, despite the losses.

Losing Flare and the two other Archangels who had given their lives hurt, though. They had been flying comrades for several years, and for a while, it was like he'd lost his own right hand.

Now he had two complete rookies in the flight, plus Jennifer Samuels.

Jen earned her wings, though, he had to admit. She'd claimed three kills in the last battle they'd fought in this very system, which was a respectable number in that particular furball. That still left a couple of new people who had yet to be blooded, and while they were working out well enough in training, he had to keep a close watch on them.

I can't imagine what it was like for Eric, he thought absently just then. *We used to get three, four new guys for practically every second or third mission.*

Times change, I guess. He supposed that was true, but now he had to worry about them changing back.

PLANET RANQUIL

▶ THE DISCUSSION HAD taken longer than he had expected, but for Eric, the time had flitted by as if fitted with wings. The story he'd just heard was just like the food, the city, and everything else about the world he currently inhabited.

So very familiar in so many ways, and yet just alien enough to make him pause whenever he thought on it. There was something about the tale that made him feel…lost and afraid, like nothing he'd experienced since childhood. He'd been afraid many times in his adult life, but he'd not felt so at a loss in decades.

"As I said, Captain," Rael finished, not seeming to notice Weston's introspection, "the Oath and its legends are rather…*complex*. The Oath Breakers were supposedly a group that didn't want to live within the confines of the colonies' beliefs."

"Religious schisms have brought about more than one break in societies back home," Eric replied, thinking about what the admiral had told him. "The closest example to this that I can think of would actually be the founding of the North American colonies that I come from. At least some of the people came over in order to avoid religious persecution at home."

Rael sighed with a shrug. "I don't know how much 'persecution' there would have been, in the event that the legends were true, but there certainly would have been a degree of friction. Even today, those who do not follow the Oath often find themselves...at odds with society in some way."

"Religions are like that," Eric replied, then shrugged. "Actually, people are like that, come to think of it."

Rael chuckled quietly as he took another drink. "Indeed. Many of our colonies were founded by groups that had slightly varying beliefs—my own, in fact."

"You're not from Ranquil?" Eric asked.

The admiral smiled at Captain Weston's butchering of the planet's name, then shook his head. "No. I entered the Merchant Service when I was young, traveled across the colonies, and even explored a couple new systems for surveying purposes. When the Drasin threat surfaced a few months ago, my name was chosen by the central computer to serve as the 'admiral' of the local defenses."

Tanner's lips twisted slightly as he said his rank, but the man shrugged fatalistically. "At least now there are some local defenses to command."

Eric nodded soberly, but saw a chance to find out something that he'd been ordered to. "You mention the central computer...I have to admit, Admiral, I'm not sure I understand that."

Tanner blinked, frowning slightly. "What do you not understand?"

"Is that how your people are governed?"

Rael Tanner had to think about it for a moment. "I'm not certain that I would say that precisely. Central is a repository of knowledge, but it doesn't give orders. It suggests, occasionally with great enthusiasm."

Eric didn't really understand "enthusiasm" and "computer" combined together, but he supposed it could be a euphemism. He just nodded. "A repository of knowledge? How much, out of curiosity?"

"I'm afraid that I don't know the answer to that question," Rael admitted. "Central is largely closed off, even to me. I can access a great deal of information—more, in fact, than I could hope to process in a lifetime—but I can't tell how much more is actually there. The system is very old, however, older than our history of spaceflight."

Eric coughed, choking slightly as he was caught swallowing some of his drink.

"D…" He coughed again. "Didn't you say that your history of spaceflight was fifteen thousand years?"

Tanner nodded, mildly amused by the reaction. "I did."

Eric couldn't help staring in shock. "You mean you've got a fifteen-thousand-year-old computer system, and it's still running?"

"Oh, no." Rael smiled. "It's far older than that."

Eric blinked and set his drink down carefully. "The information, you mean, of course. Your system must be newer…"

"No, the system has never been changed." Rael shook his head. "It's in a sealed area, completely inaccessible. There has never been a need, actually."

"So much for Moore's Law," Eric Weston muttered in disbelief.

"Pardon?"

NACS ODYSSEY

Ranquil Planetary Orbit

▶ COMDR. JASON ROBERTS was sitting watch when the ship slid into orbit above and just ahead of the *Odyssey*, and as much as he hated to admit it, he was just as awed as the others watching the main screen.

"That's one big ship," someone whispered, their voice only audible because of the silence that had fallen over the bridge.

The vessel on the screen massed out to six times the *Odyssey*'s own bulk, yet had an acceleration curve that Roberts knew the Earth ship couldn't match. Its power curve was also a frightening sight, blazing across the *Odyssey*'s passive sensor array like a supernova in the darkness. If it weren't for the fact that they'd seen a similar ship in action just months earlier, Roberts had little doubt that he'd have been even more awed by the monster that was floating just a few klicks off their bow.

This one was the *Vulk*, the same ship that had escorted them in-system on their approach. He supposed that she must be putting in for relief, or perhaps refueling. Roberts didn't really know, but whatever it was, it didn't have anything to do with him.

Couldn't have anything to do with him, in fact, since he had no way of communicating directly with the *Vulk*, even if he wanted to.

That was as irritating as anything else that had come up, in all truth. Sitting this close to that many thousands of tons of warship without even being able to say hello was singularly unnerving. Jason supposed that the captain of the *Vulk* was probably thinking many of the same things, if he weren't a complete idiot, at least. Only a fool would discount the *Odyssey* for her size, and Roberts hoped that the Colonials weren't captaining their ships with fools.

He was eyeing the big beefy lines of the ship some more when Ensign Lamont called to him. "Commander, the captain has checked in. You wished to speak with him?"

"Yes, Ensign. Put him through to my line."

"Aye, Commander."

Roberts had to wait for only a few seconds for the channel to open through his induction set and the captain's voice to echo through his ears.

"Commander?"

"Yes, Captain. How are things on the surface?" Roberts asked, then waited the necessary lag time for the captain to respond.

"Fine, Commander. Did you need something?"

"Major Brinks does, actually," Roberts said. "The major would like to secure permission for field exercises in order to integrate the fresh faces he picked up and to test some of the new hardware he was issued. I told him that I would convey the request to you. It would be a good chance to shake the rust off our guys, sir."

Another brief pause, partially from the captain thinking and partially from the time it took for the signal to reach the surface and return.

"I see, and I agree. Inform the major that I'll speak with Admiral Tanner about it."

"Yes, sir. Thank you, sir," Roberts replied.

"Anything else?"

"No, Captain. Though, just for your information, the *Vulk* has entered orbit just above us," Roberts said. "She's even more impressive from close up."

Captain Weston chuckled softly. "I'm certain she is, Commander. I'll get back to you shortly with the admiral's response."

"Aye, sir," Roberts replied. "*Odyssey* out."

▼

COMBAT SPACE PATROL

Ranquil Planetary Orbit

▲

▶ LT. JENNIFER "CARDSHARP" Samuels dropped her fighter in close behind her wing leader as they swung around the meridian of the planet below them, coming back into view of the *Odyssey* on schedule. She watched her thrusters puff just slightly, keying the controls completely through the lithe little fighter's base-flight control systems rather than the advanced NICS control system they used for combat maneuvering.

Nonetheless, she managed to come in tight on the other fighter's wing, keeping a formation tight enough that it should fool even the *Odyssey*'s advanced sensing gear into believing that there was only a single unit inbound. Assuming, of course, that they weren't looking too closely and they didn't have an IFF transponder blabbing the secret.

They did, of course, have transponders betraying them, but actual stealth wasn't the intent of the exercise. Paladin and Cardsharp just liked to keep in practice.

"Whoa. Take a look at that." Major Alexander Kerry whistled, highlighting an image on his heads-up display (HUD) and shooting it across to Cardsharp.

Jennifer keyed up the data with a casual move, then let out a short whistle of her own. "Jeez. She makes the *Odyssey* look small."

"Size doesn't matter, Lieutenant," Paladin returned back over the net, a smarmy tone evident in his voice.

"Gee, sir, I bet you say that to all the ladies," Jennifer returned in a sickly sweet voice.

"Ouch." Paladin chuckled, idly keying up a few readings he was picking up on his sensors. He frowned then, his voice turning serious. "Lieutenant...Break formation and parallel my course from two thousand meters."

Cardsharp bit down the urge to ask why and simply nodded as she hit the thrusters, sliding the fighter well clear of Paladin's before she twisted her control stick and brought her main reactors into play. The lithe fighter responded easily, twisting on its axis in response to the command and jumping away from Paladin when she pushed the throttle forward.

Two kilometers out, she killed her lateral momentum and paced Paladin as he keyed his computer in with hers. Jennifer watched the information scroll across her screen idly, seeing the same things that Paladin was seeing, but not knowing what he was looking at until he called up the combined electromagnetic interference from their displaced sensors.

"Lordy," Paladin muttered, "that baby has got some power curve. Are you seeing this, Lieutenant?"

Jennifer nodded, a little dumbly. "Aye, sir. Is she primed for action?"

"I don't know, but the EMI readings are about forty times what I'd expect from the *Odyssey*—even primed for action," Major Kerry replied. "That is one powerful warship. Figuratively, if not literally."

Jennifer chuckled. "No doubt, sir."

"Normally, I'd be tempted to swing by and have a closer look, but somehow I don't feel the urge anymore," Kerry said with a half smile in his voice. "Close back up on me, Lieutenant. We'll adjust our course to bypass the alien ship at five kilometers."

"Yes, sir," she responded. "Closing formation now."

As Jennifer brought her fighter in tighter, Kerry hailed the *Odyssey*.

"*Odyssey* Control, this is Archangel Flight Bravo, requesting landing approach."

▼

PRIMINAE VESSEL *VULK*

Ranquil Planetary Orbit

▲

▶JOHAN MARAN WATCHED the projected image of the Terran fighters as they swept around the curvature of the planet, coming head-on toward the *Vulk*.

They had some records of the small fighters from the Battle of Ranquil, but those were spotty at best, even when compared to the fighting records of the Terran starship. Maran gestured a command to the computer and watched as the ships closed with each other, coming within mere breadths of touching one another.

It was an interesting thing to do, but Maran wasn't certain of its purpose. Any transport was capable of flying at practically any distance chosen from another, even to the point of touching in flight. Normally, one kept a marginal distance for safety, if nothing else.

His eyebrows went up as they split apart a moment after he thought that, widening their stance to several hundred marks. They flew like that for several moments, then crossed back to close formation as they adjusted course away from the *Vulk*.

Pity, he thought.

It would have been nice to get a much closer view than they were going to give him.

▼

RANQUIL

▲

▸THE SUN WAS rising on a new day, the second one that
Ambassador LaFontaine had seen from this new world's perspective, and she couldn't help but rise with it to watch as it
came up from behind the oceans to the east. She thought
it was the east, actually, but now that she thought of it, she
wasn't sure that the sun rose in the east here.

Or does it automatically become the east if the sun rises there?
LaFontaine winced, gently rubbing her temple. She gave herself a headache trying to work that out.

The red giant created a spectacular display as it rose from
the light-green tint of the ocean's waters, burning its way
through the morning mist with reflected and refracted lights
that danced on the open water.

The city was immense, beyond imagining in some ways,
but she was truly stunned by how incredibly compact it was.
Millions of people fit into an area the size of a small town
on Earth, and more than a billion fit into the city without it
feeling cramped at all. She understood that the vast majority
of the planet was effectively a nature preserve, but a population that exceeded that of Earth still managed to exist there.

It was a fantastic planet, one she dearly looked forward to discovering.

"It is a glorious day, is it not, Ambassador?"

LaFontaine looked up and smiled at the approach of the familiar face of Elder Corusc. "Indeed it is, Elder. You have a marvelous city here."

"We have grown used to it," Corusc returned with a matching smile, coming up beside the ambassador and looking out over the vista alongside her.

They were standing at the apex of an enormous pyramid of what the ambassador would call glass and steel, if she didn't know better. Neither material would be strong enough to stand up to the sheer weight of the construct she was currently living in. Whatever the materials, however, the pyramid itself was a monumental achievement in her eyes.

It was over a kilometer on each side at its base, and its apex reached similarly high into the sky. The ambassador's rooms and offices had been provided from the apex of this particular structure, an area she was told was in extremely high demand among what might be considered the highest strata of society.

Julia believed it without the slightest doubt.

The view, of course, was staggering. She could see countryside to the horizon in one direction, looming mountains so far off that they appeared to float in and out of existence according to the heat shimmer in the air on another, and an ocean that stretched out farther than she could remember any on Earth doing.

It was probably the height and the psychological effect of actually being on an alien world, she supposed, but it was a heady feeling, anyway.

"The Council will meet with you for initial deliberations within three days," Corusc informed her, standing by her side as he looked out over the scenic vistas. "The first meeting will be largely occupied in formality, including official introductions, ceremony, and the like."

"Of course." She nodded.

Ceremony was something that she was intimately familiar with. As chief negotiator for the Confederation during the cessation of hostilities with the Block, it was LaFontaine's patience that had enabled her to push through the terms of the cease-fire. For better or ill, much of the Block's leadership was deeply entwined in the traditions of their culture, and with China as one of the founding members, not to mention their population advantage, tradition meant ceremony in spades.

Sitting through it was as much a test of character as any actions one might take, and one thing that Julia LaFontaine liked to believe she had was character.

▶▶▶

Nero Jehan wasn't watching the sunrise from the command pit where he had spent the night. The day before, he had met with Colonel Reed, who had been sent by the Terrans to train a core of Nero's ground forces. Much as he had his doubts, Nero had, as promised, delivered the names of one thousand of the best troops, along with their files, to the Terran advisors. They had then cut his list by half, tossing one name after another by virtue of computer searches and factors known only to them, it seemed.

The five hundred that remained were in front of him now.

It bothered him to see his men reduced to little more than names and numbers at the whim of someone else, someone he didn't really know. But he didn't see what choice he had, either. Even if he didn't believe that his people needed something, anything, to help them in their fight, the Council was backing the elder's arrangement with the Terrans.

So he was bound both by duty and necessity to swallow what little pride he had left.

He hoped that eventually the bitter taste would fade.

For the moment, however, he had another matter to determine. The forces on the *Odyssey* had requested permission to conduct "training exercises" on Ranquil, and the Council had agreed to allow it.

On the surface, it was a simple matter, but as usual, the Council had left the complexities up to someone else. Nero didn't have a problem with the Terrans conducting their "exercises"—not in principle, at least. However, finding a suitable area for it wasn't as simple as one might suppose.

Within or near the cities was, of course, out of the question. That went without saying, and Nero doubted that the Terrans would actually wish to deploy in such an environment, anyway. However, the law protected all areas beyond the range of the cities and prevented their exploitation by people.

And while Nero didn't think that the Terrans wanted to cause damage, necessarily, he had no illusions that they would be treating the land with the respect of the Priminae. Of course, that brought up another problem that was both related and unrelated.

Namely, where were his new forces to train?

Originally, each division had trained in their own underground facilities, practicing their aim and skills with simulations and low-powered lasers. It had been determined that such methods would suffice.

Nero didn't think that Colonel Reed and his men would be impressed, however.

The big man sighed, knowing that he was going to have to bite down and face the problem head-on. There was only one solution, and as much as he hated the problems it would cause, he would do his duty.

"Cathal," he said aloud, glancing up.

Cathal Mana, a midranked aide, looked up at the word. "Yes, Commander?"

"Contact Admiral Tanner for me. Ask him if he would receive me this day."

"Yes, sir." She nodded, stepping back, and crossed over to the naval command pit.

▶▶▶

"Yes, Nero, you wished to see me?" Rael Tanner asked as he walked into the ground forces command pit.

"Yes," Nero said gruffly, not looking up right away.

Rael, knowing his friend's tendencies, waited patiently for him to finish what he was working on. Nero was a more calculating man than one might expect. His size made people underestimate his mind, something that Tanner knew well to be a massive mistake that could prove fatal if you were arrayed against the man. That said, for all his intelligence and calculating manner, Nero had been pushed to his limits by the nature of his work over the last months. His frustrations only seemed to grow as he saw both what he was up against and also just how far he and his men had to go.

Finally, Nero set his work aside, sighed, and looked up. "I have a problem, Admiral."

"Well then, tell me about it." Rael smiled.

"I have to file a request for a land grant," Nero said seriously.

Rael blinked, becoming serious. "Is that necessary?"

"The Terran military advisors wish to do live-fire training, and a great deal more than our simulations will allow," Nero replied. "In addition, the Council wishes to allow them to conduct 'exercises.' I do not believe the Council is aware of what this entails. I know for certain that I am not fully aware of it, yet I know enough to say that there are few areas that will suit."

Tanner frowned, considering it. "I suppose that you are correct. However, opening a section of preserved land is not to be taken lightly."

Nero grunted, nodding. "I'm aware."

"Do you have any selections?"

The big man nodded, calling up a large map of the planet. On it, there were nine sections highlighted in various places, all well away from the cities Rael noted. He looked over the map, nodding. "I'll help you run this request through, Nero... However, we'll never be able to get it approved quickly without Central's endorsement."

"Do you believe that Central will agree?" Nero asked, genuinely in the dark concerning the workings of the ancient repository of knowledge.

"I am not sure," Rael admitted. "A cycle ago, I could tell you with confidence that Central would categorically deny any such request. Today, things are different. We shall have to see just how different."

Nero nodded in agreement.

"These are large areas you have marked off," Rael said, looking at the map again. "Are you certain you will need this much space?"

"I had to ask Colonel Reed for a recommendation," Nero admitted grumpily. "He listed a large array of requirements for a training facility of the nature we are discussing, not just for our immediate needs, but for future growth as well."

"I see." Rael nodded, retrieving the file to his own process. "I will examine this information, Nero. Expect me later today with more questions. Then we will go to Central together."

"Thank you, Rael." Nero nodded his head politely, a gesture he often forgot.

"Not at all, my friend," Admiral Tanner said softly, eyeing the map.

Afer a long moment, he shook his head.

"These are trying times," he said regretfully, thinking of the areas that they may have to despoil in order to defend their world.

Nero grimaced, but didn't say anything. After all, the world he'd come from had no areas left to despoil. Not even in its defense.

▶▶▶

"Admiral?" Eric Weston tapped lightly on the door of the admiral's office. Rael Tanner had asked him to come up a while earlier, saying that he had questions concerning one of the requests made by Colonel Reed.

Tanner was inside, sitting in front of a projected interface with which Eric was only somewhat familiar. The system was the locals' equivalent to Eric's desk back on the *Odyssey*, only it made use of their ability to project tangible "holographs," for lack of a better description.

"Come in, Captain. I'm afraid that I may not be the best company today. I sent my staff out some time ago rather than expose them to my...*frustrations*."

"Oh?" Eric raised an eyebrow.

Tanner smirked suddenly and fell back in his chair, wiping away the entire interface with a gesture. A map appeared with a detailed relief of a wilderness area. "Commander Jehan has begun filing for a land grant in accordance with Colonel Reed's recommendation for an appropriate training area. Is all this space really necessary?"

Weston blinked, eyeing the map and trying to get a sense of scale. The script along the side of the map was in the local dialect, something that the translators didn't do much for since they depended on vocal keys. After a moment, he shrugged and shook his head. "It looks about right, but I'm really not certain about the sense of scale, Admiral. Is there a problem with ownership of the land?"

Rael blinked, shaking his head. "No one owns the land, Captain. The land is protected by custom. We do not use more than we need. That is how we live, Captain."

"Admiral," Eric said after a moment's thought, "I'm not certain what you're asking of me."

"Exactly what I said," Rael replied. "I need to know if this space is really needed. Applying for a land grant is no simple matter, and it will require certain favors if I am to push it through the Council."

Eric wished almost desperately that Colonel Reed were here to field these questions, but the admiral wasn't asking Reed. Since the admiral undoubtedly knew where Reed was housed, the admiral didn't want to ask Reed.

"Admiral, the colonel and his men are trained to take indigenous people and turn them into fighters. They generally work with very little but space, and not a lot of that," Eric said truthfully. "I'm quite certain that, even without the space they've asked for, they can turn your soldiers into some of the finest irregulars you'll ever see. *But* for a regular standing army, you'll need every square foot of the space he's laid out for you, and maybe more besides."

Rael Tanner leaned forward, his expression interested but troubled. "What is the difference between the two, Captain?"

Eric Weston wasn't a foot soldier by profession, but he was a former member of the USMC, and that meant he had been trained as a foot soldier first and foremost, his flight training coming later. He was also a student of recent military history, specifically focusing on the adaptation of tactics to technology as had occurred in the last century and a half on Earth. He hadn't spent time studying Roman tactics or replaying Civil War battles, though he knew a great many military people who did. His had been an air war, and that was the era he studied.

So this was a question he felt at least somewhat qualified to answer.

"Irregular troops can be, and often are, superior individuals in a lot of ways, Admiral," he said, frowning as he thought about it. "In fact, quite often, they are better in many areas than the people training them. Often scouts, for example, are taken from irregular groups for their skill with the land and in tracking. Others sign on to fight because fighting is something they know intimately and do extremely well. They often bring a wildly varied yet extremely high proficiency in a certain set of skills.

"They are not, however, a functioning unit. Regular troops can have a lesser degree of these skills, on average, because of where and how they are recruited. However, unlike irregulars, they function as a unit—they become something greater than the sum of their parts," Eric said with a smile. "And for a strong defense, you need regulars. In the long run, at least."

"I see," Tanner said, sighing. "I'm afraid that I do not know much about the military lifestyle from which you derive much of your knowledge, Captain. I had always considered it to be rather archaic, actually—even if I accepted that we must have weapons though we did not use them. I do know, however, that teams in the field are the way we prefer to operate when staffing our transports and exploration ships, so perhaps there is something to what you say."

"Admiral," Eric said, "for a good, solid defense of your people, what you need is a strong corps of soldiers who serve, not because they must, but because they see honor in it."

This was an old debate, and he'd practiced his arguments with a good deal of gusto in university when he'd attended so many years earlier.

"Irregulars are fine for short-term defense," he went on. "They can be superb fighters, in some situations even devastating regular detachments several times their size, while using inferior equipment and weapons. Irregular forces defending their homes are never to be underestimated. But when the immediate threat is over, these people will want to go *back* to their homes."

Tanner shrugged. "I do not see the problem with that, Captain."

Weston smiled, shaking his head. "There isn't a problem with it. My own people maintain what I would call irregular troops, though we train them to operate much like the regulars do. They come together when there is a crisis and disperse back to their homes and jobs when it is over. They are a vital part of our national security."

He paused, then went on seriously. "They are not, however, our first line of defense. Regular troops are maintained during peacetime at great expense because one thing we know to be certain is that an enemy won't announce his attack. Admiral, your people desperately need a strong corps of people who take *honor* in serving as the first line of defense. Not just people fighting because it is necessary at the moment."

Tanner nodded slowly, seeming to understand, to some degree, at least.

"And for that"—Weston reached out and tapped the semi-substantial projection of the relief map—"for that, you need all this space."

Adm. Rael Tanner nodded finally. "I see. I will forward the request for land with my endorsement, then. If Central agrees, then we might be able to clear it up relatively quickly. A few days, perhaps. If not, then it will require a great deal more time, I am very much afraid."

Eric nodded. "It will be time well spent, Admiral. You know, I think that, in some ways, you have some advantages over us in this matter, Admiral."

Rael looked up quizzically. "How so?"

Eric smiled. "Our people—my people have a very powerful tradition of heroics that tends to work counter to the unit concept."

"I'm afraid I do not understand." Tanner shrugged, shaking his head. "Heroes are to be valued, are they not?"

Eric watched that gesture, suddenly marveling at the first time that they used the same head gestures for yes and no. He pushed that thought aside, forging on. "Most military commanders hate to have a hero in their command, Admiral."

When Rael looked confused, he smiled and said, "We have a saying…Heroes happen when things go wrong. If a unit is working smoothly, has a good plan, and nothing goes wrong with it, then heroics shouldn't be needed. A hero generally shows up just after Mr. Murphy's already made a mess of things."

Rael, of course, completely missed the implied joke, so Eric immediately had to backtrack and explain.

"Sorry, Admiral," he said with a smile, "Murphy is the name we give to bad luck. The kind of luck that invariably happens when you take a group of very complicated people, equip them with equally complicated weapons and equipment, and set them on a mission that's probably a lot more complicated than you realized when you gave them the plan."

Tanner smiled dryly, recognizing that form of luck a little too well. "Such as when the enemy attacks just before your shipyard facility is able to release its first warship."

"That would be a visit from Mr. Murphy, yes, Admiral." Eric grinned.

"And, as you said, heroes showed up just after." Rael nodded, understanding. "Yourself, Captain, and your ship. You are certainly heroes to my world. However, if things had gone right, then you would not have been needed as such. Yes, I can see what you mean. I am grateful for your help, but I remember at the time being...*frustrated* that it was required. We don't have a tradition of 'heroics,' as you put it."

"Exactly," Eric said, then, "but there's another aspect to it as well. In a regular military unit, the first thing you do is try to hammer down any people who actually aspire to heroics. Irregular units, on the other hand, will often enshrine them."

"So we would be doubly benefitted by training regulars, then, having the 'advantage' of lacking your people's enshrinement of the heroic ideal," Admiral Tanner said with a wry smile. "I believe I understand you, Captain."

Eric grinned. "Good, 'cause I was starting to forget where I was going there."

Rael laughed, his small frame shaking with the chuckling motions. "I feel quite certain that you would have eventually found your way."

"One would hope, Admiral," Eric replied. "Otherwise, I'd make a poor ship captain, I'd say."

Tanner nodded. "Indeed. Indeed. Very well, Captain. I thank you for your insight. With some luck, Central will accede to the request, and things will progress quickly. Perhaps we will be able to start within a week."

"That would be welcome, I'm sure. Colonel Reed is undoubtedly itching to get started," Weston said with a thoughtful smile. "Admiral, I was wondering…Would it be permissible to see Central?"

Tanner shrugged. "Of course. Though, there is little enough to see, Captain. Merely a stone wall. Central is completely sealed."

"Even so, I have to admit that I am curious."

"Then I invite you." Rael shrugged and nodded deeply. "Officially, as it were."

"Thank you, Admiral." Eric nodded in return. "I accept."

"Good." Rael's eyes danced with amusement. "Though, I fear you will be sorely disappointed. There is really very little to see."

"I'm sure it'll be worth my time, Admiral."

▶▶▶

Colonel Reed scowled as he poured over the list of five hundred men his staff had compiled from the thousand put forward. Each file they had been given by the commander of the local ground forces was…*Thorough* was the best word he could use to describe it. *Information overload* was a close second.

The mass of information on each of the five hundred was compounded by the fact that each file had to be dictated by one of the locals so that the computer systems Reed and his men had brought with them could compile a half-decent database. The result was extremely slow going as they worked through the files, Reed trying to get a sense of what kind of men he was going to be training.

"Look at this one." Master Chief Wilson snorted. "He was some kind of lumberjack or something."

"We've trained worse than that, Chief," Reed said flatly, reminding the former Navy SEAL that the actual training would begin with the Special Forces detachment. Besides, he didn't want the staff members who had chosen the men getting any flack.

Reed also knew that the skills the men began with weren't as important as their motivation, not by a long shot. And a man defending his home and family…Well, that was a powerful motivation. "What's his physical shape?"

"Looks good, near as I can tell," Wilson replied. "Big guy. But most of these guys are."

Reed nodded as a murmur of agreement passed through the group.

"They are from the outer colonies." The men looked over when the "naval attaché" assigned to them by the commander spoke.

"What?" Reed asked her.

She was a small woman, decidedly unlike the men they were trying to filter through, an "Ithan" in the local military command structure. Reed had given up trying to puzzle out the exact rank structure that predominated here and supposed that his was as confusing to them. Her name was Milla, which he'd thought was rather nice and easy to pronounce compared to a lot of what they had run into lately. As a bonus, she'd also spent time on the *Odyssey*, and while he'd never run into her, she was more comfortable with the translators and technology than someone right in from the cold would be.

"They are from the outer colonies," she repeated, as if it were obvious. "The colonies are—were—not easy places to live."

Reed exchanged glances with Carson, a moment of communication passing between them. The combat engineer nodded after a moment, with a shrug of his shoulder.

"Makes sense in a way, Colonel," he replied. "A new colony would probably select for hardier stock, and only the hardiest is gonna volunteer for this shit."

Reed nodded. "I suppose."

"I think we need less data, Colonel, not more," Wilson spoke up then.

"Excuse me, Chief?"

"This"—Wilson widened his arms to take in all the work they were doing—"I think it's a mistake."

"What part?" Reed asked, curious. The master chief was an expert in some very technical fields and, despite how his size and twice-broken nose made him appear, not given to rash action or judgement.

"We should just get Commander Jehan to give us the basic information, not the full files," Wilson said. "It was a good idea, don't get me wrong, but the truth is, we don't have time to determine who's best suited for what. We have to trust Jehan."

Reed leaned back, interlacing his fingers, and considered the chief's statement. After a moment, he sighed and looked around at the other two. "Opinions?"

"I concur," Carson said, tossing a data plaque to the table. "It's a hopeless task to try and shift all this data over to our system, and they don't seem to even record all the same things we would."

Randal Scott, former Marine Corps captain, nodded in agreement. "I guess I have to agree, Colonel. This is just a mess. I think we should trust them to know their people."

Reed took a moment, then nodded reluctantly. "Agreed."

He turned back to the young woman who had been assigned to help them and smiled a little ruefully. "I think we got a little too big for our own good, here, Milla. Do you think you can ask your people to give us just a few individual pieces of information about each that the master chief will provide to you? It'll make things better all around, I think."

She bobbed her head in agreement. "I can have that for you immediately, Colonel."

Reed raised an eyebrow, amusement flickering in his eyes. "You have it already prepared?"

She flushed a little, not meeting his gaze, but nodded. "The commander..."

Reed responded with a tight smile. "That's fine, Ithan. Could you get the list?"

"Of course." She nodded, then rose to her feet. "I will return."

After she had gone, Reed glanced at the others who were looking about as ruefully amused as he felt. "The commander seems to have already thought of it. I wonder if he meant to drown us in information."

The dry, self-effacing humor in the statement drew some chuckles from the others.

"Well, sometimes you want to test the people training your irregulars, Colonel," Wilson said in a dry tone. "See how many piles of bullshit they're willing to climb."

"At any rate"—Reed flicked off his data plaque—"now we just need the space, and we'll be ready to get started."

"Oh, joy," Wilson muttered, but smiled slightly to take the edge off his comment.

"By the way, Colonel, have you heard about the maneuvers?" Scott asked.

"No." Reed shook his head. "What maneuvers?"

"Brinks asked the captain to get clearance for some training maneuvers while they were in orbit," Carson told him. "The brass loaded them up with so many new faces and gear that Brinks wants to make sure it all works the way it should."

Reed snorted. "Can't blame the man for that."

The others agreed as Reed thought about it, then slowly smiled. "You know, we can use that."

"What's that, sir?" Wilson asked.

"Think about it, gentlemen." Reed smiled. "A live-fire exercise is damned impressive, even if a few people foul up. Could be a good way to get our recruits' attention."

The others considered that, then slowly began to nod.

▶▶▶

The ambassadorial suite was one of the nicer workplaces LaFontaine had ever worked out of, which was saying something, all things considered. She'd done her time in the less impressive, meaning *hellhole*, spots, but much of her latter career was spent in upscale residences and offices, and this one beat them all.

"What do you think of the city, Daniel?" she asked her aide.

The two were sitting in the large and spacious "housing" they had been provided, drinking one of the local beverages that tasted like a strong fruit juice, though they weren't able to pin down the precise fruit in question.

"It's impressive, Madam Ambassador," Daniel Kane told her. "I haven't seen much of it, of course, but I get the impression that a person could spend a lifetime exploring just this one city."

Julia nodded in agreement, thinking about what she'd seen of the great metropolis in which they were located. It was a unique place, to be sure. There were signs of a conventional city in the area around them, including immense skyscrapers that were so large and tall that they seemed to defy the laws of physics; however, the main populace was located in three massively large pyramidal "supercities."

With over forty billion people on the planet, Julia supposed that the Priminae had to have some very impressive cities to house them all, but what was really impressive was how *few* people she'd seen. She could walk the corridors outside her rooms all day and run into no more than a handful of people, if that.

Public transportation appeared to be not only the norm but the only way that the average person could get around, and the transport was integrated so tightly into the design of the cities that it was virtually invisible. Within the immense pyramids were equally impressive habitats, suspended in a grid of tubes and supports, in which Julia had been informed a billion people could live comfortably.

The number was boggling, especially when you consider that there were two other pyramids just like it as part of the same metropolitan area.

Combined with the city that existed around the three immense habitats, there were over three and a half billion people in this one city alone.

That was over a third the population of the entire Earth, and Julia had seen the orbital images of Ranquil in her briefings. The Priminae people used less than 10 percent the land area that Terran humans did, the rest being a wild preserve devoted to the natural world.

There's just something about these people, she thought with a smile. *I just don't know how to react to them, though. They just don't...fit.*

LaFontaine put that thought out of her mind, trying not to dwell too much on it. It was her job to figure out where and how they fit, after all. To place the people here in a framework that made sense to people back home so that some form of communication could be effected beyond the simple exchange of words.

Julia LaFontaine smiled, looking out on the incredible vista beyond her suite.

She loved a good challenge, and this was one of the best she'd ever had.

▼

INTERSTELLAR SPACE

▲

▶ IN SPACE, THERE is light on all sides, the stars an unblinking companion to the ships and species that move through the limitless vacuum, but for humans who ventured into the blackness, it was very much a reminder of the old expression "Water, water everywhere, but not a drop to drink." Those distant sparks of light that surrounded you in the depths were completely inadequate to the task of lighting the local area, leaving everything very much in the dark.

So dark, in fact, that despite the omnipresent starlight, there is too little ambient light for most planet-bound species to see even as far as their hands if they were held up in front of their faces. Those species suited to space travel, however, make use of other senses than what humans would call visible light.

To them, the universe is a very different place. Alien, in fact, to the eyes of a human. Colors are completely different, determined not by what frequencies of light that a substance absorbs or reflects, but often by what energies an object generates of its own accord.

Very few things in the living universe are truly inert, so those with the eyes to see it can perceive a very different realm from the mundane world of men, indeed.

The Drasin were such a species.

They passed through the empty depths, unaffected and unmoved by the stark beauty around them. Their perceptions were turned to the life they saw in everything they passed. The tiny spark of it in the few rolling, tumbling rocks that existed in deep space. The almost imperceptible hint of it in the micron-sized particles of dust that collided with them.

And the blazing purity of white flame that they saw when they approached a star system.

Most systems, they simply bypassed, uninterested in the life they found there. The natural white flame that arose from the combinations of planets and suns was peaceful to them, and perhaps, someday, when they were finished, they might return.

For now, though, it was the crimson slash that drew them in. The life's blood hemorrhaging from the living universe was anathema to them, and they could not pass it by.

This was such a system, the Drasin determined as it slowed its velocity and moved in closer. The tug of gravity on its skin was a pleasurable tickle of sensation, but was also ignored.

The Drasin had more important matters this time, and it alerted its extensions.

This system was filled with the crimson band.

In the past, many others had vanished into this pass, so the Drasin were cautious.

To a human, the caution might have translated to a superstition, something expressed as a joking phrase or statement. To the Drasin, it was simpler, more instinctual than that, but the sentiment remained.

Here be dragons.

▼

PLANET RANQUIL

▲

▶ TO GET TO Central, Tanner led Weston down through carved tunnels that were cool and moist. Unless Weston was mistaken, they had passed from the pyramidal habitats a few minutes earlier, walking deeper into the ground as they followed the path through a complex branching labyrinth. The halls through which they now walked were of stone carved from a single slab, unlike the glass-and-steel-like construction above, lending a feeling of antiquity.

In fact, he half expected the place to be lit by torches rather than the unobtrusive lighting systems that the Priminae favored.

"Here we go," Admiral Tanner said as they came upon a large room, empty save for Commander Jehan, who was standing at the far end. "Nero, sorry we are late. I was showing Captain Weston some of the Old City."

Old City. Eric had to suppress a choked laugh at that comment. The pyramids above them were over ten thousand years old, constructed of materials that the translator couldn't accurately render when someone tried to explain it. The city that surrounded them, just over sixteen thousand years old, was constructed of hardened stone that used a surface-molecular bonding to create a surface nearly impervious to the elements.

The "Old City" was what Rael had called the tunnels. Even he wasn't certain of their exact age, since the building materials and preservatives used by the locals defied such mundane processes as carbon dating.

"It isn't a problem, Rael," Nero Jehan said in his somber way. "I would not have proceeded without you, in any case."

"Precisely why I apologized, Commander," Rael said cheerfully, shrugging as he and Weston came shoulder to shoulder with the commander. "Have you the prepared request?"

"Yes," Nero rumbled, nodding once.

"Good. With luck, we'll be done here momentarily," Tanner said as he reached forward and tapped a polished plate on the wall.

Eric blinked as the wall rumbled and scraped, sliding slowly apart, opening a way for them to continue in. Tanner started walking brusquely, not bothering to look back, catching both Nero and Eric by surprise for a moment before they hurried along behind him.

The room in which he found himself was of polished metal, almost mirror smooth, about fifteen meters in diameter. There was nothing else in the room, just the walls, the ceiling, and the floor. Those were all made of the same metal, all polished quite carefully, but without any other distinguishing marks whatsoever.

Eric was looking carefully around when Tanner and Nero stepped toward the center of the room with their files and request, so he turned to watch them.

Nero looked distinctly uncomfortable, but Tanner nodded simply to him, and he returned the nod and prepared his files carefully, drawing out one of the electronic data devices the locals used.

"Central," he said carefully, "I have a request here…"

Strange. Eric's brow furrowed. *I thought they didn't have voice interfaces here.*

"They do not."

Weston nearly jumped out of his skin as the deep baritone voice echoed through his skull, though that was only part of his shock. As he'd watched Nero speak, the big commander and the small admiral had both vanished like someone had thrown a light switch. One instant, they were there; the next, he was standing alone in the circular room.

"What the…?" he muttered, rushing forward as he cast about for them. *Where the hell did they go?*

"They are here," the voice said again, startling him a second time. "They continue to make their petition for a land grant."

"Who said that?" Eric cast about again, this time looking for the source of the voice.

"I am what the Priminae, as you call them, refer to as 'Central.'"

Eric froze, eyes darting around. The door through which he had entered was gone, like it had never been, and he could see no way out. The voice seemed to come from inside his own skull, but it reverberated like the deepest voice he'd ever heard, sending a tangible sensation along his spine.

"You're Central?" he said after a moment.

"I am."

An AI? Eric thought wildly, trying to grasp the situation. Artificial intelligence research on Earth was as yet an extremely rudimentary science at best, even the best systems being a long way from being considered "intelligent" in the slightest.

"I am not," the voice replied, this time a hint of emotion in its voice. "There is nothing artificial about my intelligence, I assure you."

He froze again.

It read my mind.

A cold chill ran down his spine, a series of fearful scenarios playing across his head as he began to look even more urgently for a way out.

"I read your FirstMind," the voice replied. "Humans record data in two known ways, though there are some indications of a third process that I have yet to prove. You need not worry about my learning state secrets and the like. First, I have no real way to use such things, being immobile as I am, and second, unless you think of those matters and load them from your SecondMind, they are not available to me."

Of course, as soon as it said that, Eric immediately thought of the security codes for the *Odyssey*'s main computers.

Oh, hell.

The voice chuckled softly from within his mind. "Do not feel bad, Captain. That trick almost always works on you humans. The first point is, however, still in effect. I am unable to access the computers on your ship."

"What are you?" Eric asked, almost fearfully. Thoughts of Gordon's directions to learn more about this...*Central* flitted through his mind. *This is not a computer.*

"Indeed, that would be a poor descriptor of me, though I'm hardly surprised that people are interested in me," the thing said, amused. "In response to your more relevant question, or perhaps in the hopes of clearing up your meaning... What are you?"

Eric blinked, thinking about the question. "Ah...human, I suppose."

"Ah," the voice said, slightly mocking. "Then you mean, 'What species am I'?"

"Sure," Eric said, beginning to wonder if he was hallucinating.

"I'm not," the voice returned serenely.

"Not what?"

"A species."

By this time, Eric wasn't in the best of moods. He didn't react well to being entrapped at the best of times, and the fact that both Tanner and Commander Jehan were missing was both suspicious and worrisome.

"You may relax," the voice said calmly. "As I informed you, they are both still asking for permission to use the land they desire."

"Where are they?" Eric demanded, shelving the issue of the mind reading for the moment.

"Here. With you."

Eric closed his eyes and counted slowly to ten, forcing back the angry retort that had been on the tip of his tongue.

"I don't have a mother, Captain. So I would not take offense."

He started counting again.

This time, the voice let him reach ten without further cause for outburst, and he took a deep breath. "Why can't I see them?"

"Ah, a good question," the voice said with a hint of humor. "Would you prefer the simple answer or the truthful one?"

Somehow, Eric had the immediate impression that he was being asked a trick question. "Hit me with the truth."

"I've taken the liberty of altering the temporal-dimensional structure of the space you inhabit."

Eric closed his eyes, groaning as if in pain. "Simple answer."

"I masked them from you."

"Why?"

This time, there was a long silence.

"Central?" Eric asked finally, looking around. "Are you still there?"

"I am, Captain," the voice said again. "The answer to your question is…complex. For one, I wished to speak with you… to…thank you."

"Thank me? For what?"

"For saving me," the voice said simply. "Your interception and destruction of the Plague Ships, and their Virii here on the surface, saved me as much as the other people here."

Eric considered that, wondering if a computer were able to be grateful.

"I told you before, Captain, I am not a computer," the voice replied.

"What are you, then?" Eric asked, still deeply frustrated.

"I am the heart," the voice replied. "But then, so are you."

"That's not answering the question."

"Not in the way you wish, no," the voice conceded. "However, I do not have a better way to respond to it at this time. I haven't been asked that question in more then twenty thousand cycles of this system's primary."

Twenty thousand years. Eric's mind spun from the implications, and he finally had to move over to the side of the room and lean against the wall.

"That long?" he asked unsteadily.

"Yes, Captain. I suppose that I am what you might call 'immortal.'"

Push it aside, man! Eric told himself, trying to get a grip. *Come on, think straight, dammit!*

"It's my experience that humans rarely, if ever, 'think straight,'" the voice replied dryly.

"Stay out of my head!" Eric snarled, glaring around him.

"I'm afraid that I'm quite unable to help it," the voice said, actually sounding vaguely apologetic. "You see, your neural impulses fire in a coded sequence as unmistakable to me as someone yelling in your ear would be to you. Energy fields are something of a natural order of things to me."

"How come you can read my 'neural impulses'?" Eric demanded. "Shouldn't I think differently than the locals?"

"Not perceptibly so," the voice said with a thoughtful tone. "I've read minds from several worlds and three separate species, in fact. Mental thought is a universal standard, as near as I can tell from such a limited sampling, of course."

"The Drasin?" Eric asked, his mind racing as he tried to put things together while still keeping track of the conversation.

The voice paused for a moment, then spoke quietly. "No. The Drasin don't read as intelligent beings."

Eric pursed his lips. "They have to. You don't build ships—or fly them, for that matter—without being intelligent."

"Perhaps you are right, Captain. I don't know," the voice replied. "However, for the moment, they are not the subject I have in mind."

Eric nodded slowly. "All right. What is it you have in mind?"

"I want to know you, Captain. And your people," the voice said. "I want to know what you intend here…"

"Intend?" Eric frowned. "We don't intend anything except contact."

"Contact is precisely what I am afraid of."

NACS ODYSSEY

Ranquil Planetary Orbit

▲

▶ BERMONT DRIFTED IDLY by a far wall as he watched the show from a safe distance, arms hooked loosely into hand-holds so he could float withough moving too far.

"Turn out!" Master Sergeant Greene snarled, his foot clomping in a steady staccato as he crossed the open deck in front of the flailing soldiers.

They'd suited up in powered armor for parade drill, but most of the people who made up the *Odyssey*'s newly filled troop complement were less than familiar with zero-gravity drills, and the added complexity of the power suits resulted in some interesting definitions of the word *formation*.

Bermont winced as he watched Greene lay into a soldier who was floating upside down and flailing in an attempt to right himself.

"Sweet Jesus," Bermont whispered as he shook his head, "when did we become a day care facility?"

Beside him, Sgt. Jaime Curtis glanced sideways at him and smirked under her helm, keying a local burst transmission in a private channel. "About the same time as the word got to the brass that aliens were coming and they probably needed to start recruiting again. Anyway, they can't all be old men like you, LT."

Bermont scowled at her, though the effect was pretty much wasted since she could neither see his face directly nor did he open a vidcom to her heads-up display. "Don't start that old man bullshit with me, Sarge. I'm only twenty-five, and it ain't my fault that these guys came straight out of boot."

Jaime returned a chuckle, but shook her head slightly. "It's not that bad, and you know it."

Bermont reluctantly nodded in agreement.

She was right, of course. The soldiers they'd been given weren't out of boot by a long shot; most of them were graduates from some of the toughest schools of military Special Forces in the Confederation. The problem was that they were graduates, and only barely that. The *Odyssey* had originally enjoyed the pick of the crop, literally the best of the best the Confederation had to offer. Why not? After all, she was unique, and there had been very little competition for the services of people like Sean Bermont, or even legends like Eric Weston.

Since they had returned home and dropped the bomb on Congress, however, things had changed. The *Enterprise* had to be staffed, and she was slated to be one monster of a ship by all accounts. With the *Valley Forge* and the *Ticonderoga* on the list to be constructed within two years and eight more unnamed keels being floated in Lagrange points from Earth to Mars, the demand for people was reaching critical mass.

Soon, he supposed, the Confederacy was going to have to open up wholesale recruiting again, and wasn't that going to be a fine mess?

Along with the military boom, the commercial construction had more than tripled. The exact nature of the events of the *Odyssey*'s first mission was still more than a little clouded in the mind of the general public, but the conglomerates knew a new market when they smelled it, and they were banking on finding some way to exploit it.

How exactly they expected to do that, Bermont didn't have a clue, since the transition drive system had suddenly become the most highly classified thing in history. Not that it hadn't been secret before, of course, but the security around it had reached insane levels, even on board the *Odyssey* herself.

"Sweet mother of mercy, son!"

The scream brought Bermont crashing back to reality just in time to see one of the floating troops kick Greene across the helmet. The master sergeant snapped his leg up with one hand and unceremoniously whipped the unfortunate trooper across the length of the deck to where he crashed into the far wall with a bang.

"That is what you call basic physics, you sorry sons of bitches!" Greene snarled. "Action, reaction! His action was to kick me in the face because he was too stupid to plant his feet! My reaction was to plant the rest of his body for him! You got me, soldiers?"

The line of troops snapped out in agreement. "We got you, Master Sergeant!"

Greene gave them one last glare, doubling it up by using a clear helm and piping them a close-up of his snarling face through the HUDs. Then he turned and stalked off toward the soldier who was trying to crawl along the far wall by his fingertips, his crash having bounced him just far enough out that he couldn't get any real purchase.

"Lieutenant!" Greene called. "You mind taking over for a minute?"

"Not at all, Master Sergeant," Bermont replied with a smile. "You go do what you have to do."

Bermont kicked off the ground, killing the electromagnets in his suit, and glided away from where he had been standing. Halfway through his flight, he calmly flipped end for end and reactivated his magnetic clamps in midair.

He touched down on the "ceiling" and looked "up" from his position to the troops lined up beneath him without saying a word. After almost a full minute of nothing but his stare, some of the figures below started to get visibly antsy.

"Well?" he growled. "Form up!"

They were quick enough, he supposed, as almost half of them got the idea in a hurry. First, they kicked off the ground and flipped with varying degrees of grace and its lack, then the rest, and in a few moments, most of the line was clomping awkwardly into position in front of him.

"Better," Bermont told them evenly.

He might have said something else if they were raw recruits, but they weren't. Many of them had even seen action toward the end of the war, though none of them had seen it from their last units. He walked the line slowly, feet clomping with authority as the magnets sounded against the metal deck. Each time he passed within a few feet of one of the soldiers, his suit automatically RFIDed their ID tags and gave him their service records.

Army, Navy, Air Force, Marines. Bermont smiled thinly. The yet-unnamed space service didn't discriminate when it came to the sources of their men.

"Better," he said again, nodding in the manner of someone used to suit work. The gesture was exaggerated, enough so that it was visible to an outside observer. "But not great. I know that zero grav is hard to get used to, but this is all we have to do suit work in until we get permission to go groundside, so you'd better get used to it."

They shuffled slightly, but he ignored it and went on. "In fact, get used to it anyway! You're not in whatever unit spat you out and gave you to us. This is space, and believe me when I tell you that gravity up here, it is a privilege. It ain't a right. Formation drills, roof to floor, move it!"

They moved.

▼

RANQUIL

▲

▶ ERIC WESTON LOOKED around, still seeking the source of the voice that seemed to reverberate directly inside his skull. "What are you talking about? Why are you afraid of us?"

Something like a dry, deep chuckle echoed for a long time. "Afraid of you, Captain? I'm not afraid of fleas or ants, am I? I never said I was *afraid* of you, Captain," the deep voice replied. "However, I do not believe that contact with you is in the best interest of the Priminae."

Eric could feel his hackles rise over the casual confidence in that comment. "Aren't you the one who just thanked me for saving them?"

"I am. Interesting quandary, I must admit," the voice of Central replied. "On the one side, a fast and certain death at the hands of the Drasin. On the other, the uncertainty of further contact with a species that appears to be very nearly as bad."

The featureless silver polish of the room was as frustrating to Eric as the disembodied voice's words. As he turned around, casting out for the source, he could only see himself in a blurred and warped reflection.

"Just as bad?" he challenged angrily. "We're the same species as your Priminae!"

"Are you?" the voice mused, sounding quite unaffected by Eric's anger. "What constitutes a species, I wonder? Genetically, you are identical, this is true—or at least to within acceptable divergences. There are some differences in those humans from your world I've been able to observe. Your adrenaline production is 43 percent more than a comparable Priminae, muscle mass is 6 percent denser, on average, which I am unable to comprehend, as I've determined from your conversations that your world has a slightly lower gravity…"

Eric blinked, still casting about helplessly as the voice went on, listing facts with a dry, flat delivery.

"Your brain power is significantly less, and you have a much higher degree of emotional expression—"

"What are you talking about?" Eric finally cut off the voice.

"And you have a disturbing lack of patience," it finished without missing a beat. "Still, these are within acceptable parameters to define the nature of humanity. By a physical degree, at least."

"I told you that."

"However, your mental aberrations are quite perplexing," the voice continued. "In fact, judging from your FirstMind, and those others I have been able to monitor, there are a number of startling and quite disturbing implications of your presence on Ranquil and within Priminae space."

"Wait, wait, wait…" Eric held up his hands. "Excuse me, did you say 'monitored'?"

"Of course."

"You've been eavesdropping on us?"

▼

INTERSTELLAR SPACE

▲

▶THE SYSTEM WAS alive with malignant colors. At least three of the worlds within were infected, the ugly red gashes marring their tones, but that was only one part of the problem the Drasin hive mind felt as it sank a little deeper into the well of the sun. There were powerful, blazing colors moving within the well against the natural plane. They, too, carried the crimson bane, though it was harder to detect on them, as the colors were too young to have absorbed much of it yet.

It was a pity, then, that they would have to be eliminated as well.

Previous experience had warned it, though, that the young colors were to be considered dangerous. They harbored power out of proportion to their age and size, and while only rarely a significant threat, those few times could result in the loss of many.

It settled into a deep elliptic then, staying with the natural flow of the system, and calmly called upon more of its own to purge the discolored system.

It had time. It was patient.

▶▶▶

"Eavesdropping?" The voice sounded more curious than anything else. "A fascinating concept, Captain Weston. I'm afraid that it does not, strictly, apply to me, however."

"You're reading people's minds without permission!" Eric snapped, becoming more than a little frustrated. Honestly, though, he half suspected that it was from the lack of an actual person to talk to than the conversation itself.

Just as he thought that, of course, the air in front of him shimmered and a radiant image appeared in front of him. It was a humanoid figure, bathed in white light like something celestial from ancient myth.

Not original, by any means, Weston thought as he stared, but effective enough at grabbing his attention.

It was something to look at other than the silver walls.

"True," the figure said, shifting slightly, lifting one radiant arm to brush along its "head." "However, the term implies some intent on my part to overhear the thoughts or communications of others. That's not the case."

Eric stared for a moment, trying to get his mind back in gear now that he was looking at something that could, for all intents and purposes, pass for an angelic being. Finally, he managed to wrench his thoughts back to the present and quickly review what had been said.

"What are you talking about?" he asked finally. "How can that not be the case?"

"Would you consider it eavesdropping if someone were constantly yelling in your ear?" the figure asked mildly and gave a very human shrug. "I'm afraid that all sources of electromagnetic disturbance within the planetary field are effectively the same as 'yelling in my ear,' as it were. I am quite unable to avoid it."

Eric had been about to snap at the voice, or figure, again but was brought up short by that answer.

"But…" he said, blinking hard as he took in the full extent of what was being said, or what he hoped was the full extent. If it went any further than what he was thinking, he was going to be frightened. "That would mean that you could read the minds of every person on the entire planet."

"Essentially correct, though not entirely so," the voice replied, still mildly commenting as if on some clinical experiment. "There are locations within the field that are scarred, or blocked, from my sense. Like all things I have observed in my lifetime, what is theoretical and how it works in practice are two very different things."

Eric found himself nodding in agreement before he caught himself. "That's billions of people!"

"Forty billion, three hundred and eighty million, ninety-eight thousand, and…forty-two, as of thirty seconds ago. The number fluctuates moment to moment."

"I'll bet," Eric replied dryly.

"A wager would be unwise…Oh, that was sarcasm." The voice paused and actually seemed to frown as it stood there, still glowing. "It is difficult to properly read you. I wonder if this is how humans communicate with each other?"

"I doubt it," Eric told it. "We don't generally pry into each other's thoughts."

"A point, Captain. However, that's not what I mean, precisely," the voice replied. "What I mean is that, when dealing with you and your people, there is a less…*fluid* transfer of information. You think something, I 'hear' it, and then I process it and can respond. When the Priminae think something, it is more like I thought of it myself. Occasionally, I have difficulty determining if an idea was mine or theirs…"

Gestalt.

The word popped into Eric's mind like a light switch turning on, and he stared for a long moment before it really sunk in. "You're a gestalt."

The voice seemed taken aback at the comment, and it forgot to gesture in a humanlike manner, as its avatar faded for a moment before coming back.

"A fascinating concept, Captain," it said finally. "Perhaps… Perhaps, you are correct. I am unable to determine any method to disprove it that would not result in the deaths, or at least evacuation, of all humans on the planet."

"Uh…Let's not do that, OK?" Eric backpedaled nervously.

"Hardly," the voice replied, this time hitting him with its version of sarcasm. "If for no other reason than the possibility exists that the gestalt only works within the confines of the planetary magnetic core. Disrupting it would effectively 'kill' me. I am over three hundred thousand years old, Captain. I have no desire to 'end it all.'"

Thank god for that, Eric thought with equal portions of relief and grim resolve. Whatever this thing was, it wasn't suicidal, and that was one important point in its favor. At least wanting to live gave them a common ground to work from.

"That is a good point, Captain. I hadn't considered it."

"Could you not do that?" Eric growled. "I like to voice my ideas before someone compliments me on them."

"Pardon."

If he's a gestalt…then what? Some kind of unconscious psychic link?

"Not by your definition of the term, I think, Captain."

"Damn it!"

"What? Didn't you say…Oh, no. You thought that. Pardon. My mistake."

Eric curled up his lips for a moment, then glared at the radiant figure. "All right, fine. You know what, if you're omnipresent on this world, then why do you make people come here to talk to you?"

This time, when the voice spoke, Eric was virtually certain that it sounded embarrassed.

"I didn't at one point, Captain," it said. "However, the results were not to my liking."

"Such as…?"

"I accidently created several deity myths that persist to this day."

Eric covered his face with his hands and groaned.

This is what I get for accepting the captaincy of an interstellar vessel. Stupid science fiction writers…After all the wild stories they spin, how was I supposed to know that the real universe was even screwier?

A long silence followed that thought, and Eric found himself looking around.

"What? No comment?" he asked finally.

"Sorry. Did you say that out loud? I thought it was something I shouldn't respond to immediately."

Eric sighed, slumping slightly.

It was becoming a long conversation.

▶ ▶ ▶

"You did enter the petition, right, Nero?" Rael knew the answer, but asked anyway in his impatience.

"Yes, Admiral," Nero Jehan said, glancing over his shoulder. "Central should process it momentarily."

Tanner nodded, but frowned ever so slightly as he gauged the time. "Seems that it should already have passed, don't you think, Nero?"

"I am uncertain, Admiral." Nero shrugged. "You have more experience with Central than I do."

"I suppose it hasn't been that long," Rael said. But it definitely felt like something was…off.

Nero gestured toward Eric Weston. "Is Captain Weston all right?"

Rael glanced over to where Eric was standing off to one side and staring at the wall. The admiral shook his head, frowning in an amused sort of confusion. "He's fine, Commander. He was quite surprised at the concept of Central. I'm sure he's just taking it in."

"Taking what in?" Nero asked with a roll of his eyes. "It's a polished wall."

"All things are fascinating to those who have never seen them, I suppose."

"There are polished walls on spaceships, Admiral."

▶▶▶

"I believe that our time will be cut short," the voice said with what almost sounded like a sigh.

"Oh?" Eric asked dryly. "And why is that?"

"Admiral Tanner has noticed that my response to the land grant is coming slower than normal, and I believe that Nero is wondering why you're staring blankly at a wall."

Eric pursed his lips in irritation. "Gee, imagine that."

"I may not be entirely used to having sarcasm aimed at me, Captain, but that doesn't mean that I am unaware of it," the voice replied dryly. "At any rate, I am not entirely satisfied with our conversation, but the time has come to end it for now. We will speak again, Captain Weston, although it may be a while if you should happen to leave this world."

That sounded almost like a threat, Eric thought as he frowned at the apparition.

"No, Captain, a fact," it told him.

"I said cut that…"

▶▶▶

"…out!" Eric snapped, glaring at the silver polished wall.

Nero and Rael moved back away from him in surprise, eyeing him with some trepidation.

"Cut what out, Captain?" Rael asked.

Eric looked around slowly, as if waking from a dream, and finally shook his head. "Nothing, Admiral. Stray thought."

"I see," Rael said in the tone of someone who did not.

Eric paid him less attention than he normally would, still almost dizzy, trying to make sense of what had just happened. He looked down at his hands as he slowly opened them and then clenched them into fists, just focusing on the muscle motions while he strove to put his thoughts in order.

There was a chime then, and Nero looked down at his handheld processor. "The response is back, Admiral."

"And how much work do we have ahead of us, Commander?" Rael asked with trepidation. A negative response from Central would require a lot more energy to drive the grant through the Council.

"Central has approved the request," Nero said, sounding slightly surprised. "We've been granted a large tract of land on the eastern side of the Discor Mountain Range."

Rael's brow furrowed in thought. "That's mostly desert. It will require considerable effort to install appropriate facilities, but it will cut down on damage to the available land. Good, I will present this to the Council at the next gathering."

Weston, at least, was glad their attention was off of him. He didn't care to imagine how very off his game he must appear, let alone how very off his game he really *was*.

▼

NACS ODYSSEY

Ranquil Planetary Orbit

▲

▶MAJ. WILHELM BRINKS looked around the table at his officers and senior noncoms, nodding a greeting as they finished settling into place at the table.

"Gentlemen," he said with a smile, then tipped his head to the single woman at the table. "Lady."

The lady in question was 2nd Lt. Tasha McGuire, who nodded in return, showing no discomfort at Brinks's singling her out. Brinks always hazed the newbies, and she was a recent transfer to the *Odyssey* who didn't know many of the people at the table much more than by their names.

Lieutenant Bermont was the last one in, which Brinks had come to expect. Brinks gave him a quick nod, and in response, Bermont said, "Sorry, Major, I was on the parking deck when the call came in."

Nothing I didn't already know. Brinks gestured to an empty position.

"The good news," he said without preamble, "is that we've been given clearance to conduct maneuvers planet-side. Captain Weston communicated the Council decision to me an hour ago, and we're clear to begin final preparations for the exercises."

"And what would the bad news be, Major?" Lieutenant Savoy asked dryly.

As far as Brinks was concerned, there were two pieces of bad news. The first was that the *Odyssey* only had a few areas where any sort of training could take place, and among them, the parking deck was literally the only one in which a unit could practice any sort of tactical movement. It was a less-than-ideal solution, of course, since it was patently unlikely that they would be conducting infantry combat in zero-gravity situations. At least, the major genuinely hoped that it was unlikely, an ugly thought rearing in his mind as he tried to imagine a boarding operation with near-green troops.

But everyone at the meeting already knew that, so he wouldn't belabor the obvious, and just move onto the news that was really news: "Well, it seems that Colonel Reed and his Green Beanies want someone to give the locals an example of what a real soldier can do…So they invited five hundred of them to the show."

Bermont winced noticeably, and Brinks heard a slight groan from his direction.

"Problem, Sean?" he asked, knowing already what the problem was.

"Yes, sir." Bermont nodded, then shook his head. "We've got a lot of green people, Major. That was one of the reasons we wanted to conduct exercises. I'd hate to fall on our face in front of the locals."

Sometimes Bermont missed the point, Brinks thought. Messing up in front of the locals wasn't the worst thing that could happen.

Brinks fixed Bermont with a steady stare, though his words were addressed to the entire table. "Well, it's your job to make sure that doesn't happen. Especially since this has been upgraded to a live-fire exercise."

Someone hissed, but there were no more comments ventured, so Brinks tapped a command and the tabletop was lit up with the light from a floating cross section of land.

"This is the LZ, ladies and gentlemen," Brinks said, high-lighting a mountain range that made the border to the west. "The captain has decided that, under the rules of engagement for this exercise, it is to be considered hot. That means a hard entry in the shuttles, without CM aid."

There were groans, and someone cursed, but Brinks expected that and only smiled thinly. What would a planning meeting be without complaining?

"Local engineers are in the process of setting up targets for us, but we don't know where they'll be or how they'll be defended. The colonel and his boys have promised me, how-ever, that they will be defended...So I want an assault plan for all contingencies."

He looked around the table and nodded with satisfaction, choosing to see nothing but agreement and determination.

"All right, let's do this."

▶ ▶ ▶

Amherst watched with curiousity as Comdr. Stephen Michaels accepted the data plaque from the petty officer, who saluted quickly and turned on his heel to leave. Stephen quickly read through the text he'd been given.

"What's up, Steph?" Amherst asked after a moment.

Stephanos shrugged a little unhappily. "The Archangels are being assigned to ground support for the exercises."

Amherst winced. It wasn't all that bad, of course. The Archangel platform was more than capable of handling minimal ground support operations, but it wasn't what it was best at, either. Normally, the fleet was used to secure air superiority or to execute precision strikes on targets deep within enemy territory.

Close air support was a horse of a different color, however, and even the veteran flyers on the fleet were out of practice in that area, to say the least.

"I guess they're planning on shaking the rust off of everyone, sir," Amherst said after a moment.

Stephen nodded, then seemed to shrug it off and looked back over their fleet. "All right, sim time! We'll do precision flying drills and atmospheric maneuvering sims first. Let's move it, people!"

But Amherst knew Stephen still wasn't happy.

PLANET RANQUIL

▶ ERIC WESTON WATCHED as the sun set, the deep red of the sky reminding him of a cabin he had stayed in for a few months between services back home. He hadn't been back there in years—over a decade, actually. He would have to see if it was still available when he returned to Earth; he had a feeling that he would need the downtime by then.

The first thing he'd done after coming out of the chamber that supposedly housed "Central" had been to order the *Odyssey* to a higher orbit. The orbit would cost them more fuel, but it should be well clear of the planet's electromagnetic field and, hopefully, far enough not to be in danger of being read by whatever "Central" was.

Central bothered him, in some ways more than even the Drasin. The Drasin were a known quantity to Eric, something he could understand, even if not completely. Central was something else entirely, a being that was obviously different from anything he'd ever imagined. If he was right, and it was a gestalt, then it was possibly the amalgam of every being on the planet.

Possibly even Eric Weston himself, though the conversation seemed to cast doubt on that.

Even if not a gestalt, the entity was still dangerous. Central had manipulated either the laws of physics as Eric knew them or Eric's mind, and done it with apparent ease. The worst of it was that, to be honest, Eric couldn't decide which frightened him more.

Since that very discomforting meeting, Eric had been kept busy working alongside Rael and Nero as they pushed the proposal for the land grant through the Council. The Council had made their decision a lot faster than Rael had thought, giving the *Odyssey*'s troops permission to conduct live-fire exercises within only a couple of days. The idea of building a full-time facility out there wasn't as pleasant to them, but from what the ambassador and Rael were telling him, they were coming around.

He'd had the numbers converted in the *Odyssey*'s labs and knew that the territory they were talking about ceding over to their military was roughly the size of the state of Texas. Which was a big part of the problem, actually, since the Priminae had a hard time understanding why anyone would need such a massive tract of land.

But Eric kept wondering if it was going to be enough.

Nero and Reed were already sketching out plans for a large training facility, enough to process probably twenty to thirty thousand boot soldiers in a month. Officer training facilities were also being sketched out now, though those were longer term, of course, and as of a day earlier, Rael Tanner had entered the fray, dragging Weston along with him.

The territory in question was now being considered as the potential primary training area for the Priminae Navy as well as their ground forces.

If things worked out as intended, it was likely that more then a hundred thousand people would be living, working, and passing through there within sixty days. God knew that the Priminae could be slow at making critical decisions at times, leaving things until the last-possible moment, but Eric was learning now that, when they made a choice, they moved very fast, indeed.

It made him wonder, actually, what they'd become in a few years if this war weren't resolved quickly. Would the city he was watching become an armed camp? Did the people here have the steel it would take not just to survive that but to flourish? There was something about the military, about the idea of living under that kind of discipline, that was anathema to some people. They didn't thrive in those conditions, at least not in the long term.

If it happened, the Priminae would have to get their people behind the military, actively supporting it rather than merely tolerating it. Honestly, they would have to do that anyway if they wanted an effective defense force.

A soldier fought better when he knew that he was not only needed, but appreciated back home. There were few things as degrading to man than to come home to the people you served, only to be shunned and reviled by them. It would sow a bitter vein in the forces here if it wasn't prevented and cut down now—and quickly.

Something Eric knew to be dangerous, indeed, was a bitter military. It didn't fight at its peak, and it could turn on those who had hurt it. The military sowed a spirit of brotherhood in its members, by necessity as well as plan, and that spirit was a vengeful one when its ire was aroused. The Priminae needed to learn that now, peacefully, before it was taught to them later.

▶▶▶

The entity known as Central observed Eric Weston's thoughts with a certain grim concern.

The concern came from the solid belief backing up the captain's thoughts, and therefore, Central had to consider the possibility that he was right.

Central knew that there was even less sympathy for the military throughout the population of Ranquil. Most people felt distanced from the threat of the Drasin; even those within Mons Systema were largely untouched by the deaths that had overtaken their city only a few months previously.

The fact that it hadn't been the local defense force that had saved them didn't help, turning much of their fear into contempt.

For the moment, it wasn't a threat to the structure of the society, Central concluded; however, it was a threat to the survival of the society. If that attitude didn't change, then recruiting would eventually reach a plateau beyond which the defense forces would not be able to progress, and that would be disastrous in the event of another attack. They had to be unified against any invaders, Drasin or anyone else. Even the Terrans, if it came down to it.

Central, however, was a very old entity. It could look beyond the war; it had to do so, in fact. If the military emerged from this war victorious, then the future became uncertain.

Weston believed that the military might be a threat to the society it protected, though he believed that threat to be a minor one. Central wasn't certain if it agreed with that sentiment, and it did not wish to save the society from one threat only to have unleashed another upon it.

▶▶▶

A familiar voice called out Colonel Reed's name as he supervised the construction of the final few emplacements being built by he and his team. *Nero?* Surprised, he looked over his shoulder.

Sure enough, it was Nero. There was no mistaking that wide stride, those hulking shoulders. He walked with a gait Reed had seen many times in the past, not that of a soldier or a warrior, but rather, the walk of a man who worked for a living. He'd seen it before, in more countries than he cared to name. The commander may not be a career soldier up to the standards of the forces, but if the Priminae could give them five hundred men like Nero…He liked his odds of creating a truly excellent irregular unit.

"Commander." He nodded respectfully to Nero Jehan as the big man approached.

The commander didn't mind getting dirty, and that was something that Reed approved wholeheartedly of, but he wasn't out on the site that often, either. Considering that he was the de facto, if not official, commanding officer of the Priminae ground forces, Reed supposed that it was surprising that he had time to show up as often as he did.

It had been a week since the Council had decided to allow the land grant, and Reed was impressed with the speed of construction. There was an area carefully cleared to construct training facilities in, one that would occupy a hundred acres of land and be constructed complete with its own public transportation system and heavily fortified underground barracks and offices.

That was a long way from where Reed and the commander were standing now, though—on ground zero for the training maneuvers to be executed by the *Odyssey*'s assault contingent the next day. The area was dotted with quickly molded bunkers, each of which was equipped with throwaway laser emitters and primitive computer control systems. When the *Odyssey*'s crew attacked, they would be broadcasting their IFF systems in a manner decidedly unwise for actual combat, but the signals would allow Reed and his team to control the low-powered lasers they'd installed all through the assault area to create a credible defense.

Nothing really distinguished the place. It looked like any number of similar places where Reed had conducted exercises in the past. Which made him feel oddly confident about their efforts.

"So how are the preparations progressing?" Nero asked, coming up to stand beside the colonel and overlook the field below. Reed couldn't deny Nero exuded confidence; it could be intimidating. Not to mention, you might be shoved aside by a stray Nero shoulder if you didn't watch yourself.

"Very well, indeed, Commander," Reed said, nodding to the nearest group of workers. "You have some very good people here. Once we showed them how to do it once, they caught on fast, and I have to compliment you on the administrative work. Ithan Chans is a miracle worker."

Nero seemed about to register that as an insult, but said evenly, "Building things is what we do."

Reed gave him a crooked smile. "Well, we try for a more balanced approach. Sometimes you have to be able to rip them down as well."

"Indeed," Nero said, his inflection not giving away any of his thoughts on the matter.

"We'll have the field ready for tomorrow, Commander. No problem."

Nero nodded. "I can see that. I will be very interested to see the assault, Colonel. When the *Odyssey*'s soldiers were last on Ranquil, I was occupied with other matters."

"I'll bet," Reed said a little sourly.

The fact that his world had been under a planetary assault by creatures intent on utterly destroying it would tend to take up a commander's time, Reed was certain. As far as the colonel was concerned, it was a minor miracle that Nero hadn't tried to blow away the *Odyssey*'s soldiers when they came tramping through the streets in full armor.

Reed knew that, if matters had been reversed, he would have blown the *Odyssey*'s soldiers right out of the sky, along with their Drasin counterparts, then lasered their remains into ash for good measure. There were times when it was better to beg forgiveness than ask for identification.

Reed glanced to one side, eyeing the imposing figure that was Commander Jehan, once again. The man stood a full head and then some over Reed himself and was built proportionately to his size, which made him probably more than a little scary of a figure. But it was his craggy, impressive face, with the weathered yet experienced look of a man who had spent his youth outside, that gave him such authority. Reed liked to imagine he looked a lot like Nero, except with a slighter build.

In the past decade, Reed had started to see a lot of changes in the Earth military. Too many good-looking soldiers, for one thing. The new armor had become a mainstay of a lot of the units, turning the hard and tough exterior of the soldiers who wore them soft. It didn't mean that they were soft, Reed supposed, but the armor that protected them from bullets also kept the sun from baking in that leathery look of dangerous competence common to Reed's generation of soldiers.

Added to that was the fact that, with the newer munitions, there were fewer scars on surviving soldiers. If you were hit, you died, and if by some miracle you didn't, well, then the near-infrareds and medicines in your suits usually closed up anything short of an amputation, and as long as you stayed on treatment, modern medicine had pretty much done away with the scars that had once been badges of pride among some of the hardier men.

Modern soldiers were gym fit, and suit drills had replaced three-day marches, making a mere hundred-kilometer march something to be joked about rather than groaned at. Every time Reed saw some baby-faced master sergeant he winced, his first thought being that the service had gone to hell to be letting kids reach that age. Then he'd watch the "kid" rip into some poor recruit, and damned if he didn't feel like an old man who was playing out of his league.

Maybe all of this explained why he liked Commander Jehan and the troops the man had offered up for training. They were all hard men who'd spent their lives outside. In the case of the Priminae, it was because they were Colonials in the true sense of the word, working a new planet and opening new resources to the use of their people. They weren't military, it was true, and they weren't Special Forces caliber by any stretch of the imagination, but Reed had made a career of turning lesser men than this into a workable, fighting force.

Nero suddenly broke into Reed's thoughts: "I have something to show you, Colonel."

He looked up to meet the commander's eyes. "Oh?"

Nero nodded, waving a hand over his shoulder.

Reed turned around as two men came forward with cases in their hands, delivering the metallic-gray bundles to the commander and setting them on the ground when he motioned.

"Prototype weapons," Nero said, crouching down to one knee as he popped open one of the cases. "We were hoping for your opinion of them, Colonel."

Reed nodded, looking on in interest. He'd seen the Priminae lasers in action and had been duly impressed with their power. The only problem he'd seen with them himself was the fact that they had proven ineffective in battle.

Which, he had to admit, was a pretty damned big problem.

It was through no fault of the weapons themselves, though, from all accounts. The Priminae lasers were lethal beyond anything Earth technology had been able to develop in hand-held equipment, and the reports from Lieutenant Savoy had indicated that they would have charbroiled a power suit in seconds at most.

The weapon that Commander Jehan was now retrieving from the case was a bit chunkier than the laser rifles he'd seen, though, and looked quite a bit solider. It was still smaller and lighter looking than the M-112 assault rifles, but that wasn't a surprise. Reed had never liked the M-112 himself; he considered the weapon to be too clunky and heavy for a proper rifleman to use, and the contrails left behind by the scramjet-propelled rounds drew such a nice path through the air directly back to the shooter.

It was moderately acceptable for a man in a power suit, Reed supposed. They could move fast and survive almost any return fire from small arms, so counter sniper fire wasn't a big concern for them. When Reed pulled the trigger on a rifle, though, he preferred that he have more than a few seconds to decide whether or not it was time to abandon his position.

"We don't have a name for this yet," Nero said, coming to his feet and presenting the weapon to Reed, "but it is most likely to be what we issue to our soldiers."

Reed nodded and accepted the weapon, checking it over carefully while taking equal care not to actually push anything that even looked like a button or control. He hefted the rifle-sized weapon, carefully gauging it in his hands.

"It's light" was his pronouncement a few moments later.

"That is because it is activated" was Nero's response.

Reed's eyes flicked down to the weapon, noting the glowing lights for the second time, and then back to Nero. "I don't follow you."

Nero took the weapon back from him and thumbed a catch, causing the lights to die out, then handed it back. Reed accepted the weapon and blinked as he immediately noticed the increase in its heft. It weighed perhaps twenty pounds when its power systems were off, instead of the four to five pounds he'd estimated when it was powered up.

Reed placed his thumb over the power catch, then glanced up at Nero again. Nero nodded, so he flipped it on. The rifle instantly felt lighter in his hands, and he lifted it up to his shoulder to look down the sights.

Priminae weapons were designed more than a little differently than anything Earth made, but their proportions were nonetheless in the same degrees as would work for any human. The grip of the weapon was a little out of place for his comfort, but Reed recognized that as an ingrained response and not a physical one. The weapon would undoubtedly feel right for any of the locals.

"How does it work?" he asked after a long moment of reexamining the weapon.

"The firing control is here." Nero pointed. "It is designed as simply as possible. Point and…What is it you say? Shoot?"

Reed nodded with a half-smile. "That's right, Commander."

He turned around, looking intently until he found a clear line that led far out and away from the work area and a large boulder to aim at. Then he hefted the weapon again and glanced to Nero. "May I?"

"Please," Nero Jehan said, stepping back and out of the way.

Reed leveled the rifle at the boulder, judging the distance to be about eight hundred yards. With a good rifle, it was an easy shot, and one that he could make without the aid of advanced optics, though he'd like a good pair of binoculars to help him judge the wind closer to the target.

For now, though, he didn't need to be perfect. As long as the shot landed within sight, he'd be happy. The onboard optics were clear and easy to read, so he centered the boulder in them and automatically adjusted for the drop a bullet would encounter over that range, before shaking his head and lifting the muzzle again.

There was no telling what, if any, drop this rifle would have, so he'd start with a dead-reckoning shot.

Reed held his breath for a moment, steadying his aim, then let it half out, paused, and touched the firing stud gently.

The weapon didn't do more than vibrate slightly in his hands, but the air around him made up for it with a sharp sonic boom that rattled every tooth in Reed's jaw. He blinked as an eruption of flame burned into his retina, causing his eyes to water involuntarily as he lowered the muzzle of the weapon and cleared his fingers from the trigger automatically.

*Holy…*Reed cursed mentally, rubbing his eyes with his free hand.

When they were cleared again, he looked for the boulder, only he couldn't find it in the cloud of settling dust that was raining down around his target.

"Jesus…" he whispered, shaking his head. "What the…?"

"This will surprise the Drasin, I think?" Nero asked with a half-smile.

Reed was still staring downrange, trying to find the boulder that wasn't there anymore. "Jesus, Commander…What the hell is this thing?"

"A…gravetic impeller?" Nero said. "We took the idea from your assault weapons."

Yeah, except we use rail guns, and they don't fire nukes! Reed shook his head. "Commander…These might be a little overpowered for use in, or even near, your populated areas. Can they be toned down for urban operations?"

Nero frowned. "I'm not certain. I suppose so."

Reed chuckled dryly. "Let's hope so. So, what does this thing fire, anyway?"

Nero shrugged. "Aligned carbon crystals."

"Aligned carbon?" Reed frowned. "Can't say I've ever heard of it."

Nero reached down into the case again and tossed a small piece to Reed. He caught it easily, then looked at it and almost dropped it like it was searing hot.

"Sweet Jesus, Commander! This is a fucking diamond!"

"Diamond?" Nero shrugged. "Easiest thing to make that wouldn't burn up in air when fired."

Reed suppressed the groan as he looked down at what had to be the most expensive piece of ammunition he'd ever seen in his career.

▼

PRIMINAE COLONY, THEORA DEICE

Orbital Station

▲

▶COMDR. LORA BREEM had been looking forward to another uneventful shift aboard the orbital station. Usually, in addition to being a sentinel, they had scientists up conducting experiments, and sometimes a politician would make the trip. But nothing more stressful than that.

That was before Ithan Kav Brenna said something to her that, at first, she didn't register.

"What did you just say, Kav?"

Kav was staring down at his console, seemingly lost in thought despite the fact that he had just asked for the commander's attention. He looked up, and Lora noted immediately that he was white as a comet surface, and not much healthier looking.

"Kav? What is it?" she said again, demanding his attention this time.

"Incoming bow wakes, Commander," he got out a moment later.

"Ours?"

The question was pro forma, required protocol, but Lora was already moving toward her command station and slapping the combat stations alert. She knew that her signals officer wouldn't look so sick if the incoming ships were anything but—

"Drasin," he said in a strangled voice.

"How many?" she asked, falling into her seat as the alarms began blaring around them.

"Too many" was the only answer.

Lora cursed, punching up the information he was seeing.

Too many, indeed, she thought, swallowing the wave of despair that washed over her. "Get me the captain of the *Heralc*."

"Y…Yes, Commander."

There was nothing for her to do as Kav called up the communications options, and she sat there in turmoil, heart beating fast, as she was finally put through to the captain of the single Priminae vessel stationed in the system. A moment later, a projection appeared on her ship, and the captain of the warship *Heralc* nodded politely in her direction.

"Commander, I'll be with you in one moment," he said, before turning to one side and issuing a series of orders to someone beyond the reach of the projector. Finally, he turned back to her and nodded again. "Sorry, Commander. I presume that this is concerning the Drasin."

It wasn't a question, so Lora didn't answer it. She nodded her head and rose from her command chair, extending her hand to the projection. "Yes, Captain. I'm sorry for disturbing your readiness preparations."

"Not at all," he said, taking her hand lightly and inclining his head. The ghostly touch of the projected form felt chilled against her hand, but she nodded in return and they parted. "We have time, after all, before they arrive. Are the evacuation procedures ready?"

"Yes. The colony is being shuffled aboard what few transports we have. They won't be enough," she said.

"A million of them would not be enough, Commander," Capt. Kierna Senthe said with a shake of his head. "Never enough."

She nodded, turning back to her screens as he stood like a wraith by her side. "We have enough lift capacity to remove almost half of the colonists. Approximately five million people. Captain, these ships are freighters. They—"

"I know, Commander," he said, a note of fatalism in his voice. "The *Heralc* stands ready to do our duty."

NACS ODYSSEY

Ranquil Planetary Orbit

▶ "GEAR CHECK!" SERGEANT Greene growled as he strode through one of the aisles that had been created when the troop restraints had been locked into place in the large shuttle. "You and the men on each side of you! We're heading for a hot insertion in twenty minutes. I want everything tied down and every man ready to hit the ground shooting! I see anyone slacking off just' cause it's an exercise and you'll be regretting it all the way back to Earth!"

On either side of him were men in power suits, locked into place by heavy hydraulics that prevented them from flying around on a drop that was bound to get a lot rougher than any normal shuttle landing ever would. Their rifles were mounted at the immediate left of each soldier, locked into place by the same restraints that held each man, with ammunition and other equipment locked into a bin above their heads.

While most of them hadn't worked together for long, the sergeant's order was one that they were intimately familiar with, so they carried it out quickly and efficiently, checking their own suits with a quick diagnostic, then a visual examination, and then finally moving on to the suits of their neighbors as well.

There were no surprises expected. All of the equipment had been carefully checked several times before it had been cleared for use in the maneuvers, but there was always the chance of failure, so the check was mandatory. So far, though, Mr. Murphy wasn't making any appearances, and the fifty occupants of the first drop shuttle all cleared their gear and the all clear was given.

Greene grunted in satisfaction and stepped up to the front of the troop deck, slapping his own rifle into the slot built to receive it, and then spun around and backed into the cradle while keying the lock with one hand. The hydraulic system locked the braces down over his suit, and he looked out through his clear helm at the rest of the men who were similarly suspended in their suits.

"By the numbers, people. Nothing fancy," he said grimly. "I don't want any fuckups. Just remember, it's just another training run…Don't get nervous, remember your training, and you won't have me kicking your ass all the way back to the ship."

Dry chuckles were heard over the radio network, some of the soldiers recognizing the humor in the sarge's words, though they also knew the truth of them as well.

Greene just half smiled, his lips curling up into an almost sneer, and signaled over the command band, "Alpha Group, ready to drop, Major."

▶▶▶

"Thank you, Sergeant," Major Brinks said as he checked off the first shuttle's complement from his list and keyed the command band closed. He was standing in the bay of the fourth shuttle, which had undergone some rapid and annoyingly slapdash retrofitting to accommodate something that he wasn't even certain he wanted on the mission. "Lieutenant, if you can't get that thing locked down safely, it is not leaving this ship."

"I'm almost ready, Major," Lieutenant Crowley grunted from where he was pulling a two-ton test strap down over the exoskeletal tactical armor. "It'll hold, sir!"

Brinks twisted his lips, but glanced over to where Chief Corrin was examining the tie-downs and threw her a questioning look.

The chief looked at the young lieutenant, then back at the major, and nodded discreetly.

"All right, Lieutenant," Brinks said reluctantly, "you'd better get yourself ready to drop. We're leaving in fifteen minutes."

"Yes, sir!" The lieutenant saluted quickly, then keyed open the back of his currently immobile armor.

The back slip at the top, where the neck of the humanoid-shaped armor was located, opened up quietly, hissing pneumatics until it reached the point where Crowley could grab ahold of the twin handles inside and swing himself down and into the armor.

A moment later, the suit hissed shut again, and Crowley's voice came over the command band. "Locked in, sir. I'm ready."

Brinks nodded briefly, pushing himself off the perch he had observed from, and floated down to the deck of the shuttle. "See that you are, Lieutenant."

Brinks paused as Corrin passed him, keying over to a private channel. "That thing isn't going to come loose and kill half my team when we bounce off the atmosphere, is it?"

"It'll hold, Major. You have my word," the chief petty officer told him then.

Brinks nodded. "Good enough, Chief."

Then he keyed over to the unit-wide command band. "All shuttles, make final preparations for deployment."

PRIMINAE COLONY, THEORA DEICE

Orbital Station

▲

▶LORA BREEM WATCHED as the screen showed the liftoff of the second wave of heavy-lifter evacuation starships. There were about three-quarters of a million people on those ships, packed into the hulls with little regard for the comfort of the people involved. All that mattered in the emergency evacuation plans was that they got as many off the planet as possible.

"There they go, Commander," Kav said in a worried voice.

"It's going to be tough for them," Breem said. "All of them."

A lot tougher than for the staff of the orbital station. All they had to do was survive the nearly two weeks that they would be spending in close quarters. It was better, after all, than what those left behind were going to get. Better than a lot of people were going to get, in fact.

She turned to the tactical projection that showed the bow wave of the incoming Drasin ships as they breached the system's outer orbitals and began their approach. The first wave of evacuees was already pulling hard in the opposite direction, scrambling to climb up and out of the gravity well of the system's primary.

She settled into her command chair again, tapping out a command on her interface. "Laser command to my station."

"Yes, Commander. Orbitals are being directed to your station."

The powerful orbital laser arrays were the first defenses that had been created when the threat of the Drasin had been realized so many months earlier, each floating pod stashing twelve of the most powerful laser crystals in the colonies. From the reports available to her, Lora expected that the nine pods under the control of her station should be roughly equivalent in firepower to three of the heavy warships like the *Cerekus*.

They couldn't, however, chase enemy ships or maneuver to dodge incoming fire, so Lora didn't think she'd get more than one unopposed shot, and after that, it was a matter of luck and fate and the hand of the creator.

"Activating arrays," she said, flipping the safeties up and open one by one, bringing the powerful energy sources on each array to life.

Around them, the fire-control sections of the orbital command center came to life, lighting up with telltales.

"Hold on active sensors," Commander Breem ordered, leaving one safety still on. "Transfer targeting coordinates from the *Heralc*."

"Yes, Commander," came the response from the signals officer as everyone bent to their task.

"Here we go," Lora said, whispering the words softly as she watched the clean computer-generated graphics project in front of her, and for a brief second, she was almost able to forget that it wasn't just another simulation.

Almost.

▼

PLANET RANQUIL

▲

▶ "HERE THEY COME, Colonel."

Colonel Reed nodded to the man who had spoken, but turned to where Commander Jehan, Admiral Tanner, and Captain Weston were standing on the overlook around two miles from the LZ. He took just a moment to spot the lights that were moving against the backdrop of stars, then pointed them out to the other three men.

"There. See them?" he asked as the lights of the ships involved in the exercises began to streak against the sky, flames blazing behind them as they began atmospheric braking maneuvers.

"Yes." Nero was the only one to speak right away, his eyes focused on the incoming ships.

"They're coming in faster than we'd do for any other situation," Reed said for the benefit of the admiral and commander, "with their CM systems deactivated."

"Why?" Admiral Tanner asked, frowning.

"Because counter-mass fields send up a flare that's visible to a half-blind signals tech," Reed replied. "With stealth technology, if they're lucky, the first hint that they're in the atmosphere is the flames from the friction heat."

As Reed spoke, a distant rumble began to reach their ears, and he smiled thinly. "And by that time, it's probably too late."

▶ ▶ ▶

The heavy shuttle body vibrated under him as 1st Lt. Aaron Bixx fought the controls with one hand and adjusted the flex of the atmospheric control surfaces with the other. The wings of the big shuttle flexed in response to his demands, twisting the vehicle as they bit into the thickening air around them, and he put her nose down.

"We're through the breach point!" he yelled over the roar that was filling the cockpit even through all the insulation built around him. "Nose down! Stand ready on the CM!"

His copilot nodded tensely, her face white with tension as she handled the minutia of the approach, keeping Bixx free to worry about the key details.

Like not plowing into the ground at Mach 5.

"Mutherfucking son of a..." Bixx cursed as his forward view cleared for a brief moment and he saw the twin reactors of an Archangel only meters away from his nose, pacing the shuttle uncomfortably close for any pilot on a rough entry.

His string of curses kept up, and his copilot winced because she knew that they were all getting recorded in the flight log, and they'd both have to explain it later. She tried to ignore both him and the occasional glimpses of the fighter craft just outside, trusting them both to do their job as she did hers.

"Cav Flight, this is Cav One," Bixx said a few seconds later, finally eschewing the cursing for something useful. "Stand ready to go to full atmospheric braking on my signal."

There was no response as they continued their headlong rush toward the surface of the world, doing what would have been considered insane just a few decades before and wasn't considered very bright even today.

"Mark!" Bixx snarled, yanking back on his control stick.

The headlong rush of the four shuttles halted at the same moment, the fighters staying in perfect formation with them as their wings flexed under the commands of their pilots and each of them tilted back up and showed their bellies to the world below.

The large delta-shaped shuttles were designed as one-piece lifting bodies, their entire airframe intended to catch as much air as possible during just the sort of hard reentry maneuvers that these were being put to. Their control surfaces didn't rely on the old ailerons and elevators of their early brethren, but instead extended along the entire surface of their wings, controlled by flexing memory metals.

Each wing could flex of its own accord, and that of the pilot, changing the characteristics of the shuttle effectively without the added complication of a separate control surface that could become jammed.

The results of the flex were fast and effective and, above all, very predictable, so when the shuttle instantly began to buck and shudder around them, neither Bixx nor his copilot were surprised, startled, or nervous. Not very nervous, at any rate.

"Hit the counter mass on my mark!" Bixx snapped as the LZ came into sight ahead of them.

His copilot gripped her seat with one hand as her other rested on the controls for the counter-mass field generators. The timing had to be perfect on this, or at least it couldn't be late. Early was fine, early they could survive since it was a training operation. In combat, of course, it might be another story, but here and now, early was survivable.

Late, however, would result in them plowing their shuttles right into the ground in a rather spectacular display of pyrotechnics.

The ground was racing up at them, counted in the hundreds of meters instead of thousands now, when Bixx finally yelled out above the roar.

"Mark!"

▼

PRIMINAE COLONY, THEORA DEICE

Orbital Station

▲

▶ "FIRE."

Commander Breem was surprised at how calm her voice sounded, an odd detached feeling infusing her as she watched the numbers count down to the Drasin approach. The ships were less than a light-minute out now, the twenty of them that the sensors had finally managed to count, and she knew that it was almost over.

The last of the refugee ships had lifted off over an hour earlier, taking the last of the people who would—who could—be evacuated from the surface of the planet. Now it was just a matter of the final tune being played.

The laser pods made no sound, they didn't even flash or wink as they fired, but on her enhanced projections, she watched the beams race out from the pods, slashing across space toward the enemy.

"Impact in forty seconds," someone said in the background, but she didn't pay any attention.

Lora Breem had learned her lessons from the battle records of her predecessors and had focused the entire force of her arrays on only three of the incoming ships. The Drasin vessels had proved already that they were incredibly tough and resistant to laser attacks—from Priminae laser crystals, at least.

Even so, they weren't invulnerable. The *Cerekus* had proven that in the final moments of the Battle of Ranquil.

The screens showed the shots intersect the enemy flotilla and marked the three ships as unknown as they waited for confirmation of the strikes.

"Hit!"

Two of the ships winked out, the sensor information being fed back to them from the *Heralc* listing them as destroyed. The third began to twist in the three-dimensional projection, its drives dead and the pluming ejection of gas and flame causing it to lose stablity.

The cheers in the background only underscored both Breem's dark rapture as she watched the two ships flicker out, and also her despair as she watched the eighteen others shift their course to better target her positions.

"Scanners!" she called. "Full power!"

They knew she was here now; the time for hiding was past.

▼

PLANET RANQUIL

▲

▶ THE FOUR SHUTTLES seemed to come to an unnaturally fast stop as they leveled out under a hundred meters over the ground, their retrothrusters burning brightly in the early morning light. Reed watched the maneuver with approval, recognizing the skill needed to pull a tight maneuver like that, especially in tandem.

The skill of the *Odyssey*'s pilots, however, was never in question.

The Archangels split up as the shuttles slowed, a third of them staying with the slowing troop carriers as the remaining eight pulled up in a shallow arc that bled of precious little of their speed. The radio chatter that they were listening to keyed over to the fighter jocks then as the first phase of the attack began.

"Archangel Lead to Archangels, weapons free! I say again, weapons free!"

Tanner and Nero flinched slightly as the ground suddenly lit up, bathed in flames and smoke as the fighters passed over the LZ with their weapons blazing. Guided submunitions, released from missiles in flight, erupted in airbursts over the battle zone and turned the land into pitted, smoking craters. Lasers from the four linked cannons mounted on the Angels' wings scorched the ground as they passed, frying one defensive installation after another, and the gimbal-mounted 80mm cannons roared in the distance as the pilots let them fire free at any target on their screens.

"Watch the shuttles," Reed said then, knowing that the spectacular destruction caused by the fighters would distract the two men beside him. "This is important."

Tanner and Rael turned their focus to the shuttles, watching through an advanced projection even as their eyes flickered occasionally to the reality in the distance. The shuttles had turned side-on as they came sliding to a stop over the field, nothing but smoking wreckage below them.

Then, from just over forty meters up, the first of the troops vacated the shuttles. The whining crack of assault rifles was lost in the distance, as was the damage they inflicted lost in the general carnage of the Archangel's pass, but the figures themselves were dropping to the ground and instantly rushing away from the landing zone.

"Air cav tactics—adapted slightly, of course," Reed said calmly as he watched, glancing at his watch.

▶▶▶

"Move! Move! Move!" Greene snarled, wondering when he would get tired of yelling at people, as he slapped the armored backs of the men as they leapt from the shuttle. *Meh, haven't gotten tired of it yet, don't see it coming anytime soon.*

They were going out five at a time, suits already picking up possible defensive emplacements as they jumped, their assault rifles leading the way as they dropped. Those that hit the ground seemed to bounce as their suits absorbed the impact, then allowed the soldiers to arc back into the air in shallow leaps that carried them across the devastated terrain.

Greene noted one soldier whose rebound jump carried him about five meters and winced as his suit vitals flickered almost instantly to "dead." The trooper in question hit the ground hard as his armor locked up and let him bounce across the terrain.

The sergeant made a note to ream the soldier out later, but then the shuttle was empty and it was his turn out the door.

▶ ▶ ▶

Lieutenant Crowley cursed as the straps that secured his tactical armor in place refused to give properly, keeping him pinned in place as the others exited the shuttles.

"Move it, Lieutenant!" Brinks shouted as he sent the last of the troops on their way. "This is a combat drop!"

Crowley activated his armor and reached up with one metal-shod hand and simply ripped the two-ton test straps in two. Then he levered himself up and tromped across the shuttle to the door.

"Sorry, sir," he said. "Ready to go."

"Then do it, soldier!" Brinks snapped, gesturing to the door.

Crowley nodded inside his armored shell and stepped out of the shuttle.

Brinks watched him fall for a second, then threw himself out as well.

All eyes were on the skies as the radio chatter filled the observation area with the sound of the incoming soldiers.

Colonel Reed carefully split his attention, paying some mind to the exercise, but he was really more interested in the reactions of the Priminae observers.

"Troops clear!"

"Cav Flight, this is Cav One. We are clear!"

Reed and the others watched as the shuttles twisted in the air and pulled immediately out of the LZ, staying low as they pulled away toward a predetermined rendezvous.

"They'll hide themselves well away from the battle, taking their air wing with them," he explained to Nero and Tanner as four of the Archangels stayed close to the retreating shuttles. "But they won't be far."

The dance of the battle was intricate, almost pure chaos to the untrained eye, but Reed saw the patterns under the surface of that chaos, and he liked what he saw.

Mostly.

"They're a little late on the drop," he said idly a moment later, speaking to Captain Weston now. "Shuttle Four was a good minute over their allotted time."

Eric nodded. "I noticed. I'll have a word with the major about it."

Reed just nodded in response, not needing to say anything more. A minute in battle was a long time, and the entire point of air cavalry operations was to get in fast, hit hard, and be able to get back out.

PRIMINAE COLONY, THEORA DEICE

Orbital Station

▶ "WE'VE LOST ANOTHER pod!"

Lora nodded, her face set in a grim rigor as she watched the *Heralc* take out another of the enemy ships. They were down to fifteen Drasin now, but the wave of fighters from the lead cruisers were in among the laser pods now, and they were going up one by one.

"Keep firing," she ordered calmly.

Too calmly, part of her mind whispered to her. She couldn't feel much besides this strange detached sensation that made her feel as if she weren't really there, like she was just watching.

That was true, in a way. She was sitting safely in the orbital command station, and they had yet to be fired upon. There was no indication that the Drasin had even noticed them yet; they were too occupied with the *Heralc* and the laser pods, so the command center was entirely untouched by battle.

A light flickered on the screen, and someone groaned as another laser pod vanished from the screen.

Well, perhaps not entirely untouched.

▼

PLANET RANQUIL

▲

▶ "THEY'RE ON THE ground, Colonel Reed. Defenses are active and engaging the assault force."

"Thank you, Chief," Reed said, eyeing the battle through the projected enhancement of the field. "Increase the attack power of the field defenses by 40 percent."

"You got it, Colonel," Wilson said, tapping a command into his computer control.

Through their computer-enhanced view of the battle, Reed and the others could see the figures through the smoke and flames that obscured their direct line of sight. The system added in generated images of each of the soldiers as they moved in shallow leaps and fast-paced sprints across the field. Even the beams of lasers and return fire from the soldiers was added in using a real-time algorithm, making the entire thing look very much like a Hollywood movie.

"Most impressive," Rael Tanner said quietly, watching the madness of destruction as it was echoed to the screen in front of him. Oddly, though, he had to admit that it was the distant smoke and thunder that was somehow more impressive.

"Actually, it's not," Reed said, frowning.

"Pardon?" Nero asked then, speaking for the first time since the exercise had begun.

"He means that the assault team is rusty," Captain Weston said, stepping closer to look at the numbers. "They've lost too many people for this level of defense, and they're behind schedule by almost two minutes now."

Reed nodded. "That's the problem with a newly formed team, Commander. These men haven't yet learned to work together properly, and it's telling. Wilson?"

"Yes, Colonel?"

"Double the attack force."

"Aye, Colonel," the former Navy SEAL replied automatically, then increased the numbers on his system.

Behind him, he noticed the Priminae observers exchanging glances that were a decided mix of confusion and apprehension. Milla, a little more used to the Terrans, leaned closer to Nero and Rael to whisper to them.

"They seem to enjoy making things harder for each other, Admiral, Commander," she said softly.

Tanner and Jehan shrugged, but couldn't find the words to comment as they focused once more on the action unfolding.

▶▶▶

"We're getting hammered here!" someone screamed over the tactical network, causing Lt. Jackson Crowley to wince in annoyance.

He didn't know why anyone was yelling; it wasn't like that would actually help anyone hear them. He adjusted his computer to regulate the volume of the comm chatter as he bounded the EXO-12 across the terrain, keeping lower and moving slower than his suited companions.

"Keep up, Lieutenant!" Brinks snarled, an image of the major appearing in the corner of Crowley's HUD. "We aren't coming back for you!"

"Yes, sir!" Jackson said, tapping in a command sequence. "Initiating NICS interface, Major. I'll be with you in a second."

The major grumbled something and signed off, but Jackson ignored it and flipped up the shielded switch that protected the NICS activation sequence. The metal shield locked the switch in place, and the suit flashed a brief warning over his HUD as the NICS molecular needles slid from his helmet and right into the back of his neck.

"Ahhh..." Jackson grimaced, though the pain fled a moment later.

"NICS engaged," he said over the command band, adjusting his grip on the control wands in each hand as his feet worked the pedals that controlled his steps. "Engaging maneuvering thrusters."

The EXO-12 hard suit was designed as a medium armor intended originally to provide a strong armor support to urban operations in hostile territory. Its twelve-foot stature was a little too big for clearing out most buildings, but it could move through city streets with a level of skill and efficiency that even the most nimble and fleet of conventional armor couldn't match.

One of its primary design considerations was that it be able to keep up physically, not only with foot soldiers equipped with powered armor, but also with the high-speed APCs that had seen more and more use as the previous battlefield mainstay, the main battle tank, fell into disfavor.

Powered and supplemented by the NICS interface, the EXO-12 was capable of running at speeds in excess of fifty miles per hour over relatively level ground. Impressive as that may be when compared to an unpowered human, it wasn't the equal of the high-speed attack APCs used in modern urban warfare, nor was it the equal of the jumping speed of a soldier using the latest in powered armor.

So the designers had added a few things to make up for its bulk.

The twin thrusters on the back of the tactical armor were one part of that solution, a part that came into play as Crowley jumped his armor off the ground and engaged the thrust for a powered leap that reached just over 120 miles per hour at its peak.

Jackson had purposely kept the arc low, which made things harder for the local defenses to find and kill him but also made the landing a lot trickier on him. He threw himself back, bringing the armor with him, and landed at better than a forty-five degree angle to the ground.

The "feet" of the armor dug in as he landed, digging deep furrows as Jackson brought the armor to a stop almost two hundred meters from where he started, and right in the midst of the formation of soldiers led by Major Brinks.

▶ "POD THREE IS gone!"

Commander Breem didn't bother to acknowledge the report; she just ordered her two remaining pods to target another Drasin as it approached. The beams from the powerful satellite pods slashed out through space, hitting the Drasin ship almost instantly at the close range they were now fighting at, and gutted the enemy ship in a ten-second-long rage of fire that proved to be their last.

As the Drasin flared and burned, two more of the cruisers turned on the offending pods and blasted them out of existence.

Lora threw back her control system, letting it scatter as the hard projection that sustained it lost positive contact with her, and slumped back in her seat.

"That's it, Captain," she said over the open communications link to the captain of the *Heralc*. "We're out."

The projection of her subordinate didn't look much better than she felt, she supposed. He was in a marginally better situation, of course, being that his ship was still intact, and so he still had weapons with which to fight, but the projection also clearly showed that his bridge was in a frenzied state as people struggled to keep it that way.

Still, he spared her a glance over the open channel and nodded. "Understood, Commander. Your orders?"

Breem stared at him for a moment, almost unable to understand what he was asking from her. She was out of the fight. There was nothing he could do to help or save her any more than either of them could help or save those still on the planet.

She closed her eyes, then slowly shook her head. "Withdraw, Captain."

"What?" He paled, staring at her in shock. "Commander, I—"

"That is an order. Withdraw. Your duty is now to the evacuees. Defend them until they reach sanctuary, Captain. Then report to the fleet," she said, opening her eyes and glaring at him. "Withdraw. Now."

She could feel the eyes of those in her control room as they matched the captain's stare, but ignored them all as she glared at the subject of her thoughts.

He nodded reluctantly. "Yes, Commander...Walk the Path, Commander. You and yours."

"Walk the Path, Captain," she said in return, then shut off the commlink.

PLANET RANQUIL

▶"WE'RE PINNED DOWN, Major!" Lieutenant Bermont snarled from where he'd thrown himself behind a large boulder. "They've got a good cross fire set up here."

"Tell me something I don't know, Lieutenant," Brinks said through a smile that was as much a sneer as anything else. "Give me a—"

"Major," Jackson interrupted. "Pardon me, sir, but I might have something that can help."

"What is it, Crowley?"

"The EXO-Twelve is equipped with heavy ECM capabilities, sir. I might be able to get a couple clean shots—"

"What kind of ECM, soldier?"

"The works, Major," Jackson replied. "Everything from squealers to chaff."

Brinks eyed the big suit for a moment, then half laughed. "I guess they had to cram something into all that extra space."

"Uh...yes, sir."

"All right, hit it," Brinks ordered. "Hit everything. We'll move together. A three-layer pincer, with Crowley at the center, everyone got it?"

"Sir," the men responded, shouting the word as an affirmation, not a question.

"Good. Let's move!"

Crowley nodded automatically as he pumped the legs of the big machine to bring it to the front, keying open the ECM menu with the eight-way "coolie hat" under his left thumb and flipping them all to active.

▶▶▶

From the observation room, Weston could tell it wasn't going as planned when Wilson suddenly winced, shouted *shit*, and yanked his earphones off. They could all hear a sudden squealing sound coming from them.

"What the hell is going on, Chief?" Reed asked as Weston hung back, watching.

"Someone down there is cheating, sir," Wilson said with a grimace that was at least partially amused. "Heavy electronic jammers. Real heavy."

Reed frowned. "Who? Those are just Power Suits. They don't have enough power or mass to mount those kinds of systems."

"Don't know, sir, but I'm cut off," Wilson said, tossing the earphones to the control panel. "The defenses are under full computer control now."

Reed half laughed, shaking his head. "Well, good for them."

"Yes, sir."

Rael and Nero exchanged glances, somewhat confused as they looked to Milla, who seemed just as lost as they were, but Weston just smiled.

"That's battle for you, Admiral," he said with a shrug. "Even mock battle. Surprises are the one thing you can't hope to plan for."

Reed chuckled in agreement. "That's why they call them surprises, Captain."

"Indeed," Nero said stiffly, pointing to the projection in front of him. "However, we appear to have lost our view of the exercise."

Reed looked at the projection and nodded with a sigh, an acknowledgment that the jamming had indeed skewed the computer-generated images badly, probably causing it to report entirely wrong positions and actions.

"'Fraid so, Commander," he said with a shrug. "Nothing to do about it except turn it back to plain optics."

He did so, and they soon had a view of the battle that was clearer, but now muddied by smoke and debris.

"How is this going to affect scoring, Colonel?" Weston asked Reed.

Reed shrugged. "Not too bad, sir. It'll just take longer because we'll have to compile the data from the suits after the exercise. We just lost our real-time numbers, is all."

Weston nodded, then turned his attention back to the scene.

▶ ▶ ▶

Eight of the automated defensive stations covered the area on the other side of their rocky cover, so Brinks had split the team into three groups, with Jackson Crowley at the center so that his jammers would be given the maximum coverage. The lieutenant took the position eagerly enough and was at the front of the line as the soldiers made their move from cover.

They led with indirect fire from the grenade launchers saddled under their assault weapons, dropping thermobaric munitions and a mix of smoke and HE rounds into a short-range arc that landed less than fifty meters away. The *hiss-bang* of the TB rounds going off was at first overpowered by the loud cracks of the high-explosive rounds, but the thunderous rumble and lightning crack of the noxious vapors detonating shook the ground itself as the ten-psi overpressure wave rocked them, even in their suits, and provided the team with the signal to move.

Jackson pumped the legs of his oversized tactical armor, bounding over the cover in two small jumps, and extended his weapons arms out forty-five degrees from his center, allowing him to cover the widest area. The HUD of the tactical armor began reporting back with likely targets with the first second of the rush, leaving Jackson with the simple yet critical task of simply giving the machine permission to engage.

He thumbed the coolie hat controls on each handgrip, selecting weapons and prioritizing targets, then squeezed his index trigger down on the firing selectors for both arms.

Despite being at the cutting edge of technology, the EXO-12 and its onboard computers suffered from the same issues all computerized weapons systems had. For all their intelligence and capability, they weren't equipped to make moral choices. That was Jackson Crowley's job.

He was the moral conscience, the emotive factor, of the machine. He had to make the choices that it couldn't, like any rifleman did for his weapon.

Is this a viable target?

Should it be destroyed?

Fire or hold?

Crowley fired.

Around him, men in power suits were bounding over the cover, their own weapons rattling his ears as the sound was echoed to him by the suit's sensors. His own weapons fire, however, was nothing but a mild vibration that rung through the armor, the suit itself filtering out the sound of its own making in order to leave him open to sounds that others might be making in his direction.

From the outside, however, the air was filled with the rattling sound of the EXO-12's three-barrel gun whining up to speed as it began to pump over five thousand rounds per minute down range, firing the same 15mm scramjet rounds that the M-112 fired, only about four times faster.

Anti-armor lasers whined as well, their capacitors dumping power in a series of fast pulses that tore up targets in a fury of hellish radiation, vaporizing the defenses as he moved. Step by step, Crowley began to feel a growing confidence. After this, they wouldn't be making jokes about his armor anymore. The EXO-12 was proving itself, once and for all.

Of course, that was the time that Mr. Murphy tapped him on the shoulder.

Actually, it was on the foot, though the difference was of little import to Jackson. He had shifted his attention away from the action of walking, coming to relax into the natural feel of it, and then had the misfortune of stepping on a loose stone about the size of a bowling ball.

One second he was eliminating a series of hostile targets, and the next the EXO-12 pitched sideways as its center of balance was disrupted and he went down in a three-ton tangle of limbs.

Crowley cursed, throwing the armor's limbs out in all directions to flatten his tumble quickly, and began to flip himself over and climb back to his feet. He was about halfway up when the closest active defense station tagged him and shut his armor down.

Everything went black, and the armor shook as he hit the ground again, and Lt. Jackson Crowley pursed his lips in disgust as he lay there in the dark.

"Well, *fuck*."

PRIMINAE COLONY, THEORA DEICE

Orbital Station

▲

▶ "THEY SENT MOST of the remaining fleet after the *Heralc* and the evacuees, Commander."

Lora Breem nodded grimly, not saying anything else. She could read the screens as well as her subordinates could, but telling them that wouldn't do any good. They needed to feel like they were doing something, so she let them do whatever it was that they normally would.

The Drasin "fleet," or what was left of it, had indeed broken off for the most part to pursue the escaping ships. Only two badly damaged ships remained there in orbit of Theora, but she didn't even have hand lasers to fire at them.

They dismantled the pods that were still more or less intact first. Though the weapons had been irreparably damaged, they weren't taking any chances with them. Swarms of the little Drasin drones were thrown over the pods, quickly reducing them to rubble and more little Drasin drones that quickly began to die off in the vacuum of space.

She supposed that it should shock her, on some level, the disregard for their own lives that was inherent in Drasin tactics, but Lora just felt oddly numbed to it all as she watched. Soon the first fiery traces were cutting through the atmosphere, the Drasin drop pods cutting down to the planet below.

"Maker, preserve us," someone prayed, and it was followed by a hushed agreement that rolled around the command center. Lora, though, didn't take her eyes off the screens as she counted the trails of fire that led to the planet below.

At ten, she stopped counting, the numb feeling taking more and more of her senses as she just watched and waited for the inevitable.

▼

PLANET RANQUIL

▲

▶MOP-UP TOOK LONGER than Brinks would have liked, because the Green Beanies had hidden the defenses better than he'd expected, but it was done quickly enough, he supposed. Just looking at the numbers, though, told him that they had a lot more drills in their future in order to bring the teams up to their peak performance.

A short distance away, he could see a group of soldiers chuckling and joking as Lieutenant Crowley looked over his rig for damage. He supposed that it was inevitable that the lieutenant catch some flack for tripping over a rock—Lord knows it wasn't a shining example of how to get through a firefight—but Brinks was actually somewhat impressed with the armor the kid was using.

He'd seen suits that were bigger, suits that were faster, and suits that were better armed, but he'd also seen them all fall over at times, and this was the first one he'd seen actually get back on its feet without outside help. That was a big plus for the armor in his book, as long as it didn't fall too much.

The extra room for power, weapons, and jammers didn't hurt, either, of course.

"Major."

Brinks turned, stiffening in his armor, and saluted. "Sir!"

Eric Weston returned his salute with a casual crispness that came from practice, and the major let his arm drop as the captain turned to survey the field.

"You were a bit off the mark, Major," Eric said then, not looking back at him.

"Yes, sir. We have some work to do."

"Well, I wouldn't worry about it," Eric said. "I expect that you'll be getting plenty of practice."

"Uh…sir?"

"Colonel Reed has asked permission for your temporary assignment to his command," Eric told him. "Just while the *Odyssey* is in orbit. As we'll probably be here for a few more weeks, at least, if not the next couple of months, I've agreed."

"I see, sir," Brinks said slowly. "Did the colonel happen to tell you what he wanted us to do?"

"I asked that question, actually," Eric said with a half-smile.

Brinks bit his tongue. Of *course* the captain had asked that question. That wasn't an answer, however.

Eric went on, not knowing, but guessing what reaction was going on under the major's armor. "It has to do with the training of the Priminae ground forces, of course."

Brinks winced. "Captain…My people aren't instructors—"

Eric held up a hand and turned back, silencing the soldier. "I don't think you'll need to be, actually. Colonel Reed asked if I could spare you to operate as an opposing force."

Brinks blinked. Then a slow smile crossed his face under his battle-obscured helm. "You mean we get to pretend to be Drasin, right, sir?"

"That's what I understand, Major."

"Sounds like fun, Captain."

▼

PRIMINAE COLONY, THEORA DEICE

Orbital Station

▲

▶HELPLESSNESS.

It was just a word until you really experienced it.

Powerless, stricken, torture, anguish.

All words meaning nothing to someone who hasn't experienced them each in turn.

Lora Breem knew the meaning of each of those words now, in ways that she never had before. Being unable to do anything other than watch as the Drasin began the dismantling of what was a thriving colony only hours earlier.

In days, it would be a lifeless world, nothing but the crawling, swarming drones of the enemy moving on its surface. Under the world's crust, they would be teeming, chewing up the material of the planet itself to further their own suicidal propagation.

In weeks, there would be nothing in this place but a rapidly expanding field of debris that consisted mostly of the Drasin bodies themselves. Those and the cooling core of the world would make up a new asteroid field that would circle where a world had been until then.

Lora was a witness to the death of a world, and there was nothing she could do to stop it.

In a vaguely sickening way, it was actually a relief when the limping cruiser turned on her command post, finally noticing that she was floating there.

Floating there and watching them.

Someone screamed behind her as the cruiser came wheeling at them, the energy surges from their position indicating weapons fire.

Breem didn't scream; she just watched and waited.

If the Drasin had aimed properly, she would see a flash of light in the visible spectrum in the brief instant before she died. Waste energy from their lasers, flying ahead of the truly destructive force. It was the only thing she could think to do— to watch death coming rather than try to vainly evade it in some futile effort of denying reality.

So she straightened up in her chair and watched the screen.

Which promptly flashed a bright pure white and then went completely dead.

Lora closed her eyes then, just a bare scant moment ahead of the whirling lance of hellish fire that engulfed her command.

▼

NACS ODYSSEY

High Orbit, Planet Ranquil

▲

▶ THINGS WERE COMING along well as far as Eric Weston could tell. In the past couple of weeks, ship time, the new training facilities had progressed to a state of operational construction, meaning that while the overall boot camp, officers corps, and academy were still under construction, the Priminae had begun passing students through each of them in turn.

Primarily the boot camp so far, of course. With Reed's influence, that was inevitable. The reports from the Green Berets detachment were of a mixed bag, however. The troops were eager enough—some of them excessively so, according to the rough psych evaluations Weston had been forwarded—but they had a lot of problems with the idea of "controlled violence." In some ways, Eric supposed that it made a weird kind of sense; violence was one of those things that could easily be considered a "black or white" sort of situation.

However, it wasn't black and white, not for a proper army. Not if you wanted your military to actually defend the society that birthed it.

A soldier had to stand ready to fight, provide humanitarian aid, teach, learn, and do a multitude of things according to the needs of society. Specialization, as one prominent author once said, was for insects. Just because you were better at one thing didn't mean you ignored everything else.

And just because you were trained to fight didn't mean that you had to dredge up some insane antiquated notion of bloodlust to cover the moral question of whether violence was right.

All things considered, Eric had to admit that he was just as pleased that it was Colonel Reed's job to explain the difference between "justifiable" and "right." To be honest, he'd often had the same question in mind when he was going through training with the Marines.

They'd been pretty much purged the first time he'd been shot at, however. There was just something very crystalizing about bullets whining over your head; it tended to put questions of morality in perspective.

He expected that the Priminae would probably learn the same lessons, eventually, though he hoped for their sake that it wasn't anytime soon.

In the meantime, he had other concerns. Admiral Tanner had taken a personal interest in the development of the naval academy section of the new military training center and had come to him for suggestions. Unfortunately, being a product of the Marine Corps, Eric wasn't exactly the most knowledgeable person on the vagaries of naval training.

That in itself probably wasn't a bad thing, of course, since the relationship between starships and naval units was a lot farther apart than people on Earth generally assumed. There were some correlations, of course, and even more with the submarine service, but the fact was that controlling the *Odyssey* required disciplines from a wide variety of sources of which the Navy had only been a relatively small one.

"Captain?"

Eric looked up. "Yes, Ensign?"

"I need you to look these over, sir, and sign off on them," Lamont said, handing him a chip for his data plaque.

Eric accepted it and dismissed Lamont, sighing.

Sometimes he wondered if the "wide variety" of sources that contributed to the *Odyssey* was really such a good idea. It seemed that they all contributed at least one thing in common—their paperwork.

▼

PRIMINAE VESSEL VULK

On Patrol, Outer Ranquil System

▲

▶ "CAPTAIN, WE'RE DETECTING an incoming bow wake."

Capt. Johan Maran turned to look at the screens that his lead sensors officer had put up at the front of the command deck. "Analysis?"

"Working on it."

Johan nodded, closing down the analysis he was running on one of the shipboard systems and reluctantly setting it aside for the moment. He believed that they could get far more effective power through some systems if they just got the settings right, but for now, the matter of the moment took precedence.

Bow wakes were caused by faster-than-light craft as their dimensional shift fields impacted with matter in normal space. The energy discharge was impressive—at least given the minute amounts of matter involved—and caused a "bounce" in the matter's energy state that could last for several light-seconds to over a light-hour, depending on the speed of the ship involved.

The energy state had to be measured in the distance that light could travel because conventional energy measuring sticks were meaningless when dealing with FTL particles. It was generally easier to measure how long they had the energy to remain in an FTL state than to try to quantify the imparted energy of the collision.

This did, however, make it rather difficult for one ship to determine the exact range to an incoming contact. Two or more could triangulate the energy states and determine a location, but a single ship could only analyze the frequency of the energy and match it to known bow wakes in hope of determining if the incoming ship was friend or foe.

That matching process took time, however, and while it was being done, the contact was hurtling toward you at several factors of light-speed. It could be unnerving for a captain and crew.

"Unknown," Sensors Officer Jira Kath said after a moment. "The computers can't make a match."

"Opinion?" Johan demanded tersely.

"Multiple incoming contacts," she answered, not hesitating. "Enough variety to scramble the drive frequency."

Johan nodded, pursing his lips. "Agreed."

He walked to his command chair, pivoting easily on one heel and sinking into it. "Sound combat stations."

The alarms went off then, jarring enough that no one would mistake them for anything else, and behind Johan, the rear section of the bridge became a mass of action as people rushed to their combat stations.

"Communications," Johan said, "please inform the admiral's command center that we are exiting the system to investigate possible Drasin contact."

"Yes, Captain."

"Turn us into that wake then," he said calmly. "And ahead, full sublight drive."

"Yes, Captain."

NACS ODYSSEY

High Orbit, Planet Ranquil

▲

▸WESTON WAS READING when the message came in, indulging in something he rarely had much time for anymore. So he was annoyed by the chirp of the comm, but resigned all the same.

"Captain to the bridge."

Eric rose from his chair with a fluid motion, scattering a pair of data plaques to the desktop with a casual maneuver, and was around the desk and halfway across his ready room before they'd stopped sliding. He exited to the right side of the bridge a few seconds later, absently brushing his uniform down from where it had ridden up as he sat at his desk.

"Report," he asked briskly, crossing to his central command chair.

"Priority traffic from the Priminae Admiralty, sir," Roberts replied smoothly.

Weston raised an eyebrow at that. That meant the source of the traffic was from the single new station on the bridge, installed in the last couple of weeks by Priminae technicians and Master Chief Wilson.

Eric was no slouch when it came to math—a fighter pilot couldn't be—and he was better than passing fair with all types of communication systems, but the system they'd installed into the *Odyssey* power grid was beyond him. First off, the sheer amount of juice it took to run, which was actually a staggering amount by any Terran measure, was exacerbated by the flawed conversion technology that took the *Odyssey*'s electrical grid and converted it to a compatible form for the terminal.

It was bad enough that Eric didn't think that it could be run under combat conditions, unfortunately, but at least it gave the *Odyssey* real-time ship-to-shore communications.

"The *Vulk* has detected incoming FTL signatures, sir," Roberts told him. "They've moved out of the system to investigate."

Eric nodded, checking the numbers. "All right, if they're hostile, we're probably looking at the better part of twenty-four hours before they get here, but we'll assume that they're in a hurry."

"Aye, sir," Roberts agreed.

"Have all stations report in. Make sure that they're battle ready in twelve hours," Weston said after a moment.

"Yes, sir." Roberts nodded again, half turning. "Anything else?"

"No, I..." Eric paused, thinking.

"Sir?"

"Have the Archangels move up to Ready One positions. We've been fooled by the Drasin's stealth technology before," Eric decided. "And prepare for a tachyon ping of the system."

Now, this was certainly more interesting than exercises and training, although Weston hoped it didn't get too interesting...

PRIMINAE VESSEL VULK

Outer System, Ranquil

▲

▶SOON ENOUGH, THE *Vulk* had cleared the minimum safe distance to engage the dimensional drive. Johan Maran tapped a command into the projected interface in front of him. "Power up the converters. All weapons stations stand by on combat alert."

"Yes, Captain."

The command deck was a mass of activity as the crew prepared for a micro-jump that would propel them away from the system at forty times the speed of light. The incoming contact was still well beyond the range of their active sensors—only its own FTL radiation giving any evidence of its approach—so Maran had elected to meet them as far from the system as possible.

"All stations report ready."

Maran gave the order: "Execute jump."

There was no change in the apparent state of the ship as the power was channeled into the dimensional drives, but the stars outside shimmered and then blinked out as the incoming light shifted out of their detection range.

"Normalizing screens," someone said from behind him, but Maran didn't look up.

The screens flickered again, the system being calibrated to the new frequency shift of the light outside. Incoming light on an FTL vessel had to be adjusted to visible frequencies, as the difference in velocity tended to shift light down and out of human frequencies. The screens had to be recalibrated to read the normally higher-level radiation that "replaced" it.

The stars returned, their color being slightly whiter, almost "purer" than before, but showed no noticeable motion as the big ship hurtled through space. They were simply too far away for even the *Vulk*'s impressive speed to create any sort of change over the attention span of the average person.

Maran didn't pay any attention to the routine vagaries of the dimensional drive, instead focusing on the sensor projection at his side, intently searching for any sign of the contact.

Unless they were approaching incredibly fast, with an insanely powerful drive, they should be coming into contact within moments.

Then there they were.

His bridge was already reporting in: "Multiple contacts! Drive readings indicate Koruun-type transports, Captain."

That was a relief. He'd expected something much, much worse. "Isolate individual drive specs. I want to know which ones."

"Yes, sir."

Maran eyed the specs, still frowning. The Koruun transports had big, powerful drives, but even as many as he was seeing on his projections wouldn't be enough to scramble a drive frequency. There had to be someone else out there—probably multiple someones, in fact—to have sufficiently scrambled the frequency so that the *Vulk* couldn't recognize it from in-system.

"Contact the lead ship."

NACS ODYSSEY

High Orbit, Planet Ranquil

▲

▶ THE FLASH-TRAFFIC MESSAGE from the Priminae Admiralty for Weston was a transcript from the *Vulk*, transmitting from several light-minutes beyond the system heliopause. Captain Maran had reported that there were incoming refugees from a Drasin attack on another fringe system.

Eric sighed, shaking his head.

"Captain?" Roberts asked, walking over.

"So much for peace having broken out," Eric said, tapping the display over so that the angle was visible to the commander.

Roberts grimaced. "They lost another planet?"

Eric nodded, flipping through the report. "Looks like they mangled the Drasin this time, though. They've got their industry cranking out some heavy weapons."

"It's about time, sir," Roberts said, his voice just a notch beneath "scathing."

Eric personally agreed with the commander, but didn't allow himself the luxury of wallowing in that "superiority" complex. It would be counterproductive, and he had to maintain good relations with the military representatives of the Priminae people. People like Admiral Tanner and

Commander Jehan had enough problems—and guilt— because of their people's deficiencies. Adding to either would only serve to alienate them.

"Do we have incoming hostiles as well?"

"Unknown," Eric said absently. "The *Vulk* is still investigating. The refugees were pursued by the Drasin, however, but they report that the vessel *Heralc* turned back some time ago to harass the pursuers."

Roberts grunted slightly, nodding.

One ship trying to harass and harry several pursuers was at a severe disadvantage, Eric and Jason both knew. The only course of action that was really possible in such a case was a violent, aggressive assault that gave the enemy no choice but to shift their focus. Anything else and the enemy would just ignore you or, at best, split up and send the bulk of their force after the original target, anyway.

"What do we do, Captain?" Roberts asked then.

Eric shook his head. "Nothing much we can do."

Again, Roberts nodded. The *Odyssey* was deep inside the gravity well of the star and would never be able to reach a safe distance for transition before the enemy, if any, were already well into the system.

They could, of course, evacuate the system. They probably had time for that, but the deal that Ambassador Corusc had signed with the Confederation militated against it. The NAC wasn't required to lend naval support, of course—the politicians back home hadn't been willing, or crazy enough, to agree to that—but it did establish an embassy with the Priminae people and loan military advisors to them under full knowledge of wartime conditions.

Defending the embassy was Eric's primary duty as long as he was in-system, and unless matters became hopeless, he was content to accomplish that in the most direct fashion available to him.

To defend the embassy, he'd simply have to defend the planet it was sitting on.

To that end, he gave the order to roll up the reactors and put all weapons capacitors on full charge.

"Nothing we haven't seen before, right, Commander?" At least, so far.

"Aye, aye, sir." Roberts nodded and turned back to his job.

EMBASSY OFFICES

Planet Ranquil

▶ "AMBASSADOR."

Julia LaFontaine nodded gracefully as she rose to her feet from behind her workspace and smiled at the older man who had appeared. "Elder."

"I have been sent to deliver a message," he told her gravely.

Julia dropped her smile immediately, becoming quite grave herself. Elder Corusc wasn't the highest member of the local government—though she was still having a lot of trouble trying to determine exactly how the government was organized—but she knew full well that he was well above "messenger" level.

"What message, Elder?"

"There has been a detection of many ships entering the range of our system, Ambassador," he told her seriously.

Julia paled. "Drasin?"

"Not yet. However, the ships we have identified are the survivors of another lost world," he said softly.

She winced sympathetically.

It was hard, actually, to comprehend the sheer scale of this war. The loss of planets, billions of people, it wasn't real to her as much as she tried to make it so. Julia had seen her fair share of atrocity, of course, though most of it was secondhand in the war crimes tribunals that had been echoes of the last war. However, at their worst, they were bare blips on any chart she could imagine when comparing them to what had happened out here.

So why, she wondered, *do the deaths of thousands feel more real, more urgent, to me than the deaths of billions?*

The old quote from almost two centuries earlier leapt unbidden into her mind.

One death is a tragedy; a million is a statistic.

For all that, though, Julia wondered guiltily if part of it was that they weren't her people, weren't from her world, that made it such a nonevent to her.

She forced that thought away, shaking her head. "Is there anything I can do, Elder?"

▶ ▶ ▶

"Shit," Reed cursed, shaking his head as he looked at the message that had flashed across his terminal. "Not good."

"What is it, Colonel?"

He looked up, noting that Master Chief Wilson had been close enough to hear.

"We might have incoming unfriendlies," he said, his lips curling.

Wilson shook his head. "Not good, sir."

"I'm aware of that," Reed replied.

It wasn't even remotely good, in fact. The men had only started being trained a couple of weeks earlier and were still in a state of near culture shock. They had truly been unready to accept the level of force that Reed's men were applying to the training, and the rough-and-ready Colonials were showing signs of crumbling under the training from the hardened Green Berets.

Reed's men had been scaling it down automatically, but then were forced to turn the pressure up when they accidently went too far. It was a frustrating process of trial and error as they retrained themselves to read an utterly alien mindset on the fly. Things were starting to come out of the crapper, but only just, and they needed more time.

"*Ask me for anything but time,*" Reed quoted, shaking his head.

"If we had time, we wouldn't need anything else, sir," Wilson replied dryly.

Unfortunately, the former SEAL was right. Reed nodded tiredly, rising to his feet. "Kevin!"

"Sir!"

The young attaché, an ensign trained under the rules of the Confederation naval tradition, snapped into the office almost instantly. Reed wondered if the young man waited, listening, outside the door for a call, but pushed it aside after a moment.

"Get a message to Major Brinks," he ordered. "He's out on maneuvers, right?"

"That's right, sir."

"Tell him to have his men back here ASAP, and then go down to the museum and tell them to make everything ready for combat."

"Yes, sir." The attaché saluted, then vanished.

"Eager little beaver," Wilson said with a smile.

"He does his job," Reed replied. "You'd better go and tell the others that we might have company coming."

"You got it, Colonel."

Reed hesitated a moment. "You'd best ask Ithan Chans to come in as you leave."

"Yes, sir."

Wilson left, leaving Reed considering his options for a few moments before the slim woman stepped into the office.

"Yes, Colonel?" she asked, her expression tense but confused as she tried to determine what was going on.

"Yes, thank you, Ithan," Reed told her seriously. "I'm going to need you to start talking to your military. Get them ready to work with us."

"Colonel?"

"It's the Drasin, Ithan Chans," he said. "It looks like they're back."

Milla blanched white, literally frozen in place for a long moment before she shuddered and nodded woodenly.

"Y…Yes, Colonel. I will begin contacting others now." She swallowed hard.

"Thank you," he said, gesturing to the door. "Dismissed."

▶▶▶

Sergeant Greene was looking over the service reports for his "charges," the powered armor suits that the *Odyssey* soldiers used as standard equipment, when Ensign Kuboto rushed into the museum with a wild look in his eyes.

The "museum," so called for the racks and racks of armor that stood up in their charging cradles, was one of the first buildings put to use since the locals had begun construction, and while it was a little spartan, it suited Greene nicely.

"What is it, Ensign?" Greene asked respectfully, or at least as close as he got with any officer who didn't completely piss him off.

"Message from the colonel, Sergeant." Kobuto was panting, and Greene had to keep from clucking his tongue at the lack of physical conditioning. "He says to get the armor ready for combat operations."

That erased any snide thoughts from the sergeant's head in short order as Greene stiffened and snapped around to give the ensign his full attention. "What was that again?"

"There are ships coming in-system, Sergeant," the ensign explained. "They might have some pursuers on their tail."

"Corporal!" Greene snarled, spinning around.

"Sarge?" A buzz-cut head popped up from behind a suit that was lying out on a forty-five-degree angle.

"Pull the training chips from the armor!" Greene ordered, already striding forward.

"Sarge?" The voice was more than a little confused by this point.

The training chips were programmable hardware that bridged a gap in the armor's circuitry, effectively closing a circuit that was normally isolated from the armor's main functions. These circuits were directly responsible for things like locking the armor up in training when the unit was struck by a mock shot, as well as other things that were distinctly unhealthy if they occurred in actual combat. Without the physical presence of the chips, those circuits could not be activated by any outside command, which, of course, was the point.

"I said, pull the chips!" Greene snarled. "We've got to make these units hot!"

"Yes, Sergeant!" was the next answer.

Greene ignored it as he tapped out a command on the closest suit of armor in order to access the training chip.

INTERSTELLAR SPACE, RANQUIL REGION

▶ CAPT. KIERNA SENTHE clung to the hardened projection that made up his combat interface, using its projected solidity to steady himself as he struggled to remain afoot as another shudder ran through the deck of his wounded ship.

His command chair had actually been torn loose days earlier when one of the Drasin attacks had not only holed the *Heralc*'s hull, but struck a secondary reactor that detonated with the force of a small sun. The ceramic decks of the powerful warship were rated to hotter temperatures, but the force of the blast had been conducted through the decks, wreaking unimaginable havoc throughout the ship.

His crew was now a tenth of what they had started with, running on adrenaline and little else as they struggled with the remains of the enemy fleet.

"Coming around twenty marks to vertical twelve!" he called, fighting with his controls as he watched the six remaining Drasin circle around.

It was almost over, that was a certainty, but the *Heralc* had done her duty. The refugees would reach the Ranquil System, and Senthe knew that Ranquil had more than twice the orbital lasers of the Deice colony, and the *Vulk* would be there as well.

They could handle six Drasin.

Or five, if Senthe had his word in the matter.

"Forward lasers!" he called. "Target the lead cruiser!"

"Targeted!" someone called, and Kierna had to think to remember her name.

Serra. That was it, he remembered. She was a junior officer, far too junior for her current position, but the reactor detonation had killed most of the weapons specialists, and she was the best he had.

The lasers hummed in the background as they fired, drawing his eyes to the projections as he watched the computer-aided images play out.

The action was taking place in dimensional space, but slightly out of phase with the normal "universe." Each of the ships, the *Heralc* and Drasin alike, were using powerful dimensional drives to phase shift into a higher frequency where light traveled faster than its "normal" pace. Unfortunately, the light from their lasers was not subject to this phase shift when it passed out from their respective dimensional fields, and that meant that the battle was taking place at ludicrously close distances.

So when the hum of the lasers caught his attention, Captain Senthe actually missed the crisscross flash of light on his projection and caught only its aftermath.

"Hit!" Ithan Serra crowed, a little too exuberantly, but Senthe wasn't going to catch her on it now.

The Drasin's forward armor flared with the application of energy, holding up for a second under the unimaginable onslaught, but finally folding as the material was ablated away. The rest of the laser gutted the cruiser from stem to stern as

Senthe manipulated the controls at the last second and violently threw the *Heralc* to the side in a last-second attempt to avoid collision.

Faster-than-light speeds and a proximity that would frighten an orbiter pilot were not good combinations, but that was the only way to fight with dimensional drives engaged. Senthe himself would have been more than happy to drop to normal space for the fight, but then the Drasin would be free to catch the refugees, and he couldn't allow that, so all he could do was wince as his maneuver was just a split second too slow and the belly of the *Heralc* grated in collision with the Drasin ship as they passed.

When the big warship was clear and flying away from the drifting hulk, Senthe called over his shoulder, "Damage?"

"Our shields are almost gone, Captain!"

That wasn't the answer he wanted to hear. The shields—or distance—were the only defense against the Drasin's "super-weapon" that they had deployed in the opening battles of the war. No one Kierna knew of could say precisely what that weapon was, of course, but its effects were both immediate and disastrous: the death of everyone on the targeted ship, and total energy drain from all systems, and the repair of all damage previously suffered by the Drasin vessel.

Without the shields, they would have to run because there was no point dying just to rejuvenate the enemy.

"Get me those shields back!" Kierna growled, watching the screens as the remaining five circled around him.

He fought for maneuvering room—and time, as well—opening the distance between the *Heralc* and the Drasin. His move took them well beyond weapons range, given the fact that the ships were currently moving a good deal faster than their lasers could, but stayed close enough that the Drasin couldn't risk ignoring him in order to pursue the refugee transports.

"We've got another 10 percent on the shields, Captain!"

"Good man!" Kierna replied. "Ithan Serra, prepare for another run!"

▶▶▶

Johan could feel the tension slowly climbing as sensing data began to come back, and they all could see just what was happening out there.

"Heavy energy discharges, Captain."

The bridge of the *Vulk* was calm, though a hint of electric tension rode through the air as her captain nodded mildly in response to the status update.

The word *heavy* was a woefully pitiful description of the flashes of power that were being registered on the *Vulk*'s forward sensors, in his opinion, but Johan supposed that it was adequate enough a description.

"Drive frequencies?" he asked stonily.

"Five Drasin and one Priminae warship."

The tension relaxed slightly, and Johan leaned forward with a thin smile on his face.

They weren't too late.

Maybe.

"Target the closest Drasin; prepare for dimensional combat."

The order set off another series of alarms similar, though distinct from, the combat stations alert that had sounded only shortly before.

"Sensors, get me a reading on the *Heralc*. Communications, try to hail her captain."

"Yes, Captain," both stations responded at once.

"And inform the admiral that we have located the enemy and are preparing to engage."

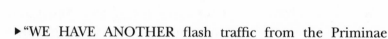

NACS ODYSSEY

High Orbit, Planet Ranquil

▶ "WE HAVE ANOTHER flash traffic from the Priminae Admiralty, sir."

Eric nodded and just flicked two fingers in the air, telling Lamont to send it to his root drive, where he could read it himself.

The message was short and sweet, as such things went, just an update on the situation as they received more intel from the *Vulk*. The contents of the message, however, were more than a little disturbing.

Five of those things, Eric though grimly.

Five wasn't an insurmountable number, certainly not if the reports coming back from the refugees were accurate. The new ships and space-based defenses that the Priminae had begun incorporating into their systems were probably up to it, and Eric knew that, in a pinch, the *Odyssey* could easily take two of them in a standup fight.

More if they had to get creative and had a little luck on their side of the equation.

However, they were still dangerous, especially if they got close enough to the planet for the heavy orbital defenses to become a factor. At that range, they could launch dropships and have a chance of landing more drones on the surface.

Which would be a very dangerous matter, especially if they scattered and landed in multiple areas, as Weston doubted whether the Priminae had planet-wide seismic sensors or enough satellite coverage to guarantee that their local troops took them all out.

A successful insertion of that nature could potentially turn planet Ranquil into the guerrilla warfare capital of the universe.

"Captain," Roberts spoke up, causing Eric to look up. "We're getting light-speed readings on the refugee ships now."

Eric nodded, thinking for a moment, then took a breath.

"Ensign Lamont, have all hands secure for acceleration. Commander, could you please contact the ambassador and Colonel Reed and inform them that I am taking the *Odyssey* out of orbit so we can better cover the planet in case any of the cruisers break through."

Roberts nodded. "Aye, Captain."

Eric forced a smile. "Once more into the breach, ladies and gentlemen."

▼

PRIMINAE VESSEL HERALC

Interstellar Space, Ranquil Region

▲

▶ "NEW CONTACT!"

Kierna Senthe grimaced, teeth showing in his displeasure. The Drasin had been fading in and out during the entire long pursuit, making keeping a good count on them infernally difficult. They'd believed that the enemy had gathered their entire force for the last push, but apparently, they had been wrong.

"It's coming on a vector from Ranquil!"

Or perhaps not.

"Identify!" Kierna ordered tersely, keeping his attention on the ones he knew were trying to kill him.

"Working on it."

Captain Senthe let his people do their jobs, not having much choice to the contrary, and focused on the people trying to kill them instead.

The Drasin were faster than his ship, especially with the damage they'd incurred over the past two weeks of running battle, and were netting them in from all sides as he tried to snake the heft warship through the cracks.

A rumble shook the bridge, causing Senthe to grip the projected controls a little tighter to keep his balance, and he looked over his shoulder. "What in the Maker was that?"

"Laser strike, Captain!" someone replied. "Glancing blow, but it blew out one of our aft bays!"

Senthe nodded, understanding. The after bays were among the few external sections of the ship that still had positive pressure controls, so the sudden shift in atmospheric levels would have caused the rumble. They'd been lucky that's all it caused, in fact. At the start of the battle, a strike there would probably have killed a hundred people.

Of course, those people were already dead now.

"Ventral lasers, return fire!" Senthe growled, gritting his teeth.

The Lympa'an-type warships, like the *Heralc* and its brother ships, were tough ships designed to take abuse far in excess of anything that nature threw at them. In fact, there were less than a handful of natural events in space that could even hope to damage one, and almost all of those were so insanely powerful that they'd crush even the thick ceramic armor of a Lympa'an in the wink of an eye.

Space was like that—very few gradients of danger existed. Either it was harmless, relatively speaking, or it was lethal.

The Lympa'an type was not, however, impervious. Even with the massive redundant systems, heavy bulkheads that prevented ship-wide blowouts like those that had happened to the converted merchant ships in the initial Drasin incursion, and all their other systems, ships like the *Heralc* were still constructed by man and not the Maker.

Which meant that they could be deconstructed by the actions of mortals and monsters alike.

And deconstruction was the aim of the Drasin, who had been slowly picking the *Heralc* and her crew apart from the early rounds of their running battle. Now the five incoming cruisers were preparing to end it, and Senthe could only stretch out the outcome just a little longer.

"Laser fire!"

"Vector!" Kierna shouted over the din, calling for the information that he needed to ensure that he didn't run into the beam that had been fired.

At the speeds of battle they were currently conducting themselves at, it wasn't so much about getting shot by laser pulses as much as it was about accidentally, or not so accidentally, running into the damned things. Even damaged, the *Heralc* could outrun any laser fired in her direction, as could the Drasin ships. So the trick was to maneuver your enemy into the slow-moving energy beams or, preventing that, get so close that it didn't matter if they saw it coming or not.

"Hold course!" someone else shouted in return. "It's not for us!"

Captain Senthe held his course, trusting the voice the way one had to when there were too many things going on at once to handle alone.

On the projected screen, a few seconds later, one of the rearmost Drasin cruisers suddenly broke up and vanished into a ball of expanding debris.

"It's the *Vulk*!"

PRIMINAE VESSEL VULK

Interstellar Space, Ranquil Region

▶ "LINE UP THE next one," Johan Maran ordered calmly, watching his projected readings as he let his helmsperson do her job.

"Yes, Captain." The woman nodded, plotting the next intercept carefully.

The Drasin knew they were there now, if they hadn't been certain before, so it wouldn't be as easy as the last one, but Maran was confident that they could at least whittle the numbers down a little.

"Is the *Heralc* responding on any frequency?" he asked, tilting his head toward the back of the command deck.

"No, Captain."

Johan nodded, tapping a command into his system as a portion of his projection enhanced the image of the *Heralc*. He eyed it carefully for a brief moment, then shook his head. "Battle damage, no doubt. Probably why they didn't warn us of their approach."

"Yes, Captain."

The *Heralc*, like all Priminae ships, had limited faster-than-light communications. The limit was a solid 3.29-light-year range for transmission, the half-life of the transmission particles. They could boost that, much like life pods did with their emergency burst transmitters, but it would blow out the communications package in short order.

The *Heralc* should have been able to call ahead from several days earlier, at least. In fact, they should have been able to call for help before the attack on the Deice world had even occurred, using the repeater stations that were installed throughout the colonies' space.

It was apparent that the Drasin were using new strategies this time and had probably taken out all the repeaters within the immediate range of the Deice world.

The amount of damage that the sensors were reading on the *Heralc*, however, explained quite clearly why they hadn't made any calls.

"Ithan Kanna."

"Captain!"

"How is your laser code?" Maran asked.

"It's been a few cycles, Captain, but I can make myself understood."

Johan smiled at the wry humor he heard in the young man's voice and nodded gravely. "Good. Contact the *Heralc*. They obviously still have sensors since they're evading the enemy fire."

"Yes, Captain. What message, sir?"

"Tell them to make for Ranquil. Best speed," Maran ordered. "There's damned little more they can do here."

"Yes, sir."

"Cori."

"Captain?" the weapons officer asked, not looking up.

"Kill us another Drasin."

"Yes, Captain."

PRIMINAE VESSEL HERALC

Interstellar Space, Ranquil Region

▶"THE *VULK* IS moving on the Drasin again, Captain. They're breaking formation—ignoring us, sir!"

That wasn't surprising, per say, but Senthe was surprised at how it made him feel. He and his crew had been battling them for days, had destroyed three of the ships in a long-running battle that had cost him over 90 percent of his crew, and now suddenly being ignored felt most irritating.

Of course, it was also a major relief.

"Damage Repair Reams, get me shields and communications back!" he ordered over the intercoms, gritting his teeth as he felt another small rumble run through the deck. "And for the love of the Maker, someone fix those hull breaches!"

People, the few that were left on the beleaguered ship, were scurrying around trying to do three and four jobs at once, while the powerful ship slowly died around them, but they still had a duty to the world they'd left behind and the people who had died on it.

"Serra, line up an attack run for the closest enemy ship."

The young woman nodded tiredly, too worn out now to respond in the affirmative, but bent to her work. Kierna wasn't about to criticize her on her lack of protocol, not when she was doing a miraculous job at least two grades over her head.

Seeing how tired his weapons chief was made the force of his own fatigue slap Kierna in the face, but he refused to allow himself to succumb to it as he stood there in the middle of his wrecked command deck and clung stubbornly to the projected helm controls that he had been forced to take over from the body of their previous commander.

"Captain…"

Kierna looked over his shoulder, eyeing the man who was standing the communications post. "What is it, Beh?"

Cornal Behhan Hann was a low-ranked hand who normally handled damage control and maintenance, certainly not the complexities of the communications station. However, the normal officer who would stand there was dead, and most of those both alive and qualified to stand that post had other places to be at the moment, so Behhan had been half drafted, half volunteered into place.

"I…I'm not sure. We're being hit by laser pulses, Captain."

Kierna blinked, frowning. "I didn't feel any more decks blowing out, Cornal," he said grimly.

"That's just it…They're low powered, Captain. Really just high-intensity light…"

"Show me," the captain ordered.

"Yes, Captain," the man said, grateful that the problem wasn't on his shoulders anymore.

Kierna called up the energy spikes as soon as Beh had sent them to his station and eyed them critically. Behhan was right—they were little more than light, powerful enough to register as lasers, but nothing more than that. He tapped up the vectors and ordered the computer to plot their origin points, along with the location of all ships at that time.

"Laser code," he said softly a second later.

"Captain?"

He waved his hand, shutting up the speaker. Laser code wasn't used very often, it was more for kids to play with than anything else, but it was standard and Kierna had learned it once, a long time ago. Luckily, he didn't have to translate it himself. The computer had a full library of it on board, as long as that section hadn't been damaged.

It hadn't, and in a few moments, Kierna was looking at the translated message.

"Chaos blood," he muttered a moment later.

A shocked silence filled the bustle of the bridge, people looking over at him as his curse reached them.

He ignored the looks and shook his head. "Prepare to withdraw from contact."

▼

PRIMINAE VESSEL VULK

Interstellar Space, Ranquil Region

▲

▶JOHAN WATCHED THE graphical image of the *Heralc* as it began to arc away from the battle, and nodded appreciatively to the communications officer. "Good work, Kanna."

"Captain!" the officer at the helm called then, his voice tense. "They're grouping in on us."

Johan returned his attention to the projections as the computer began tracing a projected line of laser light in the space crossing their path just to the rear. The beam crawled along as the computer projected its course in both directions as it calculated the beam's origin and destination, but Johan ignored it.

The beam had missed, and it wasn't anywhere near their projected vectors, so it didn't matter for the moment.

The fact that it had come close enough to be detected and plotted, though, did matter. Lasers were notoriously hard to detect unless you had the misfortune of running directly into one, or had one run into you, it really didn't matter which. In fact, only the most powerful lasers were detectable at any real range unless you were directly in their path. Detection methods varied from analyzing the flare when they intersected random particulate matter that floated throughout even the emptiest regions of space all the way to detecting and analyzing the unique spectral flare that even the most tightly beamed laser gave off. In either case, detecting a laser beam was almost always a matter of seeing it too late. Either it had missed you or it hadn't—there wasn't really a lot you could do about a beam you'd already found.

However, if you survived detecting a given beam, there were things you could do about future attacks.

"Evasive maneuvers!"

And running was always a good option.

The *Vulk* twisted in space, carving a path though the airless void that was impossibly complex and devilishly quick, the Drasin twisting and screaming at their heels. The four remaining ships had teamed together, undoubtedly hoping to deny the *Vulk* and her crew the opportunity of taking them piecemeal.

Johan had seen enough from the battle records that survived the first wave of Drasin attacks to know that his ship was more than a match for a Drasin cruiser, one-on-one. Given that the *Vulk* outmassed the average Drasin cruiser by a ratio of almost ten to one, that wasn't a surprise.

Its mass of firepower, however, only exceeded the recorded Drasin beam by approximately two to one, so the extra mass was a vital necessity. Size, though, did have other advantages. The *Cerekus*, during the last moments of the Battle of Ranquil, had taken damage that would have destroyed any prewar fleet of Priminae ships. The *Heralc*, from what Johan had seen on his sensors, had exceeded even that.

The Lympa'an-type warships were large enough to absorb damage and remain in fighting trim, able to inflict heavy damage even with the majority of the vessel blown out from under its captain's feet.

Johan would, of course, prefer to avoid that situation, if he possibly could.

"Return fire. Continue evasive maneuvers. Prepare for detailed vector changes," he ordered as he punched a series of vectors into the projected interface, then shot his orders over to the helm and weapons stations.

Combat in dimension drive wasn't something that his people had ever really practiced, at least not in recent memory. There were, however, files on the subject buried deep in the classified files that had only recently been opened to him.

They were complicated matters of math and tactics, often an alien subject to Johan, but he did understand the basic precept of combat at FTL velocities.

Ships were faster than light; lasers were not. That was the core tactical center of everything the old files had on dimension drive tactics, and it was what he had to work with now. Basically, there were two ways to hit the enemy with a laser.

First, you could fly your ship so close that your dimensional fields practically, or actually did, come into contact with each other. In this case, your laser would cross the distance between the two ships at light-speed relative to your current velocities, or fairly close, and strike the enemy in much the same way as normal space battles were conducted.

The advantages of this were obvious, of course, but so were the disadvantages. At eighty times the speed of light, the standard frequency shift of Priminae dimensional drives in interstellar space, collisions were uniformly fatal unless you and your enemy were moving on practically parallel courses.

The ancient files Johan had read described battles in which more ships were destroyed by collision than enemy fire. Of course, those ships normally took out at least one enemy ship when they died, but that wasn't the way Johan would prefer to go. Especially since the Priminae people didn't have enough ships to defend them already.

The other primary tactic was deception. It basically amounted to a war of maneuver that depended on outguessing and outthinking the enemy.

Johan was going to start with that option.

"Acknowledge your orders," he snapped after he'd sent the vector data to the two stations that had to be operating in near-perfect sync to make his plan work.

"Orders understood," both the helm and weapons snapped together, bringing a smile to Johan's face.

So far so good.

"Then execute stage on my order," he said seriously, hiding all hint of his smile.

Outside, the rush of interstellar gas and particulates flashed against the *Vulk*'s sheilds as they dashed through the "empty" void, the four Drasin baying at their heels like angry hounds. Johan ignored both, though, watching his tactical display and not the real-space screens.

Then it was time.

"Stage one! Now!"

▼

NACS ODYSSEY

Ranquil System

▲

▶ "THERE'S SOME HEAVY power being thrown around out there, Captain."

Eric Weston nodded, not looking up from his display. He could see what Lieutenant Winger was seeing, though she probably understood it better then he, but for the moment, there wasn't much to do about it.

The *Odyssey* was under full "sail," her passive sensor arrays extended all around the ship like glittering silver sails on an ancient schooner. The apparently flimsy materials of the arrays were surprisingly tough, but after this trip, Eric knew that they'd probably have to toss most of the material despite its engineered strength.

Each "sail" was a carefully engineered reflector that directed incoming energy of most types, even extremely high and low bands, to a central reception point that housed multiple sensors receivers. The entire system operated much like a parabolic dish the size of a couple of football fields, though the resolution was actually better than that hypothetical structure would be, thanks to a few advances in molecular engineering.

Even so, they were only passive, and they couldn't give him anything that wasn't already long over with.

Well, almost anything.

Tachyons themselves didn't reflect particularly well, their velocity being too high and their mass being nonexistent, so they mostly just tunneled right through matter like it wasn't there or were absorbed into heavier materials as they gave up their energy and reverted to normal matter.

They did, however, tend to rip electrons from matter as they tore through. Not many, as they were so tiny that they didn't often run into an actual atom, but enough for their passage to be read by the lines of woven sensors built directly into the huge sails.

At that moment, those sensors were telling one hell of a story.

"Five...six...six contacts, Captain," Winger announced after a moment. "One of them is inbound on the system; the others are moving in this direction—but they're not coming in a straight line, sir."

"Thank you, Michelle, excellent work." This time Eric acknowledged her statement verbally and nodded in her direction.

She bobbed her head quickly, not speaking, but instead just blushed a little.

Winger was probably the best hand with the sensors that he had, and Eric knew that he didn't acknowledge her nearly enough. She was also able to read patterns when chaos was all that Eric saw on his tactical repeater, which made her just one step shy of a miracle worker in his opinion.

"Plot us an interception course for the inbound contact," Eric decided, idly tapping in a course calculation and then double-checking it through the computer. "Bring us up along their southwest bulkhead at...ninety light-seconds."

Eric pushed his tactical board away then, shifting himself back comfortably into his command chair, and looked over at Commander Roberts. "I think we should strike the main arrays in...two hours? Sound about right to you, Commander?"

Roberts nodded. "Aye, sir. Two hours would be just about right."

"We shouldn't be reflecting anything back at them, any-way—not with the Primary at our back. But no sense taking any chances," Eric went on. "In the meantime, Commander, take our adaptive armor to the black hole stealth settings."

"Aye, aye, Captain."

Eric glanced over his shoulder, looking for the person he knew would be standing just against the back wall of the bridge. "Yeoman, I think the bridge could do with a round of coffee, if you please."

The young man nodded briskly before leaving the area. "Yes, sir. Two minutes, Captain."

Eric smiled, glancing over at Roberts. "Two minutes."

"Must have caught him by surprise," Jason Roberts suggested, amused. "Between brews, maybe."

"Maybe."

▼

PRIMINAE VESSLE VULK

Interstellar Space, Ranquil Region

▲

▶JOHAN MARAN WAS sweating, though he'd been able to mask it from the sight of his command staff up to the present. His hands were slick, his hair matted against his skull, and the cloth of his uniform clung to the length of his spine as he sat ramrod straight and continued to work the projected controls.

The battle had been raging for the better part of an hour now, contact almost constant as the two sides flashed through space at eighty times the speed of light, each trying to nail the other with clever maneuvers and traps built using light-speed weapons. Neither side having much luck at it.

The *Vulk* had fired a heavy barrage of lasers about thirteen minutes earlier, lancing the lethal beams of radiation across the depths of interstellar space, then raced along on a ragged course that eventually brought them back across the beams' path, thirteen light-minutes farther along. The Drasin, hot on their tail, had been raked by the lasers, but the hits were scarce, just the same, and at thirteen light-minutes, the beams attenuated beyond lethal focus when dealing with the hardened armor of the Drasin cruisers.

The *Vulk* itself had almost been caught in a fiendish cross fire when three of the four remaining Drasin had tag-teamed them while the last kept up the pressure from the rear. They'd just evaded that by dropping briefly out of dimensional drive and letting the enemy overshoot.

Overall, Johan had come to the conclusion that fighting in dimensional drive was even more insanely difficult than it had been implied on the old files. The attacker in this situation was fighting at a massive disadvantage as he pressed the fight. One practically had to be suicidal to take on a prepared enemy and come out victorious.

"Two of the Drasin are breaking off, Captain!"

Johan growled under his breath as he examined the vectors involved and spotted their destination easily enough. He felt it like a physical blow, even though it was something he'd been expecting. They were heading for Ranquil.

"How much time have we bought the *Heralc* and the refugees?" he demanded quickly.

"They should be several light-cycles into the system, Captain."

Johan nodded.

It would have to do.

"Redirect our course for the Ranquil System. Inform the admiral to have all defenses brought online and readied for use," Johan told his crew. "Time to see if they'll be stupid enough to drop into the gravity well."

"Yes, Captain."

The signal went out then, and the *Vulk* arced away from its frenetic battle and made a run for its home system. With the Drasin just slightly in the lead, Johan knew that he'd be playing a game of catch-up when the war continued in normal space.

NACS ODYSSEY

Ranquil System

▲

▶ "HERE THEY COME, sir! Five contacts, beelining for us like bats out of hell."

Eric's lip twisted at the unnecessary color commentary Michelle had added to her report, but he didn't comment on it as he ordered, "Strike the sails!"

"Striking sails. Aye, Captain," Michelle Winger replied instantly, tapping in a command.

Outside, and around the big ship, the massive reflectors of the *Odyssey*'s huge passive sensor arrays rippled, then began to roll up as the material was withdrawn within her hull on command. Each sail took several minutes to withdraw, eventually leaving the matte-black surface of the *Odyssey*'s black hole stealth mode floating almost invisibly against the backdrop of stars.

While that maneuver was ongoing, Eric Weston was looking over the last information that Winger had shot over to him from the sensor array, the vectors of the incoming ships.

As he'd expected, they were coming in solidly on the same course as the refugees and the sixth contact had, and unless they maneuvered wildly, they would wind up coming right across the *Odyssey*'s firing arc at less than three light-minutes.

"Any update on contact six?" Eric asked, looking up.

"Aye, sir." Winger nodded. "It looks like one of the Primmy ships, sir. Beat up pretty bad."

Eric raised his eyebrow at the nickname but, again, let it pass. He'd have to see if that was starting to spread, though. Somehow he didn't think he wanted to slip up and call Commander Jehan a "primmy."

For the moment, though, he had other things to worry about.

"Do we have visuals?"

"Aye, sir."

"On-screen," he ordered.

The screen flickered then, and a dark shape blurred out the stars in the center of it, occasional flashes of light jumping from its surface. Eric grimaced as he looked at the lousy optics, but knew that it was difficult at best to get truly clear images at long range in space.

"Clearing it up now, sir," Winger said in response to his unspoken thought.

The image wavered, then brightened as Winger applied light amplification, then abruptly jumped into near-perfect clarity as she used the computer records of Priminae warships to fill in the lost details.

Like the *Vulk* and the *Cerekus*, this one was a large, uneven cylinder that had blunted ends. The laser tubes were visible on the screen composite, bristling from the "front" visible section of the ship in something that would flash a warning light up for any military man despite its alien origin.

"Jesus," Daniels cursed quietly.

Eric didn't blame him, either. Whoever was over there was in pretty lousy shape. The ship was partially obscured by venting gases, and large chunks of the misshapen cylinder were missing, burned away by the heavy lasers of the enemy.

If the *Odyssey* had taken a quarter of that level of damage, Eric knew, they'd be nothing but expanding gasses.

"What's their vector?" he made himself ask, no hint of his thoughts in his voice.

"They're going to pass just over two and a half light-minutes from our position, sir," Jason Roberts said quietly. "Would you like to send a couple shuttles with medical teams?"

"Negative." Eric shook his head. "We're running silent, Commander. Let them slip past. They have help not too far away."

"Aye, sir," the commander replied with equanimity.

"Weapons," Eric said softly, his voice carrying just the same.

"Sir?" Waters stiffened, glancing back.

"Status on the pulse capacitors?"

"Fully charged and waiting, sir," Waters replied with a grin.

"Excellent." Eric took a breath. "It's a waiting game now."

▼

INTERSTELLAR SPACE, RANQUIL REGION

▲

▶ THE DRASIN SHIPS were approaching one of the Crimson Systems, one that had defeated several brethren in the past, pursuing and pursued. Ahead of them, they saw the band that encompassed almost the entire life of the system, even infecting the Primary, the life-giver itself.

They knew that this system had to be destroyed.

The ships didn't know of any other systems where a star had been infected by the band; it was inconceivable, and yet it had happened. Deep in the pure white energy of the local Primary, there was an ugly flare of crimson blood, the infection rotting away at the heart of a star.

Cutting that band out might not even be possible, but the rest of the system could be cleaned, sanitized. The star would be quarantined then; none of the horde would ever reenter this system once its outer infections were cured. That would prevent any further contamination.

Immediately, however, the problem was on a smaller scale. It was anathema to the horde to allow any to escape a cleansing, and there were many ahead who could be destroyed. In the clutch of the Primary's gravity, the sting of the warrior ship ahead would be deadened, and its damage would allow the horde to cleanse it quickly.

Interception had to happen well before the planet, however.

The defenses in the last system had been impressive—better than expected, even. The ships would not risk approaching the planet.

There was a brief rumble as the gravity of the Primary disrupted the drive bubbles, and the two ships flickered back into normal space, on a pursuit course for the wounded ship and its fleeing sheep.

▼

PRIMINAE VESSEL VULK

Ranquil system

▲

▶THE RUMBLE OF the dimensional drive cutting out shook the bridge as the screens flickered white suddenly, the energy overloading it in a flash.

"Equalizing screens."

The screen faded back to black; then the stars flickered into place, beaming steadily out at them as the bridge crew ignored them as they milled about their work. There were more important things out there to find than the stars, and each man and woman on the deck was deeply involved in finding objects much closer.

"Two enemy cruisers directly ahead! Three-point-two light-cycles!"

Johan nodded. "Lock lasers onto them. Position of pursuing ships?"

"They'll be entering Ranquil gravity well in…two marks."

Johan grimaced, but acknowledged the report. He'd allowed himself into a bit of a nasty situation as things stood. Pinned between the enemy ahead and the enemy behind, things were far from perfect, but the *Vulk* and its crew had a job to do. He was fully aware that sometimes the ideal action was not one of his possible options, not when there was a planet full of people to defend and limited resources with which to defend them.

"Stay on course. Accelerate to full velocity."

"Yes, Captain."

The ship rumbled a little, the powerful drive systems actually making themselves felt as they wound up and began to drive the big ship down the well.

"Contact the arms section," Johan said stiffly. "Have them break out the nuclear explosives and arm them."

There was a brief silence, but finally, someone nodded.

"Yes, Captain."

▼

PRIMINAE VESSEL HERALC

Ranquil System

▲

▶CAPT. KIERNA SENTHE stared at the projected screens with a sickly look, eyeing the enemies that were pursuing them to the end.

"Maker blasted fool," he said under his breath as the *Vulk* flickered into the system. "He's let them right in."

"Ranquil has some of the best defenses now, Captain," his young weapons officer offered weakly. Fatigue came through in that voice. "At least, since the battle…"

"I'm aware of that," Kierna said tiredly. "But neither we, nor our transports, will reach those defenses before we're overtaken."

There was a silence, and into that silence Kierna issued an order.

"Take us about."

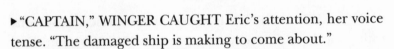

NACS ODYSSEY

Ranquil System

▶ "CAPTAIN," WINGER CAUGHT Eric's attention, her voice tense. "The damaged ship is making to come about."

"What?" Eric frowned. "Send me their vectors."

"Aye, sir."

Eric looked down at his tactical mirror station, the slim screen repeating what the tactical and sensor stations were looking at, and frowned at the changing graphs and numbers.

The damaged ship was indeed coming about, though they were slow, and now he had to worry about their bulk coming into his line of fire.

"Give me a plot on the main screen, Lieutenant," Eric ordered. "All players with a projected time compression of ten to one."

"Aye, sir," Michelle Winger said, fingers working furiously along the composite panel she was lightly working.

Modern interfaces owed a lot to their historic ancestors, but some of the major changes had required a certain flexibility in the mental attitudes of the users. The panel Michelle was working furiously on would once have been a keyboard attached to a computer that processed the information she was gathering, but on the *Odyssey*, it was a featureless black panel of glass-like plastic that detected her commands through proximity and motion sensors buried under the sealed surface.

The interface itself was adaptive, as most of the *Odyssey*'s equipment had been designed to be, and could effect multiple layouts according to Winger's needs of the moment. The biggest problem this sort of interface had created when they were introduced was actually quite serious, however, as most of the operators who initially used them were hospitalized for carpal tunnel syndrome in short order from trying to "punch" the commands with their fingers rather than merely brush the interface lightly.

Winger was an old hand at the system, Weston knew, and had grown up with similar models, so her fingers glided over the smooth surface, never leaving contact by more than a few fractions of a centimeter as she followed her captain's command and sent the processed information to the main screen.

Eric looked up as the screen flickered, showing the compressed vectors he'd asked for, watching the numbers fall toward that "zero hour" when all of the players would be in effective combat range of each other.

"It's going to be messy, Captain," Jason Alvarez Roberts said quietly.

"Yes. Yes, it is, Commander."

"Shall I contact the Priminae Admiralty and ask them to call off that ship?" Roberts suggested.

Eric pursed his lips, considering and weighing the risks. There were some complex issues involved and possibly no right decision. Finally, he shook his head. "No, Commander. I don't think so. We don't know how well the Drasin can locate and track Priminae communications, but we do know that they are pretty decent at tracking power signatures."

Roberts nodded reluctantly. "True, sir."

"Helm," Weston called.

"Sir?" Daniels glanced back, waiting for his orders.

"Thrusters only. Adjust our course ten degrees above the elliptic," Eric told him. "We need to clear our guns."

"Aye, sir."

▼

PRIMINAE VESSEL VULK

Ranquil System

▲

▶ "DEPLOY WEAPONS."

Johan Maran had given the command without flinching, but he was the only one on the command deck who wasn't shocked. Still, his weapons officer nodded and tapped in a command, and a moment later, a half dozen blinking lights floated away from the ship on the projected display.

"Deployed."

Johan nodded, watching the lights for a moment as they floated oh so slowly away from his ship, then forced his attention back to the matter at hand.

"Continue on course," he ordered. "Prepare a firing lock on the Drasin ahead."

"Yes, Captain."

He didn't say it aloud, but everyone knew that the orders were just a formality. They had no choice, not with survival itself on the line.

The *Vulk* powered on through the emptiness of space, lumbering toward its enemy as it laid a trap in its wake for its pursuers. The big ship's acceleration was the equal of its quarry, however, so it wasn't gaining any on them as the command crew watched the screens.

"Time to detonation?" Johan asked tensely.

The weapons officer checked the numbers, then looked up. "Forty cycles."

Maran nodded, taking a breath.

Forty cycles was enough. More than enough, in fact, for the *Vulk* to get clear of the blast radius of the weapons-grade nuclear munitions. Like everything else on the *Vulk* and its brother ships, the prohibited weapons were considerably enhanced over those carried by the fleet's previous incarnation of converted transports, but even with those enhancements, the *Vulk* was armored and hardened to survive much, much worse.

Maran tried not to focus on the thought of the weapons at his back, instead looking to the tactical situation he was flying into. On the projection, there were several dots of light and projected courses, one of which caught his eye immediately and made him wince.

"What is that blasted fool doing?" Johan growled, looking at the lines. "Status on the *Heralc*!"

"Damaged, Captain. Badly," came the response, "however, they're coming about to engage the Drasin."

Captain Maran had to bite down the impulse to send a scathing message to his fellow captain, but instead considered it for a moment and finally shook his head as he settled back. "Fine. Signal the *Heralc* and inform them that we will catch the Drasin in a cross fire."

That still left one wild card out there, he knew. The messages from the admiralty had made it clear that the *Odyssey* had departed orbit with the intentions of engaging any Drasin that made it into to their weapons' range. They had, however, also engaged their stealth measures, and the *Vulk*'s sensors weren't reading them anywhere out there.

Given Captain Weston's reputation among the people on Ranquil, however, Johan was unwilling to assume that the *Odyssey* wasn't much closer than he might otherwise believe.

"What is the last-reported position of the *Odyssey*?" Johan asked, feeling more than a little tense about the entire matter.

NACS ODYSSEY

Ranquil System

▶WESTON WATCHED THE display plotters as the *Odyssey* clawed for "altitude" relative to the system elliptic, using only thrusters and minimal counter-mass power, trying to clear her line of fire from any well-meaning but pushy "friendlies."

Inside the big ship, the crew was hanging on to anything that was available, since without the full power of the big ship's CM generators, they could feel the g-forces of even the relatively weak thrusters. Anything that hadn't been secured carefully was tossed to the back corners of whatever room it was in, resulting in the destruction of a few hundred thousand dollars' worth of equipment, but nothing that was particularly valuable or important.

The crew was well drilled for acceleration, but some things always slipped through the cracks.

One crewman was quickly dispatched to the medical labs when a half-secured tie snapped in the cafeteria and he was pelted with three hundred and fifty pounds of flour in twenty-five-pound tubs. Another walked himself into Dr. Rame's tender care when he was caught off guard by the thruster burn and sprained his arm while keeping himself from slamming into the back wall.

Relatively light damages and injuries, all things considered, for a hurriedly prepared thruster burn.

On the bridge, the main screen was now split into three sections, each displaying a different angle of the tactical map as the *Odyssey* continued to rise above the common plane of the other ships involved.

Space was, of course, a three-dimensional environment with no true up or down. However, for practical purposes, most common maneuvers were conducted along a very narrow plane of action that generally coincided with the system elliptic, or basically the plane that the majority of planets orbited on.

Eric wasn't really certain why, at least not when it came to warfare, except perhaps the personal momentum that tended to infect even the most tactically minded person. Under normal conditions, one remained on the elliptic because the shortest distance between two points almost always followed it, and fuel was a concern when one traveled the immense distances involved in space travel.

For whatever reason, the other ships in the battle were remaining on that rough plane as they closed with each other, much like Eric would have had the Priminae warship not forced his hand. Tactically, the move "above" the elliptic would clear the *Odyssey*'s guns and give them an advantage in one respect.

In another respect, however, it was a tactical pain in the ass.

Due to the immense distances normally considered, even within a given star system, the elliptic was a relatively "flat," or two-dimensional, plane. It allowed the tactical station to project ship movements over a two-dimensional display with a relatively high level of accuracy and tactical precision.

Now, however, the display had to be projected in three separate cutaways to give any sense of perspective to the matter, and Eric was finding that he really didn't like trying to think in three dimensions.

It was weird, actually, to realize that. He was a pilot—a fighter pilot, at that—and thinking tactically in three dimensions was integral to his training. However, those instincts were channeled to think in terms of plus or minus forty thousand feet or so, not plus or minus forty million kilometers!

The scale was warping his mind as he tried to keep it all pictured in his head at once. The lightning-fast calculations and instincts he'd developed for flying Archangel One were working against him now that he had the time to second-guess himself, and it was infuriating.

"Commander," he said after a moment, looking over to where Jason was examining the screens with a similarly distressed look, "remind me to have a...*vigorous* discussion with Admiral Gracen about clearing a holographic projection system for bridge use."

Roberts gave him a pained nod of agreement.

▼

PRIMINAE VESSEL VULK

Ranquil System

▲

▸ "DETONATION, CAPTAIN!"

Johan Maran looked at the tactical projection and nodded gravely. The nuclear detonations were appearing on the scanners now, meaning they had detonated just under forty cycles previously. The leading edge of the radiation was now being reflected off the *Vulk*'s shields, and it wouldn't be long before the main force of the expanding wave struck them.

"Brace for shield turbulence," he ordered, his voice going out over the entire ship.

A few seconds later, the *Vulk* shuddered, then shook, then calmed again as the radiation passed and its energy stopped interacting with the *Vulk*'s energy fields. The entire event took only seconds, but it was unnerving, just the same. Ships in space didn't normally suffer from any sort of turbulence. Any impact large enough to shake a ship was normally fatal; however, the energy shields did their job by absorbing, reflecting, and refracting dangerous radiation away from the ship, and certain laws of the natural world applied. In this case, in order to push the radiation away, the shields had to push against their projectors and the ship in an equal fashion.

Luckily, it ended as quickly as it had begun, and Captain Maran nodded grimly as he watched his projections. "Inform me when the scanners have reset from the pulse."

"Yes, Captain."

In the meantime, his forward scanners were still quite active, and they showed things coming to a head in short order. The *Heralc* would intercept the Drasin before the *Vulk* could close with them, and that was likely to be bad news for the damaged vessel.

"Drive Room," he called out in a low voice.

"Yes, Captain?" the voice of the master engineer came back a moment later, sounding distant over the communication system.

"I need more acceleration," he demanded.

"We can't give you any more, Captain. We're already beyond the recommended specifications as it stands."

"Blow your engines, if you must," Johan snapped, his frustrations coloring his voice. "But give me more acceleration. The *Heralc* will be engaged for twenty-two seconds before we can interfere. I will not lose a ship this close to home. Is this understood?"

There was a silence, until finally the voice came back. "Yes, Captain. I'll see what we can do."

Maran closed the connection then, satisfied that the man would try.

"Scanners clearing, Captain!"

One thing after another. Maran turned to the projections again, eyeing the information as the scanners began to coalesce into a distinct picture. He was forced to bite his tongue then, grimacing against the pain, in order to prevent an epithet from escaping his lips.

They were still there.

Through that nuclear hell, they had survived and were still closing.

NACS ODYSSEY

Ranquil System

▲

▶ "GIGATON-LEVEL DETONATIONS, Captain!"

"What?" Eric Weston snapped upright in his seat, his relaxed posture ramrod straight in an instant. "Where?"

"At the edge of the system, sir," Winger reported. "I'm reading…no less than five separate detonations in the multiple-gigaton range."

"Jesus…" someone whispered.

"Someone really needs to take all these dangerous toys away from the children, Captain," Commander Roberts said dryly as he shook his head.

Eric grimaced at the comment, thanking God that there were no members of the Priminae people aboard at the moment, but couldn't exactly disagree. Every weapon these two combatants seemed to field was a masterwork of brute force and sheer overkill. Further, both sides had developed general systems and armors that defended themselves against weapons of a similar nature.

Which meant that, for the *Odyssey*, it was like standing between two clumsy giants intent on batting each other's brains out with very large, and very unwieldy, clubs.

"We've got a problem, Captain," Jason Roberts said a moment later.

"What is it, Commander?"

"Radiation levels are rising—fast."

"This far out?" Eric asked, unbelieving.

"Aye, sir."

"Send me the data," he ordered crisply, pulling his display closer.

A moment later, he let out an unhappy sound as he noted that the sudden increase in radiation levels had gone far beyond the normal levels for a star system of this nature. The *Odyssey* was, of course, well protected against radiation. It had to be, in fact, since any given star put out a lot more than any bomb.

However, those bombs were a lot closer then the system primary, and they were also, apparently, very, very, dirty. The levels outside continued their fast rise as the *Odyssey* slid through the leading wave of the blast, and the slower-moving, but more lethal, particles began to slam into her hull.

Worse, the adaptive armor was the first line of defense against radiation, and in its black hole stealth setting, it was all but inviting the lethal doses in for coffee. The *Odyssey* had more protection, of course, including layers of carbon fiber sandwiched with graphite and other composites that also served to insulate the big ship, and those secondary defenses were, or should have been, more than enough for any near strikes from nuclear sources.

Something here wasn't adding up.

"Michelle," Eric snapped, "confirm the range."

"Aye, sir," Winger said, recalculating range to targets. "Five-point-two-one light-minutes, Captain."

"Damn it, Lieutenant, that's not possible!" Eric growled, running the figures in his head. "The maximum lethal range on an enhanced-radiation warhead is no more than a hundred and fifty thousand kilometers at these sizes."

Winger gulped, but nodded. "Aye, sir. I…don't know what to say, Captain."

Eric forced himself to relax. There was nothing she *could* say, of course. She knew as well as he did that the inverse square law was supposed to be on their side in this matter; the radiation from the explosions should be barely detectable at this range, except as an impressive flare in the distance.

Whatever it was doing, it sure as hell wasn't supposed to be bombarding his stealthed armor and rendering a third of his outer hull just as radioactive as the nastiest dirty bomb he'd ever heard of. And that was the biggest problem at the moment, not the theory of why the situation was impossible, but the very real fact that the neutron flux was building in the *Odyssey*'s armor, and in short order, the *Odyssey* herself would be perpetuating the situation by generating her own lethal rads.

"Damn it!" Eric cursed. "Radiation alert! Secure from black hole settings. Take our armor to best general reflection."

"Sir, our stealth—"

"I know, Commander," Weston said, interrupting. "And this blast of radiation is going to light us up like a Christmas tree, but it's better than dying slowly of radiation poisoning in twelve months."

Roberts nodded grimly, saying nothing.

Weston activated the intercom. "This is the captain speaking. This is a general quarters alert. Prepare for combat and high-stress maneuvering. I say again, this is a general quarters alert."

The general quarters alarm sounded then, joining the radiological alarm that was already echoing throughout the ship.

"Take us to full military power, Mr. Daniels. All power to drives and counter-mass generation," Eric growled. "Mr Waters, have all weapons brought up from standby and release the safety locks on the pulse torpedo tubes."

"Aye, sir," they both responded as the hum of capacitors charging began to whine through the hull.

"Ms. Winger, distance to lead Drasin vessel?"

"Three-point-two light-minutes."

"Very well," Eric told her. "Begin a countdown, Michelle, starting from the moment of armor shift."

"Aye, sir." Lieutenant Winger nodded instantly.

"That's it for hide-and-seek, ladies and gentlemen," Eric announced then. "We know that they're going to see us, and we know *when* they're going to see us. Now, let's make sure that they never, ever forget the sight."

▼

PRIMINAE VESSEL HERALC

Ranquil System

▲

▶ "THE *VULK* HAS deployed nuclear explosives, Captain."

Kierna nodded grimly, though he'd expected nothing less. The *Vulk* was not pulling any of its blows, but that was fine. He didn't intend to do so, either.

"Shields?"

"Low, but enough to protect us, sir."

"Continue on course, then," the captain of the injured vessel growled, his eyes watching the projections intently.

Only minutes were left now, and he could once again be in contact with the enemy. He'd deny it to his dying breath, but there was a part of him that eagerly anticipated it, courted the violence that was to happen, even. He didn't reflect on what that meant, didn't consider how deeply he'd been changed from the man he had been only a short time earlier.

Such things didn't matter to him now.

Only the enemy did.

"Sir!"

"What is it?" he growled, shaking away the chill that had filled him, and glared at the young woman at the scanner station.

"Another ship, sir! It just appeared."

"Where? Show me!"

The ship in question blinked into being on the main projection, blazing white against the black of space as it shifted in space and came under power.

"Is it Drasin?"

"Nothing I've ever seen, Captain."

Capt. Kierna Senthe glared at the projection. "But it's not one of ours?"

"No, sir."

"Acquire it," he ordered, a deathly calm in his tone.

▼

NACS ODYSSEY

Ranquil System

▲

▶ "TWO MINUTES TO detection."

The calm way Michelle Winger said it merely underscored the thread of tension filling the bridge as the *Odyssey* continued to increase speed as she vectored in on the enemy ships.

Eric watched the screen carefully, mentally running the figures himself to be sure of their accuracy, waiting as the probabilities ran down. Since the *Odyssey* had been waiting in stealth, while the approaching Drasin cruisers had not been even trying to hide their position, they had a significant advantage at the moment.

Those numbers, though, were offset by the fact that the *Odyssey* didn't really know precisely where the Drasin were. If they were to fire lasers at the enemy positions from this range, the computers calculated a 4.3 percent chance of scoring any hit and less than a quarter of 1 percent chance of disabling or destroying the target. The odds were slightly better with the pulse torpedoes, due to their homing ability; however, the energy-cost ratio made risking those prohibitive.

The *Odyssey* had to close the distance to their enemy quickly so that they were close enough to open fire at or before the time that the enemy finally received the glare of radiation reflecting off their armor. Once that first contact was made, Eric estimated that they had five, maybe ten seconds before the Drasin realized that the new contact wasn't, in fact, sitting still but was actually accelerating right down their throat like a "bat out of hell," as Winger had put it earlier.

At that point, the Drasin would react, returning fire and/ or commencing evasive maneuvering.

Given the fact that, even under full weigh, the *Odyssey* had certain basic physical limitations that would prevent her from accelerating much past a third the speed of light under the current time and distance restrictions, the enemy was going to know they were coming while the *Odyssey* was still almost two full light-minutes out.

He certainly could have wished to get closer.

"Waters?" Eric asked.

"All systems ready to fire, Captain," Waters replied instantly.

"Good. We'll lead with the pulse torpedos," Eric told the young man. "Arrange a staggered firing pattern. I don't want any more than a one-degree variance at two light-minutes."

"Aye, sir. Programming now."

"Helm?"

"Tactical evasion maneuvers are being compiled as we speak, sir," Daniels said confidently. "We're ready to make things just a little hard on their gunners."

"Excellent." Eric permitted himself a smile as he counted himself lucky for the men and women he'd been privileged to command. "Commander, I think we may as well go ahead and sound battle stations. Let the crew know that we'll be in the thick of it in just a few more minutes."

"Aye, sir."

The general quarters alert had long since faded, but was now replaced by the urgent signal that denoted imminent combat.

PRIMINAE VESSEL HERALC

Ranquil System

▶"THE SCANNERS ARE registering high acceleration from the new ship, Captain."

Kierna frowned at the projections as he stood at his place just above his wrecked command chair. "I see them, Ithan. Are those power readings correct?"

"I believe so, Captain."

He frowned, shaking his head.

Something was wrong here, very wrong. The power levels on the new ship were flat, ridiculously so. It appeared that almost the entirety of their profile came from reflected energy as opposed to the *Heralc* and other ships of its class with radiated immense power curves. Even transports showed higher power curves than this ship, which meant that it couldn't possibly be a threat.

Yet something was gnawing at the back of his fatigued mind, something Kierna thought he should remember but couldn't quite place.

He shook off the feeling. "Very well, Ithan. Do we have an active target lock on the vessel?"

"Not yet, Captain. It's moving too fast. We're trying to project its course now, but the ship is still accelerating."

He nodded. "Understood. Use active sensors. The Drasin?"

"Still on course, Captain. We'll close with them in just over two cycles."

Decisions, decisions, Kierna thought as he eyed the icons that represented the two distinct threats on his projections.

The Drasin were a known problem—and a lethal one, to be sure. They were closing on him of their own accord and, if they got past him, would destroy the refugees and possibly attack the core world of Ranquil. The new contact was an unknown, its profile not appearing in the computer, at least not that his weapons officer could find, and it was too damned close to the projected zone of battle.

Further, it was much closer to him than the Drasin, and for all its flat power curve, it was pulling some impressive acceleration. Not as high as the *Heralc* could manage, to be sure, but high enough to make him wonder why that power curve was so low, after all.

The numbers on the new ship were still changing, so he couldn't tell one way or the other which one he would be contacting first—Drasin or unknown.

Either way, Kierna Senthe would be prepared.

"Status on forward lasers?" he growled, tapping a command into his projections.

"Repairs complete, Captain. All banks report ready to fire."

"Excellent. My compliments to the repair team." Kierna nodded grimly. "Ithan, please inform the crew that we will be reentering combat shortly. They have a few minutes to prepare."

PRIMINAE VESSEL VULK

Ranquil System

▶ THE TWO DRASIN ahead were undeterred by the blast of radiation from the war charges the *Vulk* had dropped in her wake, but Maran didn't find that surprising. Even at near-point-blank ranges, the Drasin armor had stood up to the massive detonations and the subsequent chain reaction triggered by the explosives, so there was no reason to expect it to do any better at range. Still, it had been worth a shot.

The Drasin, though, weren't the main thing occupying his attention at the moment.

He grunted once as he watched the projections, one eyebrow lifting as he saw the blaze of light erupt from the depths.

"Well, that answers *that* question," he said, speaking to no one in particular.

"Sir?"

Johan glanced over to see his first approach from the side and nodded at the projection. "The *Odyssey*."

The woman looked at the screen and nodded. "So that is where it was hiding."

"Yes. But it's out of hiding now." Johan frowned. "I wonder why. They were in a good position, had a clean shot at the Drasin from there. From what I know of Captain Weston, which I will admit isn't as much as one might hope, I expected him to stay dark until he fired."

His first shrugged. "Perhaps it is a tactical strategy."

"Perhaps. In any event, it hardly matters. I wish him luck, but in the meantime, we have our own matters to attend to."

"Captain!"

Johan jerked around, his attention locking back to a red blossom on the projection that mapped the *Odyssey*'s position. "What happened?"

▼

NACS ODYSSEY

Ranquil System

▲

▶ "WE'VE BEEN PAINTED!" Winger's call startled the bridge, shocking them out of the building tension they had been enduring as they waited for the countdown to run down.

"What?" Eric jerked around, one eye on the clock.

The Drasin shouldn't have detected them for another minute, thirteen.

"Triangulating directionality now, Captain," Winger announced. "It's a high-energy tachyon pulse!"

"Shit!" Eric cursed. "Velocity?"

"Way the hell over light-speed, sir," Winger said grimly. "Calculating now."

Eric bit back another curse, the dull, agonizing tension that had been building long gone now, replaced by the bleeding-edged terror that made up about 1 percent or less of military life. Someone had spotted them and painted them with a high-energy tachyon pulse. That meant they were basically visible to anyone who had FTL receivers within tactical range.

Which meant that their element of surprise had been well and truly blown to hell.

"Fourteen times light-speed, Captain." Winger groaned. "They've sure as hell seen us now, sir."

Eric bit back his own groan, but nodded. "New countdown, Lieutenant. Start it from when they would have received the sensor reflection."

"Aye, Captain." Winger nodded, tapping in another command that started a countdown from when the Drasin would have a confirmed course and speed for the *Odyssey*.

"New game, everyone," Eric told them calmly. Then his voice shifted to a harder edge. "Adapt."

PRIMINAE VESSEL VULK

Ranquil System

▶"WHAT HAPPENED, ITHAN?" Johan Maran growled, watching his projections as the two Drasin vessels ahead shifted their course to intercept the *Odyssey*'s projected image.

"It was the *Heralc*, Captain," came the answer. "They acquired the *Odyssey* on their active scanners."

"What?" Maran blew, his voice roaring across the bridge. "Contact them! Now!"

"Yes, sir."

Johan Maran glowered at the projection as the *Odyssey* continued to accelerate into the maw of the alien ships. Did they realize that they had been spotted? He couldn't know, but they hadn't altered their course in response.

Would they have?

It was another question he couldn't answer. How could he get into the mind of an alien, even a very human one like Captain Weston? It was obvious that the man thought very differently than anyone Johan had ever met. It was even obvious that his…race, for lack of a better term, had different psychological leanings than Johan's own people.

Unlike many people in Ranquil, Maran wasn't entirely convinced that this was a good thing. The local population and even some members of the fleet, not to mention the admiral's office, seemed convinced that Weston could calm a solar flare.

Johan was more skeptical.

He was willing to admit, however, that Weston and his people were a force to be contended with. And so long as that force was aimed away from Ranquil and at the Drasin, he wasn't stupid enough to complain too loudly about the armed alien ship in orbit of one of the core worlds.

That did not, however, help him with his current problem. As he understood it, the *Odyssey* had been given a trans-comm for communications with the admiral's office as well as emergency use. However, the power systems on the ship were not entirely compatible with it, and the military protocols that the *Odyssey* followed didn't stretch so far as to permit the installation of a foreign power source.

Not an entirely unwise rule, he supposed, but it did limit the response options that he had at the moment.

"Captain Senthe is waiting, sir."

Johan turned to glare at the secondary projection that appeared beside his chair. "What in the destroyer of worlds are you doing, Senthe?"

NACS ODYSSEY

Ranquil System

▶ "TEN SECONDS TO zero point, Captain."

Eric nodded, acknowledging Winger's report, and made a motion to Lieutenant Daniels. "Execute evasive patterns."

"Aye, Captain."

The *Odyssey* rumbled then as its big thrusters fired, shoving the ship out of its current line of travel.

"Two...one...zero point," Winger announced.

The bridge tensed, waiting to see if the coronal flare of one of the enemy's powerful lasers would light up their sensors. The zero point that Winger had calculated was the exact time it would take a laser to reach their position, if they operated on the assumption that the Drasin had instantly returned fire when they detected the *Odyssey*.

Moments passed, and it quickly became obvious that the enemy ships hadn't been so quick to act.

Whether it was because they were slow or because they were smart didn't matter so much at this point. What did matter was that the *Odyssey* was now maneuvering to stay well clear of the likely lines of fire, while the weapons people under Eric

Weston tried like the devil to predict what the alien minds downrange were thinking and doing at that exact moment.

Eric wondered if the problem was driving the other minds on the *Odyssey* as batty as it was driving him. He found himself alternating between hoping that it was and hoping that it wasn't. One the one hand, he really needed someone to pop up with a miraculous view into the thought processes of the alien mind, but on the other, he'd honestly hate to be the only one on the ship with a migraine over the whole situation.

Survival versus personal satisfaction—it was a terrible choice to have to make.

DRASIN FORCES,
RANQUIL SYSTEM

▶ IF THE IDEA of "taken aback" could apply to the command consciousness of the Drasin fleet, then it had been taken aback when the third enemy ship appeared on the detection grid, already accelerating toward them at six-twentieths of the normal space maximum and climbing. It was more than merely the fact that a third ship tilted the odds against the fleet, making the likelihood of them eliminating the fleeing band much slimmer, but also that it had been able to hide at all.

Now that the consciousness was focused on this ship, it was obviously one of the band. Its scarlet scent was so strong that it should have been visible from out-system, yet it had remained undetected until this point.

That was wrong.

The command was given then, and the lead two of the fleet turned to meet the third ship. The injured and lame of the band were limping toward them, but at a reduced speed, and were of no import. Behind them was a more powerful, and hale, warrior of the band, but behind him, there were two more of the fleet.

To this point, the battle had gone well for the fleet, but the new factors could easily turn the pull of gravity against them. For all that, however, there was no real choice. If they could not eliminate the dregs of the last system cleansed, they would at least remove one of the system threats, then turn to deal with the others.

The units of the fleet accelerated to full normal velocity and prepared to engage the enemy.

▼

PRIMINAE VESSEL HERALC

Ranquil System

▲

▶ KIERNA SENTHE WATCHED as the Drasin cruisers altered course to intercept the *Odyssey*, still seething from the scathing words blasted at him just minutes before by Captain Johan of the *Vulk*.

He should have known that it was the *Odyssey*; every military vessel of the Priminae people had to know of that ship by this time. He could defend his ignorance. It was unlikely that the *Odyssey* would be in Ranquil at this time. He and his crew were tired, so tired, in fact, that they had begun having problems sleeping when they had the time, as it was alien to them to do so now.

Even more truthfully a cause, though he would never speak it out loud, was that the young woman standing the weapons station was far too inexperienced to be running that station. She should have located the *Odyssey* in the computers, as they did have a minimal profile on the ship, but she had not.

Senthe would never let those words see any report, however. Ithan Serra had done a heroic job since the death of her superior, and he would be damned to the destroyer before he or anyone was critical of that.

Besides, it was on his head, not hers or anyone else.

He should have double-checked when it came back unknown, but it seemed unimportant at the time. The Drasin themselves were far more urgent, so he'd thought.

"Engine report!" he growled, in a decidedly bad mood.

"We're stressed badly, Captain. The reactors are down by a third mass and dropping."

The reply wasn't one he wanted to hear. If the reactor mass dropped below half, it would begin to adversely affect the ship; if it fell below a third, then the reactors would fall below the stable point and collapse, or rather, cease collapsing.

That would leave them dead in space—in more ways than one.

"Very well. Increase draw from the reactors, and direct it to the primary thrust."

"Captain!"

Senthe slashed his hand through the air, cutting off the shocked protest. "Do it!"

There was a long, tense silence.

"Yes, sir."

It didn't take long—power draw from the cores was nearly instantaneous—so in short order, the numbers were changing quickly as the *Heralc* jumped from its relatively low acceleration to a full tenth over its rated maximum, leaping forward through space toward the enemy and the ally.

NACS ODYSSEY

Ranquil System

▶ "CORONAL FLARE!" WINGER announced, with a sudden burst of instinctive terror. Winger, Weston noted, always gave them the best news.

"Analyze," Eric ordered, though he supposed that it wasn't strictly necessary to do so. His people knew their jobs.

"Working," Waters replied by rote, leaning over his panel as he turned the computers' attention to determining the beam frequency of the enemy laser.

"Which ship fired that, Michelle?" Eric asked as Waters worked.

"Vector indicates the lead ship, sir," she informed him. "It was aimed at our projected position, if we had stayed on course."

Eric nodded.

So far so good. They were following a predictable strategy so far, which meant that he could outthink them and then outfight them.

"Analyzed, sir," Waters announced.

"Adapt our forward armor to compensate," Eric ordered. "And, Daniels?"

"Yes, sir?" The young man at the helm stiffened, glancing back.

"Try to keep the lead ship between us and his friend as much as you can."

The bridge was a smoothly operating machine, a fact that pleased Weston to no end. He only hoped that the rest of the ship was operating to the same degree.

We're all depending on just that.

▶▶▶

"Suits, you dumb bastards, suits!" Chief Petty Officer Corrin screamed as she swung over one of the knee-knockers that separated the forward armaments berth from the corridor behind. She hooked her hand in one of the overhead locker handles and stopped her forward momentum as she grabbed one of the racked vacuum suits and threw it at its owner.

"Sorry, Chief," the man babbled quickly, grabbing the suit in midair and struggling into it.

"Don't forget again, Jenkins," she snarled through her own unsealed suit helmet. "We lost five guys in this goddamned station last time we tangled with these bad boys. Three of 'em died from exposure to hard vacuum. You got me?"

"Yes, Chief," the men responded quickly, nodding as they checked their suits again.

Corrin gave the section a quick once-over, then nodded curtly as she kicked off the wall and propelled herself back out and into the main corridor outside.

The men exchanged relieved looks for a moment, until her voice came floating back.

"Don't let me catch you unsuited after a battle stations call again, or I'll make you wish you were exposed to hard vacuum!"

Jenkins paled and redoubled his efforts to get into his suit while the others finished checking their own and their buddies'.

▶▶▶

"We're maneuvering again," Cardsharp said, pulling an ace of spades literally out of the air as it sailed past her position.

"A-yup." Stephanos nodded, not looking up as he completed his checklist.

"Captain's let Daniels loose of the leash from the feel of it," Paladin replied, dealing out another card to Centurion.

"A-yup."

"Is that all you're going to say?" Racer complained from her perch on the nose of her fighter.

"A-yup." Stephanos didn't look up, but twisted his head to one side as a joker spun past his position and clattered off the far wall behind him.

"Eyes in the back of his head," Paladin complained, shaking his head.

"Top of his head from the looks of that." Racer grinned. "Must be what makes him a good pilot."

"Must be," Paladin agreed. "Lord knows it's not his skill."

The pilots of the Archangel squadron chuckled at that, but their flight leader didn't rise to the bait as he continued to read something off his data plaque.

After a few moments, the pilots shrugged and went back to their game.

▶▶▶

It seemed to Weston that there were days when you just didn't get a chance to catch your breath. The *Odyssey* thrummed powerfully under his body as they moved to put themselves in the path of the threat that was approaching.

"Captain, the bandits are maneuvering fast. I'll need the main engine thrust to keep the first between us and the second."

"Understood. Hold for my command," Weston replied.

"Aye, sir. Holding," Daniels responded instantly.

"Mr. Waters, do you have a firing solution?"

"Yes, sir."

"You may engage the enemy. Four-pulse burst, if you please."

"Aye, aye, sir. Four pulse, firing...now."

And that wouldn't be the last time, Weston knew.

▶ ▶ ▶

A lot of the crew was in love with the massively energy-intensive application of antimatter production known among the NAC System Defense Agency as "pulse torpedoes." How could you not admire something that was at once a marvel and a monster? At least, that's the way Greene saw it. Others had their own point of view because it was easily the greediest of energy-using systems aboard already energy-poor spacecraft. The magnetically bundled pebbles of anti-hydrogen had originally been intended for power production and thrust on board ships intended to be used for in-system transport. Preproduction test prototypes of the reactors and thrust mechanisms in question had literally gone up in smoke, though precious little of it, when the reactors lost positive control of the mix rate and self-annihilated.

With the antimatter beam drive declared a failure, but the weapon potential proven beyond a shadow of a doubt, the military moved in quickly and swept up the design specs and lead researchers in a flurry of prewar paranoia, and the concept vanished from the public view for almost twenty years.

In fact, it still hadn't reemerged into the general view of the public when Capt. Eric Weston was given command of the first interstellar drive vessel (IDV) eighteen years after the spectacular failure of one of the *Odyssey*'s first true progenitors. The AM beam drive had been replaced with a more conventional chemical thrust system that burned hydrogen and oxygen to achieve thrust and used a nuclear fission pile as the primary source of power, but deep inside the *Odyssey*, there were still traces of the old experiments that brought her ancestors to such a black end.

The tokamak particle accelerators that were integral to the ship's smooth running could also generate minute quantities of antimatter, which were used in several shipboard systems, including the counter-mass system (though only as a byproduct of the anti-mass field itself), power generation, and of course, the forward pulse torpedo launchers.

Each tube launcher charged power from the capacitors surrounding it and funneled in sufficient amounts of antihydrogen to ensure a military-grade explosive reaction, then carefully tied those particulate pieces of energy together with a powerful electromagnetic field.

Once loaded and charged, every moment that passed with those weapons sitting in the tubes was another moment off the lives of the technicians monitoring the fields and praying that the captain would finally give the order to fire the hellish little specs of death, even if they would have to turn around and recharge the tubes immediately after.

So when the command for a four-torpedo burst finally came down, a sigh of semirelief and semidisappointment sounded in the fire control room as the men and women manning the systems let four devils out of their pentagrams.

▶▶▶

"Burst away, Captain," Waters said a moment later, and Weston felt an unseemly emotion—satisfaction.

He wasn't the sort to take much of that in violence, his career nothwithstanding, but the enemy they'd found was one that Eric had little sympathy or empathy for. "Excellent, Mr. Waters. Daniels, you have the conn."

"Aye, sir, I have the conn," Daniels confirmed, tapping orders into his interface.

The ship began to rumble around them as he reversed thrust on one of the outriggers, twisting the big ship in space, then fired off the main engines at full burn. The *Odyssey* leapt forward on command, dashing off at a tangent from the enemy ships, looking to keep them guessing and to keep the farther enemy ship from getting a clear shot at the same time.

"Adjust all plates to match forward armor," Eric ordered, noting that Daniels's maneuvering was bringing them around and exposing other parts of the ship to potential fire.

"Aye, sir." Waters nodded. "Adjusted."

"Ms. Winger, update location and vectors of enemy ships every ten seconds, if you please."

"Aye, sir." Michelle nodded, punching in a command. "Send to your display?"

"Yes, please." Eric nodded. "Thank you."

The new information hit his display only seconds later, showing updates on the enemy, both from the last-confirmed numbers, which were just under two minutes out of date, and the updated projections based on extrapolation.

Trying to second-guess alien minds when the information he had was almost two minutes out of date and the ships in question were all moving the better side of a third of light-speed was an interesting intellectual exercise, to say the least. That didn't mean that Eric felt he was any good at it as he frowned at the numbers and tried to make sense of the enemy's actions.

They had to know that the system they were invading was better defended than the last time, which made the situation all the more confusing. Sending two, or four, ships in alone was suicide. Yet the active tachyon blast that had "outed" the *Odyssey*'s position had also brought back a nice echo from the rest of the system, and there didn't seem to be any others in hiding out there.

So, the question he had to ask was, were they incredibly clever and planning something he hadn't forseen, or were they incredibly stupid?

Eric suspected that even if it wasn't the former, however, the latter was unlikely to the extreme.

"Pulse torpedoes will contact projected enemy positions in…twenty seconds."

Eric nodded at Waters's announcement. "Very good. Daniels, prepare to bring us around for another shot."

"Aye, sir."

▼

PRIMINAE VESSEL HERALC

Ranquil System

▲

▶ "*ODYSSEY* IS CIRCLING."

Kierna could see that, though he didn't understand it any more than did his weapons officer. He didn't say as much, of course, merely nodding sagely as he watched the numbers.

The *Odyssey* had swept out and away from the enemy, aborting their headlong charge, and had fired some sort of fast-moving projectiles into the Drasin ships. The energy readings from the projectiles were very low, as were the mass readings, so he wasn't certain what good they would do, but the *Odyssey* did have a reputation, so he'd wait and see.

Or not, as the case may be.

The *Heralc* had increased her thrust, at a cost to their reactor mass, and would be entering the battle quite soon as well. They were within effective laser range now, well under a single light-cycle, but Senthe wanted a kill.

He'd wait for it.

"Energy bloom from the Drasin! They're firing!"

Kierna stiffened, jerking up and around. "At us?"

The young woman stared wildly at her screens, then shook her head. "No...not at us."

"The *Odyssey*, then?"

"No, sir. They appear to be targeting the weapons fire the *Odyssey* sent at them."

Kierna blinked. "Are they hitting it?"

"I...I don't think so, sir...I...no...Mother!"

Kierna stared at his own screen as it suddenly went white with energy discharge. "What was that?"

▶▶▶

The torpedoes were a new thing to the Drasin.

Magnetically accelerated to relativistic velocity by the launch tubes on the *Odyssey*, each pulse torpedo traveled a course that was affected not only by ballistic trajectory but by the fact that like charges repel one another. In a four-torpedo burst, such as was closing on the lead Drasin vessel, the firing pattern had to be precalculated according to the spread one wished to achieve at the targeted range.

Firing all four simultaneously at long-range results in a relatively wide "shotgun" spread that could sweep across a fleet, or squadron, and wreak havoc, yet probably not actually kill any given ship. At close range, a similar pattern would strike almost entirely on a single target, the matter/antimatter mutual annihilation rending any armor and hull to shreds. Against the pulse torpedos, there was no effective armor known to Earth-based science unless you had an ungodly amount of it.

It was possible to repel the incoming rounds if one knew their frequency and had a powerful enough field generator, but even that was difficult in the extreme due to the incredibly high velocity they were fired at. The best one could hope to do would be to deflect them marginally and hope they hit another ship.

And if you didn't know the frequency of the incoming torpedoes…Well, there wasn't much you could do about it.

The Drasin saw the four points of destruction approximately twenty seconds before they struck, the light from the weapons traveling a third faster than the weapons themselves, and reacted in the only way they could.

They opened fire.

Beams of impossibly lethal radiation scoured the skies as they panned from one sector to another, attempting to intercept the incoming projectiles, but the Drasin soon learned a hard truth that the American military had learned decades earlier with much slower-moving targets.

That is, when a contact is incoming, even on a predictable path, and you have less than a minute to identify, target, and destroy it…You're pretty much out of luck.

Eighteen seconds after they opened fire, the torpedoes slammed into their target and erupted in a blaze of pure white flame.

NACS ODYSSEY

Ranquil System

▲

▶ERIC WATCHED THE plot intently, tracking the likely courses the enemy would be following. He'd find out if he were right in just a moment.

"Prepare tachyon active sensors."

"Aye, aye, sir." Lieutenant Winger nodded instantly. "Sensors primed."

"Narrow band, high velocity," Eric ordered.

"Aye, sir. N-band, high energy," Winger echoed.

"Mr. Daniels, bring us around."

"Aye, sir," Daniels responded, tapping in the commands.

The *Odyssey* shuddered again, swinging around as her main engines continued to thrust on full power. The big ship spun like a bottle rocket in a wide arc across space, its forward thrusters fighting hard to keep it from surrendering to the forces Daniels was putting on her.

"Single ping, if you please, Lieutenant."

"Aye, sir. Single ping."

The lights dimmed for a moment as the tachyon generation systems drew inordinate amounts of power from the system, and then the ship's computer filled the bridge with a single loud, clear tone to simulate the release of the tachyon ping.

Tachyons were a class of particles proposed in the middle of the twentieth century in response to the study of the Theory of Relativity and the apparent limit that theory placed on the maximum attainable velocity of the universe. Tachyons had no mass and were theoretically unable to travel any slower than the speed of light.

Interestingly enough, the speed a tachyon traveled at depended largely on an inverse relationship with the amount of energy that existed within the particle itself. Zero energy particles, like those the *Odyssey* used for its transition drive, were effectively unlimited in speed and could cross the entirety of the galaxy, even the universe, in the blink of an eye.

Endurance, of course, was another matter. The universe abhorred tachyons, or at least it had no love for those particles of this mysterious class that were generated by human technology. As such, it required immense amounts of power to construct a tachyon matrix that could endure a useful distance, as far as stellar travel goes.

For tachyon echo location and ranging (TELAR), the requirements were somewhat less onerous. High-energy particles with less complex structures could be used, narrowing the range according to how one charged each particle. When a TELAR pulse struck an object of sufficient mass, the tachyons would interact with the materials in question, and a small, almost minute, percentage of the particles would actually "bounce" back.

Which, Weston knew, made for a very difficult job on the part of TELAR operators like Lt. Michelle Winger.

It was a good thing that she was as good at her job as she was, and even better that she seemed to love her job, too.

"Confirmed weapons hit," she announced calmly, ignoring the short and impromptu surge of enthusiasm around her. "Two...Hold. Three weapons struck the enemy vessel."

"The fourth?"

"Unknown. I don't have a tachyon return off of it," she said apologetically. "It's too small, sir."

"Understood. Track on light-speed sensors. Let me know when you see where it went."

"Aye, sir." Winger nodded.

"Status of enemy vessel?" Eric asked calmly.

"That's unknown at present, sir. They appear to be intact and mobile, but severely damaged."

"Understood." Eric nodded, and indeed, he did.

TELAR imaging only provided the operator with a single "snapshot" of the universe along its range. What happened before the ping and what might happen after were entirely beyond the scope of the system's capabilities.

"Send the data to the labs for immediate analysis," Weston ordered, turning back to the weapons station. "Waters?"

"Aye, sir?"

"Prepare to close with and engage the enemy."

"Aye, sir."

▼

PRIMINAE VESSEL HERALC

Ranquil System

▲

▶ KIERNA WAS PREOCCUPIED with trying to figure out what had happened. The screens had cleared moments earlier, but the shocked chaos reigned as the crew around him tried to determine what had happened.

"Serra! Status!" he snapped. "What was that?"

"Military-grade explosives, Captain."

"Nuclear?"

"No, sir." She shook her head. "The blast was contained. No appreciable radiation or cascading chain reaction."

"Effect?" Kierna was snapping his questions out, quickly and without relief, but all too aware he and his ship were flying into that war zone.

"Three impacts on the Drasin cruiser...It's badly damaged, but still mobile, sir," Serra responded, frowning as she calibrated something. "The fourth weapon missed and is flying free."

"Where to?"

"Headed out-system, below the planetary orbit."

"Thank the Maker for that." Kierna shook his head. "Watch the *Odyssey*, Ithan. Inform me if they fire again."

"Yes, sir." Ithan Serra nodded, not looking up.

Kierna eyed his projections, calculating the range to the targets. Interestingly, both of them appeared to be focused on the *Odyssey* now, as if it were the only threat in the sky.

Time to show them the error of that assumption.

"Prepare weapons to fire on the undamaged cruiser," he said calmly, hanging onto the solid projection of his control interface. "We'll take them down from behind. If the *Odyssey* fires another round of those weapons, I want to be ready to evade, however."

"Yes, sir."

The reply was automatic from his crew by now, and Kierna took a breath as he accepted the instant respect, the confidence, they placed in him. Then he set his hands on the projection controls and pushed the thrust all forward.

"Prepare to engage the enemy. We're going in."

PRIMINAE VESSEL VULK

Ranquil System

▲

▶ "BOTH THE *ODYSSEY* and the *Heralc* have entered into engagement range of the enemy ships, Captain."

Johan Maran nodded briefly, eyeing the numbers on his own projection. He was still a short few cycles from interception, and the Drasin behind him were beginning to accelerate again, so they would soon be coming into range themselves.

The best bet was to continue on the present course, intercept and destroy the innermost Drasin, then turn to meet the remaining two with all remaining ships.

He just hoped that the *Heralc* and the *Odyssey* would be remaining, then.

"Understood. What is our reactor mass?"

"Both reactors are holding at point-eight-five gravities."

Johan nodded. At that level, the reactors had enough mass for a prolonged mission, even at the horrendous energy expenditure of warfare.

"Increase power draw to engines."

"Yes, Captain."

NACS ODYSSEY

Ranquil System

▶ "BOTH PRIMMY SHIPS are increasing speed and closing, Captain."

Eric hid another grimace at Winger's use of the shortened "Primmy" for the Priminae people. She'd done it again, so he had to make a note to not take her on any diplomatic missions to the surface.

"Thank you, Lieutenant," he said aloud. "Are they crossing our beam?"

"Negative, sir. They're staying clear of our firing vectors so far."

Commander Roberts smiled dryly. "How uncommonly intelligent of them."

"Careful, Commander," Eric reproved, "we already know that they don't have much experience fighting. It's no surprise that their joint-operations doctrine is lacking. In fairness, we don't even have one of our own just yet, either."

Roberts nodded reluctantly. "Aye, sir."

"That said," Eric went on, "I think that we should probably have a talk with the admiral about developing one. Don't you, Commander?"

"Which admiral, sir?" Roberts asked with a hint of a smile.

"Any of them that will listen, I suppose."

"Admiral Tanner it is, then."

Eric had to suppress a snort of amusement, which he immediately forced away before shooting a mild glare in Robert's direction. Commander Roberts didn't notice, or appear to at least, so Eric had to forgo the satisfaction of watching his first officer squirm a little as the timing dictated he pay more attention to the work at hand.

"Lieutenant Daniels, have you calculated our approach vectors?"

"Aye, sir."

"Then engage when ready."

"Aye, Captain. Engaging maneuvering program."

▶▶▶

The *Odyssey* bucked and twisted in space as her main thrusters flared again, burning the fuel stored in her tanks at an incredible rate as she began to build delta-v toward her targeted destination. The thrusters built along the length and breadth of the large ship always flared, seemingly at random, pitching and rolling her along nearly random course corrections and adjustments to keep the enemy ahead from locking onto her with their lasers.

Momentum and inertia in space are two of the biggest obstacles to serious maneuvering, the sheer mass of a space vessel working intensely against its maneuvering abilities, no matter how powerful a thrust it has. Even if thrust is powerful enough to overcome mass and inertia in short order, the humans inside are not structurally designed to withstand significant acceleration.

Across the vast expanse of even a single star system, one to ten gravities of acceleration were insignificant, and anything more would kill a person in short order, so something had to be done in order to make space travel practical, if not possible.

For Earth, that breakthrough had come at the same time, and in the same form, as the technology that finally provided the true heavy-lifting capacity needed to begin serious work in space. The counter-mass field, or CM, reduced "effective" mass of anything within its projected range, according to a geometric formula.

The lighter something is, the more effective a CM field would be. Hypervelocity missiles dropped to less than 1 percent of their full mass, while Archangel fighters operated at about 4 percent of their total mass while under full counter-mass support.

A ship the size of the *Odyssey* sat right at the point of diminishing returns, a factor that had figured heavily into her size. Power expenditures to effectively reduce the mass of a significantly larger vessel were considered prohibitive by Earth-based science.

So, as it was, the *Odyssey* massed out to just under 22 percent her total real mass while under full CM support. That gave her a reasonably fast sprint, and decent top end, but certainly prevented the big ship from making maneuvers like her smaller brethren.

So when the big ship's thrusters flared, she slid along her previous course for a time, building up delta-v until her power curve began to outweigh her inertial force.

Then the *Odyssey* plunged toward the wounded Drasin cruiser, the people on board her scrambling to keep her powerful weapons pointing in just the right direction as they awaited the order to let loose the proverbial dogs.

▼

PRIMINAE VESSEL HERALC

Ranquil System

▲

▶ "FIRE!"

The order cracked across the bridge, tension turning it into a whiplike thing that snapped everyone as the tension continued to increase around them.

Kierna watched as Ithan Serra plunged her finger into the projected interface built of photons and solidified atmospherics, feeling the satisfying rumble of feedback as the ship acknowledged her command.

The firing of the forward laser banks was anticlimactic, no sound emitting from the lethal crystals, as they were excited by direct power siphoned from the reactor mass of the ship's power cores. Outside, Kierna knew that there would be no significant light, except for a flash of visible light reflecting off the *Heralc*'s hull and perhaps a similar flash visible to the enemy ship about a tenth of a milli-cycle before the laser struck home.

On her projection, though, the scene was a bit more dramatic. The path of the laser was traced in real time across the three-dimensional view of the battle zone, the compressed nature of the projection making the beam crawl across it so slow that Kierna had the urge to yell at it as if that would alter the speed of light and the basic structure of the universe.

Serra glanced up and around to where the captain was sitting. "Fired, Captain. Beam will intersect target in nineteen-tenths, Captain."

Kierna nodded. "Thank you, Ithan."

Serra nodded and turned back to her station as Captain Senthe focused his attention on the twin power cores and their total mass.

The numbers were not encouraging, he noted quickly. The power draw from them was exceeding their capacity, and the total reactor mass was now down to under two-thirds of standard gravity each.

He could almost imagine that he could feel the difference already, though he knew that it wouldn't become noticeable until they dropped to about one-half standard gravity. At that point, the *Heralc* would begin to founder in space like a lame animal, unable to maneuver either to attack or evade. When that happened, they were as good as dead.

▼

NACS ODYSSEY

Ranquil System

▲

▶ "FIRE WHEN READY, Mr. Waters," Eric Weston said calmly, taking a sip from a cup of coffee the Yeoman had fetched him.

He and the rest of the bridge crew had managed to crawl into their vacuum suits some time earlier, but none of them had either their helmets sealed or their gloves on, as both of those would reduce the effectiveness of their control over the shipboard systems.

In space war, there were long periods of time, even during the most ferocious firefight. Time to think, time to panic, time to die, even—all before the enemy weapons could even reach your position. But like in any form of combat, there were also short scant seconds of pure, unadulterated panic.

In those seconds, time was everything, and suddenly, you didn't have enough of it anymore. The bridge crew wore their vacuum suits, as per regulations, but kept their hands free and eyes clear so they could make better use of those few rare seconds they sometimes had to endure.

If a shot burst close enough to the bridge to cause explosive decompression, they were probably dead, anyway. Otherwise, the rate that atmosphere would escape from any survivable leak would give them all plenty of time to don their gloves and rack their helmets shut.

"Aye, Captain," Waters replied, tapping in a few last commands. "Firing."

The bridge filled with the distinctive snap/whine of the superconducting capacitors discharging, then being recharged with power from the reactors, and the forward lasers burned forth, lighting the way as another barrage of pulse torpedoes spat out into space.

▶▶▶

In space, they say no one can hear you scream.

That is something that only holds true for those species, like humans, who rely on the vibrations through atmosphere to conduct what they refer to as sound. Other species, especially those born to the harsh environment of space, hear things in other ways.

For the Drasin, a scream is a thing of raw animal fury, however, and never something as draining as terror. So when the scream of one Drasin ship crossed the void and alerted the other to a known danger that had now become intolerable, the tactical situation was even more muddied for the lead ship.

The sheer malevolent scarlet of the target it was tracking was anathema to the entity, as it was to the entire hive. It *must* be destroyed. The reaction was as simple and unavoidable as the jerk of a human knee when tapped with a hammer.

Survival wasn't of particular concern, except that the numbers of the Drasin hive were still building, and now was not a time to lose ship minds so easily.

So instead of continuing on to hammer the hated crimson band, the injured ship hesitated for a moment in space.

That hesitation cost the ship mind, and the hive, when it was suddenly forced to deal with another problem that compounded its dilemma. First, a low-powered beam of coherent light struck its hull, confusing the mind for several seconds as it tried to determine the reason for the beam.

A moment after that, the beam suddenly leapt up ten thousand fold in strength and began to heat up the damaged hull. Again, the situation was confusing. The beam, though stronger, was not appreciably dangerous, as the majority of its energy was being radiated away, so the Drasin ship mind calculated the odds for several moments instead of maneuvering.

Those moments proved fatal.

The moderately warm beam shifted frequency suddenly, this time dumping all of its energy into the armor and suddenly vaporizing several cubic meters of it every second.

Instinctual instincts kicked in then, and the Drasin leapt away from the beam, accelerating under all available thrust to avoid the searing energy.

And it flew right into a second burst of those deceptively low-powered projectiles, and the ship mind had only a few seconds to scream its own rage before it was blotted out by the malevolence of the crimson band.

NACS ODYSSEY

Ranquil System

▶"TARGET ELIMINATED." Waters's simple pronouncement was filled with deep satisfaction as he calmly kept plotting out the vectors on the other target.

Eric examined the plot, one ear on the reports, but his mind focused more on what might happen next. The enemy only had so many options available to them, given their weapons and maneuvering abilities. He just had to outthink a completely alien intelligence.

"The Primmy got the other one, too," Winger announced. "I'm reading a powerful thermal bloom from its position. Consistent with a Prim laser strike."

Eric nodded. "Destroyed?"

"Uncertain, Captain."

"Understood. Daniels, take us in closer to intercept the second ship. If it is still kicking, I want it put down before we have to deal with its friends."

"Aye, Captain. Adjusting course now."

▼

PRIMINAE VESSEL HERALC

▲

▶ "HIT!" SERRA ANNOUNCED, flushed with a fierce sort of elation.

Kierna nodded grimly, forcing down his own bout with the bloodthirsty emotions he'd come to know so well over the past few weeks. "Hit it again."

"Yes, sir!"

PRIMINAE VESSEL VULK

Ranquil System

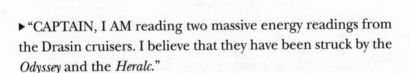

▶ "CAPTAIN, I AM reading two massive energy readings from the Drasin cruisers. I believe that they have been struck by the *Odyssey* and the *Heralc*."

Johan Maran nodded, watching the projections himself.

The energy readings they were detecting from this range were, or should be, enough to ensure that the Drasin ships were dead and gone, but so far, neither the *Odyssey* nor the *Heralc* had turned from their targets.

"They're both firing again, sir."

Indeed, they were. Flashes of energy colored his screens, denoting the destruction of any remaining remnants of the Drasin threat those two ships might have posed.

That only left the two chasing up behind the *Vulk*, then.

"Reverse thrust," Johan ordered. "Take us around to intercept the remaining two enemy ships."

COMMAND BUNKER

Ranquil

▶ "MIDLEVEL SYSTEM SCANNERS have shown the destruction of two of the Drasin cruisers, Admiral."

Tanner nodded, suppressing the urge to sigh in relief.

That sight probably wouldn't do much for morale, but he couldn't quite help it. Any amount of Drasin in his star system was too many, but two less than there were before was a good start. Some of the tension he'd been hiding was gone now, but he didn't have time to relax just yet.

"Have our orbital defenses been brought online?" he asked.

"Almost, Admiral. We'll have them ready shortly."

Rael Tanner nodded, knowing that the orbital arrays were much like shipboard energy banks, only they didn't use collapsing power cores to provide energy. The power requirements were extreme and had to be fed into the systems from the planet or from an orbital relay station. In this case, the orbital station was still under construction and wouldn't be operational for some time.

Given that the defense satellites were unable to move, it hardly mattered. There was more than ample time to fully charge them for any conceivable battle that they could win.

"Contact Captain Maran."

"Yes, Admiral."

A moment later, the projection screen flickered, and the image of the captain of the *Vulk* appeared a dozen meters ahead of Tanner. The captain was sitting in his command chair, looking away from the transceiver, so Tanner waited while Johan finished up something.

Finally, the captain turned his focus to the transceiver. "Yes, Admiral?"

"The two closest Drasin have been destroyed, Captain," Rael began.

"I'm aware of that, Admiral. I am moving to intercept and destroy the remaining two now," Johan replied.

"I see. My scanners indicate that they do not have the required acceleration to reach Ranquil before the refugees do. May I suggest that you pull back to cover the refugee ships and come into our defensive sphere?"

"I don't believe that would be wise, Admiral," Johan said, shaking his head. "If we have the power to end the threat out here, it would be best to do so."

"Very well. In that case, I am...*strongly* advising that you allow the *Odyssey* and the *Heralc* time to match your acceleration," Tanner said after a moment. "The *Vulk*, and its crew, are too valuable to risk to mischance, Captain."

Johan fell silent for a moment, then gestured to someone off-screen. "Very well, Admiral. We are reducing acceleration now."

"Very good, Captain. Good Luck," Tanner said before signing off.

A snort from behind him caused Rael to half turn and see Nero Jehan approaching from behind.

"You have something to add, Commander?" Rael asked, his lip twisting ironically as the huge six-foot-plus figure came to a stop beside his own five-foot-three frame.

"Yes." Nero smiled toothily. "I can see that the chain of command is as much a confusion to your captains as it is to my squads."

Rael grimaced. "I'm certain that you mean that as some sort of comfort, Nero, because I'm equally certain you don't intend to insult the capability of the glorious fleet of the Priminae people."

"Oh, no, of course not, Admiral."

NACS ODYSSEY

▶ "PRIMMY SHIP IS slowing acceleration, Captain."

"Interesting." Eric took note of the relative positions of the five starships currently plying the ancient art of war in this sector of space. Things were a bit crowded.

The *Odyssey* was almost three million kilometers positive to the system elliptic, her course adjusting to bring her in a rapidly flattening curve as she continued to accelerate toward the two remaining Drasin cruisers that were still in-system. The *Vulk* was far ahead of them, the planet in their rearview while the other warship was pulling hard to match relative velocity with her.

Eric's course changes would bring the *Odyssey* into the battle from above, relative to the Priminae ships, which was just where he wanted to be. The *Odyssey* would no more survive friendly fire from an accidental beam crossing of a Priminae ship than it would the hostile fire of a Drasin warship.

Likewise, the dangerously charged homing abilities of the pulse torpedoes were quite uncontrollable and didn't pay attention to IFF signals, even if the Priminae ships had any.

"What's the status on the other ship, Michelle?"

Winger tapped in a command and brought up the latest visuals of the damaged vessel, causing someone to whistle.

Eric ignored them, eyeing the damage with a critical eye. "Are they still streaming atmosphere?"

"Aye, sir," Winger replied, frowning. "Don't know where they're getting it all, sir. Even a ship that size shouldn't be able to vent like that."

"Generators on board, maybe, sir?"

"Maybe," Eric said, acknowledging the suggestion from Lieutenant Daniels. "We know that energy conversion technology is possible."

"That's true, sir. Basic theory has been around and proven since the twentieth century, but the power requirements and the computational power…" Michelle Winger shrugged.

Commander Roberts glanced up. "We know that they have power to burn, but if that's the case, then why the hell haven't they sealed off the affected sections and stopped atmosphere production?"

"Unknown, Commander," Winger said. "Maybe their system is an all or nothing deal?"

"Damned fool way to build a warship."

Eric finally shrugged. "Either way, it's irrelevant right now. Code the images. Shunt them over to the engineering labs. Let them puzzle over it. When we get back, I'll ask Admiral Tanner myself."

"Aye, sir." Winger nodded, tapping a command to clear the images.

A moment later, however, an insistent tone sounded from her station. Michelle instantly began poring over something, staring at numbers as they flashed past her screen almost too quickly to see.

Eric waited a moment, then frowned when she didn't say anything. "Winger…"

"It's the Drasin, Captain. They're up to something."

"What?"

"Unknown. I'm not getting high enough resolution off these sensors, sir. If I had my main array—"

"We struck those sails for a reason, Michelle," Eric reminded her.

Traveling at light-speed through a vacuum wasn't precisely the "null zone" that it seemed. Micrometeorites could and would punch holes through anything they collided with, especially at the speeds the *Odyssey* was moving. The forward field generators were calibrated to shunt anything larger than a spec of dust out of the path of the *Odyssey*, or in the case of certain extremely massive objects, push the *Odyssey* out of a direct-collision path if the pilot was asleep at the controls. However, the fields were aimed straight front, as far ahead as the power allowed, and didn't do a lot to cover above and below the ship on the theory that the ship didn't have any reasonable right to be traveling sideways, anyway.

There was some leeway built into the system to account for maneuvering and such, but at the speed the *Odyssey* was traveling, her reflector sails would be ripped to tatters if they extended them. Actually, large segments were already in bad shape from their earlier deployment.

"Aye, sir," Winger reluctantly agreed.

The reflector sails were meant to be used up, that's how they were designed, but there was no point in doing so when it wouldn't give them a reasonable amount of sensor time.

"Keep working on those signals. Clean them up. I want to know what the Drasin are doing."

PRIMINAE VESSEL VULK

▶ "DRASIN ARE LAUNCHING fighters, Captain."

Johan grunted, not looking up. "What are the main ships doing?"

"We can't see, Captain. The fighters are screening them, sir."

Captain Maran didn't like that, not in the least. There was no reason to launch fighters that far out. The small ships must have the same problems that plagued the Priminae equivalents, so why waste their energy supplies by flying them in when their mother ships could easily carry them?

"Increase scanning," he ordered. "Go to all active measures."

NACS ODYSSEY

▶ "WHOA!" WINGER BLINKED.

"What's going on, Lieutenant?" Eric was concerned. Every time something happened they were left with more questions and fewer answers than they had at the start.

"I'd say that the *Vulk* is wondering the same thing you are, sir," she spoke up. "They just flashed some low-energy tachyons at the Drasin."

Eric nodded, knowing that the low-energy particles would travel much faster than higher-energy ones. "We seeing anything interesting?"

"Drasin ships have certainly launched fighters, sir," Winger replied. "Two fighter screens have formed up between the *Vulk* and the Drasin ships."

Eric frowned. "Anything else?"

"Hang on, sir…I've got the computer calculating shift patterns and wave mechanics. It takes a few seconds."

Eric nodded, willing to wait if Winger said that he had to.

"Got it. Looks like the Drasin are…reversing acceleration, sir."

"What?" Eric's head snapped around.

"The FTL wave proves it, sir. They're pulling back."

Commander Roberts frowned, looking over from his station. "Are you saying that they're abandoning their fighters, Lieutenant?"

"It's possible, sir. Maybe the fighters have the delta-v to catch up with them later, sir, I don't know."

The fighters might be able to pull that kind of delta-v, but the acceleration of the Drasin wouldn't be enough to give the enemy much time for retrieval if they did. The Drasin had to come to a zero-zero stop before they could begin to accelerate out of the system, and during that time, the *Vulk*, the *Odyssey*, and the other ship would all still be accelerating right up their tailpipes.

Even if they made the heliopause ahead of pursuit, they were going to have to jump to FTL without recovering their fighters.

PRIMINAE VESSEL VULK

▶ CAPT. JOHAN MARAN glared at the incomprehensible mash of signal reflections that was his pulse of FTL particles. The attempt to identify the plans of the Drasin cruisers had resulted instead in nothing more than a confusing mix of returned signals as their fighter screen interfered with the scanners.

The Drasin were up to something behind that screen, Johan knew it in his guts.

"Full power back to acceleration," he ordered after a second's consideration. "We won't give them time to accomplish it."

"Yes, Captain."

"Signals," he said, turning slightly, "send to *Heralc*. We are increasing speed to intercept the Drasin. Join us when able."

"Yes, sir."

Johan then turned back to the primary projection and frowned at the mess that was still all over his screen.

What could they be doing?

▼

NACS ODYSSEY

▲

▶ "THE *VULK* IS increasing acceleration, Captain."

Eric glanced at the projections. "They must see that the Drasin are trying to run off while using the fighters as a screen."

Commander Roberts nodded in agreement. "Can't say I blame them."

"Who? The Drasin or the Primmies?" Eric asked, then winced.

Damn it! He groaned, shaking his head. *That damned nickname is just* too *easy to remember.*

"Both," Roberts said, not giving any indication that he'd noticed the slip. "The Drasin have seen their pals get chewed up by a ship they know to be badly damaged and us. And the Priminae captain over there is probably chewing his nails for missing the action and also undoubtedly wants those Drasin dead before they can escape with any more intel on Ranquil."

Eric nodded. "Most likely, Commander. Lieutenant Daniels."

"Sir?"

"Calculate an intercept course for the Drasin ships, if you please."

"Aye, sir." Daniels nodded, continuing the calculations he'd already started.

Intercepting a ship at solar ranges wasn't quite as easily done as it was said. Given the disparity between action and perception due to light-speed differences and the extreme energy cost of real-time sensing, a ship could potentially make several maneuvers before its pursuer saw even the first one.

So it often came down to an educated guess, judging from what one knew concerning the enemy's intentions and the best course of action to achieving them.

In this case, the Drasin were withdrawing according to the best available data the *Odyssey* had, and their course should be fairly predictable. They wanted to evade the *Odyssey*, as well as the *Vulk* and the third Priminae ship, so they needed a least-time course to the heliopause. If they got creative, Daniels's projection would probably become worse than useless, but it was still the best chance they had.

"Calculated, Captain," Daniels announced only seconds after the order had been made.

"Plot and engage, Mr. Daniels," Eric ordered. "What engagement time do you project?"

"All things optimal, we'll have them in extreme range for no more than two minutes before their superior acceleration lets them get ahead of us," Daniels responded.

Weston nodded grimly, expecting nothing less. "Very well. Ensign Lamont?"

"Aye, sir?" Susan Lamont turned.

"Contact the Archangels and have them scramble for immediate deployment," Eric ordered. "I want them ready to deal with the fighter screen in case they break off to harass us."

"Aye, Captain. Archangels on scramble," Lamont confirmed.

"We've got a job to finish—let's get it done."

▶▶▶

"Archangel Squadron," the voice came over the speakers, causing a flurry of action even before it continued, "this is your scramble notice. Prepare for possible engagement with the enemy fighter screen. I say again…"

Stephanos grinned as he jumped into action, simply because no one was listening by that point, of course.

Paladin was juggling about forty-three cards that he'd accidently let scatter in zero gravity, barely managing to pluck them back out of midair before they floated too far away. "Shit!"

Steph had already pulled a reverse somersault that ended with him hooking the ridge of the cockpit seal with his hands and swinging himself down and into the padded seat. He snapped up his helmet and jammed it on, not bothering to seal it right away.

"Archangel Lead, we confirm the scramble order and are preparing to taxi."

"Confirmed, Archangel Lead." Susan Lamont's voice was warm as it came over the link. "Be advised, two enemy cruisers have launched fighters to screen their withdrawal. We do not expect that the fighters will be recoverable."

Ouch.

Stephanos grimaced as he toggled his fighter's twin power plants to standby, letting the powerful machine start to whine eagerly under him. "Acknowledged."

Anyone without a way home was a lot more dangerous than someone who thought they might have a future. At least, that worked for humans. Stephanos wasn't certain that would hold true for the Drasin, but he had little choice but to treat it the same way.

Of course, as he considered the matter, *the Drasin hadn't shown much care for personal survival in their past engagements, anyway.*

Stephanos pushed the thought away, instead focusing on the whine as his craft finished its preflight checklist and asked for his manual confirmation. He ran down the list, punching in the affirmation as each question was green-lighted, then keyed his communications gear to *Odyssey* flight control.

"Odyssey Control, this is Archangel Lead."

"Roger, Lead. Control standing by."

"Archangel flight has passed preflight. Requesting permission to taxi," Stephanos said as his helmet's HUD fed him the data from the other fighters.

"Roger, Lead. Permission granted."

"Thank you, Control," Stephanos said, then punched the command to taxi.

Unlike on the ground, where gravity would keep the wheels of the fighter nicely in place until the pilot decided otherwise, the process of taxiing on the *Odyssey* was more about waiting in place until one of the lumbering loaders came over, linked to the pin built into the front of the fighter, then physically towed you to the massive airlock elevators that connected to the flight deck.

So Stephanos and the rest of the team had little to do as they waited to be moved to launch positions.

PRIMINAE VESSEL HERALC

▶CAPTAIN SENTHE WATCHED unhappily as the *Vulk* pulled away from his ship. He didn't like being left out of the fight, but there was no help for it now. Maran had decided that whatever the Drasin were up to behind that damnable fighter screen of theirs was too potentially dangerous to leave them at it for long.

Kierna couldn't really disagree, either, unfortunate as that was.

There was nothing he could do as the brother ship of his own *Heralc* began to pull away, driving forward into the fighter screen, and the Drasin cruisers beyond it.

"Captain"—Serra frowned—"the *Odyssey* has altered course."

"What? To what heading?" Senthe demanded, confused.

"I'm projecting it now, Captain."

The new course appeared on the main projection a moment later, showing the *Odyssey* on a flattened curve rather than the more direct line he had seen earlier.

"That doesn't go anywhere near the Drasin's projected course."

"No, sir."

Kierna frowned, trying to make sense of it. The *Odyssey* was not crewed by cowards or fools, that much had already been determined, so why was it avoiding the conflict? Better still, if it was avoiding conflict, why in the Maker do so in such a way as this? It would be far simpler to just reverse course and return to Ranquil.

"Orders, Captain?"

Kierna looked up, then shook his head. "Stay on course."

"Yes, Captain."

He turned back to the new projections for a brief moment, then looked up again. "What is our reactor mass?"

"Three-fifths of standard gravity each."

Kierna managed to keep from cursing, but only just. He was starting to feel the difference in the ship from the low reactor mass. He was a little lighter on his feet now, but the acceleration was beginning to pull at his arms as well. It wouldn't be long before they would have to reverse course, or risk being trapped on a vector that would take them out of Ranquil space with no power.

▼

NACS ODYSSEY

▲

▶EYEING THE NUMBERS, Weston punched open a communications channel. "Archangels, this is the captain. We are approaching optimal launch. Get ready."

"*Odyssey* Actual, this is Archangel Lead," the cheerful voice of Commander Michaels came back a moment later. "We're in the Ready One position and ready to fly."

"Good," Eric returned. "Happy hunting, Archangels."

The channel shut automatically as Eric lifted his hand, then gestured to Commander Roberts, who was handling the timing of the maneuver.

"Killing main thrust," Roberts announced, an eerie silence falling over the ship as the heavy thrust faded away in time to his words.

The *Odyssey* slipped onto a ballistic course then, just for a short time, running on pure momentum.

"Firing maneuvering thrusters," Commander Roberts announced as Lieutenant Daniels executed the maneuver.

Outside the *Odyssey*, the big ship shuddered briefly, then dropped her nose even deeper toward the system elliptic as she brought the open maw of her flight deck to bear on the projected course of the Drasin fighters. Momentum continued to sweep the *Odyssey* along on its previous course, ignorant of the ship's current bearing, and deep within the big ship's flight decks an order was given.

"Archangels are go," Roberts said stonily, keying in a command.

▶▶▶

"Go, go, go!" Stephanos yelled, slamming his thrust to full the instant he had the order.

The invisible flame from his bird's twin reactors lit up the blast plate that had been erected behind him, turning the metal several hues of red in the first few seconds of exposure. Then the powerful fighter leapt forward and slammed him back into his seat.

With CM fields on full power, he only felt a fraction of the force that was exerted upon him, allowing the Archangel fighter to roar from the flight deck at over a hundred g's acceleration and climbing by the time Stephanos saw open space.

Once the black had surrounded him, he forced a hand forward and keyed the command that retracted the landing gear back into the plane. It wasn't strictly necessary for aerodynamics, of course, but the extended gear would throw off the center of balance he was used to and maybe blunt the edge of his abilities.

Besides, he didn't want to look stupid.

Stephanos chuckled at that thought and keyed open the squadron comm channel.

"Archangels, this is Archangel Lead. Check in."

One by one, the other eleven members of the squadron checked in by the numbers while Commander Michaels finished his in-flight checklist and made a point to listen to the reactors.

You never knew for sure how they were working until you were in flight, he had found, and able to listen to the distinctive hum the two power plants put out. Sometimes he knew he was in trouble just by a slight shift in the background whine that rode the mechanics of the craft back up to the cockpit.

And sometimes he could just tell when everything was purring along just right.

Stephanos smiled.

This was one of those times, thankfully.

Fianlly the in-flight and the squadron checklist were complete, and Stephanos keyed open the tac channel again. "Let's ease into diamond formations. Four-fighter teams. Staggered vertically."

The confirmations echoed as Steph kept the throttle up, easing his plane over to slide into the tip of the diamond spear his wingman and the second team had formed. Once that was done, all that was left was the screaming.

▶ ▶ ▶

"Repositioning *Odyssey*."

Eric acknowledged the report while he checked the status of the ship, and the thrusters flared again, bringing the *Odyssey*'s nose back up and on course following the launch of the final Archangel fighter and signifying the closing moments of the launch maneuver.

"Igniting main thrusters."

The familiar roar returned to the background, shaking the deck for a moment as the main power plants of the NACS

Odyssey began throwing their particulate thrust back out into space and pushed the big ship along its intended course.

Commander Roberts turned from his post and nodded to Eric with a satisfied look on his face. "Maneuver complete, Captain. We are back on course for the retreating cruisers."

"Thank you, Commander. Mr. Waters, status of the pulse launchers?"

"We have all but two charged to capacity again, sir," Waters replied. "The last two should be ready by the time we're into range."

"Excellent. Good work, everyone. That was a textbook launch," Eric said approvingly.

▶ ▶ ▶

"Someone get me the numbers on the number eight tube!" PO Sharon Tate growled, pushing away from her station and turning to look at another display. "We've got to keep those little hell beasts on ice for another freaking hour, so let's not fuck it up."

The crew in the control room for the pulse torpedoes nodded in enthusiastic agreement, knowing as they did the results of fucking up, and a young crewman quickly fetched the numbers.

Sharon nodded, looking them over. "All right, we're looking good here, people. What about tubes eleven and twelve?"

"We've got containment up and ready, waiting for the tokamaks to throw some anti-hydrogen our way."

"All right, good. Who's turn is it to supplement the magnetic containment, anyway?" Sharon asked, a half smirk in her eyes.

The other people in the room all pointed to the youngest member of the group, a male crewman by the name of Cade Harlan. He looked around nervously, not knowing what the hell they were talking about.

"Ma'am?"

"Here." She shoved a can of spray paint into his hands and pointed him toward the sealed-off section that held the housings of the magnetic containment tubes.

"What's this for?"

"Just something we do every time we have to charge these blasted things. Call it a tradition," Sharon told him.

"Ma'am...?" Cade was getting really nervous by this point, but didn't have much choice as three people shoved him toward the hugely massive door that was even then being opened for him. "I don't know what to do, ma'am!"

"You'll figure it out." Tate smirked, shoving him through the door.

▶▶▶

The crewman sailed through the door in the free fall of the weapons control room, just as the other members of the group closed it behind him. Harlan could swear they were laughing when the door shut, but he was busier catching himself from slamming into the far wall.

"Great. What the hell am I supposed to do with this?" Cade muttered after he'd gotten himself under control, shaking the paint can slightly to hear the rattle.

He pushed off the wall and looked back to the large pane of transparent aluminum that separated him from the others in the control room and saw that they were all pointing at the large grate that covered the magnetic containment tubes directly below and above his position.

"What the hell?" He frowned, noting a trace of color on the grates.

It took him a moment to catch on, and when he did, he had to laugh.

Supplementing the magnetic containment.

Right.

Cade Harlan shook up the can and traced over the lines he saw below him, brightening them up, and let the quick-dry paint do its job. When he was done, he kicked off and sailed back to the door.

It opened this time, letting him pass through into the control room, where the others were laughing and Petty Officer Tate took the can from him and clapped him on the back. "Nice job, Crewman. Now we'll be safe."

Harlan laughed. "Where the hell did that tradition come from, anyway, PO?"

Tate shrugged. "Seemed obvious to us, kid. Those torps are the fucking stuff of hell itself. We all feel better if we've got something a bit more powerful than magnetic containment holding them in place."

Harlan just shook his head, but he was grinning as the mood in the control room buoyed him up. Suddenly, things didn't seem so tense anymore, so he supposed that it must have worked, after all.

Back in the sealed tube room, the quick-drying paint finished its job and brightly marked a large circle with a star enclosed.

After all, what better to hold back the demons of hell than a pentagram?

PRIMINAE VESSEL VULK

▲

▶ "THE *ODYSSEY* HAS altered course, Captain."

Johan looked up, a frown crossing his features. Lately, it seemed that the only expression that did cross his features was a frown.

"Show me," he ordered.

The new line traced across the projection then, showing the new course and its intersection with the Drasin line. Only, it didn't intersect with where the Drasin were going to be; it intersected with where they had already been.

"Are you certain?" Johan asked on reflex, wishing he'd bit it back.

"Yes, sir."

He puzzled at the line, then looked to the fuzzy patch that indicated the current Drasin position and their course.

Finally, Johan Maran templed his fingers. "What is going on? Am I missing something? Or is Captain Weston?"

In the end, he didn't see anything he could do differently, however, and continued with his current plans as they stood. The *Odyssey* could take care of herself, and while he would have appreciated their added firepower, he didn't think he would need it.

Two Drasin cruisers against one Lympa'an Class warship should be a workable battle.

"Ignore them," he said after a moment. "Stay on course and confirm the status of all our laser crystals."

"Yes, Captain."

▼

ARCHANGEL SQUADRON

▲

▶ "EQUALIZE CM FIELDS at 20 percent power," Stephanos ordered, tapping in an adjustment to his controls.

The fleet called back acknowledgments, setting their counter-mass fields to an energy-conservation setting, then feeding the excess power from their reactors into charging the superconducting capacitors that would be used when they entered into combat maneuvering.

The enemy fighters were ahead of them, about five light-seconds closer to the elliptic plane than they were, and either unaware of the Archangel's launch or uncaring of it. Either way, Stephanos was going to make certain that they understood the gravity of their error.

For all of the two seconds they had to consider it.

The three staggered diamond formations of the squadron had drifted a few kilometers apart as they raced down along the course they'd launched on, vectored to intercept the Drasin at the end of an acceleration curve, and on board each fighter, the pilot was running through the last pre-combat checklist.

Each of them carried ten hypervelocity missiles, each massing one-quarter ton apiece, and the CM systems on each of those had to be charged and confirmed before they could be launched. Much the same way the four linked lasers in the Archangel's wings had to be primed, their tubes "pre-exited" so that they'd fire on command when needed.

Stephanos didn't expect to need the lasers much; they hadn't proved exceedingly valuable in battle against the Drasin before. The small fighters simply weren't capable of carrying the expensive and bulky heterodyne systems that allowed the *Odyssey* to adapt its laser fire to specific armor reflection frequencies.

The only system on board that didn't need some per-combat preparation was the forward 80mm. The electromagnetic accelerators were pretty much an on-command system and would fire in almost any environment.

"Three minutes," Stephanos announced as the clock ticked on by. "Wing Leaders, check in with final numbers."

PRIMINAE VESSEL VULK

▶ "FIGHTERS."

The single word was quiet and uttered with little emotion, yet managed to convey a sense of curiosity, just the same. The light-speed sensors had just detected the fighter group as it launched from the *Odyssey*, and they were presumably en route to engage the Drasin force.

Why fighters?

Johan Maran was beginning to feel like he needed a diagram to understand the captain of the *Odyssey*. Captain Weston had met the enemy with fighters before, during the Battle of Ranquil, but he had a reason to leave his fighters to do battle then. He had to slip between the other ship and the planet, otherwise the Drasin would have destroyed Ranquil.

So what was he doing now?

The only thing in the direction he was going was...

"Pulse the Drasin formation again!" Johan snapped. "I want a confirmation on the cruisers' location."

▼

ARCHANGEL SQUADRON

▲

▶ "ARCHANGEL LEAD, GOING Fox Actual," Stephanos announced, watching the enhanced graphics of his helmet show him the Drasin ships.

With the naked eye, there was nothing to see out there. The ships were dark enough to be blots against the black of space, and their drives were pouring radiation in the other direction. Still, they weren't looking to hide themselves particularly well, so they gave off waste radiation in the form of heat, some gamma bursts, and even the occasional flashes of visible light for the Archangel's sensor arrays to pick up, then compile into a very pretty image that was filled in from archive images of the enemy fighters.

It almost looked like a movie.

A silent buzz tingled through his arm as the computer located and locked on the target, calculating its course along the ten-light-second distance between them, then announced that the firing solution had been plotted.

"Archangel Lead. Fox Three," Stephanos announced as he flipped up the cover over the thumb button and slammed down on the stud.

The smooth underside of the Archangel popped open at his command, and the rail system built into the sleek fighter ejected one missile out the port-side tube. It fell away from the fighter, launched by a low-powered electromagnetic launcher, until it briefly jerked free of the fighter's CM field. Then its own CM field kicked, powered from onboard capacitors to "supersurge" the field, just as the solid rocket fuel booster ignited.

The missile cleaved through space like a laser beam, accelerating to almost 0.8c in just a few seconds. After those seconds were done, its CM generator burned out, though the rocket booster kept burning, and the quarter-ton sledgehammer continued on course at 80 percent the speed of light.

One by one, the other wing leaders called out "Fox Three," launching their own missiles into space as the Archangels continued screaming silently toward their target.

NACS ODYSSEY

▶LIEUTENANT WINGER STIFFENED in surprise. "Archangels have engaged, Captain."

Eric looked over. "How long ago?"

"Just now, sir," she told him. "The *Vulk* has pinged the Drasin fighters again."

Eric nodded, understanding. The Priminae ships had power to burn, from what he could tell, and the speed with which the *Vulk* was using active tachyon-location systems was only one more proof.

At least it gave him real-time data on his fighters, and maybe something else.

"Updated course on the cruisers?"

"They're pulling away approximately as predicted," Winger told him instantly.

"All right. Commander Michaels can handle the fighters. Let's nail those cruisers," Eric Weston said coolly.

▼

ARCHANGEL SQUADRON

▲

▶ "CONFIRMED HIT!"

Stephanos bared his teeth slightly as the huge plumes of energy showed on his sensors as at least two of the four missiles tore through their targets, ripping them apart. The other two were unconfirmed, but he was pretty sure that at least one had missed completely.

"Secondary Fire Teams, choose your targets."

The secondary teams in each diamond accelerated slightly, edging ahead of their flight leaders, and locked up the second array of targets.

"Enemy is maneuvering. I'm having trouble getting a lock," Cardsharp said a moment later. "No joy. No joy."

The HVM system, while fast and packing massive power delivered on target, was lacking in at least one area—maneuvering. The missiles were basically very, very heavy-beam weapons in their own peculiar way. Once fired, they went straight into the target with very little ability to maneuver.

"Roger that, Twelve," Stephanos returned. "Anyone having better luck?"

The other two fighters responded quickly in the negative.

"Distance is now five. I say again, five light-seconds. Hold positions. Fire when you have a positive lock."

The team called back, confirming receipt of the order. On board the fighters, the pilots watched their sensors with practically religious attention, watching not only for the moment their weapons systems rewarded their patience with a lock, but also for any sign that the enemy was firing back.

Seconds passed as they continued to barrel in, the lock percentages slowly climbing as the distance dropped and the computers started to develop predictive algorithms for the evasion patterns. What they didn't see was what they both feared and expected.

Cardsharp was the first to voice it.

"Damn it, why aren't they shooting back?"

"Can it, Twelve," Stephanos called.

He wanted to know the answer to that question himself, but Commander Michaels knew how easily people, even well-trained people who knew better, could let the unknown get to them. Letting speculation start to run back and forth would only hurt their chances and dull their edge.

Again, it was Archangel Twelve, Jennifer "Cardsharp" Samuels, who made the first call. "I have tone."

"Take the shot."

"Archangel Twelve…Fox Three."

Mere instants later, the other members of the secondary fire team received tone and opened fire as well.

Three more havok HVM missiles blazed across the alien sky and ripped into their targets only seconds later.

"Hit! Hit! Hit!" Stephanos called. "Three confirmed. Good shooting!"

Three more targets lit up, three more put down. Which left one question burning in the minds of each of the pilots.

Why weren't they returning fire?

"Ten seconds to knife range!" Steph called. "Switch to combat maneuvering and hook up the interface!"

The fighters shifted to their combat-maneuvering systems and brought their CM fields up to full combat levels. The fields would quickly drain their energy reserves, but while they lasted, the Archangels would be able to pull high-g maneuvers like the laws of physics were looking the other way.

"Archangel Lead. Guns, gun, guns!"

Calls of Fox Three and guns ranged through the tactical network as the team went weapons free and opened up on any available target.

First one, then three, then a dozen blooms of heat and light lit up the sky as the Drasin fighters died in the blaze of fire from the Archangels.

Yet, through it all, there was no return fire.

Stephanos had only a few seconds to worry about it; then the enemy was upon them.

"Tighten up! Stay with your wingmen! Here they come!" he called out as the enemy fighters appeared from the dark of the black sky, appearing like a wave from the night and rushing right into the throats of the Archangels.

And then passing right by without skipping a beat.

Stephanos twisted and jerked around in his fighter, looking over his shoulder at the computer-enhanced HUD that was projected all around him. "What the...?"

Archangels Four and Eight cursed, rolling as the Drasin fighters nearly collided with them, the pilots yelling into the ether.

"Where the hell are they going?"

Stephanos's eyes widened, something clicking in his mind, and he slammed his fighter over. The Archangel flipped nose for end as his abrupt change of vector caused his wingman to jerk around in a slower move. Then Stephanos fired his reactors and slammed the throttle full up.

The fighter screamed around him as it began to shake against the sudden change in vector, and even with the CM field at combat levels, he felt the pressure slam him back into the seat—hard.

"Steph! Damn it, Steph!" Lt. Franklin "Burner" Amherst yelled over the tac-net, already throwing his own fighter around in an impossible slide that culminated in a full-power burn from his twin reactors.

Stephanos ignored his wingman's demands, trusting the younger man to catch up as he could, not wanting to lose any time on the Drasin.

"All Angels," he called out tersely over the tactical network, "watch for kamikaze attacks on the Prim warship."

That was all it took.

The Archangels erupted in a series of curses, their flight profiles curving tighter and harder than they had before, and within moments, the entire wing of twelve fighters was pointed in the same direction as they poured on the power.

Ahead of them, the mammoth size of the Priminae warship was nothing but a tiny blip on their forward-scanning sensors, but its distance was "only" a few light-seconds away, and they, like the Drasin, were going very, very fast.

"Spread wide, Angels!" Stephanos called, his left hand coming off the throttle control as he tapped in a series of commands, sliding his finger along the touch screen between his knees, to clarify his order.

Within a little over a minute, the twelve-man group had let themselves drift out and away from the direct "six" of the Drasin group, taking up positions all along the periphery of that exalted place in a fighter jock's heart, their engines still throwing them through space after the alien craft.

"That should keep us from getting fried in friendly fire," Stephanos muttered, trying not to put too much emphasis on the word *should*. "In case you hadn't figured it out, weapons are free, ladies and gentlemen. Vent those bastards."

PRIMINAE VESSEL VULK

▶CAPT. JOHAN MARAN watched the details from his light-speed sensing systems with growing alarm.

"Target all weapons on the approaching Drasin fighter craft, Ithan," he ordered grimly, wondering if what he was worried about was even possible.

"Yes, Captain."

The answer was immediate, and the actions that followed only marginally less so, but Maran was still worried. The vectors he was reading off the Drasin fighters were difficult to interpret. They were using highly active evasion courses, after all, but unless he was losing his mind, they were going to actually engage his ship at close range.

Certainly, it looked that way.

Drasin fighters were exceedingly difficult to target, their maneuvering ability made them very elusive to larger weapons, and the few smaller lasers he had capable of locking onto a target that fast were of little use against the Drasin armor.

Now, if only the *Odyssey*'s fighters would get clear of his...

"Captain, new motion on the *Odyssey*'s fighters."

Maran's eyes widened, and he watched the signals of the fighter craft as they spread out, changing their pursuit vectors enough to clear themselves from his fire arc.

What? Are they mind readers, too?

Maran shook off the bizarre and largely unproductive thought and merely nodded in satisfaction.

"Fire on the Drasin with the main lasers. Full sweep."

"Yes, Captain."

Deep inside the cylinder of the Priminae warship, the large spinal-mounted laser crystals hummed at a frequency just above human hearing, sending shivers up and down the spines of those few who were close enough to that range to feel it instead. The ship's reactors fed power to them at a steady rate, the prodigious energy requirements of the massive laser crystals being dwarfed by the output of the twin reactor system buried deep in the armored hull.

In seconds, they reached a critical point, and the massive crystals began to fluoresce. A second or so after that, a beam hotter than the inside of a star leapt out into the empty void and lanced across the endless sky.

▼

ARCHANGEL SQUADRON

▲

▶STEPHANOS IGNORED THE screams of triumph coming from the others around him as his system automatically clamped down on his sensors to avoid burning them out as the corona of the laser swept over him.

That was one powerful laser.

He shook his head, checking his sensors, and tried to determine what, if anything, it had accomplished.

Three of the alien fighters were unaccounted for, which was a pretty piss-poor use of energy, in his opinion, but probably a pretty good average for using the main gun of a capital ship to "swat" fighters.

Certainly, the *Odyssey* would never be able to match it against fighters actively trying to evade. The one time Eric had used her main guns against a fighter group, the Drasin had been so supremely overconfident that they hadn't even bothered to evade, if they'd even acknowledged the *Odyssey* itself as a threat.

Unfortunately, whether it was good or not, there were still at least forty more fighters, all screaming through the vacuum on their mission.

And he did *not* like what their mission looked to be.

"Angel Lead," he muttered grimly, his finger tightening on the firing stud for the forward 80mm autocannon, "guns, guns, guns!"

The high-powered projectiles flared in his enhanced viewers, crossing space silently and invisibly in the real world, but in his encapsulated environment, Stephanos could practically count each heavy round in the stream as the computer filled in their location, speed, and vectors.

Across the distances they were fighting at, things that moved at merely the speed of a bullet took time to arrive, but when they did, they delivered their kinetic impact loyally, and Stephanos watched in satisfaction as the stream of cannon rounds tore up the fighter, sending it spiraling out of control when he got a piece of its engines.

"Vent one," he growled over the net, letting the flight recorders register his voice and log the event along with his comment while the others in the fleet continued pouring their weapons into the unflinching aliens.

PRIMINAE VESSEL VULK

▶ "THEY DO NOT seem to be engaging the *Odyssey*'s fighters…"

Johan Maran nodded, frowning as he tried to determine what, if anything, that meant.

The Drasin were known, or at least purported by legend, to be single-minded killers. Destroyers of worlds and devourers of civilizations. Literally, the greatest horror in his people's combined history, but like most of his generation, Maran had never really believed in the stories. They were told to teach lessons, they were fables, lessons in morality, and such things were always exaggerated to better make their point.

The Qirt didn't actually lift the boulder because he believed he could. The Predatory Sora did not spare the helpless kin in return for a future favor. And the Drasin did *not* really exist.

And yet they did, and where some truth lay, could the rest be more than mere myth?

"Continue firing," he ordered grimly, watching as the lead elements of the approaching Drasin fighters entered into the range of his smaller laser emplacements. "All available weapons."

ARCHANGEL SQUADRON

▶ "DAMN!" JENNIFER "CARDSHARP" Samuels growled, twisting her fighter into a tight spiral, her timing thrown off by the sudden dimming of her display as the Archangel threw up its sensor shielding in self-defense, blocking out the more dangerous frequencies of the laser's corona as it passed over her.

"Lost my lock," she said, matter-of-factly, though her calm words didn't hide the frustration in her voice. "Moving to reacquire."

"Negative, Cardsharp," her wingman, Paladin, said as he came up. "I have tone, taking my shot."

"Affirmative," she replied reluctantly, pulling back on her throttle just enough to let Paladin slide out in front of her.

She watched the sleek form of the fighter move, barely a hundred meters away from her, sliding gracefully against the startlingly brilliant background of stars around them. While he stayed on his target, her job was to watch his back, which was just what Jennifer intended to, so she threw her sensor net wide and watched for trouble.

Not that there was any lack of trouble to be found, of course, but none of it seemed to be near her or Paladin at the moment, relatively speaking, so she relaxed slightly as he murmured over the tactical network.

"Slippery little bastard," he growled. "Lost tone...Hang tight, Jen, I'm going in."

"Right behind you, Paladin."

Paladin's Archangel flared brilliantly in her enhanced environment display, his CM and reactor energies producing a brilliant glow that surrounded his fighter like a celestial halo, and he began to accelerate away.

She kicked in her own burners, her hand pushing the lever that controlled the CM field all the way up at the same time, and was pushed back into her seat as the former outraced the latter by a few instants. Then the counter-mass field caught up with the thrust, and Jennifer was floating free in her cockpit again, following her wingman in as he chased the evading Drasin down toward the suddenly imposing bulk of the Priminae warship.

▼

PRIMINAE VESSEL VULK

▲

▶ CAPTAIN MARAN WATCHED in a shocked kind of awe as the *Vulk*'s main computer had to reduce the magnification into negative numbers as the lead Drasin closed.

"What in the name of the Breaker are they—"

His question was cut off as the final approach vectors came back, and his eyes widened, as the only possible answer suddenly formed in his mind. "All hands! Impact alert! Impact alert!"

His warning came a few seconds too late.

The Drasin fighter slammed into the forward shields at a combined velocity of over 0.7c. It delivered its kinetic impact with a force that surpassed the combined power of the *Vulk*'s onboard nuclear munitions.

The screens, rated to observe the corona of a star, overloaded and went black.

The bridge shook under Johan's feet and pitched wildly. Johan was hurtled across the deck as his hands flailed out for something, anything, to grab hold of.

Around him, people were yelling or screaming. Some cried out in shock and pain as they were slammed around like straws in a hurricane. Then Capt. Johan Maran hit the far wall, and everything went black.

ARCHANGEL SQUADRON

▶ "HOLY...SHIT!" PALADIN cursed, yanking up his stick as he barely avoided being engulfed in the fireball ahead of him, adjusting his vector to skim over the wounded ship. "Pull up! Pull up! Pull up!"

Behind him, Cardsharp was following suit, staying close on him as she inverted her flight profile and put the heavier armor of the plane's belly between her and the explosion.

"Watch out for the shock wave!" she yelled, watching the eruption reach out for her plane.

"Can't avoid it! Going through!"

Paladin's last signal broke up as the flames finally reached up and swallowed his fighter, and a moment later, Cardsharp followed him into the maelstrom.

The enhanced environmental display gave her a look out into the very face of hell as Jennifer fought the stick to keep from being buffeted by the residual shock wave as she rode through the edge of the energy release and tried to get some cover from the other side of the *Vulk*.

Then, as abruptly as it had happened, she broke out into space on the other side, and the stars were clear and unblinking ahead of her once again.

"I'm through! I'm through!" Paladin called as he adjusted his course to skim the surface of the *Vulk* as he whipped past the huge starship. "Coming around in five...what th—Mayday! Mayday! Wind Shear! Wind Shear! I can't hold it! I'm going—"

His signal broke off as Cardsharp stared in shock as Paladin's fighter suddenly slammed into the *Vulk*'s shields, caroming off as it began to break up.

"Paladin! Come in! Come in, Paladin!" she screamed into her comm, staring in shock as the fighter continued to fall to pieces before her eyes.

"Wind shear? What the fuck?"

"Cardsharp! Pull up! Get out of—"

Then it had her, too, and her stomach lurched in her belly as her fighter was suddenly yanked from its flight path and plummeted toward the *Vulk* just like she'd run right under a heavy rain cloud at the edge of a hot dry air barrier.

Forewarned, Cardsharp threw her thrusters full out and surged forward, angling her nose up and away from the ship, and managed to turn her plunge into an arcing sweep that skimmed the edge of the shields and then curved back out into space.

"Grav shear!" she yelled, almost before her mind had consciously figured it out. "I say again, gravity shear! The artificial gravity of the ship extends beyond its hull!"

Then she was out and accelerating away from the ship, passing the wreckage of her wingman's fighter and searching desperately for any sign of life in the twisting scrap metal.

She didn't find any.

▶▶▶

The *Vulk* shuddered, barely even slowing in its lumbering forward motion as the first Drasin fighter suicided right in its face, but on board, the situation wasn't as easy as it appeared from the outside.

The bridge was a scene of shock and complete disarray as crew members struggled to pick themselves up off the deck and struggled desperately back to their stations.

"Captain! Captain!"

Johan Maran was groaning, fighting the darkness as he struggled back to the pain of the real world, but was somehow already moving, crawling, back to his command station.

"Status report..." he croaked, hauling himself back up into the chair.

The ithan in charge of sensors blinked, tapping in commands as he tried to clear his eyes. "The shields held, Captain. Asymmetric generators are severely depleted, however—"

"What about the other Drasin?"

"One moment..."

"Now!"

"I believe that four were vaporized in the blast. The rest are...still coming, Captain."

"Fire! Destroy them!"

▶▶▶

"Sweet Jesus..."

Stephanos jinked clear as his fighter's telltales went off, buzzing his nerves directly with a warning he couldn't ignore.

The *Vulk*'s lasers fired a few seconds later, and suddenly, the area of space they were fighting in got a lot less friendly, indeed.

"Son of a...!"

"Mother fucker!"

"Evade! Evade! Evade!"

Screams of fright and anger were echoing over the tactical network, but Stephanos ignored them as he twisted and turned his fighter through the web of laser light that was even now being drawn and updated by his enhanced environmental display.

The Archangel computers, operating as a Beowulf cluster, automatically shared all data on the lasers as they were detected and drew real-time lines across the sky for Stephanos and his team to see as they flew.

Red beams appeared to slice out from the ship, sweeping the heavens and utterly vaporizing anything that crossed their paths.

"We've got to pull back!"

"Negative!" Steph ground out, interposing his will on the squad. "Get closer!"

"*Closer?*"

"Jesus fucking Christ, Commander!"

"Are you nuts?"

"Closer!" he ordered again, then cut his throttle and spiraled his bird around one of the sweeping beams. "I want these genocidal bastards venting whatever the fuck they breathe all over this sector of space! Closer!"

Then he pushed the throttle up and aimed his fighter down toward the big cylinder of the *Vulk*, and Archangel Lead began to chase the closest Drasin in, weapons blazing.

"This is Archangel Lead!" he snapped angrily. "Guns, guns, guns!"

NACS ODYSSEY

▶SOMETIMES EVEN WESTON could register surprise on a large scale. When Winger yelped in shock and reported a major flash point from the *Vulk*, Weston wondered for a second if they were going to make it out all right.

"It looks like a nuke," Winger said.

"Nuke?" Weston asked tensely, thinking furiously about the nuclear weapons, or whatever they had been, already in use so far in this battle. "Not a laser strike?"

"Negative, sir. Widespread frequency release. Not merely a laser bloom," Winger confirmed. "Either a nuke or maybe... I don't know...reactor breach?"

"The Angels?"

"I'm still reading telemetry from..." She trailed off.

"What is it, Lieutenant?"

"I just lost telemetry, sir."

Eric Weston closed his eyes for a moment, pushing down the worry he felt trying to force his actions. Steph and the Angels could handle themselves. He had bigger issues.

"It...It might be interference, sir."

"It doesn't matter," he said after a moment. "We'll worry about them after we've dealt with the cruiser ahead of us."

"Uh...yes, sir."

"Range to target?"

"Two light-minutes now, sir," Waters replied quietly. "Still closing."

"Very good. Have the pulse tubes charged to active status."

"Aye, sir. Activating pulse tubes."

Eric Weston stared at the screen again, though his mind lay far behind them. Back with the squadron he'd fought and bled with so many times before.

God fly with you, Steph. God fly with you all.

ARCHANGEL SQUADRON

▶ COMDR. STEPHEN "STEPHANOS" Michaels hit the retro-rockets on his fighter as he whipped past the hulking Priminae warship, flipping the sleek craft of war end for end, and then threw full power to his reactors to kill his momentum.

The Archangel changed its acceleration in an instant, slamming from 0.4c to relative zero in under two minutes, then continued to accelerate until it was matching the lumbering warship three thousand meters to his port side. Stephanos checked his instruments, running comparison tests with the reports from Cardsharp and Paladin's flight data, then keyed open the squadron tactical frequency.

"Maintain a two thousand–meter distance from the Priminae warship, Angels," he ordered. "That should keep us well clear of her gravity well."

Confirmations came back over the network as the other fighters repeated his maneuver, ten transponders suddenly arresting their motion relative to him as they all formed up around the large ship.

The Drasin were sweeping around, their fighters showing abilities approximately in keeping with the Terran counterparts, though they seemed either unable or unwilling to engage in radical braking maneuvers of the ilk Stephanos and his team had just executed.

"Looks like the explosion shook them up some, sir."

"Negative, Burner," Stephanos replied, his voice quiet as he focused on the numbers. "They're just regrouping."

Indeed, that's what he was seeing on his instruments as the remaining Drasin fighters, almost thirty of them, circled back around and came in for another run.

"Here they come, Angels!" Stephanos growled, tapping out a weapons query to the flight computers.

The answer came back quickly and wasn't quite what he might have hoped. He'd used his forward 80mm quite a lot, trusting the gimbal-mounted weapon to both track and kill the enemy fighters at the ranges they were dealing with, but many in the flight had relied more heavily on their havoc HVM missiles, and the numbers were running low.

He was down to three thousand rounds in his forward cannon, and five of his twelve havocs were expended. The gigawatt lasers on his wings were powerful against human craft and missiles, but in the last battle with the Drasin, they had proven to be a minor factor at best, which meant that he was going to be bingo for weapons after another engagement.

The rest of the squad was generally worse off.

"Line up your shots," Stephanos ordered calmly, not letting his thoughts reach his voice. "Make 'em count. The engagement time is going to favor the enemy this time."

Again, the team acknowledged his orders while he haloed five of the inbound fighters in his HUD, then transferred the markers over to the tactical network, effectively stating, "These are *mine*," to the other flight members. Moments later, similar marks began appearing across his HUD, and Stephanos nodded silently in approval as the incoming targets were quickly split up.

The Drasin were coming back around on another intercept vector, increasing their speed to combat velocity, and that was going to make the engagement window very, very narrow, indeed.

In fact, despite how little he had left, Stephanos didn't think that a lack of weapons was going to be the problem this time around.

The problem was that they might not have sufficient time to launch all their birds before the Drasin closed to terminal approach.

"This is Lead," he said over the tactical net. "Go to rapid fire on havocs, and prepare to engage on my command."

PRIMINAE VESSEL VULK

▶ "REPORT ON DAMAGE!"

"Captain"—the young man turned, looking back at Captain Maran as he wiped a stray trail of blood from his forehead—"the Maintenance Department reports that they can't bring the asymmetric fields back to full power. The impact strained the generators past their ability to repair."

Maran grimaced. "Tell them to get those fields back up. We won't survive another impact like that."

"Yes, sir!"

Maran turned away, wiping his eyes again as a trickle of blood from his forehead got into his eyes.

"Here, sir." An ithan wearing medical planets on her shoulders handed him a cloth as she leaned over his console and applied directed healing treatments.

The sharp pain of the cut vanished quickly, leaving only a dull throb in its place, and Maran used the damp cloth to wipe the remaining blood from his face before handing it back to the young woman. "Thank you, Ithan."

She nodded and accepted the cloth back as he passed it off and turned back to his controls.

"Corun!"

"Captain!"

"Adjust fire zone to intercept incoming fighters. Recode all computers to track those targets. Forget about the Drasin ships—they're too far away to matter. I want all available lasers retasked to intercept those fighters."

"Yes, Captain!"

"And, Corun!"

"Captain?"

"Try not to hit the Terrans."

"Sir!"

Maran looked around, picking out another officer in an instant as the young medical ithan chased him across the bridge, trying to apply deep heal to his head injury.

"Mackin," he said softly, coming up beside his third-in-command, "we need to start thinking about clearing as many people to the evacuation centers as possible."

"Captain?"

Maran shook his head. "I don't think we can stop them all."

▼

ARCHANGEL SQUADRON

▲

▶ "HOLD YOUR FIRE."

Stephanos watched the incoming ships as they entered into the Archangel's range, watching the numbers as his locks formed up, but still held the missiles back.

"Sir, they're getting close."

"Hold your fire," he repeated himself, his voice tense. "I want them all."

"We're not going to get them all, Steph," Burner replied grimly. "They've got more ships than we have birds."

Stephanos nodded grimly, conceding the point. The remaining eleven Archangels had precisely twenty-eight havocs left, and the enemy had at least thirty fighters still dedicated to their kamikaze operations.

A nerve tingler snapped him out of his reverie, though, as the Drasin closed to less than one million kilometers, and he nodded grimly.

"All Archangels, rapid fire on havocs! Take 'em out, boys!"

In the fuselage of each Archangel, up to twelve havoc missiles were nestled in twin rotary dispensers that whined up as the motors attached to them were fed full power. The hefty

HVM weapons spun in their holders until the clamps were released on each in turn, and they were thrown clear out into space.

Once spun up, each rotary dispenser could clear its racks in less than ten seconds.

The Archangels put twenty-seven HVM missiles into space in just under eight. Each weapon was tracking on a preset target, tiny reaction thrusters making minute adjustments as the kinetic kill weapons powered up their CM fields, and then the space between Archangel and Drasin was suddenly slashed by lines of lethal power accelerated to 0.8c.

At seven hundred thousand kilometers, space was suddenly lit up by the release of multiple megatons of kinetic power, and the battle was joined again. Yet, through all the power and all the dying, the enemy kept right on coming.

"Weapons free!" Stephanos yelled. "Ventilate 'em!"

Missiles already expended, the fighters opened up with their remaining arms, loosing thousands of 80mm rounds and hundreds of gigawatts of laser energy into space as they poured everything they had into the oncoming enemy.

Through the multimegaton explosions, through the 80mm hail, and through the crossing beams of gigawatt level lasers, they came. One Drasin, then two, four, eight exploded, and still, the force came in. Through it all, time slowed for Stephanos as he watched the enemy come on, and he knew then that no matter what you had on your side, if the enemy were willing to court death, he had an advantage that could so very easily prove insurmountable.

The Priminae ship opened up, its massive terawatt lasers cutting swathes of destruction across the vacuum, and even more of the enemy ships vanished into balls of expanding gas and energy. Five more, then ten, and fifteen.

Fully 90 percent of the enemy's surviving force died in that last-ditch locked phalanx of fire, and still, they rushed onward into the breach.

"They're getting through!" Cardsharp yelled over the network.

She was right, Stephanos could see it. Three fighters were through the wall of light and steel they had cut in the space between them, still accelerating even now. His HUD displayed their speed emotionlessly, as well as the speed of the Priminae ship, and Steph did the math in his head in those last few seconds.

They'd impact at a relative velocity of 0.73c.

If the Priminae ship survived, Stephanos could hardly imagine anything in the entire universe that could harm it.

PRIMINAE VESSEL VULK

▶ *SO IT CAME down to this,* Johan thought.

"Collision imminent!"

The yell was calm, at least as calm as one could expect, and Johan was proud of his crew in that moment.

They had done all he had asked of them, all he could have asked, and he only wished that he had done as well for them as they had for him. It was easy to see the mistakes made in retrospect, perhaps especially since this one had been so glaring and so short a time past. He should have engaged the fighters farther out, but had expected them to engage like his own small craft might, and didn't believe them to be a credible threat to his ship.

He'd been wrong.

And now he was going to die for it.

The pity was that he wouldn't die alone.

Johan watched as the fighters wheeled in on terminal approach, and issued one last order.

"Launch the life pods!"

His ship shuddered under him, the smaller explosions the forerunners of what was to come, and he knew that some of his people were getting away.

Not all, that would have been impossible in the time they had, but some.

He only wished that he could have held off on the order just a few seconds more.

And then it was too late for regrets.

ARCHANGEL SQUADRON

▶ "TAKE EVASIVE ACTION!" Stephanos ordered over the network as the last two Drasin fighters passed through the last-ditch fire from both the Angels and the Priminae ship. He rolled his own fighter as he spoke, throwing full power to the CM field as he did, and activated the fighter's blast shields.

The armor plates slid out over the sensor pods that normally had to be exposed to space to one degree or another, cutting them off and effectively blinding Stephanos inside, but he already knew what was going to happen, anyway.

His mind filled in what the sensors could no longer see, graphically illustrating the cataclysm that was passing just outside his cockpit.

The two fighters would be crashing into the Priminae's shields about now, he thought, wincing slightly at the thought.

He imagined the shields flaring under the force of impact, either holding or failing, he couldn't say, but turning brilliant white under the impact even as the fighters' mass was converted into energy by the impact.

On a planet's surface, there would be a mushroom cloud, but in space, it would be spherical.

No, no, Stephanos corrected himself, the ship had its own gravity field.

How would that affect the explosion? Stephanos didn't know, couldn't even guess. For a moment, he was tempted to lower his blast armor, just to find out, but then his mind filled in the next thing that would happen.

The shock wave would reach out like the angry fist of God, swatting his Angels from the skies.

The universe then shook and rolled and tried to turn Stephanos inside out as his imagined scenario came entirely too true.

PRIMINAE VESSEL HERALC

▶ "BREAKER BELOW."

Someone hissed at the curse that escaped Kierna's lips, but the captain of the *Heralc* couldn't care less. On the screen was the same thing that had been there when they overloaded, the last image of the *Vulk* before it vanished into an inferno of heat and light, and over fifteen thousand people died in the endless night.

"Weapons status!" he called out, trying to shake the feeling of stunned shock that threatened to swallow him whole.

There was a pause before anyone responded, but he let it pass.

"W...Weapons active, Captain. Ready to deploy."

He nodded. "Increase all forward scans."

"Yes, Captain."

"Captain!" A too-young woman at the engineering station called sharply, turning to look at him.

"Yes, Ithan?" Kierna asked, though he knew what she was going to say.

"We do not have reactor mass to engage the Drasin in a prolonged battle, Captain. We're down to under 60 percent of gravity, Captain."

"Understood, Ithan," he said in a too-calm voice, not looking at the young woman. "Weapons are to be charged."

There was a silence on the bridge, and for a moment, no one wanted to meet the Captain's eye, which was fine with Kierna. If he miscalculated, if he simply chose to ignore the threat, then the *Heralc* would become a derelict, forever falling away from the world it was supposed to defend.

There was nothing they could do that would repower the reactors once their mass dropped below critical levels.

Not a thing in the universe.

ARCHANGEL SQUADRON

▶STEPH STRUGGLED WITH his fighter as he bucked around, relying on nothing but inertial guidance and his own inner ear as he tried to bring it back under control. Finally, the system smoothed out, rocking a bit as he overcompensated for the last correction, and an awful sense of calm passed over him.

It was strange; it shouldn't be. He was physically unconnected from the explosion and the ship by anything—vacuum isolated him more effectively than anything else could—but Stephanos felt what he was going to find before he secured the fighter from its highly armored mode.

Lights came back as the sensors were free to look out again, and instantly, new data began pouring in. The Angel transponders were all there, the first thing he queried, and Steph gave a brief prayer of thanks for that before he looked to the ship.

Or what used to be a ship.

The hulk of the once great ship was twisting slowly in space, well astern of Steph or any of the other Angels, and he flipped his fighter in response, firing his reactors to kill his momentum.

"Jesus…" Burner's voice came back over the network, whispering in shock.

Stephanos didn't blame him.

As the sensors got a better look, the computer filled in the image with as close to real-time data as he was going to get, and Stephanos watched the dying ship as pieces of its hull twisted and collapsed inward. First one section, and then another, until finally the rest of the ship itself twisted horribly of its own accord and sank into itself.

And then finally, there was nothing left.

No hull.

No debris.

Nothing at all.

"Holy shit."

"Sir, this is Cardsharp…Recommend we avoid that area."

"What?" Steph blinked, not that he was planning on flying through it. "Why?"

"Don't know for sure, but judging from what we just saw…I don't think it's all gone yet, sir. Something's still under power in there. And it eats ships."

Stephanos blinked, trying to shake away her words with little success, the very concept boggled his mind. Finally, he managed to say, "Agreed."

He marked the area as a hundred thousand–kilometer no-fly zone, choosing the number mostly at random except that all of his fighters were at least that far away and seemed OK, then shot the waypoint orders to the flight.

"Sir," Burner came on a moment later, "I think I'm picking up survivors' beacons."

Steph checked the data, then cursed. "Archangel One to *Odyssey*, request immediate search and rescue units. I say again, we request immediate search and rescue at the following coordinates…"

Everything slowed down then for a while, took on normal dimensions. The Archangels lazily orbited the escape pods from the downed Priminae warship, unable to do anything more, but unwilling to entirely abandon the stricken people to their fates, either. Stephen eyed the screens carefully as the second big Priminae warship approached, growing with every passing moment.

"They'll be here in a few more minutes," he announced over the squadron link, finally. "When they start search and rescue operations, we'll peel out and meet up with the *Odyssey*."

Most of the team acknowledged, but there was a silence from Cardsharp's fighter. He waited a moment, then quickly checked the status of her fighter. When everything showed green from where she was currently flying "overwatch" position, he flipped over to her channel.

"You all right, Jen?"

There was another pause, and he was just on the brink of heading his fighter over in her direction. Her voice over the network put a halt to that a moment later, however.

"Yes, sir. Fine. I'm just tracking something odd here."

"Odd how? We have more bandits inbound?"

"Negative. I think the *Odyssey* has launched shuttles."

"OK. Probably SAR birds. How many?" he asked.

"Uh…I'm thinking all of them," she answered. "And I think that the *Odyssey*'s signal is starting to Doppler blue again."

Steph thought about saying that she was reading her instruments incorrectly, but this was Jennifer Samuels. She was space qualified on everything with a reactor; she wouldn't be misreading the Doppler signal of her gear.

Just the same, he linked into her feed and double-checked against his own gear.

Damn, she's right. They're accelerating out of the system again. Why the hell are they doing that? No way they catch that bandit now. He stared at the numbers as they continued to show an increase in the *Odyssey*'s speed. *What the hell are you doing, Eric?*

"All right, change of plans, everyone," he said over the squadron's tactical network. "We're going to sit right here until the *Odyssey*'s shuttles arrive. No way we can catch the *Odyssey* if they're determined to chase after that bandit, so we're not flying out of bingo fuel range from the planet."

The squadron acknowledged the change in orders, not overly concerned. Whatever the *Odyssey* was up to, they'd find out soon enough, and for the moment, they had their fighters strapped on, and that was everything they could ask for. Steph, however, was trying to puzzle out his friend's actions as he watched the screens.

The *Odyssey*'s blue shift continued to accelerate until, suddenly, there was a momentary surge, and then the ship's signal was completely gone.

"Holy shit, were you watching that, sir?"

Steph swallowed, acknowledging the signal sent over the private channel from Cardsharp. "I was, Jen. Tell me that wasn't what I damn well know it was."

"Had to be. They just transitioned out, Commander."

"Crap. Well, that explains the shuttles," he said finally. "Resupply birds."

"Have to be, but…Why did they do it?"

"I wish I knew, but the cap will have his reasons. He always does," Steph said. "Hopefully he'll have told someone on the shuttles what the hell they were this time."

Steph could tell from a certain hesitation that Jennifer had decided, perhaps wisely, not to comment on her captain's peculiarities.

Steph swapped over to the squadron channel and checked everyone's fuel and weapons status. The Archangel Class fighter burned straight liquid hydrogen with pure oxygen as the oxidizer, which was not the most effective fuel under normal circumstances, but it was cheap and plentiful and, with their CM fields, more than handled the job they needed. The constant maneuvering required at high combat levels would kill their fuel levels fast, however, the CM fields notwithstanding.

Everyone had more than enough to have rendezvoused with the *Odyssey* as originally planned, but when calculating the cost to send a wing out to escort the shuttles in, Steph was coming up short on fuel to make it back to the planet. In theory, it wasn't a big deal. They could easily get picked up by the locals, but he didn't want to be doing that.

Not that he mistrusted Priminae technology, but it wouldn't look good to be towed in, and unless he had a damned good reason, he wasn't going to be making the Angels look bad. So he settled on his initial call and elected to settle in to wait for the approaching shuttles, no matter how much he really wanted to get within network link range of them so he could ask just what the *fuck* was going on.

NACS ODYSSEY

▶JUST OVER TWENTY light-years away, what was going on was a lot of retching and general misery as the *Odyssey* drifted in an empty section of interstellar space following its jump. On the bridge, Eric found himself forcing his light lunch and coffee back down where it was supposed to have remained while everyone else seemed to be doing much the same.

"Is it just me, or was that worse than usual?" he asked, not really aiming the question at anyone in particular.

"Not just you"—Susan Lamont groaned before adding a belated—"sir."

"Oh, good." He put a hand to his face, noticing that he was sweating and clammy. *This is worse than usual. God, what the hell? Must be because we were all mentally worn out by the fight.*

"Bring us about," he ordered through the pain. "Extend the sensor sails."

"Aye, sir. Extending sails," Lamont responded.

"Coming about, sir," Ensign Waters chimed in.

The deck shuddered as the *Odyssey* swung slowly around, bringing its most powerful sensors, scopes, and detection apparatus to bear on the estimated location of the enemy starship.

"Ensure the sails are stealthed."

"Aye, sir. Black hole settings, as ordered," Lamont replied calmly as her sails unfurled.

Because the *Odyssey*'s sails had the combined area of several football fields, they created one of the most powerful mobile telescopes and sensor arrays ever designed by Terrans. There were better ones in Sol, of course, positioned at most of the Lagrange points in the solar system by this time, and a couple sitting outside the heliosphere, but for a system mounted on a ship, the *Odyssey*'s size was unmatched.

"Target spotted."

Eric turned to the screens, gaze falling on the fast-traveling contact they were centered on. "Any sign of a course change?"

"Negative. Still on their original course," Lamont said. "They passed within three light-minutes of us, about five minutes ago."

"Understood, pull in the sails, Ensign. Helm," Eric ordered, "recalculate for next transition."

"Aye, sir."

The cringe in the helmsman's voice was echoed in Eric's mind, but he did his best to ignore it. They had a lot to do and surprisingly little time to do it in, and there was no time for squeamishness. Not even when it really was that bad.

Their current task was a great deal more complicated than it appeared, and it was absolutely vital that everyone work to his or her peak despite the effects of the transition drive. Tracking a ship in FTL without using active sensors was tricky enough, since no matter where it appeared to be when you spotted it, it was actually much farther along its projected course.

In order to hop ahead of them, the *Odyssey*'s crew had to calculate the Drasin's acceleration and course, then make a best guess on where it would be when they transitioned back into real space. Guessing wrong meant either being spotted by the enemy or, more likely, losing them entirely in the expanse of interstellar space.

The situation was further complicated by the need to remain entirely undetected, and so Eric had ordered that they transition far enough ahead that the tacyon burst was completely burnt out before it could reach the projected position of the alien ship. That gave them a very small window to work in and expanded the possibility of a critical fault in their calculations.

Still, there was nothing to be done about it. One way through, and that meant doing the job, doing it right, and doing it the first time, every time.

"Coordinates calculated, sir."

Eric nodded, thumbing open the ship-wide. "All hands, stand by to transition."

Whatever happened next, it would be something new...

PART 2:

Delivered From Darkness

TRAINING FACILITY/TEMPORARY TERRAN COMMAND AND CONTROL, RANQUIL

▲

▶COLONEL REED STOOD shoulder to shoulder with Major Brinks, their support staff and liaison in behind, as the approaching shuttles and Archangel fighters slowed and circled the hastily cut landing field before firing retrorockets to stabilize their descent. The big shuttles came down on the north side of the field, where there was plenty of room for them to space out their final positions, both for safety concerns and because they had significant loads to disembark.

The fighters came in tighter, showing off, in Reed's opinion, landing with wing tips practically touching on the south section. It was an entirely pointless display of precision and completely in character for the Archangels.

Reed ignored the fighters—they didn't have anything he needed, anyway—and headed over to where the clouds of dust were settling around the big shuttles. One of those would hold someone who could answer his immediate question—namely, what in the name of all that was holy was going on?

For some reason, Captain Weston had seen fit to take the *Odyssey* out of the system, leaving him saddled with a ton of people he wasn't normally supposed to be dealing with. With them at least technically outside his chain of command, being assigned to the *Odyssey* while he was assigned to the Confederation Embassy attached to Ranquil, that could potentially get dicey.

The men and women in the shuttles were fast and efficient; they had already started unloading some of the equipment by the time he'd arrived. He glanced at it and noted that most of it was munitions for the Archangels, so he guessed that they were prioritizing the rearming of the fighters.

Understandable.

Reed came to a stop near a senior master chief who was snapping orders, and simply waited for the man to notice him. It didn't take long since the chief would have had to be blind and stupid to miss the stares of the men and women he was ordering. He glanced back, saw Reed, and snapped off a couple more quick commands before turning and saluting.

"Sir."

"At ease, Chief. You have something for me, I'm hoping?"

"Yes, sir. Dispatch from Captain Weston, sir," the chief said, handing over a data plaque.

Reed accepted it. "As you were, Chief."

"Aye, sir," the chief replied before returning to snapping out orders to the men and women swarming off the shuttle.

Brinks approached from behind him, pausing at a respectful distance while Reed finished with the brief on the plaque.

"Huh."

"Mind if I ask for an elaboration on that, Colonel?"

Reed shrugged. "Captain Weston is trying to follow a damaged ship back to its base of operations. You, the shuttle crews, and the flyboys over there are seconded to my command, officially, until the *Odyssey* returns."

"Well, I was already technically there, sir," Brinks replied with a grin. "But it's an honor to serve under you and all that rot."

Reed rolled his eyes. "Yeah, yeah. Go let your guys know what's going on. I'm going to have a quick chat with the chief flyboy. I'll catch up with you later and we'll get a planning op in progress."

"Yes, sir." Brinks saluted before heading off.

Reed took a breath before he headed over to where the pilots of the Archangels were milling around their fighters. It wasn't that he didn't respect the abilities of the fighter wing, or even actually dislike any of them personally, but they had a reputation for being glory hounds. Probably, the Confederacy's propaganda division manufactured a lot of that, but it still irritated him. He and those he'd served with before and after the war were shadow operators—they lived in the shadows, worked in the shadows, and more often than not, died in the shadows. Maybe someone had to stand in the light, but it often rankled to watch when you were always in the dark.

He put that aside, however. Being able to act like a professional was a prerequisite for his duties as a SF trainer. Had he felt the need to like everybody he worked with in the past, there'd have been a lot less well-trained guerrillas harassing the Block's forces during the last war. Working well with assholes was actually in the job description.

He found Commander Michaels leaning back against his fighter, eyeing the goings-on carefully as flight crews from the *Odyssey* rolled gear into place to rearm the squadron.

"Commander."

Michaels looked over at him and pushed off the fighter, standing more or less straight. "Colonel."

"Orders from the *Odyssey*," Reed said, flipping to the appropriate section of the data plaque with a swipe of his thumb before handing it over.

Steph accepted it, eyeing Reed for a moment before he skimmed through it quickly. His eyes widened. Finally, he nodded slowly and handed it back to the colonel, correcting his posture just enough to be considered "acceptable" as he saluted.

"Sir, the Archangels are at your disposal."

"Thank you, Commander. What do you need in the short term?"

"Judging from what I'm hearing here, I'd say a supply of H and O2, Colonel. We're low on fuel, but everything else was shipped out before the *Odyssey* left the system."

Reed nodded, turning to the Priminae liaison that had accompanied him. "I understand. Ithan Chans, can you get in contact with someone to bring supplies of hydrogen and oxygen out here?"

Milla nodded, noting the order on her personal computer. "Yes, Colonel."

"Thank you," Reed said before turning back to Commander Michaels. "In the meantime, we've got a decent temporary housing here, so check in with my aide and get yourselves assigned some bunks. I can't promise much on this kind of short notice, but there's no reason for you to be sleeping in your planes."

The commander smiled. "Wouldn't be the first time we had to, sir, but thanks. Wilco."

Reed nodded. "Well, as you were, then. I'll get back to you when I know more about the fuel situation."

"Thank you, sir," Steph said, turning to Milla. "Good to see you again."

"You as well, Commander," she said with a hint of a smile, though it was strained by the circumstances. "It would be better in another time, I believe."

"Most likely." He nodded with a wistful look.

Milla followed the colonel, taking the first few steps backward as she shrugged in the pilot's direction. "I apologize. Duty, yes?"

Reed walked away from the fighters, reasonably pleased that the encounter was fairly painless. He'd encountered pilots with more bluster for less cause, so maybe it wouldn't be too bad dealing with them until the *Odyssey* got back.

In the meantime, however, he had to get ahold of the ambassador and let her know about the current state of affairs. He was reasonably certain she knew that the attack on the planet had been warded off, but whether anyone had informed her of the *Odyssey*'s departure was another matter entirely.

As he headed for the transport section so he could visit with the ambassador, he wondered for himself whether Weston's actions were intelligent and forward thinking or reckless and foolhardy. Sometimes, particularly in the midst of an armed conflict, it was hard to tell the two apart. Genius and insanity were often separated only by the results. Unfortunately, sometimes it could take generations before you really saw the full scale of the results, and this was one of those times, Reed thought.

The effects of involving the Confederation and Earth in an interplanetary war was quite likely something only the survivors would be able to judge, and even then, it would hopefully be some time before they were qualified to do so. The new technology the colonies had to offer the Confederation and Earth was a huge incentive, but they all could have done without the introduction to the Drasin, however.

No matter, what was done was clearly done. The clock didn't turn the other way, and they had to deal with the results of the *Odyssey*'s first mission as it stood. That said, however, Reed was beginning to wonder if this wasn't a pattern in the actions of her captain, as his latest move was certainly following similar lines. Weston clearly wasn't someone who had trouble making decisions, which was generally a good thing in a commanding officer, mind you. More men had died because their commander wavered in his action, too afraid of making the wrong decision to make any, then had been killed by poor decisions.

The problem was, being willing to make a hard decision that risked so much was a lot like playing no-limit Texas Hold'em and going all in. It was an incredibly powerful move that worked every single time, except the last time.

I hope this isn't Captain Weston's last "all in."

▼

RANQUIL

▲

▶ THE BEING KNOWN only as "Central" observed the vanishing dot that represented the *Odyssey* from many different perspectives. It saw it on the instruments used by the Priminae to monitor the system and in the eyes of those watching said instruments. The *Odyssey* was most vibrantly viewed through the minds and imaginations of those people, however, as they filled in the details of the ship's vanishing all on their own.

From the range it was sitting at, there was no way for Central to know what the captain of the ship had elected to do precisely, nor the reasons why. Having spoken to Eric Weston, however, Central had some ideas, all the same.

Weston seemed like a kind of premeditated risk-taker to Central, someone who took calculated chances—great leaps followed by careful analysis and planning on the fly. If he was leaving now, he would have a good reason—in his own mind at least—and it might dovetail with Central's own goals.

Central was not known for believing in luck, nor the supernatural; however, it was aware of both of these things as they existed from the human standpoint. Even the most enlightened of the Priminae had some beliefs that were not entirely rational, after all. An entity like Central could not really express frustration, but it felt frustrated that Weston was moving well beyond its powers of observation. Still, he was ostensibly an ally, so Central bade the starship a wish for both luck and guidance before turning its focus to tasks more within its sphere of influence.

▼

DEEP SPACE,
NEAR RANQUIL SYSTEM

▲

▶A TERRAN WOULD describe their behavior as that of a wolf pack, circling a particularly confounding prey. The descriptor would even be accurate, save for one significant difference: a Terran wolf pack knows when the game is up and it's time to move on to easier prey, but the alien ships that were holding almost half a light-year outside of the Priminae star system had no such limitation.

The system had to be cleansed. There was no other option. The crimson band that infected the system had to be eradicated, even if the star itself had to be destroyed.

With that kept firmly in mind, however, the few Drasin ships in the area were painfully aware that the losses incurred in this single system had slowed the cleansing of an entire sector by a now significant level. The Drasin had conferred after each defeat, the few survivors relaying a little more information each time, and they'd come to realize that there was an unknown factor in the middle of the cleansing.

That made things far more complicated, as this generation of Drasin had been specifically tailored for the crimson band of this sector. Weapons, armor, even tactical selections were based on information culled specifically for dealing with the *life* in this place.

The new and unknown weapons and tactics used by a single small combatant were delaying them, and that was unacceptable. Long-range observation of the system indicated that the unknown bearer of the crimson band was not present; however, it had been shown in the past to be able to almost entirely mask its presence even at close range. Losing more of the cleansing here would not be optimal.

The Drasin decided on an alternate option.

On an atypical orbit of the local sun, the picket forces located the system's comet clout and plucked up several of them for the next phase. Estimated probability of success of a purely kinetic bombardment was less than one in ten thousand, but that was not the goal. The picket forces sent the chosen comets sunward and, along with them, a cloud of warriors in their wake.

▼

MONS SYSTEMA, RANQUIL

▲

▶ "THAT'S WHAT THE *Odyssey* reported, ma'am." Reed was standing easy as he delivered the information to the ambassador, arms crossed behind his back and legs set about shoulder width apart.

Ambassador Lafontaine examined the information, scowling at the screen of the plaque as if she could intimidate it into reporting something different. While the *Odyssey* wasn't assigned to Ranquil or her office, she would have preferred some notice before Weston took the ship haring off after some new shiny thing that caught his attention.

That was saying nothing of the soldiers and pilots he'd saddled her with here. Certainly, she was confident that Colonel Reed could find things for them to do, but it hardly seemed professional and could leave her with awkward questions to answer when she dealt with the local parliament.

"Your thoughts, Colonel?"

"On what, ma'am?"

She looked up at him, her eyebrow arching as she pinned him with a stare. "About Captain Weston's actions."

The colonel just shrugged. "Judgment call, ma'am. He had to decide then and there if he was going to pursue the target. Everything else just fell from that decision."

"And you believe it to be the correct decision?"

Clearly, Reed hated it when he was put on the spot like that, but the ambassador didn't particularly care what Reed hated. She knew he probably resented interference from the civilians in his chain of command, but what choice did he have but to ask for assistance? Unlike Weston, Reed was unlikely, in the ambassador's opinion, to take wild risks.

Reed sighed, shaking his head. "Situational, ma'am. I can't say, and that's not me trying to weasel my way out of anything. I really can't say. From here, it seems a little over the top, particularly given that he left the Archangels behind, but from the bridge of the *Odyssey*? Hard to say. I wish he'd kept some of his shuttles, but I can see the logic in leaving them behind."

"You can?" she asked, skeptical. How much was Reed covering for the man? "I certainly cannot. Without his shuttles, he can't abandon ship in case of an emergency or even investigate anything he may find up close."

"While that's true as far as it goes, Madam Ambassador," Reed conceded, "I believe the point is that if the *Odyssey* encounters a situation they can't run from, they're not making it back, shuttles or no. Also, this is a recon mission. There won't be any planetary exploration or the like. It's as I said, I wish he'd kept a couple birds on a gut level, but honestly, I can't imagine what he'd do with them."

The ambassador sighed, rubbing her face tiredly. This was going to wind up giving her migraines and more gray hair to cover up, she just knew it. The bright, shiny allure of being on a planet new to her had already begun to wear off.

"Very well," she said finally. "Thank you for the report, Colonel. I'll see to it that your materials requests are given high-level consideration, just to help move things along. You're dismissed."

"Ma'am." He nodded, heels clicking as he turned and left her office.

She stared at the information on the portable computer plaque for a long moment.

Why did I volunteer for this posting again? Oh, yes, adventure and the history books. I'd feel better if Captain Weston weren't so intent on making certain those books were such fascinating reading, however.

She checked her schedule, noting that she had a meeting with a senior administrator in less than an hour, and decided not to arrange any special meetings over the matter. She'd let him know what was going on and let it run up the Priminae chain that way. It may not be the fastest way, but she could do with the experience of how their politicking was handled.

She didn't think that the requests would be anything overly troublesome, either, so there really wasn't any need to fast-track any of it. Hydrogen and oxygen were easily available, and while they'd have to fabricate adaptors for whatever system the Priminae used for storage, that would be easily handled as well.

More than likely, they already had adapters, now that she thought of it, or at least schematics for them. The Priminae had provided the *Odyssey* with additional oxygen the last time they were in the system, after all.

She supposed that Captain Weston would have been well aware of that when he made his decision. One less headache for her, at the very least.

She checked her timepiece and closed down all the files.

There was work to be done, after all.

BRIDGE, NACS ODYSSEY

▶ WESTON TRIED VALIANTLY to keep his stomach from voiding its contents all over the deck, just barely succeeding as he curled over in his chair and listened miserably to the sounds of others failing in the same task.

Have to make a note that multiple transitions in succession are to be avoided under almost any circumstance. He groaned, forcing himself upright as the first scents of stomach acid reached his nose. His gut tightened up, and he had to fight through the repeating urge to vomit alongside so many of his crew.

There was work to be done first.

"Deploy sails," he ordered. "Bring us about and locate the enemy cruiser."

"Aye, Captain," Winger said miserably, clinging to her controls to keep from sliding to the deck.

"Coming about, Captain." Daniels groaned, his hands working the controls more by instinct and muscle memory than his will.

As the *Odyssey* rumbled and slowly came about, her large sensor sails unfurling to catch the enemy trace, Eric placed his fingers to his temples and tried to soothe the throbbing he felt there. *We're going to have to do a full medical after this. The side effects are going beyond motion sickness. We're going to need to know if it's temporary or cumulative.*

It was the *Odyssey*'s fifth successive transition, and each time, the jump through transitional space seemed to become exponentially worse. The normal rush of fear and gut-level nerves he experienced had been replaced by a deep sickness that had grabbed him at his core and made him want nothing more than to go to his cabin and curl up in the dark. If it became any worse, he could easily add sob softly until he fell asleep to the list, though Eric figured it would take about two more transitions before he'd admit that aloud.

They already had more than twenty men and women in sickbay, sedated to various levels. The worst were in medically induced comas, though Palin assured him that there were no signs of any permanent damage at this point. He wasn't sure he could authorize too many more transitions in rapid succession, though. The risk of losing more of his crew to medically ordered sedation would be high, and soon he'd run the chance of losing crew he couldn't stand to lose.

He'd already crunched the numbers after the last transition and thought he could possibly order three more. Realistically, however, Eric didn't think he'd chance more than two, and he was really pushing it to say that.

"We have them. They've executed another evasive maneuver."

Eric groaned as quietly as he could. Every damned time they thought the enemy was heading for a star, the little bastard changed course and left them running themselves ragged to catch up. "Calculate and prepare transition drive for new coordinates…"

"Hold on, sir." Michelle snapped straight up. "Enemy contact is red shifting! They're slowing down!"

"What? There's nothing out here." Eric's eyes snapped to the screen. "Show me the plot."

"Aye, sir."

The star field appeared on the screen, with the computer highlighting the decelerating Drasin cruiser. It was clearly slowing its relative speed, but there was nothing in range that it could be meeting.

"Is there another ship out there?" Eric asked.

"Can't say yet, sir. We're working on passives, but unless it just arrived a short time ago, I don't think so," Michelle said, equally confused.

Her computer beeped at her, calling her attention to an error in the system.

"Hold on, what's this?" she mumbled, confused.

"Lieutenant?" Roberts spoke up for the first time since they'd arrived at this point of deep space.

"Computer error, sir. There's a mismatch between our records and the current scans," Michelle said, fingers skating along the controls of her panel. "Computer wants to know if it should update the logs."

"What kind of error?"

She called up the offending record, and her eyes flickered back and forth between the real-time view and the original mapping made decades earlier by the James Webb Space Telescope. The computer helpfully pointed out the error in the original file, as well as suggested that they update their data with the most recent observational and clearly correct version.

She stared at it for a moment and then flicked her hands across the board to send both images up to the main screen.

"The image on the left is from the James Webb Space Telescope, mapped in twenty twenty-eight," she said in clipped tones, still uncertain as to what she was seeing. "The one on the right is from our own scans, two minutes ago."

"They look like stars to me, Lieutenant," Roberts said, eyes nonetheless flicking between the two.

"They're identical, except for the area our bogey is decelerating into," she said, highlighting the offending sections of the images.

On the Earth-based scan, there was clearly a star sitting right there where the *Odyssey*'s instrumentations insisted nothing but empty space was currently sitting. Eric stared at it for a long moment, unable to quite believe what he was seeing.

"Michelle," he said slowly, "how could we possibly have misplaced an entire *star* sometime in the last few decades?"

"Unknown, sir. We'd have seen a nova, and even a singularity collapse would show us something from here on the higher band sensors," she answered. "I'm getting nothing on any of those, however."

"Range to the star from our current position?" Eric asked. "Assuming the Webb scans are accurate."

"Just under half a light-year, sir."

He nodded, thumbing open the ship-wide. "All hands, this is the captain. I believe we may have tracked our quarry back to his den. The *Odyssey* will stand down from transition alert for the next twenty-four hours while we observe the area. Medical checkups will be scheduled—they are mandatory. Other than that, we're on minimal watch starting now. Get some rest. You all deserve it."

The comm blinked off, and he addressed the people around him. "That goes for you all as well. Nonessential stations can be left unattended; essential stations please be certain to schedule yourselves at least two free shifts out of the next three. Get the observation running, then get some rest. I have a feeling that we're going to need it."

After seeing that everything was settling down, the jobs needed doing being done, Eric handed the bridge over to Commander Roberts with a firm admonition for him to do the same as soon as someone suitable to replace him was freed up. He then headed down toward medical to check in with Dr. Palin over the effects of the last set of rapid transitions.

The *Odyssey*'s CMO took one look at him as he stepped into the medical labs and shoved a pill pack and a small cup of water in his hand.

"Take them."

Eric might normally have argued a bit, or at least demanded to know what he was taking, but given how he was feeling, he decided it could wait. He swallowed the two pills from the pack and washed them down quickly before returning his attention to the doctor and the actions beyond him.

"How bad is it?"

Palin, who had returned his attention to a computer screen, shrugged without looking up. "In the short term? Reasonably bad. It's like better than 70 percent of the crew has come down with near-crippling motion sickness. If you hadn't called a stop when you did, there might not have been anyone to run the ship."

Eric winced, though he'd been reaching that conclusion himself. "And the long term?"

"Indeterminate at this point." Palin scowled. "In theory, there shouldn't be any repercussions. Tacyon radiation is too highly energetic and the particles too small to interfere with human cells. In practice? This is dark territory, Captain. We may not know for years—or decades."

Eric sighed. "Understood. How long before the affected people come back to duty?"

"The worst? I'm not waking them until we're going to be stable for a reasonable period," Palin answered. "Most of the crew will be back on shift by the end of the twenty-four hours."

"Good. Thank you, Doctor," Eric said, turning to leave. He paused as his stomach growled just before he exited the lab, however, and half turned back. "What was in those pills?"

Palin smiled. "Hungry, are we?"

Eric nodded, a little wondered at it, actually. A half hour ago, he would have sworn to never eat again.

"Let's just say that it's a good thing you don't have any surprise drug tests coming up."

"Doctor..." Eric growled, eyes widening.

"Relax, Captain. I was mostly joking." Palin was in far too good a humor for Eric's liking. "It was, however, a cannaboid derivative. Civilian drug tests often pop positive for cannabis if you've taken it. It has no mind-altering effects, Captain. It's just a very effective nausea suppressor and appetite enhancer. Go get something to eat and then get some sleep—doctor's orders."

Eric left, casting doubtful glances over his shoulder at the doctor until the doors closed. When his stomach growled again, he shrugged and headed for the commissary. Judging from the brisk business being done there when he arrived, he figured that the doctor had been giving a lot of people his little munchy pills.

I hope those things have been cleared by the military board for use, he thought wryly as he got in line with the rest. He could have had a meal brought to him in his cabin, but there was hardly any need, and by times, it seemed like a good idea to be seen rather than just heard.

A couple of the younger sorts tried to skip him ahead in line when they recognized him and then tried to simply step out of line when he refused. Eric hid a smile when one of the chiefs behind the counter clubbed a lieutenant across the wrist.

"If the captain wants your spot, he'll take it from you," the older man growled, reasonably low. "Don't make a production of things when people are trying to eat."

The poor butter-bar lieutenant looked honestly caught between wanting to take the NCO to task for smacking him with a ladle and not wanting to gather any more attention than he already had. He finally, wisely, chose to get his food and let the line continue as efficiently as it had before Eric had joined it.

As Eric stepped past the chief, he nodded to the ladle. "You are going to be washing that before you use it again, right?"

"Course I am, sir." The man looked affronted. "Lord only knows where that officer's been, begging your pardon, sir."

Eric laughed softly. "Tell you what, Chief, why don't you double my serving of the mystery meat, and we'll call it even?"

"Brave man," the chief replied as he fetched another ladle and spooned a double portion onto the captain's tray. "Sounds like a deal to me."

"Good enough. Thanks, Chief."

"Anytime, Captain."

The mood in the mess seemed positive. He'd expected a quieter and possibly even sullen group when he arrived. Multiple transitions were far more taxing than he'd expected them to be, so he'd come in with the worst firmly in mind. He wasn't sure what it was, over all, but Eric guessed that it was probably more to do with his having ordered a twenty-four-hour reprieve than the doctor's munchy meds.

They probably helped, though, he thought dryly as he took a seat at an empty table and began eating.

He already missed the squadron, he found. Their presence in the mess was a comfort, a place he could sit where there was no awkward question of rank. He was in command, they knew it, but it didn't make the slightest bit of difference to any of them. Flight leader or captain, he was now and would always be one of the Angels.

Now, though, he sat alone in the middle of the crowded commissary, his thoughts more focused on the current situation than anything else.

The fact that they had, for all intents and purposes, misplaced a star was bothering him. All right, that was more than a little bit of an understatement. He was flat-out terrified by the possibilities that brought to mind.

Did those monsters destroy a star?

It seemed impossible on the face of it, but he'd watched and rewatched the drone data of them dismantling a planet piece by piece. Certainly, they couldn't have done that to a star, but could they have done *something?* If they'd blown it up, then the *Odyssey*'s sensors would have picked up some sign. Similarly, if they'd somehow managed to cause it to collapse on itself, Eric was familiar enough with stellar phenomena to know that, even then, they'd likely have noticed *something.* A perfect singularity seemed the only possible answer, but why would they fly *into* something like that?

In the end, he couldn't make any sense of it with the information they had available, so he shelved it and finished his meal. Afterward, he ambled slowly through the ship, taking his time to check on the goings-on at various stations and generally make his presence felt. He didn't want to be seen as looking over their shoulders, but Eric felt like it was sometimes good for morale to see the captain involved on the ship elsewhere than merely on the bridge.

He guided his wanderings to end at his quarters, where he finally turned in for the "night." Actually, he had to check his watch to realize that it was the middle of the afternoon, shipboard time. It hardly mattered, of course. Not in deep space, light-years from a star (the misplaced one notwithstanding), but it was still disconcerting to feel as suddenly worn as he did just then.

Especially when I've not been jerking my fighter around in the air for the past forty-eight.

Between the food, the fatigue, and he suspected the doc's munchy pills…Well, he was beat, so he stripped down and called it a night. So what if it was the middle of the afternoon? He was the captain of the only source of daylight for one hell of a long way. If he said it was night, it was damned well night.

▼

RANQUIL, ARCHANGEL TEMPORARY FLIGHT BASE

▲

► COMMANDER MICHAELS LET his hand run along the armored skin of his fighter, eyes falling to the large tanks of O2 and hydrogen resting on a pallet nearby. His own bird was due to be tanked up next in line, as soon as they finished fabbing the adaptors to the Priminae gear.

Until then, he felt like he was chained down. Oh, certainly he likely wouldn't be flying, even if he had more than a couple more hours of fuel, but the lack of the possibility was wearing on him. His bird, now designated Archangel One since Eric had handed his own over to Cardsharp, was rearmed and fully checked. It was ready to fly as soon as it got a drink.

Like more modern fighter craft, the Archangels took several hours of maintenance work for every hour of flight, but Captain Weston knew that better than most and had sent along the people, equipment, and parts to handle the job. The remaining fighters of the squadron were all ready to fly, ready to fight, just as soon as the fabbers finished printing out the new attachments for the Priminae storage tanks.

They were all sitting together, wing tip to wing tip, where they'd landed, but the crews had thrown up some UV reflective tents over the lot to keep any degradation of the armor systems to a minimum. He'd always found it funny how something as simple as sunlight could cause so much damage to some of the toughest, most technically sophisticated armor suits ever devised. The stuff could take military-grade laser strikes with ease, but a month out in the sunlight would fade half the effectiveness from the cam-plate adaptive structures.

It was funny how things worked sometimes.

Stephen couldn't help but toss the occasional glare over at the fabbers, matched by another at the patiently waiting tanks of fuel. He was feeling a little disenfranchised, he could see that, and knew that most of the other Angels were in the same boat. They should be on the *Odyssey* with their captain, not sitting grounded here on an alien world waiting for some fancy desktop printers to finish building a damned nozzle for a gas pump.

He knew why Eric had taken off, but that didn't mean he liked it.

"Checking on your bird?"

Steph rolled his eyes as he half turned, amused by the suggestive tone in Jennifer "Cardsharp" Samuels's voice. "Always."

"Everything intact?"

"Always," he repeated, not taking the bait. "What are you doing down here, Jen?"

"Checking on my bird," she replied, shrugging as she smiled. "It's a nervous habit."

"I know. We'll all be down here a few times today, I expect—until they're refueled, at least."

He knew that even though it didn't actually make any logical sense, Jennifer would feel a lot better about her fighter once she was certain it wasn't anchored to the ground. The ability to scramble and get it off the ground would make her feel a hell of a lot better. It wouldn't actually change anything in terms of the fighters sitting there, but at least they'd be able to get them off the ground if they needed to.

So far, the local officials had been pretty helpful concerning getting them fueled and fed, but most of those who were normally assigned to the *Odyssey* didn't really feel too comfortable depending on an alien early warning network while sitting in the center of a war zone. It wasn't that they distrusted Priminae tech, per se, but it had been clear from the get-go that the enemy out here knew all the Primmies' tricks. They'd come in loaded up with armor, weapons, and tactics all aimed at screwing the Primmies over, which was the only reason the *Odyssey* had such an easy time of it.

So sitting grounded on a world Michaels knew had a big bull's-eye painted across it, they all really wanted to have the *Odyssey*'s eyes out there watching for trouble.

▶▶▶

Tanner strode into the command center for the system defense network, summoned by an urgent chime from the night watch. He could have hoped for a night's peace after recent events, but was unsurprised to find it denied to him. For all that, he was reasonably satisfied with how things had progressed and might normally be feeling almost happy. It was that, of course, which led him to believe that his doom was hovering just overhead and would soon be falling upon him.

"What is it?" he demanded as he stepped into the center of the room.

"Contact on the first system picket line, Admiral."

Tanner looked over the projection, his eyes locating the signal the young officer was speaking about. The lights were showing an unpowered object passing the outer line, and he followed the track carefully to see that it was headed on a ballistic course directly for Ranquil.

"Natural track?" he asked, though his voice clearly sounded skeptical.

"No, sir. Nothing that size tracks toward Ranquil without being noticed many orbits in advance."

Tanner nodded. He'd been well aware of that. "So, they're trying to crush us under a cometary collision?"

"It seems so, Admiral."

"Fools, then," Tanner said. "Dispatch a freight tractor to readjust its course."

"Of course, Admiral."

"Make certain that the *Cerekus* is detached to cover them," Tanner ordered after a moment's thought, "in case it's some type of trap."

With his orders delivered, Tanner stepped back and took a seat at his personal station. He accessed the outer line stations and began looking over the raw data.

What are they up to? He couldn't believe that the Drasin thought that a purely kinetic assault would ever possibly work. The Priminae colonies had been capable of shifting immense mass in defense of their planets for thousands of cycles. There was simply no conceivable mass that could be tossed their way that they couldn't deflect.

His first thought was, of course, that they intended to somehow escort it in. They could possibly pull that off; however, with the level of warning the outer picket lines permitted, the defense forces had other options than a direct intervention. Continuous laser fire from extreme range could easily be enough to deflect even huge masses, the tiny amount needed to create huge differences at their destination.

However, there was no indication of anything but some scattered ice and mineral, completely as expected in a cometary tail.

What are they up to?

It almost had to be a trick. He knew it, and the Drasin likely knew that he knew it, but in the end, Tanner had to send his ships out, anyway. He couldn't just ignore a mass that size aimed at a populated world, to say nothing of it being *the* populated world of the entire sector.

The problem was, he was all too aware that they also knew that, and that meant he was being forced to make moves that his enemy could easily predict.

Even he, as inadequate to the job as he sometimes felt, was fully aware of how bad a position that was, strategically speaking.

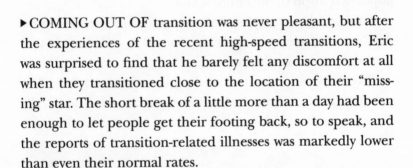

NACS ODYSSEY

Deep Space

▶ COMING OUT OF transition was never pleasant, but after the experiences of the recent high-speed transitions, Eric was surprised to find that he barely felt any discomfort at all when they transitioned close to the location of their "missing" star. The short break of a little more than a day had been enough to let people get their footing back, so to speak, and the reports of transition-related illnesses was markedly lower than even their normal rates.

Of course, several of our most illness-prone crew members are in medically induced comas at the moment, which is probably skewing the results, Eric thought darkly. Those crew members were weighing heavily on his mind ever since the end of the rapid succession of transitions left them permanently in the medical labs.

The doctor assured him that they would be fine, but the fact that they were confined to medical beds and kept from waking for their own good was something that troubled his sleep. He didn't know how long they'd be like that, simply because he didn't know how long the *Odyssey* would be committed to its current mission.

They'd come out of transition several light-days from the recorded location of the "missing" star; he'd ordered that range to keep any chance of detection from being a possibility. They were now approaching the area where they'd lost the enemy's signal, falling in on a pure ballistic descent.

"We're starting to pick up some strange low band readers, sir."

Eric looked over to where Michelle Winger was frowning as she stared into her instruments. "Define strange."

"Heat. Lots of it," she replied curtly, still glaring at her displays.

"Heat? But no light?"

"Nothing much. Occasionally, there's a ghost echo, like something is out there…But it's nothing I can pin down. Even our best scopes just show flashes and shadows, and then only for a split second. The only constant is the heat."

"Is it a threat to the ship, Lieutenant?"

"Negative, sir. Not that hot, just well above the average. Heat doesn't propagate well in space, so we're close to the source, but I'm not seeing anything on any of our passives besides the infrared," she answered. "If we could just go to actives…"

"Not a chance, Lieutenant. This is a scout recon. We sneak in, sneak out, and hopefully never get seen. Blasting the entire sector with tacyons and high-energy radiation would be counterproductive," he told her dryly.

"Aye, Captain."

Eric was almost amused by the slight pout he could hear in her tone and easily imagined her face with an expression to match. He suspected that it offended her professional sensibilities to be limited to such a degree, but that was the way things worked sometimes. You used what you could, what the mission permitted, and you made yourself satisfied with it, even if you couldn't be happy.

Michelle went back to work without complaint, however, as he expected of her. Sensibilities aside, he knew she was both competent and professional.

"There's something else, Captain," she said after a moment.

"What is it?"

Michelle grimaced, shaking her head. "I'm not sure… Here, sir."

She flicked her hand, sending what she was looking at to the main viewer. Eric's eyes focused on the screen, but all it showed was a dark-red mass.

"What am I looking at?"

"The heat source, sir."

Eric frowned. "What magnification?"

"Sir, this is the widest-angle lens our scopes have. There is no magnification."

Eric leaned forward, then stood up as he circled around the bridge to where Michelle sat. He leaned over her shoulder to read the raw data himself.

"How big is this?" he asked, perplexed.

"I can't tell, sir," she said, shaking her head. "There's nothing to use to compare it against. I have no frame of reference. It's big, but without some sort of parallax or ranging beams, I can't tell how far away it is. We can't range using parallax because it's too big from our frame of reference, and the *Odyssey*'s scopes aren't set far enough apart. Without the actives, I can't say how big it is."

"Best guess, then, Lieutenant," Eric growled.

Michelle was quiet for a moment, then shrugged helplessly. "Maybe as little as a few light-minutes across to as much as light-years. It depends on how close we are to it."

"On the low end, how long until we make contact with the target?"

"At current speeds? Sometime in the next twenty-four to forty-eight hours."

"Any idea what it might be?"

"No, sir. There's nothing in any of the listed natural phenomena that match this," she told him. "But honestly, I don't think we'd be able to detect it from Earth, anyway, so we could be looking at some very common physical event in the galaxy."

Eric shook his head. "Nice thought, but I don't buy it. The enemy flew in here; they didn't come out. This isn't natural."

"Then it's not my department, sir." She shrugged helplessly.

Eric sighed, straightening up. "Then whose department would it be?"

"Engineering?" Michelle offered, uncertain.

Eric considered it for a moment. "All right. I'll try that."

"Sir? I was just guessing…"

"It's better than what I had, Lieutenant. Keep monitoring the scopes."

"Yes, sir." She nodded.

"Commander, the bridge is yours."

Roberts nodded, stepping over to the command station. "Aye, Captain. I have the bridge."

Eric nodded, stepping away from the sensor station and heading off the bridge. He caught the first lift from the command habitat, heading back toward the engines and life-support systems in the aft of the ship. He didn't know if anyone in Engineering would have an answer, but it was better than any of the ideas he'd come up with.

The majority of the *Odyssey*'s Engineering Department was in microgravity, back in the aft of the ship where the engines were located. Eric pulled himself along the handrails, sliding into the main rooms where he located the ship's chief.

"Sam, I have a question I want to spitball past you," he said as he hooked the corner of a wall to bring himself to a stop.

"Shoot, Cap. I'm listening," Sam Wilson said, looking over from where he was monitoring the output temperature of the *Odyssey*'s reactor.

"You paying attention to what's going on outside?"

"The missing star, you mean? Heard about it. Not my section." Sam shrugged.

"No, well, maybe not," Eric said. "We're picking up a lot of heat coming from up ahead."

"You think we're heading into an invisible star?" Sam blinked, his mind suddenly racing as he began calculating the *Odyssey*'s heat tolerances and whether the ship could pull away from a stellar mass if it got too close.

"Not that much heat. This is a lot lower in temperature, but it's everywhere."

Sam frowned. "It can't be everywhere."

"It's so big, Sam, that our forward scopes can't see the edges. But here's the thing"—Eric frowned, thinking about what he was saying—"the enemy ship we've been tailing, it went in to this sector and didn't come out. I don't think it's a star. Detection and sciences say it's no natural phenomena they're familiar with, so I'm thinking it isn't natural at all."

"You think it's something the enemy built? How big are you talking, Captain?"

"On the low end? Numbers say that, if we're right on top of it, at least forty, fifty light-seconds across."

Sam whistled. "That's the low end?"

"Extreme low end of the scale, based on the angle of our scopes." Eric nodded. "More likely to be several light-minutes across or more."

Sam shook his head. "Can't even begin to imagine, Captain. Sorry."

"Uh…sir."

The two men turned to see a crewman first class with his hands in the air, as if he were seeking permission to speak in class.

"What is it, Sanders?" Wilson asked.

"You say this thing is giving off heat, sir?"

Eric nodded. "That's right."

"And it's probably several light-minutes across?"

"Yes."

"Can I see the raw data?" The crewman looked eager.

Eric half twisted and tapped in a set of commands at a nearby terminal. The engineering screen changed over to the raw feed coming from Winger's scopes.

"This is all we've got, besides occasional flashes of light."

"Flashes?"

"Yes," Eric said. "Indistinct, fuzzy, but certainly broad-spectrum light."

"It's a mega construct," Crewman Sanders said a few seconds later. "Has to be."

"I need more than that, son," Eric said tightly.

"Well, it's only theoretical on Earth, sir," Sanders said, "but what we're looking at here fits the expected readings you'd see if you were on approach to a Dyson construct. First glance, you'd think probably a Dyson sphere, but that's unlikely. Those are almost impossible to build, even in theory, and the light flashes are probably sunlight from the star within."

"So it's not a sphere," Eric said, confused. "What is it?"

"Best guess, Captain? We're looking at a Dyson Cloud," Sanders said softly, almost reverently as he looked over the raw data.

"Which is?"

"Sorry, sir. OK, the sphere is the easiest to describe." Sanders shook himself, turning to the Captain. "Imagine a shell around a sun, about eight light-minutes in diameter. Along the inside of the shell, you build your civilization, right? The sun gives you massive amounts of energy, all of it captured and used, and because the shell is so huge, you can have a society of trillions of people or more living there."

Eric stiffened, his mind racing.

"The Dyson Cloud is a little different, not quite as elegantly perfect, but a lot more realistic to build. Instead of a shell, you surround the sun with orbiting platforms in a cloud formation. They don't have to be perfectly balanced like the shell, and you gain some redundancy protection, but you give up a little space and a few other things."

"You're telling me that the *Odyssey* is currently diving toward possibly *trillions* of Drasin?" Eric's eyes were wide, his jaw slack. The implications alone were staggering, but for the moment, he was more concerned with the immediate repercussions. "But this had to have been built in only a few decades. How could they have done that?"

"Decades? No, sir. This is Class Two megastructure. You can't build that in a few decades." Sanders shook his head.

"In twenty twenty-eight the James Webb scope mapped this star," Eric growled. "Even accounting for light-speed lag, this thing can't be more than...two hundred years old, tops."

Sanders paled. "Sir. We really don't want to tangle with a Class Two species."

Eric rubbed his face. "Son, you need to stop talking in code."

"Class Two species, on the Kardashev scale," the crewman said, looking for a reaction.

Unfortunately for him, Eric didn't have a clue what he was talking about. He knew enough about the physics of the ship to be considered conversant in a lot of science-heavy topics, but this one was completely alien to him.

Sanders winced. "Sir, we're not even considered a Class One species yet—at least not unanimously by the scientific community. General consensus is that humans—from Earth, anyway—rank around point-nine-eight on the scale."

"That's pretty close to one," Eric said, frowning.

"Yes, sir, but the scale isn't linear," Sanders said. "Where it starts exactly is debated, but a species probably first registers when they tame fire. Call that a Class Zero species, if you like. A Class One is a species that can produce energy equivalent to the total power potential of a planet. We're close...but not quite there."

"And these guys?"

"If this is a mega construct like a Dyson Cloud, then they're a Class Two species," Sanders said, "a species capable of tapping the total power potential of a star. That's so far past us, sir, it's not even the same *game* anymore."

"If it's the Drasin, we've been handling ourselves all right so far," Eric said firmly. "It's quality against quantity."

"Just remember, sir," Sanders mustered his nerve, "quantity has a quality all its own."

Eric half smiled, looking at the young man closely for a moment. "Now you're talking a language I understand. I'll keep that in mind."

"Yes, sir. Sorry if I was out of line, Captain."

"No apologies. I asked, you answered."

"Yes, sir."

Eric nodded to the chief and spared a second for the crewman, then kicked off the wall and headed back up toward officer country. Crewman Sanders's words were ringing in his mind as he moved, so he headed straight back to the bridge.

"Any change in status?" he asked as he stepped onto the command deck of the *Odyssey*.

"No, sir." Commander Roberts shook his head as he stepped up from the captain's station, clearing the way for Eric to step in. "Did you find out what you wanted to know?"

"Wanted? No." Eric shook his head. "Needed? Maybe. I need to check a few things, Commander. Keep an eye on the sensor track, if you please?"

"Aye, sir."

"Thank you," Eric said, slipping into his chair and calling up information on mega constructs, Dyson clouds, and the Kardashev scale.

It took only a few minutes of skimming the files to see what Sanders was talking about. The Kardashev scale was a geometric progression, from a theoretical zero point through to Class One, Two, and Three. Class One was the capacity to manage the total power potential of a planet, Two was the same but for a star, and then Three...Three was a species that could do the same thing for a galaxy. The very idea boggled his mind in ways he hadn't felt since he was a child, but luckily, he wasn't dealing with that just yet.

The power output of a star was huge, incredibly so, but it was something he could imagine. Something he could mentally wrap his mind around and keep his sanity intact. He wasn't so sure he could do the same if faced with a Class Three species.

As for the potential construct itself, Sanders's theory sounded good. He did get the names wrong, but Eric supposed that there would be some discussion over such things, which would explain as much. Freeman Dyson postulated the concept in 1960, amazingly enough, and Sanders was quite correct about it fitting the readings they were seeing.

A complex Dyson Swarm, to be specific, fit the readings best. It had to be extremely complex and much tighter woven than the more common predictions stored in the *Odyssey*'s banks, but it fit. Sunlight was blocked, absorbed by the orbiting satellites, but they couldn't insulate all of the heat transfer, so that was what the *Odyssey*'s close-range infrared scopes were detecting.

He made some quick calculations, assuming that the star was precisely where the James Webb scope said it was, and then used that as a reference point to estimate the center of the swarm. The computer spat back the numbers a moment later, leaving Eric to sit back and just think quietly for a minute.

Twelve light-minutes in diameter. My god, how do you build anything that big in so little time? We're too close. If we light up our drives, we'll never be able to cut our momentum and pull clear before we're spotted and overtaken—not if they have any kind of watch at all. What have I done?

"Commander."

"Sir." Roberts stepped over quickly.

"By my math, we're six hours from contact," he said dully. "We're invisible, hopefully, but if what I now suspect is right... we're..." Eric smiled ruefully. "Well, Commander, 'outnumbered' doesn't begin to describe it."

"Captain? I don't understand."

Eric sent the relevant notes to a slate and handed it off to Roberts. "Read that. It'll describe it better than I can.

Commander, I may have just led us into a wasps' nest, and I'm not certain we can get out."

Roberts frowned. It didn't take him long to find the relevant sections.

"Is this accurate?"

"As accurate as it can be, considering no one's ever built one of the damned things," Eric told him, "if you're asking about the swarm. If you're asking about the guess that this is what we're dealing with, I'd say we'll soon be finding out how accurate it is."

"You plan on going *into* that?" Roberts stressed, his voice dropping. "Sir, why?"

"Because I don't think we can reverse course without being spotted and overtaken, not if it is what we think it is," Eric answered. "And if it isn't, then we need to know what the hell it *is*."

"But going into the swarm, sir?"

"Run the numbers, Commander. Can we reverse course without being spotted?"

Roberts grimaced. "No, sir. We'd need full CM to pull away before we intersect the estimated boundaries of the swarm."

"And if we use CM, we may as well take out a billboard with our position and send it ahead of us."

"Yes, sir."

"Our speed compares favorably with the enemy, Commander, but we'd have to come to a zero-zero stop relative to the swarm before we could begin pulling away. They'd be on us before we could build delta-v."

Roberts clearly didn't like it, but couldn't argue. Physics weren't on their side at the moment, and that was putting things mildly. "So your plan is to penetrate while under stealth?"

Eric glanced around the room, dropping his own voice. "Calling it a plan is being generous, Commander."

Roberts snorted. "I'm glad you're willing to admit that, Captain. So that's it, then?"

"Unless you can give me a better alternative, I think so," Eric said, tapping in a couple of commands and changing the images on his station displays. "Look here, at these high-res heat readings."

Roberts examined the screen for a moment. "You mean the lines, I assume."

"Yeah." Eric nodded. "I think those are the cracks in the swarm. We can penetrate there, using nothing but thrusters as guidance. Nothing can detect thrusters from more than a couple kilometers away."

"That's because they're so underpowered they can barely shift the *Odyssey*'s bulk without CM."

"Well, we'd best plot our course as quickly as we can to give them a running start, no?" Eric suggested, his tone artificially light.

The commander grimaced, but nodded jerkily. "Aye, sir."

"Get to it, then, Commander," Eric said, "but try to keep it quiet for now."

"Yes, sir. I'll start on the course corrections—could be some tricky maneuvering."

Weston smiled and clapped Roberts on the shoulder. He appreciated the fact that Roberts didn't need to wonder at the reasons for that order, or question it. There were times to be open with the crew and times to keep your trap shut. This most certainly fell into the latter category, at least until they knew exactly what they were dealing with and had a little more to go on than just a guess.

▼

RANQUIL SYSTEM

The Cerekus

▲

▶ THE IMPOSING BULK of Syrenne Tianne's command, the *Cerekus*, slowed to a smooth stop, relative to the plummeting ball of ice and dirt that was currently tracking toward the inner system and Ranquil itself. Left unchecked, the comet would deliver a deathblow to the planet within a few more days, but despite that, no one on the ship was particularly concerned.

The small tractor vessel they had escorted out was more than enough to nudge the comet to a safe course, and in the process, they'd taken a few moments to see if there was anything of value in its composition to warrant harvesting the material for later use. It wasn't unknown to harvest the comet shield for various rare materials, or even for the water itself, since environmental protection was part of Ranquil common law.

In this case, things were a little more complicated, given that the entire comet body would have to be surveyed and analyzed to ensure that the Drasin hadn't done anything subtler with the material.

Syrenne looked out over the streaming ice and vapor, her eyes scanning the scene with little appreciation for the spectacular beauty. After months of combat, billions of dead souls, and uncountable losses in terms of property and actual *planets*...Well, she had little interest in the beauty of a comet at the moment.

Particularly not one being used as a weapon against her world and people.

"Tractor One reports ready to begin operations."

"Understood." Tianne nodded. "Inform them they have clearance to proceed."

"Clearance granted," the young ithan said as she turned back to her station.

Tianne glanced to the time check and nodded. They were on schedule to have the comet cleared from its trajectory within two marks. That would leave the *Cerekus* free to backtrack the trajectory and see if they could spot any sign of the instigators of this particular attempt on Ranquil.

Useless as it was, it was still an assault on the planet. That should not go unanswered for.

For the moment, however, all Tianne and her crew could do was wait for the small tractor craft to do its job. Only when that was done could the *Cerekus* go on the hunt.

▶▶▶

On the tractor ship, Ithan Marjir and the small-work crew under her command were focused on their jobs, and largely trying to ignore the immense hulk of the *Cerekus* that loomed above them. Probably, it was supposed to be comforting, but they saw it more as a reminder that this was anything but a normal mission, and things could well take a turn for the worse with little to no warning.

Marjir pointedly ignored the screen displaying the *Cerekus*'s position as she finished the last calculations needed to bring the comet into tow.

It wasn't as simple as locking the mass in with a beam and hauling it around, unfortunately. Even with the gravitational focus of the tractor's beams, it was entirely possible to both break the mass up and lose large chunks of it in the process. Since they wanted to ensure that none of it struck Ranquil, she had to keep the mass together—or at least within the scope of her beams.

To do that took time, care, and precise calculations. Unfortunately, she was quite aware that the *Cerekus* wanted to be elsewhere, and the big ship's captain was quite eager to see this job done in a hurry. With less time, she fully intended to make up for it with more of the other two, because that was the way she did her job.

They matched pace with the comet, taking careful scans to determine whether it had any fault lines that might cause it to break up. It did, of course, so then it became a matter of making certain that they could control the breakup and keep the pieces within the sphere of effect of their beams. Once all the math was complete, Marjir ordered that the overpowered tractor ship bring its beams to full strength and englobe the falling comet.

With the big chunk of dirt and ice solidly locked in their field, the crew of the tractor slowly began to reverse thrust. Changing the course of something as massive as a comet wasn't exactly a casual maneuver, not even with the power and technology the Priminae commanded, but it had become routine a long time previously. As they confirmed that the comet wasn't breaking apart, the crew of the tractor continued to add more and more thrust to the mass, and slowly, it began to have a perceptible effect.

It wouldn't take much, not this far out, to keep the comet from striking the planet, but as long as they were doing the work anyway, the orders were to deliver it to a stable orbit. This was for several reasons, including the fact that they didn't want it in any unpredictable orbit that might later threaten the planet once more, or another installation, but they also wanted to be able to recover the ice and minerals later, if needed.

As they pulled back, however, Marjir and her crew were surprised to hear a sudden echoing bang reverberate through the small tractor.

"What was that?" the ithan demanded, spinning around as she looked to all the stations around her.

"Unknown. We were struck by something."

"That's not possible," she said. "Our screens would have blocked anything like that."

"Agreed. However, we were struck by something," the crewman said again, poring over his instruments.

"It must have been internal," Marjir countered, adamant. "Check the drive status."

"Ithan, it was an external strike. I am certain."

Marjir got up and walked over to his station, leaning over the crewman. "Our screens show full integrity?"

"They do."

"Well, then nothing could have hit us. It has to be internal."

"Ithan, there were no harmonics within the ship. It was a shallow strike on our hull."

She grimaced. "Turn on the exterior imagers."

"Yes, Ithan."

The imagers covered the hull for situations when the screens were down and a strike was a possibility. It was important to be able to check the armor of the tractor by eye, just to make certain that they wouldn't be risking anything by engaging their beams. The first few images flickered by with nothing unexpected; the hull was intact and there were none of the subtle markers that might show dangerous degradation. Almost halfway through the cycle, however, Marjir's breath hissed as she spotted a decidedly foreign body on the side of her ship.

"What the hell is that?"

The crewman paled, punching in computer commands faster than she could follow. A few seconds later, the computer ID came back, and she found herself rapidly blanching to match her subordinate.

"Drasin," she whispered. "But…how?"

Her mind locked up for a few interminable seconds, probably the most vital seconds of her life, and by the time she managed to snap herself free again, it was too late.

"It's cutting through the hull!" the crewman yelped, stunned almost as completely as his commander.

Under normal circumstances, on most ships, the few bare seconds of disbelief would have been a minor fault at most. On the tiny tractor, however, by the time either of them managed to regain control of their faculties, a hiss of escaping air erupted into a whirlwind of destruction.

Normally, explosive decompression was very much slanted to the second word and not so much the first. However, in a small environment like the tug, which only had minimal gravity generators, the sudden venting of atmosphere turned the inside into a whirlwind of destruction. Marjir was torn from her feet and thrown toward the widening hole in the side of the ship.

She had just enough time to scream before a slash of the Drasin's cutter bisected her torso.

▶ ▶ ▶

Marjir's remains, already freezing in the cold of space, were blown clear of the ship as the Drasin pulled itself in and turned its focus on the remaining crew of the small tractor.

The remaining crew had time to scream, but against the howling wind and the suddenly overworked atmosphere generators, it did little good. The crewman Marjir had been arguing with lunged for his panel, slapping the emergency panel and literally throwing open every connection there, with no eye as to what he was doing. Alarms went off as the ship systems tried to compensate for the problems, but on a ship that small, there was only so much they could do.

The Drasin rampaged across the deck for a few more seconds, only stopping when everyone was dead. Primary goals accomplished, the soldier drone paused briefly as it analyzed its environs before turning to the controls and beginning the second phase of the plan.

▶ON BOARD THE *Cerekus*, Captain Tianne found herself more than a little bored with the current assignment. With the massive sensor arrays at her disposal, she was confident that there were no Drasin ships within the system, unless they were hiding behind the Primary or one of the gas giants. As neither of those were anywhere near their current position, it seemed terribly wasteful to have the *Cerekus* stationed there to monitor a single tractor.

She felt that way right up until the alarms went off, startling everyone on the ship from their complacency.

Tianne bolted for the command deck, men and women following suit as they headed for their own stations, the same question on their minds as was on their captain's.

What in the Breaker is going on?

She burst onto the command deck in time to see the tractor ship reeling on the screen, venting gasses from a gaping hole in its side.

"What happened?"

"Unknown. Tractor vessel initiated hull breach response, but there has been no contact with the crew."

Tianne glared at the screen, mostly to keep from glaring at the crewman who she knew was faultless but was still reporting horrid news.

"Scans. Full spectrum," she ordered. "Analyze the tractor ship."

"Yes, Captain."

The *Cerekus* threw every detection system it had at the smaller ship, responding with the results in just a few seconds.

"No"—the crewman swallowed—"no life, ma'am."

"Damn it. Download their logs. Find out what the hell happened."

"Yes, Captain."

She again found herself glaring at the screens, including the long and midrange scans. She almost wanted them to show a Drasin ship somewhere in the vicinity. At least that would have made sense! Instead, they were all clean and quiet, with no hint at the cause of the current emergency.

"Computer refuses access, Captain!"

"What?" Tianne's head snapped around, this time her glare clearly focused on the crewman handling the interface systems. "Do it again."

The crewman blanched, but did as ordered while the captain approached and watched over his shoulder. The results were the same, however, as the computer flashed a standard *Access Denied* message and went merrily about its way.

"Impossible." Tianne leaned over the crewman, punching in her own access code.

Access Denied.

Simply not possible. There wasn't a ship in the entire star system, now that the *Odyssey* had left, that would—or could—refuse her codes. Not even within the Forge itself.

"Tractor systems coming back online!" another crewman called out.

"What?" Tianne twisted, again finding herself scowling at the screens.

The small tractor ship was now stabilizing its position, and he could see the gravity well forming on the space-time readings. It was apparently going back to work.

Computer error caused by the accident? she wondered, frowning as she moved over to the life sciences station. *But no, the* Cerekus *still reads no living people on board. What* is *going on?*

"Captain..." The crewman at the sensor stations spoke, this time hesitantly.

"What is it?" Tianne couldn't quite keep the weary dread from her tone.

There had been too many impossible things, too fast. She could feel herself waiting for the next.

"The tractor is beginning to accelerate the comet."

Tianne shrugged. "So? That is what we're here for."

"It's plotting a trajectory *toward* Ranquil, Captain."

Ah, there it is. She didn't snap or snarl this time; she just straightened up and walked back over to check the readings for herself. They were indeed aiming the rock at Ranquil, which, to her mind, confirmed that the crew was indeed dead. *So, the Drasin are out here, after all. How did they evade detection?*

It was no matter, to be honest, except for the crew of the tractor and their families. Tianne returned to her command station as she mentally catalogued the orders she would need to give.

"Weapons stations to standby," she ordered as calmly as she could. "Target the tractor."

There was a hesitation, fleeting, but she noted it and wasn't surprised. Being ordered to fire on the demons from the dark was one thing, but Tianne wouldn't want anyone under her command who'd jump to fire on their own.

"Yes, Captain."

"Fire."

The powerful lasers of the immense vessel discharged silently into the black of space, intersecting with the tractor ship almost instantly. It flared brightly on their screens for a brief instant before its hull was overpowered and the small ship simply vanished through laser-induced state change.

"Target destroyed."

"Deep scan," she ordered. "I want the entire area probed, crewman. If there's anything hiding out there, find it."

"Yes, Captain."

Tianne sat back, waiting for the results, but didn't really expect to find anything. Whatever had hit the tractor ship had managed to slip through all their surveys the first time; she didn't think it would be found now.

They almost had to get an agent on board, but that's impossible... isn't it? Tianne didn't know how it could have been done, but somehow the attack had managed to redirect the tractor ship's efforts into hammering Ranquil even harder. That took someone on board changing the computer settings directly, so far as she knew.

The very idea that it might be done from a distance scared her to the core, so Tianne was practically praying that the Drasin had somehow gotten someone or something on the ship as the gaping hole in its hull would seem to indicate. The alternative was honestly too terrible to consider.

"All scans show clear, Captain."

Tianne nodded. "Ready the *Cerekus* to take over the comet-redirect assignment."

"Yes, Captain."

The *Cerekus* was quite capable of managing the mission, she reflected as the crew went about the business of the moment, but it was far from ideal for the job. The small tractor ship had gravitational-warping capabilities almost on par with the *Cerekus*, but with far better fine control. Tianne knew that the *Cerekus* would almost certainly break the comet into fragmentary pieces that they'd then have to clean up, either with gravity beams or lasers, but there was little else to do at the moment.

The major concern was how the Drasin managed to infiltrate the tractor in the first place, and whether or not they were still nearby.

Syrenne Tianne had a bad feeling that her current assignment was to be far from the straightforward matter it should have been.

BRIDGE, NACS ODYSSEY, UNCHARTED DYSON CONSTRUCT

▶ "HOLY MOTHER..." THE voice trailed off before it could finish the statement, leaving Eric glad that he didn't have to possibly reprimand one of his officers for profanity beyond acceptable limits. Particularly since he was physically stomping on the urge to spout a few choice epithets himself.

"*Odyssey* is penetrating the swarm, Captain."

Possibly the most useless status report I've ever received, Eric thought. There wasn't a man or woman on the bridge who wasn't fully aware of that, and likely no more than a handful on the entire ship. *And most of those are in medically induced comas.*

Every screen on the ship was dedicated to one part of their penetration of the cloud swarm or another, from straight visuals to radio interferometry scans. Granted, the visual-spectrum images were pretty dull, as such things went. Mostly just blackness that was occasionally punctuated by refracted or reflected light from farther into the swarm.

More interesting was the thermal images, now far clearer, as they were much closer and had been enhanced through constant exposure and computer adjustment. The slabs of material that made up the swarm were thousands of kilometers on a side, orbiting within a few thousand kilometers of one another in a loose, cracked shell around the star they were assuming was in the center of the structure. Within that, however, was another swarm that interlocked with the orbits of the outer shell. The general belief of the department heads was that this was done to minimize energy loss from solar collectors, a belief founded in the fact that there weren't many reasons any of them could imagine for building such a massive structure save for energy collection.

What bothered Eric most, however, was what they could be using all that power for.

The Drasin and Priminae both have energy-generation capacity so far beyond Earth's that it's almost staggering. What could they possibly need to chain up an entire star system to power?

As they glided, silent and blacked out, through the outer swarm of the Dyson Cloud, it became clear that the inner swarm was radiating noticeably more heat. The structure of the mega construct was amazingly complex, interlocking orbits dancing with a precision that Eric couldn't hope to understand, even with computer aid, and he was far from a slouch on the mathematics side of things. This was a construct that used complex formulas to balance a tangled set of interactions that made the three-body problem look like grade school arithmetic.

"The inner swarm is counter-rotating, relative to the outer, sir," Waters spoke up softly, his voice holding a touch of awed reverence for what he was seeing.

"I see it, Ensign." Eric nodded. "That's why we caught occasional flashes of sunlight from the outside."

"Yes, sir."

"Aim us for one of the cracks in the inner shell," Eric said. "Thrusters only."

"Aye, Captain. Thrusters only."

While the complexities of building a mega construct such as he was seeing were beyond him, Eric was quite capable of computing orbital trajectories in his head without using his fingers and toes to remember the numbers. On thrusters alone, they could just redirect their course enough to catch one of the rotating gaps, if they began firing as quickly as possible.

If they missed that window, they'd have to light off their CM systems to make the needed maneuvers, and that was one thing that Eric had no intention of doing. CM systems affected local space-time to reduce the relative mass of any object within their reach and, as such, would be visible to any sophisticated gravity sensors for a significant range.

Even old-school accelerometers would pick up a CM field powering up, and Eric was pretty damned sure that whatever the systems in use by this structure were...They were considerably more advanced than accelerometers.

He wouldn't have been surprised in the least if the *Odyssey* were already being tracked by gravity sensors, in fact. While on ballistic trajectories, however, the chances that such a track would be brought to anyone's attention were slim to none. Space was far from empty, and despite how large the *Odyssey* was in human terms, its mass was essentially insignificant in gravity terms. As long as they kept course corrections to an absolute minimum, and didn't show a collision trajectory, Eric was reasonably confident that the *Odyssey* wouldn't trip any automated red flags.

On EM sensors, the *Odyssey* was blacked out, completely invisible against the background spectrum of the area. Even active scans would be lost in the scanner absorbing settings of the camplates.

So they were running silent and deep again, only this time Eric knew that they were sailing right through an enemy harbor. Which, actually, made a fool of the concept of "deep." They were about as shallow as it was possible to be, given the imposing slabs of construct orbiting all around them.

And all we have to do is cruise right through and try to avoid hitting any mines before we can break clear, Eric thought darkly as he flipped through the results of the multitude of scans the *Odyssey* was in the process of making.

Even without their active sensors and sails, the *Odyssey* was still an exploration and science ship at its heart. She had more instrumentation per square foot than anything else that had ever been built by man, all predicated on her originally assigned mission.

If we survive this, the raw data alone will be worth the cost of every space program on Earth since the Moon Race.

The ship shuddered lightly as the thrusters puffed, altering their course just slightly. Eric hoped that the changes wouldn't be enough to flag them for a closer look on any gravity sensors, but he suspected that wouldn't happen.

This has to be an incredibly complex system to track. Every one of those plates will affect orbital mechanics within the cloud. Minor ballistics changes must be commonplace and hopefully hard enough to predict that they won't even notice.

That was the theory, anyway.

Whether the practice would bear out the theory was something that they were about to prove, but Eric was confident enough that he didn't even have to wipe away the sweat from his face.

Well, it's either the confidence or the air-conditioning.

▼

PRIMINAE VESSEL CEREKUS

Ranquil System

▲

▶TIANNE CHECKED THE calculations for the maneuver against her notes. "Status?"

"*Cerekus* stands ready to begin, Captain."

"Excellent. Engage the gravity beams."

"Yes, Captain."

A low hum filled the air in the big ship, caused by the increased power draw from the *Cerekus*'s big twin cores. Tianne watched as the computer showed the gravity warping of space-time envelop the comet, firming up slowly as they tried to grab it rather than crush it or accidentally yank it into a collision course with the *Cerekus*.

"It is breaking up, Captain."

"Just keep the pieces within the gravity depression."

"Yes, Captain."

The work was slow, painstakingly so, and the forces involved were immense, but slowly, the big ship managed to get its grip on the comet. It was taking twice as long as the tractor would have been able to manage it in, but they were getting it done, and that would have to be enough.

So long as that mass of ice and rock does not impact Ranquil, I will consider this a success.

Pacing the comet and gathering it in their gravity beam was only the first step, however; the second began when they applied power to the ship's drives and began to pull the rock back from the path it was on. Once that happened, then the stress of the move would surely shatter the remaining chunks of the comet into shards that could potentially escape their field and continue on course.

So long as they got the biggest pieces, that would be fine, though she was well aware that the odds of putting the crumbled chunks into any sort of stable mining orbit would now be all but impossible. The *Cerekus* didn't have the deft touch of the tractor, so the best they could hope for now would probably be scattering the pieces of ice and rock across the orbit of one of the system's gas giants.

A planet the size of Deus would make short work sweeping the pieces from the skies over Ranquil, which was a solid second prize in Tianne's opinion.

"Apply reverse power," she ordered, "gently."

"Yes, Captain."

The *Cerekus* rumbled low, a feeling felt deep down in the bones by the crew as the big ship began to slowly reverse power and pull at the comet body.

▼

RANQUIL SYSTEM

▲

▶ MOST COMPLEX SPECIES in the galaxy developed in environments humans would find familiar, no matter how superficially different it might have been from Earth or similar environs. Atmosphere, gravity, day and night. Even the largest of life-bearing planets, or the smallest, had enough lines of similarity for a person to extrapolate and begin to understand the nature involved.

The Drasin were born of the stars themselves, lived their lives in the black of space, and were bred for one purpose alone.

To a human, there was no comprehending either the perspective that gave them or the lengths to which they would go to achieve their purpose. Lengths such as launching themselves through the cold black of space, scattered in the tail of a comet, knowing that, at best, only a few would even strike the target they were aimed at. Of those few, most would not survive, but that did not concern them.

They were Drasin. One was all it often took.

The large warship of the red band was looming in the distance, growing fast as it slowed relative to their fall. The first little ship was so small that dozens had fallen past it, still tumbling along on their trajectory to the ultimate target, but this new ship was large. It had a gravity of its own; they could see the warp and twist of space as they closed on it.

Silicate claws and mandibles flexed, the moment of action bearing down on them, and like a hard rain on a tin roof, the Drasin fell to the *Cerekus*.

▶▶▶

A faint echo of sound—something exploding, almost—was the first hint of trouble to reach the bridge of the *Cerekus*. Tianne looked around, trying to place the sound, but before she could ask anything, an alarm sounded from the damage control station.

"Captain, we're venting atmosphere. Sector Twelve, Deck Nine."

She didn't bother ordering them to control the problem; they'd already be doing that. "Bring up the external viewers of the hull in that area."

"Yes, Captain."

The screens flickered, showing a gaping hole in the armor of the *Cerekus* with atmosphere venting wildly through it.

"We must have been struck by something, Captain."

"That's impossi...ble." Tianne barely finished the word as she considered what she was about to say. There was a feeling deep inside her now that she couldn't identify, and wished that she would never have to. In theory, nothing could penetrate the debris reppelling fields used to keep the ship from being holed through by small bits of flotsam and matter as they barreled through the black of the voice. In theory, however, there were no Drasin in the vicinity, and she knew that wasn't true.

Tianne took manual control of the screens, flicking through the camera views quickly enough that they flashed by in a blur until she stabbed her finger down onto a control and stopped the screen on an image that caused her blood to run cold.

"It—It's cutting through the hull."

That feeling in Tianne's gut turned ice-cold, and she reflexively gripped the console in front of her to hide the emotion.

On the screen, everyone could see one of the Drasin drones slicing through the composite hull of the *Cerekus*, pulling the slagged material apart without even waiting for it to cool.

Tianne ignored the talking that had erupted, instead palming open the ship's communications channel. "All crewmen, this is Captain Tianne. We are being boarded. Draw weapons from the armories, and prepare to combat the Drasin boarders."

She then turned back to the crew surrounding her. "Seal this deck. Nothing comes in. We have a job to do."

They stared for a moment, still clearly shocked.

"Now!" she snapped, jolting them back into action.

A moment later, the blast doors protecting the command deck slammed shut, leaving the deck entirely sealed from the rest of the ship. Tianne nodded, taking up her station again as she checked on the progress of the *Cerekus*'s current mission, the comet they were towing. It was breaking up, but most of the material was remaining in their control. They had to pull it clear of any threat to Ranquil, regardless of the current threat on board.

"Bring the drives to eighth power," she ordered, "slowly."

"Yes, Captain."

"Venting atmosphere, Sector Forty-Three, Deck Twelve!"

The *Cerekus* rumbled a little more, its powerful drives fighting the mass of the large comet fragment as they powered up a few more degrees. Tianne felt the shudder through the deck and into her bones, leaving her uncertain as to how much was caused by the drives and how much by the knowledge that her ship was infested with an enemy that she and her people were still coming to grips with how to combat.

"Security reports contact with Drasin, Sector Ten, Deck Nine!"

"I want every free crewman scanning space around us. Use visuals, if you must! Find where they're coming from!"

In that moment, she realized that she was deep into something she'd not trained for. There were no procedures for this, no steps to follow.

Fear gripped her, but she tried valiantly to push it aside, because there was work to be done.

CENTRAL COMMAND, MONS SYSTEMA, RANQUIL

▶ "EMERGENCY PULSE FROM the *Cerekus*, Admiral."

Adm. Rael Tanner turned from where he was working and approached the young ithan who'd spoken. "What's the nature of the emergency?"

"Drasin, Admiral."

Tanner scowled, moving back to his command station. "Details, Ithan. To my station."

"Yes, Admiral."

They were waiting for him by the time he arrived, and Tanner found himself not quite believing the flood of data that was still pouring in from the *Cerekus*. That they'd been boarded was shocking enough, but that it had happened the way that it had...Well, it made no sense.

How did they approach the ship undetected? He couldn't imagine how anything could get within the detection radius of one of those monster ships; they were packed with technology beyond what even his own command center used.

Unfortunately, Captain Tianne hadn't included that piece of information in the emergency pulse, so Tanner had to assume that it was unknown to her as well. He looked to the real-time screens following the *Cerekus*'s position, noting that it was even now moving to pull the comet back from its apocalyptic trajectory.

Tanner approved of Tianne's dedication to duty, but couldn't shake his concerns, either. Even a few of the Drasin drones were a serious threat as they seemed to have veritable immunity to standard-issue Priminae weapons.

The thought struck a chord with him, and Tanner headed over to where Nero Jehan was overseeing his section of things.

"A word, if you would?" he asked quietly.

Nero looked up and grunted, but nodded curtly. He stepped out of the controllers' pit and joined Tanner on the upper level of the room.

"What is it, Rael?"

"The new weapons, the ones issued to your forces," Tanner asked softly, "were any sent to the *Cerekus*?"

Nero shook his head. "No. Priority was assigned to ground forces."

Tanner winced. "I was afraid of that."

Nero frowned, perplexed. "Why do you ask?"

"The *Cerekus* has reported Drasin boarders."

The big outer colonies man stared, stunned. "That is not good, Rael."

"As our friends from the *Odyssey* would say, Nero, tell me something I do not already know."

▼

CEREKUS

▲

▶ARMED WITH MILOSEC lasers, the squad of crewmen, led by a coranth named Cirrus, cautiously advanced through the corridors of the large warship, both looking for and hoping not to see their quarry. They knew that their weapons were very nearly worthless against the Drasin, those reports had been made clear after the previous encounter in system, but what else could they do?

Scraping sounds were heard from ahead of them, just around a corridor, so they slowed and inched forward. Cirrus signaled a stop before he moved ahead to cautiously peer around the bulkhead. He blanched when he saw the mottled red-and-brown coloring of the large insect-like Drasin drone, scratching and burning through a bulkhead just ahead.

Cirrus backed off, grabbing the shoulder of an ithan he knew worked in Engineering.

"Miran, what's through the bulkheads just up here?" he asked.

She paused, considering it for a moment before speaking. "Control circuits."

"For what?"

"Atmosphere generators."

Cirrus looked distinctly ill by this point. "They're going to cut through them!"

"Don't worry," she said, "we'll just reroute control through other circuits. The *Cerekus* has multiple systems to handle every important function."

Cirrus relaxed marginally, but the nagging concern was still eating at him. "That thing out there looks terribly interested in those circuits."

"It's an animal," another crewman said in a panicked voice, "likely doesn't even know what's behind the bulkhead."

"And if it does?" Cirrus hissed in challenge.

The crewman backed down silently, so Cirrus looked back to Miran. "Any thoughts?"

She shook her head. "It could be part of a systematic attempt at sabotage, but I would think they would need more Drasin—many more, if they wanted to be sure of it being effective."

Cirrus grimaced. "That isn't out of the question, from the last word I heard. OK, Ithan, you're with me."

"Me?" Miran squeaked. "For what?"

"Come on, quietly," he hissed, "I want you to see if you can tell what it's doing."

"Shouldn't we just…you know, stop it?" she asked, more than a little fearfully.

"With these?" he asked dryly, holding up his milosec laser. "I've heard of how well they work against drones. If we must, we will, but I'm hoping for another way."

"And you want me to give it to you?" she asked, disbelieving.

"Do you see anyone else standing by my side?"

"But…Coranth, I don't know…"

"Listen to me, Ithan," he told her, deadly serious, "I've studied the conflict recordings from the Systema battle. If we run around the corner with lasers flaring, the most we'll likely do is annoy it. Do you understand me?"

She swallowed. "Yes, Coranth."

"So, quietly," he said, "look around the corner and try and determine what it's doing. Think about everything there, and tell me if there's anything we can use to improve the odds in our favor."

"Yes, Coranth."

He nodded, stepping aside for her to edge closer to the corner. When she leaned a little too far and almost fell into the open, he caught her by her uniform and held her tightly, but otherwise left her hanging there where she could watch the Drasin in action while he tactfully ignored the near-convulsing shivers that were racking her body.

Seconds passed, turning into minutes. Then she gasped softly and grabbed his arm to pull herself back.

"We have to stop them!" she hissed.

"What? I thought you said that we have alternate circuits if they cut these?"

"We do, but that...that..." She grimaced. "The Drasin soldier is not cutting the circuits. It's interfacing with them."

His breath hissed through his teeth. "You think it can break our security?"

"Impossible. It's a beast," the crewman from earlier growled.

"Beasts don't interface with computer systems," Ithan Miran said. "This is something beyond my experience, Coranth. If it can interface, we have to assume that it at least believes it can break our security."

Cirrus cringed, but couldn't help but agree. "Right. I'll call the bridge and let them know. Request more men and weapons as well."

He opened a commlink to the command center. He realized his hands were shaking and hoped the others hadn't noticed.

▶▶▶

Capt. Syrenne Tianne scowled at her command displays, willing them to change, while knowing damned well they wouldn't. The latest information explained why the tractor had accelerated toward Ranquil, to be sure, but it left her with a bad situation that was growing worse.

Like most of those who were charged with planning the defense of the colonies, she had studied the Battle of Systema and knew that the weapons she had on board were not likely to do anything against the invaders. The new gravity impeller design hadn't been issued to ships for various reasons, most notably that they were still testing the lethally powerful systems, and they weren't considered safe for use within the hulls of even large warships.

She called up the file on the impeller, just the same, checking the device specifications carefully before nodding in satisfaction and opening the comm.

"Engineering, here," the voice on the other side spoke up instantly.

"I'm sending fabrication data to your account. I want these items manufactured and distributed to the security teams as quickly as possible."

"Yes, Captain."

Tianne closed the channel, considering the situation. The shipboard fabrication systems were fast, but the kind of schedule they were on would strain even those. It would take an hour or more to get the first units out of the fabs, and the need to construct carbon crystalline munitions would slow things down further.

In the meantime, she needed a way to buy time while the *Cerekus* continued its mission.

A flick of her finger opened another comm channel.

"Security officers here," came the response.

"Send a demolitions team to Deck Nine, Sector Ten. Have them meet with Coranth Cirrus and place themselves under his command."

"Yes, Captain."

She closed the channel, knowing that, before this was over, the *Cerekus* was going to need yet another period in the Forge. There was something so very wrong with ordering the use of explosives within your own vessel, however, and it felt like a cold weight settling into the pit of her stomach.

I hope we don't wind up blowing the ship out from under our feet just to spite the Drasin.

BRIDGE, NACS ODYSSEY, UNCHARTED DYSON CONSTRUCT

▲

▶ "WE'RE PENETRATING THE second swarm."

The words were entirely unneeded in reality, but Eric knew they had to be said for the record. Like most of the crew, however, he was too busy staring in shocked awe at their screens to listen to the lieutenant's statement. Still, "penetrating the second swarm" wasn't something he'd ever expected to hear on the bridge.

As the *Odyssey* approached the second orbital swarm within the Dyson Cloud, the ship was able to detect more and more light through the cracks that existed between the plates that made up the loose shells. Once they penetrated the inner swarm, it was like moving from night to day. The brightness beyond made Eric squirm in his seat. The cold comfort the black of space provided was stripped away, and he felt exposed to the eyes of the universe.

Aside from directly aft, every single camera and scope on the *Odyssey* was returning a brilliant image of the inside of the Dyson construct. The closest areas had already been scoped carefully, but for the most part, all they could see was what appeared to be solar collectors of some type or another. Endless kilometers of solar collectors, as far as their best scopes could see.

God. What the hell are they doing with all the power?

"We've cleared the orbital plane of the swarm."

Eric admired Michelle's calm tone. The young woman was keeping the updates coming with a by-the-book assuredness that was probably helping others maintain calm almost as much as the sheer awe of what they were seeing rendered them frozen in place.

"Are we detecting anything within the inner orbits?" he asked softly.

"Compiling scope data now, sir," she replied. "There are some shadows on the initial feeds that look suspicious, but I'll need to layer images to get better resolution."

He nodded, understanding the difficulties she was working under and was willing to wait. Without the active scanners, they were limited to the passive scopes, which actually wasn't a deficit in signal *quality* due to the nature of the devices, but the scopes were slower as they were limited by the size that could be mounted on a ship like the *Odyssey*. Scanners were active systems, able to gather detailed data very quickly with relatively small receivers on the ship. The scopes, however, were very large and bulky systems that worked entirely passively. They offered the highest-resolution imagery possible, but took a while to build that data with repeated exposures over time.

With the *Odyssey* running practically every computer dedicated to the scopes, they were building very detailed imagery of the interior of the swarm, but there was no defeating physics in this aspect of the universe. Time was required to do the job, and there simply wasn't anything he could do about it but wait.

"Lieutenant Daniels, double-check ETA to transit," he spoke softly, his eyes still glued to the external feeds.

Daniels had to shake himself from his own staring, checking his calculations based on the now confirmed data they had concerning the location of the system's star. "Three days, Captain."

Three days.

Three days while they were a sitting duck in the center of what had to be the single-largest population Eric had ever heard of. *Potentially, at least.*

It was true. They didn't have any confirmed sighting of the Drasin to this point, but there was no way something on this scale got built without an absolutely staggering number of hands, or mandibles, on hand to do the work. Eric checked the numbers himself, now that they had enough data points to get a sense of the scale.

Outer swarm is one-point-three astronomical units in diameter, inner swarm is "only" point-seven AU across. This is insanity. How could anyone build something like this in less than a hundred years?

The scale of the construction was almost too large for him to wrap his head around, would *be* beyond his ability to do so if Eric wasn't aware of the cost of constructing the *Odyssey*. There were nations on Earth who couldn't have afforded simply shipping the materials into orbit to build a ship like the *Odyssey*, not even if they dedicated their entire GDP to the project. The scale of the construct they were now *flying* the *Odyssey through* was so far beyond that Eric wondered if the NAC could afford to even consider planning something like this.

It has to be automated. Self-assembled, maybe.

That still left him with the question of what they were using all the power for. The Drasin had struck him as a strange, bizarre species ever since the end of his last mission. They reminded him more of a virus, a biological weapon, than a real, thinking species. He'd opined to the admiral that no thinking species would select for destruction the way the Drasin had, reproducing until they destroyed the very planet they existed on, and he still believed that.

The question here was, what kind of bioweapon would build something so complex and awe-inspiring as this Dyson Cloud they were currently sailing *through?*

There just seemed to be a discrepancy between what he had seen in the destroyed Priminae systems and what he was seeing here.

We're going to need to check on the magnitude of the stars they assaulted, see if they're building more of these constructs.

He hadn't wanted to risk sending any other manned missions into those systems; the threat of garnering more attention from the Drasin had previously overruled any information they might have won from the expedition. Now, however, he wasn't so certain.

If they can, and are, building things like this so close to Earth... We need to learn why, and what the hell they use them for.

He stood up. "Command, you have the bridge."

"Aye, sir. I have the bridge," Roberts replied.

Eric nodded and headed off the bridge, deciding to do a little deeper digging and consulting with a few of the *Odyssey*'s experts. There had to be some advantage to having a ship filled with some of the best minds the Confederacy could scrounge up, after all.

CEREKUS, RANQUIL SYSTEM

▶ THE IMMENSE WARSHIP barely shuddered as the explosion tore through one of its decks, the mass of the big ship absorbing the force. But for those who had set off the explosives—Coranth Cirrus and the rest of his team—it felt as if the whole universe had come crashing down on them. The corridors were filled with smoke and debris, chunks of the deck and walls covering them as they slowly got back to their feet.

"Central!" Cirrus swore, glaring at the crewman who had been sent up with the demolition materials. "Were you trying to end us?"

Crewman Vasque glared back as he cleaned himself off. "That was the charge I was told to use. The Drasin are difficult to kill."

Cirrus glowered, but there really wasn't a lot more to say. "I just hope we didn't blow the hell out of something we needed."

"No worries, Coranth," Miran said, spitting ceramic shards from her mouth. "I told you, we have many alternates to use in the place of those controls."

Cirrus sighed, hefting his milosec laser as he began to move forward. The corner they'd been peeking around was now a jagged cropping of razor-sharp ceramic edges, but he didn't see the Drasin soldier drone in the hallway, at least.

"It looks clear," he said as he stepped into the open, finding puddles of slagged mineral splattering the floor and walls. "One drone down."

"How many more left, do you suppose?" Vasque asked tensely.

"At least three," Miran responded, attracting their attention. She shrugged. "That is how many holes we're currently venting atmosphere from."

"Well, on that so very comforting note…" Cirrus shook his head as he contacted the command deck. "Clear here. One drone eliminated. Orders?"

"We are tracking another three decks down from you, twelve sectors aft," an ithan responded. "We are redirecting an engineering team to meet you with the newly issued infantry arms."

Cirrus glanced at his laser, which he had yet to bother discharging, and snorted. "I hope they're better than standard issue."

"We don't know—you'll be the first to use them in combat."

Cirrus bit back his first, impulsive curse of a response, which involved Central and a vacuum cleaner, and said, "On our way now."

There were days that Cirrus wanted to just lie down and cry, and this, it seemed, was rapidly becoming one of them.

▶▶▶

On the command deck, Capt. Syrenne Tianne turned a grim eye to the damage reports from Deck 9. The solution to the problem rooting out the Drasin had a strong possibility of being almost as bad as the Drasin themselves.

High explosives being voluntarily detonated within the corridors of my ship is not a good precedent.

That said, the tactic appeared to be working as far as removing the Drasin. The fact that it also tore out several large sections of her ship was a sad side effect, but one that she would simply have to endure. If they survived this mission, however, Tianne would be insisting on a timelier issuing of weapons to her crews.

Better to have them and not use them, she was learning, than to need them and not have them.

"Captain," a crewman spoke up, drawing his attention, "I believe that you should see this."

"What is it, Neval?" Tianne asked as she walked over.

The crewman nodded to his display. "Look."

She frowned, her eyes focusing on the display. "What am I looking for, crewman?"

"Watch for it, ma'am. You'll know it when you see it."

Tianne bit back an annoyed response, watching the screen as she waited for something to happen. She was about out of patience when her eye caught what the crewman was talking about—an object adrift in space that was only showing very dimly on their visual spectrum scanners.

"Is that what I believe it to be?"

"Yes, Captain. I have spotted three like that so far," the crewman said, nodding to the Drasin drone on the display. "At first, I believed it to be a drone knocked loose during boarding maneuvers; however, they are all on the same trajectory."

"And that is?"

"Ballistic intersection with Ranquil."

Tianne paled as she heard that, her mind racking itself to dredge up everything she'd ever learned about the Drasin. There was little information on whether they could withstand uncontrolled entry into a planet's atmosphere. Certainly, they hadn't done so during their last assault, but then, they hadn't needed to, either.

If even one of those reaches the surface intact and unnoticed, it could spawn billions. She stepped back from the station, gesturing to the crewman to continue with his duties. Tianne quickly stepped back over to her own station, taking a seat as she deftly opened a comm channel.

COMMAND CENTER, MONS SYSTEMA, RANQUIL

▶RAEL TANNER FELT like he'd been struck with a hammer as he sat there, staring at the comet track as it filled the main screen. Just moments earlier, it had been a sign of optimism, a sign that they were beating back yet another attempt by the Drasin to assault Ranquil.

Now, however, thanks to Captain Tianne's warning, he saw the previous trajectory of the comet as a sign of a completely new threat. A threat he couldn't see coming, even if he now knew it was there.

They simply did not have enough optical scanners to map even that one section of the sky in the time left available to them, and it had been proven by the *Cerekus* that no other method would work to spot the incoming drones. He was much like Captain Tianne in that he didn't know if the drones could survive entry into the atmosphere, but even if one in a hundred did, it was too much.

Rael forced the shock aside, slowly issuing orders that would bring the orbital defenses to task. There was no clean way to track them before they entered the atmosphere, but once they did, then there would be an ignition trail they could see. The orbital forts weren't intended to fire inward, but they could be retasked for the duty. The only question in his mind was whether they would be able to track and target drones moving that fast through the atmosphere. They were designed to handle ships that, while they were moving considerably faster, were much, *much* farther away.

The lag time between calculating a safe vector to fire and when the Drasin were low enough in the atmosphere that they ceased burning would be close. Possibly too close for even their best fire-control systems to handle, especially if they wanted to avoid vaporizing large chunks of the planet in the process.

He walked over to where Nero was snapping orders, preparing his ground troops presumably.

"Nero, a word, if I may?"

The beleaguered soldier looked up wearily, then joined Rael on the upper section. "Yes, Rael?"

"Can you task anything to eliminate ballistic items entering the atmosphere?"

Nero sighed. "You know the situation, Rael. Orbital defense is your section, not mine. I have been calling up all reserves and preparing them to intercept anything that strikes the ground, but to answer your question, no, I have no forces that can shoot down anything above forty thousand segments. So why are you really here, Rael?"

The admiral sighed. "This also falls under your authority, Nero, but have you considered asking the Terrans to become involved?"

Nero grimaced, though he had half expected as much. "I've sent along a warning of possible planetary assault, so they are readying their forces, yes."

"Please ask them if I might request the aide of their combat craft. I feel we may need the additional support before this is done."

Nero said nothing, but he nodded reluctantly.

▼

RANQUIL MILITIA TRAINING BASE

▲

▶REED LOOKED OVER the gathered men seriously for a moment, getting a measure of them before he spoke. They were standing around a display table under an open tent that had been set up to one side of the flight field, the Archangels looking between the intel being presented and the full-bird colonel doing the presenting. The situation on the screens was far from comforting, so they all listened closely when Colonel Reed spoke up.

"While we're scrambling ready response teams to handle anything that hits the ground, the Planetary Defense command has asked that we provide additional air support," Reed said, nodding to the pilots.

"What's the game plan, then, sir?" Steph asked.

"Missile defense," Reed answered easily. "With multiple confirmed ballistic threats inbound, we need to track and eliminate them in the upper atmosphere."

"We know where they're coming from, sir," Cardsharp pointed out. "Why don't we sortie the squad and pick them off well short of the planet?"

"Because we haven't been able to confirm that those tracks are the only inbound threats," Reed responded. "If I'd been planning this mission, I wouldn't have sent any along with the comet in the first place. That would have been a distraction play, while additional forces were dropped in from other tracks."

The pilots grimaced at that thought, but nodded in comprehension.

"Glad you weren't planning this one, then, sir," Cardsharp said with feeling.

Reed smiled thinly but didn't respond. "Planetary Defense has gone to full alert, so they're blanketing the system with every detection net they've got, but these are small and relatively unpowered objects. They're the devil itself to see, and there's one hell of a lot of space out there for them to hide in."

"With full CM, we've got maybe eight hours' flight time in atmo," Steph spoke up. "What kind of mission window are we looking at, here?"

"Unknown and open-ended," Reed grimaced as he answered.

"We don't have enough pilots to keep an effective CAP on this planet, even if the window were small," Steph said, having expected an answer like that. "Engagement window against a single ballistic object entering atmo is going to be thirty seconds, maybe? There's no way we can go from scramble to intercept in time, not even if we live in our cockpits."

Steph and the remaining pilots of the Archangel fleet glanced at each other seriously for a moment, but Reed could see that was all it took. They'd willingly be living in their cockpits for the foreseeable future; it wasn't like they hadn't done it before.

"Can you arrange in-flight fueling?"

Reed was stumped for a moment, then just shrugged. "I'll have Ithan Chans kick that up the line. We may be able to work something out."

"We know that their orbiters have the precision needed," Steph pushed, "and what they lack in experience, my team will make up. Get some orbiters into the air with H and O2 to spare, and we'll be able to pull longer flights."

"I'll see what we can do," Reed repeated his position. "Until I get word from the Priminae, I can't promise anything."

"Yes, sir."

"What we will have is near total scanner saturation of space within two or three light-seconds of the planet," Reed went on. "Planetary Defense is hoping that they'll be able to beat the detection threshold of the drones with that kind of power behind them and at least give us a few minutes' warning on inbound tracks. They'll also be engaging from orbit, so hopefully they'll be cutting down on anything that actually hits the atmosphere."

"What about actual rocks and such? You know, legitimate shooting stars?" Cardsharp asked.

"Compared to Earth, space is pretty clean around here," Reed answered. "They have a lot less space junk than we do, but what little there is should be easily detected by Planetary Defense and ruled out as a threat. I've advised them to slag anything they detect that doesn't respond to an IFF challenge, but I don't know if they'll take it that seriously or not."

"If my whole bloody planet were at risk, I think I'd be taking it pretty damned seriously." Cardsharp grunted.

"No argument there, but that's not our call," Reed countered. "I'm going to be assigning men to support the local militia, who'll be standing ready to scramble to any impact sites on a moment's notice. You may be called upon for close air support, so consider the mission needs carefully and talk it over with the ground crews."

"Yes, sir," Steph responded, already thinking about the load out he'd need on his birds. "UAVs?"

"Carnivores are already in the air," Reed answered. "They're armed and ready to engage ground targets, but they're not designed to take out ballistic inbounds."

The pilots all nodded. Traditionally, ballistic defenses were ground based. The Archangels were known to be reasonably effective at taking out ICBMs, if needed, but carnivore drones were primarily designed as downlooking support platforms. They only carried a limited number of munitions, and those were rarely of the air-to-air variety. They'd probably need them badly if any of the Drasin survived to kiss dirt, anyway.

"Our best ETA for the first ballistic drones is that they'll hit upper atmo in twelve hours," Reed said grimly. "Starting six hours from now, I want every man and woman sleeping at the controls of their equipment, just like my team and Brinks's soldiers will be sleeping in their armor. Am I understood?"

"Sir!" The pilots snapped to attention as one, the word coming out forcefully and without a shred of uncertainty.

"Outstanding. You have six hours before you're chained to your planes, pilots," Reed informed them. "Get some chow, read a book, or get whatever pre-mission fumbling you lot do done. We'll shortly be at war for the fate of this world, and while that may be old hat to some of you, it feels a mite important to me, so I don't want to screw this up. Dismissed."

The pilots nodded and broke up, most heading for the crews servicing their planes while Steph remained behind.

"Any idea how many we're really dealing with here?" he asked softly.

Reed shook his head. "Unfortunately, no."

"Well, damn."

"Yeah, that about covers it, Commander."

"We don't have enough manpower to properly cover this world, Colonel," Steph said again. "You know that, right?"

"I am aware, yes."

"Have you informed the Primmies?"

Reed scowled at Steph. "Don't use that word. Call them Priminae or nothing at all. You get into that habit and it'll spread faster."

"Right, sorry." Steph shrugged, uncaring. "You did tell them, though, right?"

"Yes, I did. They're going to put some of their own craft into the air, jury-rigged with versions of their 'gravity impeller' cannons."

"Oh, fuck me." Steph grimaced, rubbing his face. "Amateur flyers with weapons of mass destruction."

"I'm not sure that I'd qualify them quite that high, but essentially, yes," Reed said dryly.

"I saw what those things did in practice," Steph countered. "And those were handheld!"

"The vehicle-mounted versions won't be significantly more powerful, apparently," Reed said. "Size and weight are big concerns, so they optimized the handheld ones pretty well."

Steph snorted. "Optimized, huh? Not sure that's what I'd call it."

"Just stay out of their crosshairs, OK? We've already lost too many of you." Reed sighed tiredly. It had been a long week and wasn't shaping up to be any better in the foreseeable future. He could ill afford to lose anyone, let alone some of the most irreplaceable men and women in the NAC armed forces. He needed them badly, but couldn't afford to spend them. It was not a good situation to be in, and that was stating things mildly to the extreme.

"Understood, sir." Steph nodded in agreement.

For him, Reed supposed that it was simpler; he'd already lost men and women to this alien sector of space. He didn't begrudge the Priminae the sacrifice his people had been called on to make, but that didn't mean he felt good about it, either. He and his were combat flyers, the sort of people who had a taste of something they could only get while doing things normal people just didn't understand. Reed suspected that they considered the risk of dying out here to be acceptable if it let them do what they were trained to do.

All the fun, none of the cleanup, he thought grimly, smiling at his own dark thoughts. At least out there they weren't tearing the living hell out of Earth.

There were, however, only so many of them left. The Archangels were artifacts of a war no one wanted to remember at the moment back home. Since the discovery of the Priminae and the Drasin, there was some talk of spooling up recruiting again, but it was just talk so far. Until that happened, the men and women currently standing here on the alien world whose air he was breathing…Well, they were the last of the kind.

And they are being picked off one at a time out here.

In the end, attrition was one enemy that not even the famed Archangel fleet could beat.

Steph nodded to the colonel one more time, stepping back from the table. "I'm going to check on my plane and the others."

"You do that, Commander," Reed said, glancing up as Steph started to walk away. "Commander?"

"Sir?" Steph glanced back.

"Good luck."

"Sir." He nodded, then turned his back to the table and headed for where his plane was parked downfield.

NACS ODYSSEY, UNCHARTED DYSON CONSTRUCT

▶ERIC WESTON STOOD along one wall of what had been their primary cartography lab until just recently, watching the experts performing analysis. As the central hub for basically all stellar mapping for the ship, the large room was the nexus for every data trunk line to the shipboard scanners and scopes. Literally every piece of information scanned by the *Odyssey* ran through this one room to be processed and cataloged.

Since the ship's entry into the Dyson construct, however, the room had been subject to a hostile takeover by Engineering. Generally speaking, engineering officers didn't have a lot of interest in most of the data brought in through the sensors—not the raw data, at least. Certainly, none of them were either ignorant of astronomy, nor were they truly disinterested, but by and large, they were more than willing to wait for the finished product of the astronomers' work.

Not today, apparently.

Arriving in Engineering earlier had been like walking into a ghost town. Oh, the ship was still fully staffed, all on-duty people were where they had to be, but during times like this, Eric was used to seeing as much as twice the normal shift working the stations below decks. He'd had to actually hunt someone down this time to learn where everyone had gone.

He'd been shocked to arrive at the cartography lab only to find that the room was literally standing room only, and not a lot of that. Still, he'd shuffled into a place where he could see what the big draw was and found that most of Engineering was poring over the raw data from the scopes showing the interior of the swarm.

Not a real surprise—most of the ship was doing the same, to be frank.

The difference here was that all the data on the central display holograph was from real-time computer-generated feeds that showed the layering as the scopes continued to take more and more exposures to improve the resolution of the overall imagery.

"It can't be purely ballistic," one woman was arguing. "The plates must be tractored together somehow to keep them from eventually drifting out of their orbit."

"Of course it's not purely ballistic," a man countered sarcastically. "I'm merely saying that any species with this level of accomplishment is surely beyond any of our magnetic tractor technology. Each slab must have artificial gravity, and so they likely have some form of gravity drive as well."

"That could explain the swarm's precision," another conceded, "but that does bring up an interesting hypothesis."

"Oh?"

"Yes, if they have gravity warp drives on each plate...Does that mean that the swarms are capable of being moved from one star to another?" he asked. "Certainly, with the technology we now suspect they have, they could easily create an

Alcubierre drive, which wouldn't be constrained by any notion of size and mass we'd be limited by."

That shut the room up in a hurry, and Eric didn't blame any of them for their shock. The very concept of a construct this huge being…*mobile*…Well, it shook him deep down just as badly. The *Odyssey* used a conventional chemical rocket drive system, something completely useless for interstellar travel and very nearly worthless for even interplanetary travel, if not for the invention of the CM technology.

Eric was knowledgeable enough to recognize the term Alcubierre drive, however, and knew that they were talking about a completely different beast. The Alcubierre drive, otherwise known as a warp drive, was based on the manipulation of gravity to warp space around a ship. In effect, it created a never-ending "hill" for the ship to glide down, constantly picking up speed until the drive was stopped or reversed. With such a system, it was conceivable to move plates like those that made up the Dyson swarm, much to his growing horror.

"Let's not buy trouble before we have to," the first woman, a lieutenant commander from Engineering named Naomi Sears, said with one hand up in a "stop" gesture. "We haven't detected nearly enough matter inside, or outside, the swarm to indicate that the swarm is *not* native to this system. They must have built it on-site, using the planets and material already here."

"Unless that's the reason for the swarm," a younger lieutenant spoke up, frowning. "What if it's a mobile scrap yard, so to speak? Move into a system, then use the system's own star to power factories that convert local materials into warships, or whatever."

"Unlikely." Sears shook her head. "If that were the case, I believe that we would have seen a great many more of the Drasin cruisers already."

These people are going to give me nightmares, Eric realized as he listened in. *As if I don't have enough reasons to lose sleep already!*

"They must be using the power for something, though," the lieutenant said, shaking his head.

"It could be as simple as life support for the entire species," Sears offered halfheartedly. "That was the original idea behind Dyson's concepts. You could create huge habitats for massive populations using any of the constructs. The swarm is the most efficient overall design when you have to balance power versus practicality."

"If they used local materials to build this thing, then they're likely here for the long haul," Master Chief Grear spoke up, quieting the room.

The engineering noncom was one of the most experienced men on the ship, and when he spoke, everyone listened. Even officers.

"I think that what we have to determine is whether these plates are locally produced," Grear said carefully, his eyes not leaving the display. "Because if they're not, then we have a real problem."

"These things built something that should be impossible to build"—the lieutenant rolled his eyes—"and you think it's only a real problem if they can move it?"

Grear just turned to pin the young man with a stare that could curdle milk. "Son, if this is a habitat, then it's a sitting target out here now that we know where it is. I'll grant you, we don't have any weapons that could do squat to it now, but I also know that it's always easier to break things than it is to make them. We could figure out some nastiness to do here, if we needed to. If they can fly those plates around the galaxy, however, we have a real problem because that implies that they were able to move in here, then clean the entire place out of all raw materials in under a hundred years. Any species that can do that, and that *does* do that, is a menace to all life everywhere."

And that is the real issue here, Eric thought as he continued to watch the debate unfold. The Drasin were rapidly showing themselves to be a threat, not just in terms of making war on another species, not even just in terms of engaging in the act of genocide, but they were actually beyond all that. Beyond every measure he could mentally call up to judge them against.

This is more than poisoning the well; it's annihilating everything a living species might ever again use to gain a foothold. Even without the mobility of an Alcubierre drive, that's what they did here. They moved in, less than a century ago, and now no species will ever develop in this system again. It's been permanently sterilized.

Forget everything else, technical prowess be damned, that was what counted. On its own, Eric could see the pro arguments for creating a construction like the swarm beyond the *Odyssey*'s hull. It was extreme, certainly, but had a lot of benefits going for it. However, when combined with the speed in which it had been built and the Drasin's preferred war fighting strategies to date, it was an ominous thing to be considering.

Capt. Eric Weston turned and left the cartography lab without a word. He'd heard what he needed to hear for the moment and had too much to consider as it stood. To Weston, it felt a little like he was drowning. He had to break it down, turn it into pieces he could handle, otherwise he knew that he would sink into the situation and be swallowed up by it.

▼

TEMPORARY AIR FIELD, RANQUIL

▲

▶ "ARCHANGEL ONE, THIS is Control."

"Go for Archangel One, Control," Stephanos said as he opened his eyes and blinked away the sleep.

"We have confirmation of inbound ballistic targets. ETA to upper atmosphere...eight minutes. Archangels are go to scramble."

"Roger that. Archangels are scrambling. Hold one," he said, his right hand reaching out to swipe the bank of switches to the on position. As the twin reactors began to whine in his fighter, Steph swapped over to the squadron channel. "We are go for scramble. I say again, we are go for scramble. Light the fires, and get off your tires, people. We have incoming."

Before most of the squad could do more than groan or moan out a reply—at least half of them had been asleep like he was—Steph swapped back over to the command channel. "Command, Archangel One."

"Go for Command, Archangel One."

"Send the plot to our computer net. We'll be in the air in two minutes."

"Roger that. Wilco."

The channel went dead as Steph completed the preflight and glanced out to see his crew chief waving at him. Steph flashed the man a thumbs-up sigh, but got crossed arms in return. He nodded and settled in to wait while the crew cleared the field. It didn't take long. Another few seconds later and the man waved at him again, then flashed him the thumbs-up. Steph returned the signal as he tapped the throttle up with the palm of his left hand.

The fight whined some more as the power multiplied, shaking slightly until the two counter-rotating turbines got back into sync, and finally settled down as everything flashed green in his HUD.

"Control, Archangel One," he said finally.

"Go for Control, Archangel One."

"This is flight double-A-dash-zero-zero-one declaring liftoff."

"You are cleared for liftoff, Flight Double-A-Zero-Zero-One."

Steph pushed the CM throttle full open and felt the fighter lift up on its piston springs as the mass of the whole craft suddenly dropped. He could feel the vibrations pick up suddenly as the weight of gravity no longer helped damp them down, his fighter literally shivering as it tensed to launch itself back into the fight.

"Flight double-A-dash-zero-zero-one, lifting off," he said by rote as he pushed the throttle wide open, then adjusted the vertical vectored thrust downward.

The fighter blasted the field below it with exhaust gases, and Steph was pushed down into his ACESXII seat by the acceleration. As he cleared the field, he redirected the thrust to the back as he lifted the nose and blasted for the sky as the other fighters called for and received clearance behind him. One by one, they lifted into the air behind him, slowly twisting in place to find their angle, then following in his tracks as they each in turn kicked in their full thrust.

"Command, Archangel One."

"Go Command, Archangel One."

"Archangels clear. Proceeding to first waypoint, engagement area alpha."

"Roger, Archangel One. Good hunting."

Steph closed the channel and adjusted his heading as his fighter passed hypersonic, still accelerating, and headed for low orbit. His targeting array was running on full power, but the sky seemed unusually clear ahead of him.

That explains why, he thought as a Priminae laser burned across his HUD, its corona hot enough to show up on his computer overlay as it intersected the upper atmosphere and vaporized something just before it started to burn on entry. *They must be firing on anything that moves. Here's hoping they have their IFF systems worked out.*

"I've got one on screen, Steph," Cardsharp announced as they reached their assigned AO.

"I see it," Steph replied. "You and Burner break from the group. Take it out, but don't forget to confirm the kill."

"Roger that."

The two Archangels accelerated away from the main group's orbit, dropping into pursuit of a rapidly descending fireball a few hundred kilometers away. Burner took the lead, locking up the target with his forward guns while on final approach.

"Target locked," he reported calmly, thumb already finding the firing stud of his gimbal-mounted cannon. "Guns. Guns. Guns."

The cannon roared in the upper atmosphere, depleted uranium rounds launching fast enough to draw a line of fire between shooter and target, and the slugs slammed into the falling object with enough force to blow it completely apart.

Cardsharp slid her fighter ahead, catching up with the debris quickly, and paced the shards as they continued to burn through their descent.

"Target destroyed," she said confidently a few seconds later. "Confirmed kill, Burner."

"Look sharp, Angels," Stephanos's voice interrupted her. "We've got more incoming."

The skies above the Archangels were suddenly alight with shooting stars, their computers scrambling to keep count as the trails of fire raced for the surface of the planet.

"Oh, hell," Cardsharp hissed as her computer count raced through the double digits, heading for triple in a hurry. "This is gonna suck!"

"Quit the bellyaching and get to work," Stephanos ordered. "Target assignments are on your computers now. Don't let them hit the surface!"

The Archangels banked hard and split apart as they began to race across the skies, literally blowing shooting stars out of the skies.

TERRAN COMMAND AND CONTROL

▶ COLONEL REED GLARED at the display in front of him, wishing he knew a little bit more about how the damned thing worked. The Priminae had provided them with state-of-the-art command and control systems as part of the training facilities they'd built and had been helpful enough to patch them into the planet's command network just before the current crisis.

What they hadn't had time to do was provide full training in how to use any of the systems, so Reed and his staff were moving back and forth between their own Terran systems and the Priminae's, basically providing a human bridge to try to keep everyone working together. Without Ithan Chans, he was certain they'd have been lost, but the young woman had managed to be part teacher, part bridge herself, and seemed to be everywhere at once when they were pressed.

It was working for the moment, with only the Archangels being controlled by the patchwork system, but Reed had his doubts if things would stay running so smoothly once the ground teams got in on the action.

And it was pretty clear that the ground teams *would* be getting in on the action—and sooner than later, at that.

The incoming contacts were multiplying quickly on their screens, most only becoming visible when they hit the upper atmosphere and began to burn through entry. Orbital defenses were burning through what few they could, either those that got unlucky enough to be picked up on visual sweeps while still well above the atmosphere or those that were in shallow enough entry trajectories to allow the orbiting lasers to track and target them without frying large swathes of the planet below.

Given the rather extreme nature of the Priminae's weapons, he understood their reluctance to aim the blasted things in any way that might intersect with the planet. Even an ocean strike would probably vaporize an unbelievable amount of water and have significant effects on planetary ecology. If one of those beams happened to intersect a city…Well, there was no point in doing the enemy's work for them.

Still, it meant that the orbital defenses wouldn't be able to intercept enough of the incoming ballistic drones. With the Archangels in play, a few more would be taken out before they hit the ground, and the Priminae armed shuttles would account for still more. In the end, though, Reed was banking on the probability that they wouldn't get them all.

That was why he'd activated all his men and got them dispatched out to work with the Priminae ground combat teams. Well, his own men, at least. They were experienced in dealing with locals who probably thought they knew more than they actually did about soldiering. The *Odyssey*'s ground combat detachment was a force he was keeping in reserve, partially as a trump card in case things got out of hand, but more because he was afraid they'd make a bigger mess than was necessary if he put them in the field with untrained local militia.

There are few things worse in the universe than soldiers who think they're better trained than the guy beside them, Reed thought, *except when the soldier in question is right.*

"We have several possible impact sites plotted, Colonel."

Reed glanced at the Priminae display table, eyeing the map carefully. "You'll be sending out teams?"

"Yes, Colonel." The young ithan nodded. "If we can eliminate any threats before they begin to multiply, things will be much safer."

"Can't argue with you there. Make sure that some of the advisors are with the teams dispatched, if you can?" he asked. "It'll give us a chance to learn what we need to work on in the future."

"I believe that can be arranged, Colonel."

Reed nodded before turning his attention back to the display and trying to work out which flashing light represented which life currently sitting in harm's way.

▼

RANQUIL, UNDERGROUND

▲

▶ FOR A HUMAN, the events transpiring around the planet of Ranquil were such as to inspire everything from awe to terror. To the being known to the populace of the planet as "Central," the awe was almost entirely missing, but deep inside, even Central would admit to the terror. The Drasin were unlike any other complex life-form in its experience—on that one area Central agreed with Captain Weston.

This is what humans feel when they're exposed to a potentially lethal disease.

Laser fire was crossing the skies, invisible to unaugmented living eyes, but Central saw the beams clearly by the bleed of their coronas. Each flare of heat was the satisfying sign of a potential infection vector being annihilated by those immensely powerful beams, but it was also a sign to Central of how very helpless its position really was.

The ancient intelligence had no weapons and exerted little influence on the world around it in a physical way. For nearly uncountable years, it had been content to watch and enjoy the slow development of the people the world of Ranquil played host to.

Now those people, and itself, were under threat of destruction, and Central found itself not enjoying the sensation of helplessness.

Within its sphere, Central could well claim to be nigh omniscient. Omnipotence, however, was far from within its grasp.

So when the first impacts began to rock across the surface of the planet, Central could only watch and wait to see if the people of Ranquil were up to the task of saving their lives, their planet, and itself.

▼

RANQUIL'S SURFACE, EXERCISES ZONE

▲

▸ MASTER CHIEF NATHANIEL Wilson had been pegged for a lot of off-the-wall duties during his tours as a SEAL, but he couldn't think of any that quite rang the bell for "weird" as much as sitting in an alien shuttle craft, surrounded by trigger-happy yokels, while about to land in a crash zone that could possibly contain an active alien monster that was looking to eat him.

Mom told me there would be days like this, but I thought she meant if I took drugs.

The compact shuttle was surprisingly roomy inside, leaving him and the twenty local militia he was riding shotgun with just short of rattling about like the lone pea in a pod. He'd feel a lot better if they hadn't shown him the melty walls trick before takeoff; the idea of a computer controlling the solidity of the bench his backside was firmly ensconced on gave him shivers. He knew it was more than a little hypocritical, given that computers were pretty much the only thing keeping a Terran shuttle flying, and he didn't mind those, but frankly, at the moment, he couldn't give a damn.

Just don't let this freaky wall melt until I'm within a survivable distance of the ground.

"The impact site is just ahead!"

The pilot's message was translated through his computer almost fast enough for real time, but honestly, in Wilson's opinion, the slight lapse between spoken word and translation made him feel like he was living one of those classic Japanese movies he grew up watching whenever he got drunk with his buddies.

Knowing computers, the translation's probably about as good as those old dubs, too, the master chief thought wryly as he checked his assault weapon once more.

He'd armed up with one of the local's gravity impellers, though he was packing his own service pistol as a backup. He'd selected the local weapon for a lot of reasons, including the fact that it was always good to be able to swap ammo with the guy next to you, but really, it was more about getting to know the weapon in field conditions. They'd run them through all the tests they could back at the training facility, and pound for pound, Wilson was certain that it was the most lethal piece of munitions delivery mechanism he'd ever held in his hands.

Especially when the gravity impeller is on.

That said, there were things you just didn't learn until you used a weapon in a fight, and this was as good a time as any. He just hoped that there weren't any of the "obvious in hindsight" design flaws that tended to congregate around weapons that were rushed into the field waiting to bite him on the ass.

The back of the shuttle melted away while he was thinking, and Wilson almost jumped up in surprise while barely keeping from cursing.

Damn! A little warning, first?

The militia troops with him seemed to expect it, however, and were immediately piling out of the shuttle in a reasonably ordered movement. Wilson followed them, thumbing the gravity impeller to active mode as he did. The heavy gun instantly lightened in his hands as he jumped down from the shuttle, stepping aside and lifting the muzzle skyward.

"Well...This is a mess," he said, accompanying the comment with a low whistle.

Smoke was slowly filtering up from the ground ahead of them, likely the impact crater, but the entire area was flattened like a bomb had gone off. In fairness, Wilson supposed that one did. He wasn't sure why the brass on both sides were so hepped up over this. No matter how tough those things were, he didn't think that they could survive this kind of impact.

If they could, I can't see how our guns would do much to them.

Still, aliens and all that, so maybe they had some kind of insulation technology. Wasn't his department, so the Navy master chief just shrugged and followed the squad in as they started to make their way through the rubble toward the smoke that marked ground zero. For now, his primary duty was just to keep a watch on the new kids and make sure they lived to learn how to play the game in the big leagues.

That, and report back to the colonel on what lessons still needed teaching, of course.

Walking toward the center of ground zero went against pretty much every instinct in his body, but Wilson followed the men as they did just that. There was no cover to hide behind as they moved, but on the flip side, there was no cover for anyone or anything *else* to hide behind, either. The blast of the impact had flattened the local flora, including some goodly sized trees, leaving nothing but open ground to cross as they entered ground zero.

The first thing Wilson thought as they reached the lip of the crater was that it was smaller than he'd expected.

He looked down over the edge and frowned. "I'm no expert on kinetic artillery, but this looks more like a deep penetrator strike than a meteor."

"Indeed," Coranth Seran Mir said, looking down into the pit from beside him. "We had tracked the object at higher velocity than expected. It would appear this was intentional."

"You think it accelerated after it hit the atmosphere?"

"No. However, it did not decelerate so much as we expected," she countered. "Likely, it adopted a streamlined aspect in midfall."

Ouch. Wilson really didn't want to think about a living species that not only was willing to subject itself to an unaided orbital drop but actually attempted to make itself hit the ground harder in the process. "We've got to climb down there, don't we?"

"Unfortunately, yes," she replied, waving some of the others forward. "We need the descent tools."

Two of the others came forward with what looked vaguely like rappelling gear to Wilson. He didn't question it too much and just set to strapping himself in while watching the others do the same.

"Do I have to worry about making sure this is cinched tight enough or anything?" he asked, not seeing the others do much more than slip the harnesses on and snap them shut.

"No, they won't fall off unless you try to remove them."
Seran shrugged. "Please don't be silly enough to do that until
we're finished with the descent, yes?"

"No worries there, lady," Wilson muttered, hooking himself up. "These things better work is all I'm saying."

"They work fine, Mister Chief."

"That's master chief."

"Someone has an inflated impression of themselves."

I'm either starting to like these people, or I'm going to shoot them,
Wilson thought dryly as the team got prepped for the descent.

The first two stepped into place, fiddling with their harnesses before they shouldered their weapons just how Reed
and his beanies had taught 'em, then stepped right over the
edge and started walking down the near-vertical wall like the
proverbial spider.

"Nice tech," he said, glancing over at Seran. "Anything I
need to know about setting it before I take that first step?"

She glanced at him, checking his harness, and twisted a
dial before slapping him firmly on the chest where the rig
crossed. "You're ready now, Mister Chief."

He shot her a glare, which was promptly ignored, and
shouldered his own weapon as he took a tentative step over
the side. There was a brief moment of disorientation, almost
entirely from the shift in visual perspective, and then he was
standing on the side of the wall and feeling altogether too
relaxed about it.

Feels just like walking normally, he thought as he followed
the lead element down, Seran stepping into place beside him.
"This is completely weird."

"What is?"

"Walking down the side of a wall."

"It's simply an extension of gravity-control technology, Mister Chief."

"Look, lady," he growled, "if you can't call me Master Chief, then just Chief will be fine. Hell, call me Nate or Wilson, or any damn thing but Mister Chief."

"I suppose I can do one of those. I do have a question, however," Seran said quietly as they marched down the wall.

"What's that?"

"What *is* a master chief, anyway?" she asked, sounding genuinely confused.

"Between you, me, and the monster we're hunting?" He shrugged. "A master chief is the dumbest man in whatever squad he's part of."

"Really?"

"Lady," Wilson said patiently, "we're walking down the side of a crater impact hole, hunting alien monsters with prototype weapons."

"Yes, but we are all doing that, no?"

"We're all doing that, yes," he admitted, "but I'm the only one here stupid enough to do it without knowing anything at all about the gear keeping me from falling to my death."

"This is not what you call courage?"

"The difference between courage and stupidity is measured only by success and survival," he answered. "So ask me again when we're back topside."

"You people from *Odyssey* are very strange," she said, shaking her head.

Wilson shrugged. "We can discuss why we're strange later. I think we're coming up on our objective."

Ahead of them, the smoke was beginning to thicken, clouding their vision and likely filling the air with noxious, if not outright poisonous, fumes. Luckily, they were all in environmental gear of one type or another, letting them ignore the majority of those effects. The glow and heat shimmer, however, spoke of more serious problems ahead, and those had attracted his attention solidly.

The shaft they were in was only a few dozen meters across and nearly vertical on all sides. They'd descended probably thirty meters, with the heat increasing as they went. Wilson wasn't certain they were going to be able to get much closer, but that wasn't the biggest problem he was seeing.

"Am I the only one, or are you guys seeing things moving down there?"

PRIMINAE SYSTEM COMMAND

▶ "MORE REPORTS COMING in from the ground teams, Commander."

Nero nodded, calling up the reports for himself. Most of the teams had already reported in from the crash sites, all with pretty much the same basic information. Extremely deep impact craters, compared to their diameter, which indicated that the enemy had actually impacted harder than terminal velocity would indicate. Best guess so far was that they hadn't been drone soldiers, exactly, but some sort of delivery vehicle designed to penetrate deep into the ground when they struck.

If that were the case, mission successful for the Drasin.

Phase one of the mission, at least, Nero thought darkly, knowing that he already had men and women moving into the danger zones to attempt to put an end to the enemy mission before phase two got underway.

"We have eight teams investigating impact sites already, and more are likely to get through the orbital and high atmospheric defenses," the ithan reminded him. "We're simply not prepared to deal with this sort of assault."

"I would have thought that the defense net would protect well against ballistic objects," Nero grumbled.

"It does. It just doesn't deal well with stealthed objects, sir."

"We'll need to speak with someone about improving that," Nero muttered. "Nature may not attempt to hide its attempts to kill us, but our enemies do."

The ithan didn't respond, probably wisely given his boss's current mood.

Nero took another look at the screens, then turned around and headed up to the top command level, where Rael was trying to coordinate the entire mess they were currently mired in. Mostly, that just amounted to watching helplessly while their teams went about their jobs, but Nero supposed it was the thought that mattered.

As long as the lack of action doesn't get us all killed, that is.

"Rael," he spoke when the admiral paused for a moment.

"What is it, Nero?"

"Operations on the ground are proceeding as expected," he reported. "The objects we believed to be soldier drones apparently...were something else."

Rael Tanner looked at him sharply. "What?"

"Uncertain. Drones would not have struck the surface as hard and fast as they did, however," Nero said. "They appeared to have been deep-penetration devices, similar to the Terrans' weapons of that nature."

"Not possible." Rael shook his head. "We have confirmed imagery of them before entry—they match the profile of a soldier drone."

"Then, Rael, the solider drones have more capabilities than we thought."

"This is not something I need to hear right now. I'm dealing with a lot already, Nero." As if it were Nero's fault.

"On the contrary, Admiral," Nero said with a twist of his lips, "this is *precisely* the news you need to be dealing with right now. It just isn't the news you *wanted* to be dealing with."

Rael Tanner groaned, but Nero knew his old friend agreed. Just trying to ignore what was happening wouldn't help anyone.

"Fine," Tanner said. "I'll see what I can learn and put some people on it. Go see to your ground teams."

"Yes, Admiral." As if he weren't already doing just that. Sometimes Nero thought Tanner underestimated him.

▼

TRAINING BASE, SITUATION ROOM

▲

▶COLONEL REED GLARED at the telemetry from the suits he had in the field, not liking what he was seeing one whit. The master chief was at the bottom of a viper pit, staring at the vipers, and the best Reed could get off the telemetry was some obscure motion readings. Thermal was off the charts, video was obscured by mist and heat shimmer, and most of the rest were clearly being jammed. Whether that was intentional or accidental was just another one of the things he needed to know and didn't.

The communications channel was one of the few systems in the suits' telemetry suite that wasn't being at least somewhat disrupted by the heat, rock, radiation, and other general elements in play at the impact site. Not really a surprise, given that they were digital systems that were designed to retransmit any missing information thousands of times per second if need be until a perfect signal and handshake response.

He queued in a message, sending it to the chief's system but not directly to the chief, because he didn't want to distract the man.

"Chief, when you get a moment, check your environment and try to get some drones down there. Suit telemetry is broken up. We're not getting anything useful here."

The message would wait in the armor's queue until Wilson had a chance to access it, with only a small icon on the HUD to let him know it was there. Reed wanted better intel, but he'd prefer getting his best commo man back in one piece, so he wasn't in a hurry to distract him.

A flick gesture pushed the chief's file to one side as Reed called up the Archangels' telemetry files in its place.

The special air superiority team was tearing across the skies over Ranquil, moving faster than most of Reed's systems could track. In teams of two, composed of a lead element and a wingman, the Archangels were tearing the ever-living hell out of anything that moved through the upper atmosphere. Unfortunately, there weren't enough of them, and while the Ranquil shuttles were trying, the local lasers were proving ineffective against the Drasin infiltrators.

I suppose that's what I should call them, Reed mused as he gestured the Archangel data aside. *They're certainly not your average grunt soldiers, whatever else they may be.*

He was growing more and more concerned about the ineffectiveness of his allies' weaponry, however. He'd read the reports, but they'd been abstract until now, and honestly, Reed had questioned Eric Weston's conclusions.

Now, however, he wasn't so certain. The fact that they appeared perfectly adapted to their chosen mission might just be an example of very good intel and planning, but he'd never seen intel so good in his military career. Someone, something, *always* screwed up.

This time, however, they seemed perfectly adapted for a conflict with the Priminae people. Laser resistant, specifically along the frequencies used by the Priminae, both in space and in the dirt. In a power-for-power slugging match it seemed almost even with the new warships the Priminae had fielded, but even then, the Drasin had counter moves to almost everything they could put into play.

Normally, if he were honest, Reed would just shrug it off as bad luck and an example of how big space really was. Statistically, it was incredibly unlikely to find another civilization in space that was at a comparable technical evolution to your own. It was just a fact in his mind that, on average, even twenty years of technical development more on one side or the other was likely to be a game changer, and in space, twenty *thousand* years was far, *far* more likely.

So, by that reasoning, it was not only possible but highly likely to find that one civilization had an overwhelming advantage over another.

Which made sense, right up until you threw the *Odyssey* into the mix.

How it was that the *Odyssey*, which came from a much lesser technical power base, could inflict the level of damage it had against the Drasin...Well, that was a really interesting and probably vitally important question. There was really only one answer that Reed could come up with, and that was the Drasin were tailor-made—literally—to engage the Priminae, and when faced with technology and weapons that, while less advanced, came from a very different branch of the research tree...Well, they showed the weakness inherent in specializing.

Which meant that there were now three species—three civilizations was more accurate, he supposed—in the same sphere of space, and all three had comparable technical development, even if it weren't entirely parallel. Statistically, this wasn't merely unlikely. It was like being struck by a three-mile-wide meteor the day you hit the Powerball jackpot and walking away from the impact.

Patently impossible was the point he was trying to make.

And yet, somehow, in the universe, they'd managed to beat the odds. In fact, if Captain Weston's supposition was correct, the odds were even worse. Four civilizations, not three. Terrans, Priminae, Drasin…and who or whatever was holding their leash.

The math says that it's so unlikely as to be impossible; the reality says that it has happened and the math can take a flying leap. Either way, Reed knew that something was wrong with the picture he was seeing. Pure chance couldn't explain the situation, but that didn't discount chance entirely.

Reed's specialty was training soldiers, and he was good at his job, so this was a little beyond his ken, but he was far from a stupid man. One of the reasons he'd been picked for the assignment he was currently on was because he had a PhD in emergent cultures and degrees in a whole slew of related fields. He was also a modestly successful science fiction author who had written several well-received, if only marginally well-read, novels on first contact and cultural contamination.

These were all situations he'd actually thought about in the past, in detail. For three to four civilizations to be at the same point in development, at the same time, in a sector of space this small, relatively speaking, Reed was certain that an outside force, or forces, were being exerted.

That, of course, brought up the question by whom and for what reason?

Of course, the philosophy and scientific inquiry would simply have to wait. He had a war running.

The screen shifted, showing cleaner telemetry from Chief Wilson's suit.

"Major Brinks, I want your men ready to lift off in ten minutes. The master chief just turned up something interesting," he said.

RANQUIL, FIRST IMPACT SITE

▶ THE ROAR OF sonic booms shook the walls of the crater shaft around them as Wilson and the Priminae militia opened fire.

"Where the hell did they all come from?" he snarled, his gravity impeller roaring as it spat diamond slugs downrange as he and the others backed slowly up the near-vertical shaft.

The walls below them *crawled*.

Not the large abominations encountered before, but smaller, faster, insectoid versions that had come charging up out of the heat and damned near overwhelmed them before they knew what was going on.

The sheer concussion of the reflexive barrage of rounds unleashed by the team had beaten them back, but only temporarily. Chief Wilson had been glad that Seran, the woman in charge of the squad, had been smart enough to call a retreat before he had to suggest it himself.

Bravery was one thing, but being swarmed by a thousand creepy crawlies in a hot, dark cave was another entirely. They fell back, however, a little messier than he would have preferred, and kept firing as they did.

The sonic shock waves rattled his teeth, even through the armor, which was scary enough to Wilson since he knew that the armor was rated to insulate against overpressure waves that could send his brains drooling out his ears. The diamond slugs were turning the crater below them into fine dust and pulverized shards of rock.

He was just about thinking that he'd be getting out of it all in one piece when an urgent comm from the colonel broke into his concentration.

"Chief, I'm going to need to ask you to get me one of those things alive and intact."

"You want me to *what?*" Wilson spat out, half in shock and the other half pure incredulous disbelief.

"You heard me, Chief."

"Yes, I heard you, and now I'm wondering if you got any of *my* messages over the past couple minutes!" Wilson snarled back. "How the hell am I supposed to get a piece of these things through all of this?"

"Not a piece, Chief. I want the whole thing," Colonel Reed replied evenly, "intact."

Wilson cursed, though not until he toggled the acknowledgment icon on his HUD and killed the direct comm.

"Intact, he says," the Navy SEAL growled. "I ought to show him *intact.*"

Nevertheless, he had his orders, and he checked his fire as he took in the situation. "Ithan."

"Yes, Wilson?" she asked, still firing as they retreated.

"I need you to hold your fire."

"Pardon me?" She stopped shooting so she could stare at him, clearly shocked.

"The colonel wants one of those things *intact,*" Wilson said, twisting the word.

"He is insane, yes?"

"He's an officer, so, yes." Wilson shrugged in the exaggerated way someone in powered armor did. "But orders are orders."

She looked at him for a moment and then said quite possibly the sanest thing she could have, in his opinion. "He is your officer, you get one."

Wilson grunted, not trusting himself to say anything remotely polite in response. He just nodded once and slung his weapon, letting the impeller hang off the back of his armor as he tried to judge his next action.

It wasn't as simple as it might be, given that he was currently standing on a ninety-degree incline, feet planted into the side of the shaft by some magical gravity device issued by the Prims. He'd paid attention when it was issued, but that was a long way from being comfortable using it in a combat environment.

Finally, however, he nodded. "All right, give me an opening."

"It is your death day." She shrugged, signaling to get the attention of the rest. "Draw back, but cease firing. Our friend here has a request from his superior."

"What request?"

"The colonel wants one of the Drasin, intact."

"Does his superior not like him, for some reason?"

Seran just shrugged. "I would guess not, but that is not for us to say."

Wilson rolled his eyes under his helm, though he knew they couldn't see it. "Har har, can we can the comedy until after I've grabbed one of those suckers for the boss?"

"Please"—Seran motioned with one arm—"as you will."

As soon as he'd started down the impact crater/shaft, Wilson had mentally reoriented the world so that he didn't feel at all like he was walking down the side of a wall. Instead, he felt like he was currently standing in a narrow tapering tunnel with the exit to his back. Mentally, he was upright, standing on the floor, with a partially fused wall and ceiling of rock around him. Physically, he knew that he was only being held from falling by the gravity manipulation of the harness he was wearing. His problem at that moment was that he really needed to get his mental and physical selves into the same place, otherwise there was just no way he was going to be able to do what had to be done without getting himself killed.

What the hell, he thought fatalistically as he steeled himself. *You only live once.*

Wilson sprinted forward, jumping clear of an outcropping and flipping in midair to plant his feet on the other side. The gravity manipulation in his belt had been set to orient his personal gravity toward whichever direction his feet were pointed, so he stuck the landing and pushed forward.

This is no way to familiarize myself with new gear, he mentally growled at himself, fighting off a wave of disorientation as his eyes told him that he was now standing on the ceiling, his inner ear told him he was on the floor, and his head told him he was walking down a wall.

With a mission to accomplish, he ignored all three and just told himself that he was standing where he damned well should be standing and anything else could wait until there were no longer any things trying to kill him. The swarm had been thinned by the concussion and fragmentation unleashed by the gravity impellers, but there were still more than enough to give him chills as they regrouped and charged back up the shaft in his face. Gravity was working for him at the moment, however, and any that got too *playful* were kicked loose and set to fall back to the bottom of the crater while he lunged to try to catch one of them without getting his armored limbs chewed on too badly.

Little bastards are fast, Wilson griped to himself, latching onto the carapace of one finally while kicking another half dozen off his lower limbs. The one in his hand was snapping and clicking at the air, helpless in his grip.

Helpless until a flash of light exploded in his face and blew him back off his feet.

He was falling, he could feel that in the pit of his stomach, blind, and still holding onto the little bastard that had shot him in the face with a death grip in his left hand. He flailed about, swinging his feet around, and caught the edge again with a jarring hit that threw him forward into a roll that shook him loose from the side yet again.

He knew where the sides were now, however, and tucked into the roll to bring his feet back into contact with the side another time. This time he kept his balance and managed to come to a running stop, knowing that he was facing down despite the fact that he couldn't see a damned thing through his helm.

"Little bastard fried my visor!" he called. "I can't even get it to go transparent. Huh, didn't even know that was possible."

"Chief!" he heard Seran scream from above him. "They are coming for you!"

"I can't see! Where?"

A roar of noise and a shock wave rattled his teeth inside his armor, leading Wilson to start sweating.

"Are you *shooting* at me?"

"Turn, Chief. Turn now and run this way!"

He shuffled around, until he thought he was pointing the opposite direction. "This way?"

"Almost, turn more!"

Another shuffle, then he heard her yell for him to stop so he did. Another roar and more rattling of his teeth was all it took to convince him to start running. When amateurs were shooting what he would normally consider field artillery in his general direction, Wilson wanted to be nowhere near where he was standing.

"Good!" she called in his direction. "Keep running! Run!"

"I'm running, lady! I just can't *see* a damned thing!" he snapped, his legs pumping while his imagination filled in the sounds of the swarm chasing on his heels.

He could hear and feel the shock waves of the others firing around him, but tried very hard to ignore the fact that there were people he didn't entirely trust unloading weapons powerful enough to crack his armor like an egg in his immediate vicinity. Tactile feedback through his armor told him that the little bastard he'd grabbed was still wriggling, so he tightened his grip and just kept running blind.

"No! Wilson! Stop!"

He heard the scream, but couldn't react in time, as his legs kept on pumping even though they suddenly had nothing left to pump against. Instinctively, he tucked the little monster in his hand into his chest like a football as he started to pray. Master Chief Wilson burst out of the crater, catapulting forty feet into the air as his legs kept running against nothing but air, flipped over twice, and then slammed into the ground on his back.

"Chief! Chief! Are you all right?" Colonel Reed's voice came over his radio. "Every vital you have just spiked!"

"I'm alive," he croaked, rolling over painfully. "Blind, winded, and barely mobile, but I'm alive."

"Your telemetry reads like something is chewing on your armor, Chief."

"What? Shit!" Wilson rolled over, slamming his hand into the ground until the little beast in his mitts stopped wriggling. "Little bastard shot me in the face, overloaded the helm. I can't see shit, Boss."

"That's not possible, Chief. When your cams are blown, it defaults to backups; if those go down, then the whole helm loses power and turns transparent."

"I read the manual, Boss," Wilson growled. "All I know is that I'm blind as hell and this little bastard is trying to eat my suit! Get me some backup out here."

"Brinks is en route with Savoy's tech team. They'll be there in a couple minutes."

"Won't be fast enough," Wilson mumbled under his breath before speaking up. "Roger that, Boss."

"Hold tight, don't get eaten, and keep that thing intact."

"Roger. Wilco," Wilson acknowledged. *I sure hope I didn't kill it a minute ago.*

He lay there on the ground for a moment, his hand firmly clenched around his prize, until he heard footsteps approaching and forced himself to sit up.

"Chief?"

Seran's voice was uncertain, so he waved with his free hand.

"I'm alive. Bruised, maybe a little broken, but alive and breathing," he said. "I can't see a damn thing. Is this thing still alive?"

He held up the hand gripping the thing that had most resembled a spider the size of his head, hoping that he was extending it generally in her direction.

"It is…twitching," she said with a hint of distaste.

"Good. There's a team coming in," he said. "They'll get this cleaned up and hopefully get my suit patched up."

"My men are covering the crater," she said. "But if these are like the soldiers…"

"Then we can't miss even one of the little bastards, yeah, I know," he said before slumping in place.

A rumble in the distance separated itself from the background noise, growing in intensity rapidly. Wilson breathed a sigh of relief as he recognized the sound of the big chemical rockets of the inbound shuttle.

"Master Chief Wilson, do you copy?"

"I copy."

"Major Brinks, here. I'm going to dispatch Lieutenant Savoy's technical team to your disposal. I understand you have a package for me?"

"Wriggly little bastard is right here in my hand, sir."

"Excellent. Hold on, we're coming overhead now."

"I can hear you, sir. Can't see you, but I can hear you."

There was a pause. "What do you mean you can't see us?"

"My helm systems are all dead. I'm looking at a black plate, sir."

There was a long pause before Brinks came back, then he spoke again.

"Roger that." The major didn't sound confident. "Savoy is pulling a spare helm and a field kit for armor repair. Hopefully he can patch you up, Chief."

"Thanks, sir," Wilson said.

The roar of the shuttle had settled in over them, and Wilson imagined that he could feel his armor being buffeted by the blast of the shuttle's thrust. Unless they were a lot lower than the book called for, however, he knew that he was just imagining things, though. There were thuds and calls from others around him, and then he felt someone grabbing his hand.

"It's all right, Chief. I've got it."

Wilson let the little beasty loose into the hand that was on his, relieved to have it out of his grip. He felt someone pulling him back up to a sitting position, hands working around his helmet.

"Give me a perimeter around that crater! Someone pop a thermobaric down that shaft, damn it!"

"Damn, Chief. You really stepped in something pungent," a new voice spoke up. "Hold with me here, I'm going to pop the seals."

"I'm not going anywhere."

"Heh, right."

The hands twisted on the helm, hard, twisting his whole body until the helm finally gave way and the seals blew. A loud hiss preceded Wilson's ears popping painfully as he swallowed and worked his jaw. The helm lifted clear, and he blinked in the daylight as he got his first look around since he'd taken the hit down in the crater shaft. He flinched as a low rumble shook the ground, but recognized the smell of a thermobaric cooking off nearby.

"Hey there, Chief," another helm said, looking down at him.

He squinted in the light, managing to read the name stenciled on the helm. "Lieutenant."

Lieutenant Savoy grinned. "You beat the ever-living hell out of your kit, Chief. Never seen damage like this. Damn hit scorched the helm at least a dozen microns deep."

It took him a few seconds to figure out what that meant. "You're telling me that I couldn't see because my face was covered in *soot?*"

"Pretty much." Savoy nodded, scraping at the damaged helm with his combat knife. "Baked in, though. Helm is totaled. Must have been some kind of plasma blast. Laser wouldn't have done it, not to this material."

"It was bright as fuck, and it came from that little prick I grabbed."

"Well, we locked it in some tough material. Should hold," Savoy said. "For now, let's get you back in the fight, Chief."

The tech lieutenant held up a fresh helm for him, and he grabbed the helm and pulled it on, twisting it to seal the pressure locks. He held his breath for a couple of seconds as it linked into his armor, then breathed in relief as the HUD came online, showing the IFF and combat network.

"All right. It's linked in. I'm good," Wilson said, getting to his feet.

"Whoa, Chief"—Savoy slowed him down—"you took some hits."

"What?"

"Look down." Savoy pointed to his legs.

Wilson frowned, glancing down and tagging his armor diagnostics. He winced when he saw the state of his armor. The little bastards had obviously been chewing on his legs, and they'd all but turned the armored sections into swiss cheese. Luckily, they hadn't gotten into the circuitry, so while it wasn't going to protect him from squat, everything was still intact and he had full range of motion.

"I can still dance, Lieutenant," he said, "Long as no one steps on my toes."

"All right, then, Chief"—Savoy grinned—"best get to your feet, 'cause I'm pretty sure I hear Charlie starting to play the fox trot."

"Roger that," the SEAL chuckled, getting up. He unslung his gravity impeller and turned back toward the crater. "Let's finish this dance before the dance floor gets too crowded."

"Right you are, Chief." Savoy nodded, hefting his battle rifle. "Yo! Burke!"

"Sir?"

"What's the readings look like?"

"The TB shook 'em. We're waiting for the aftershocks to ease up so we can see if there's any movement down there," Burke replied. "Crater walls look solid. I don't think we collapsed anything."

"Good news. I know how you like spelunking, Burke." Savoy grinned.

"Me, sir? No, sir." Burke shook his head. "Drop the squid back down there, he looks like he can't be any more beat up."

Wilson ignored the smartass, coming to a stop at the edge and peering down. "How long before we know if you got them all with the overpressure blast?"

"Won't be long now," Savoy said. "We're establishing geo-sensors now, mostly reading falling rocks and such. When that dies down, we'll get a good, clean reading. Then we'll know."

"So we wait?"

"We wait." Savoy nodded.

SKIES OVER RANQUIL

▶ THE SHUTTLE BANKED away, heading for the next impact site while Brinks coordinated with the crews they'd already dropped off. The Drasin assault this time was proving to be difficult to fend off, mostly because the defenses of the planet were designed primarily to deal with fleet assault. Granted, even those had proven ill equipped at handling the Drasin, but that focus made it all the more difficult to adapt quickly to handle the much smaller method the aliens had utilized this time around. Even a month earlier and they likely would have had better procedures in place, better trained forces, and better communications. Today, however, they would have to make do with what they had, as little as it was.

"Command and Control, this is Brinks. I've got the package."

"Confirmed, Major. Deliver the package to our base of operations immediately."

"Shuttle en route. ETA, ten minutes."

"Roger that."

The major leaned forward, tapping the pilot on the shoulder. "You've got clearance to break speed records, son. Make it happen."

"Pleasure is all mine, sir," the lieutenant at the controls replied, tapping the CM controls full open just before he pushed the throttle to the max and kicked off the afterburners.

Even with CM at max, the level of thrust the big bird put out was enough to slam Brinks back into his acceleration bolster as the afterburners lit off the waste fuel that escaped the primary burn. The added boost hammered the shuttle past hypersonic, the CM field being the only reason they didn't start to ablate from air friction.

Crossing continents at that speed was a matter of minutes, and the shuttle actually shaved four minutes off Brinks's ETA by the time they were slowing to an orbit of the landing field. The shuttle circled once, then settled into a taped-off section near the command base while the troopers remaining on board picked up the large munitions crate they'd locked the creepy crawly they were delivering in.

The crate was heavy metal, laser welded, and plated with ceramic inside to prevent any electrical discharges while transporting live munitions. It was about the most solid container they'd been able to scrounge up, but after less than five minutes of locking the creepy crawly inside, Brinks had begun to entertain doubts. The damned thing had managed to actually bounce the box off the deck of the shuttle, rattling around like loose change until they'd dogpiled it and strapped it down.

He'd be just as happy to get this particular menace off the bird he was currently entrusting his life to, thank you very much.

The shuttle dropped onto the dirt outside the temporary command center they'd thrown together, and the men jumped out, lugging the box clear as another three full squads piled in. Brinks saw them all strapped in, then slapped the back of the pilot's helmet lightly to let him know it was time to move out again.

The shuttle lifted smoothly into the air, the whole maneuver having taken less than two minutes, and they were shortly winging clear to their next AO with a full load of troopers armed to the teeth and looking for a fight.

Just as well, since we're almost certainly going to find one.

▲

▶ "CAPTAIN TO THE bridge. Captain Weston, please report to the bridge."

The voice was calm, and Eric didn't break stride when he heard the call, but he stopped his casual strolling pace and moved up to a brisk military doubletime step. While he was certain that something was up—otherwise he wouldn't have been called—Eric had no intention of making anyone skittish because they just spotted the captain running through the corridors.

It took him a little under three minutes to make the bridge, and when he got there, it only took a glance at the plot to see why he'd been summoned.

"Commander," he said as he stepped up beside Roberts, "those do not look like Drasin."

On the plot lay a small squadron of ships that were larger and sleeker than anything the Drasin had shown to date, clearly gleaming with a metallic sheen that the silicate-based Drasin vessels lacked. Eric didn't know what more the universe could throw at them, and honestly, he wished that he wasn't about to find out, but it was clear that whatever they were looking at wasn't anything they'd seen before.

"No, sir, they do not," the former Army Ranger said seriously.

"Did I screw up?" Eric asked seriously, more than a little concerned by the situation. "I thought this was a Drasin construction. Was I wrong?"

"I don't think so, Captain. Michelle, tell him what else we found."

"Uh…yes, sir," the sensor specialist said tersely. "Ensign Lamont and I located these earlier."

She changed the plot for the moment, showing clouds of familiar vessels moving in and out through the plates that made up the swarm. Those Eric clearly recognized as the familiar Drasin ships they'd been fighting.

"More to the point, hyperspectral analysis of the swarm itself shows that it is clearly of Drasin fabrication," Winger went on, "identical chemical signatures as their ships and soldier drones."

That brought a near-invisible wince from Eric. Though he'd been counting on it, it wasn't what he would term good news. Of course, it just might be better news than if the Drasin were only one of two species that were clearly capable of dismantling a solar system, but he could have wished for a nice peaceful superpower, he supposed.

Fat chance. Superpowers don't get where they are by being peaceful. Peaceful people don't have the drive to expand.

No, if there were another species out here that wasn't getting attacked by the Drasin, Eric was thinking that he had a good candidate for his "trigger men."

Maybe they're actually allies, or some variation of such, but genocidal sorts don't usually have particularly good allies anyway, so either way, these ships need watching.

"Record everything," he said quietly, but firmly. "I want every piece of data we can scan or extrapolate on those ships. Either they're allies to the Drasin, or maybe something much worse. Either way, if we ever run into those ships on our own, I want to know who they are before they get a chance to pull anything."

"Aye, sir." Michelle nodded. "We'll get everything we can."

Eric nodded curtly, then walked over and took his place at the command station, calling up the plot on his personal screens. The high-resolution scans were eerily perfect, in the way that computer-generated data often was, but Eric found himself feeling something when he looked at the new types of ships.

Familiarity.

They weren't Priminae, that was certain. The material signatures were all wrong, that was clear from the hyperspectral analysis, but the design…The designs looked very similar to the Priminae Combat Class ships they'd seen in the past. The Priminae didn't build with metal, however; they preferred ceramic composites that were stronger and lighter than any alloy possible in nature.

These people use metals. Advanced alloys, from what these scans are detailing, but metals just the same. Eric skimmed over the hull on his screen, eyeing the bulges with a critical air and generally trying to get a feel for the builders.

Who are you?

PRIMINAE VESSEL CEREKUS, RANQUIL SYSTEM

▶ THE DECK ROCKED under the feet of Coranth Cirrus and his team as they finished sweeping another deck.

"Are you absolutely certain we've tuned the impellers as low as is practical?" he demanded of the engineer who had delivered the weapons to him.

"Yes, for the twelfth time, I'm certain."

"Damn," Cirrus swore, "it feels like we are inflicting more damage than the Drasin."

They paused to look at the jagged hole they'd blown through the inner bulkhead, even now cooling from the impact and the spattering of a Drasin's molten innards, and few had a response to that. The impeller weapons were most assuredly not intended for use on board ship, and Cirrus was reasonably sure that he and everyone with him had damage to their hearing from the continuous explosive discharges they'd been unleashing.

Still, with their standard-issue milosec lasers being effectively worthless against the drones they were encountering, there were few options.

"How many left?" Cirrus asked wearily.

They'd eliminated three of the drones so far, leaving behind smashed bulkheads and rapidly cooling pools of molten silicon and other materials in their wake for the maintenance crews to manage. It didn't seem like much, but each one required a different approach depending on what the Drasin was attempting to do. The last two times they were positioned at vital circuitry that, while perhaps not completely irreplaceable, they certainly would prefer to avoid inflicting undue damage on.

"We recorded two more breaches in the hull."

At least two, then. Cirrus hoped that was it. They were tearing themselves and the ship itself apart to remove the intruders, and it was taking a toll on his team and himself. Every bone in his body ached, and he felt like he wanted to throw up with every step, something he was told was due to the continuous exposure to concussive force from their own weapons.

The Drasin hadn't even laid a finger on them during the entire engagement; they were more focused on sabotaging the ship to give a damn about the crew at the moment. No, every bit of injury he and his had suffered had been at their own hands!

It was galling almost as much as it relieved him, to be brutally honest. The enemy apparently didn't consider his teams enough of a threat to bother fighting, despite the fact that they'd been picking them off one by one since the monstrous beasts set their first pincer on board the *Cerekus*. While he certainly didn't want them to wake up and take serious notice, Cirrus had to admit that the complete lack of any sort of respect from the enemy was both irritating and worrisome.

"Come on, we've got to drag this gear over to Deck Four, Section Eighteen, next." He grunted as he slung the impeller and picked up the munitions pack.

Either way, they had a lot of work left to do before the *Cerekus* was clear of enemy intruders, and even when that was done, he shuddered to think of the cleanup.

The repair teams are never going to look at me the same again.

On the command deck of the *Cerekus*, Syrenne Tianne gritted her teeth as she actually felt the last reverberations of the explosion several decks away fade.

Ordering men to use demolitions material on my own bedamned ship! What's next? She tried to keep her expression from scaring any of the younger crewmen and women around her, but was frankly failing miserably. *Likely, I'll shortly receive a summons from the admiral to fire on Ranquil itself!*

As soon as that thought had crossed her mind, she winced involuntarily. That particular order was far from unlikely, and she realized it almost the moment it crossed her mind.

"Captain, we've redirected the comet sufficiently for it to completely bypass all Ranquil facilities."

Tianne turned to the crewman and nodded. "Thank you. Kill the beams and let it fall freely then. I want all imagers scanning constantly. See if there are any more of those things around us!"

"Yes, Captain."

Could she relax now? No, she couldn't.

▼

RANQUIL, OVER DRASIN IMPACT CRATER

▲

▶ LT. ALEXANDRA PAULSON had seen impact craters in the past, but there was an ugliness to them that never failed to send a shiver down her spine. This one she was orbiting her shuttle around was no exception; in fact, it was possibly even uglier than most, given what she knew was waiting down in its black depths. The smoke and dust of the impact was fouling visibility, and she'd actually elected to switch over from air-breathing jets to the shuttle's self-contained systems in order to prevent any of the trash in the air from equally fouling the intakes.

"Well, that's certainly one big-ass hole," she said as she directed her shuttle in a smooth orbit over the impact strike.

"Deep penetration, same as the last couple," Maj. Wilhelm Brinks replied absently. "They're consistent, if nothing else."

"They are that," the pilot replied as she flipped over the protective cover that shielded the weapons payload switches from accidental activation. "We're armed and ready to pop, sir."

"Target area is clear of friendlies," Brinks said calmly. "Fire when ready."

"Roger that," Alexandra said, composed as she overshot the target once and put the nose of her bird almost vertical.

The big orbital shuttle was a flex-wing lifting-body design despite the use of the CM systems, partly because CM was such new technology that no one had gotten around to designing completely efficient hulls for it yet and partly because no pilots wanted to trust their lives to a craft they couldn't glide in on a bet if the fancy counter-mass systems failed.

They barely felt the climb inside due to the CM systems, but the big shuttle was clawing for altitude as Alexandra let out the reactors a little. Part of it was just show—she could have dropped from a much lower altitude, to be sure—and some of it was just because she enjoyed pushing her bird to its limits, but there were real tactical reasons to drop to a higher level than they'd chosen to perform their final observations from.

For one, they didn't want to get nailed by a piece of shrapnel thrown up from the blast that was coming. She still shuddered whenever she remembered one of her academy training exercises when she was called upon to do a low-altitude strike run with live munitions. A slight error in her instrumentation caused her to be a mere ten feet under the planned drop altitude, something that shouldn't have made the slightest difference in any sane world. In the real one, however, it was the difference between getting her arse end wet and having it torn clean off by the waterspout she created.

It was only a miracle and the reflexes of her training supervisor that kept her from planting the training bird nose first into the lake they'd been using for target practice. A Mach 1, forty-foot impact was pretty much not a survivable incident in anyone's book, and since that day, she felt like puking whenever she had to do a low-altitude drop.

She still *did* the drops, mind you. She just kept barf bags beside her seat for when it was over.

Glad I won't be needing them on this run, she thought as she leveled the shuttle out and brought it around for the final run.

The entire body of the craft flexed to maximize maneuvering efficiency as she came around, arming the ground-to-surface missiles as she did. The HUD flashed red, alerting her that she was armed and dangerous just in case she had somehow managed to be a complete imbecile and activate the triple-protected weapons by accident, and she haloed the target.

A final flick of her thumb cleared the firing stud on the control stick, and the bird was hot as hell and about to unleash some on the ground below.

"Bird is hot," she said calmly, leveling the shuttle as she dipped the nose down and picked up speed. "Weapons free."

There was silence from around her; she already had clearance to fire, so the announcement was more for the records and a courtesy to the major sitting just behind her. Her thumb fell on the stud, and the shuttle rocked slightly as the heavy warheads fell free.

"Shuttle One, bruisers clear."

The "bruisers" in question, a quartet of high-yield, conventional air-to-surface missiles dropped clear of the shuttle before their CM and reactors powered up. They roared away at a relatively sedate acceleration, entering terminal guidance almost instantly due to the proximity of their launch point. When terminal guidance went active, both the CM and reactors lit off, causing each to resemble nothing more than beam weapons as they lanced straight into their target at speeds normally all but impossible in Einsteinian space, let alone within the atmosphere of a planet.

They slammed into the hole, the CM fields dropping a split second before impact, and the combined detonation and impact could be felt for well over a hundred kilometers without sensing equipment. The ground erupted upward, a volcano of dirt and rock reaching for the sky as the shuttle slowed to an easy orbit of the ground zero.

"Target engaged, Major. Please advise."

"Take us down as soon as the dirt finishes falling from the sky, Lieutenant," Brinks said from behind her. "We need to drop a team to confirm we got them all."

"Roger that. Shuttle One, mission stance changed," she replied. "We're playing air cav now. Jamie, get the troops ready to jump. I'll make a low and slow pass."

"Roger, Alex," M.Sgt. James Queen replied, getting the attention of the grunts in the back. "Time to earn your pay, boys!"

"Huah, Master Sergeant!" they called back automatically, popping their restraints as they got ready to disembark.

Major Brinks stepped back, leaning into the bulkhead as the shuttle banked into the approach turn. "We just hammered this LZ, boys, so things should be peaceful for you, but best not to assume anything. Get down, dig in, and get the seismo sensors deployed. We need to be sure that we nailed all these bastards. Got me?"

"Got you, sir!"

"Yellow light! Green in thirty seconds!" the master sergeant called, acting as the shuttle's jumpmaster.

"Watch your assets, boys. Don't make me come back with local militia," Brinks growled. "We haven't gotten them trained to shoot straight yet."

"Jump in ten!" the master sergeant called, counting down as the men readied to jump.

At just under fifty meters, Alexandra leveled out, sweeping the shuttle into a sidelong glide at just under forty knots when the lights in the belly of the bird shifted to green and the master sergeant ordered the jump.

The armored troopers cast from the open belly of the bird, jumping in pairs, as that was the maximum width they could safely cast from the shuttle. Two at a time, they dropped, landing with powerful flexing of their armored legs and immediately setting about to securing the area against possible attack.

From the shuttle, Brinks and the master sergeant watched the last of them away before they signaled to Lieutenant Paulson that the men were clear.

"Next stop, Lieutenant," Brinks called.

"Aye, sir. Strap in. We've got a distance to cover, sir."

▼

RANQUIL, BRAVO AO

▲

▶ LT. SEAN BERMONT glared about him as he and his team looked over the mess they'd just been dropped off beside.

"This one's gonna be trouble," he announced, shaking his head.

"That's about the single-most useless thing I've ever heard come out of your mouth, Lieutenant," one of his men responded. "And I've heard you talk about what you get up to on leave."

Several others snickered, but Bermont really wasn't listening. The Drasin strike had really nailed a lucky placement in this situation, at least for the Drasin. For Bermont, his team, and the two squads of local militia that had arrived to clean them out, things were not looking so good.

The ballistic inbound, whatever the hell those things were, had come down on the outskirts of Mons Systema. Whether this was intentional or not, Bermont figured he wasn't the person to say, but the net result was that, in addition to burrowing deep into the ground, the damn thing had literally brought several buildings down and effectively buried itself in the debris.

Bermont shook his head, waving to his men. "Get those seismo sensors placed, we need to see what's going on under that mess."

"Yes, sir."

While his men were doing that, Bermont stepped over to where the militia groups were and zeroed in on the man in charge.

"Have you got anything that'll get us through that?"

The coranth shook his head. "Not here, no. I've put in a call to System Command, but I'm not certain how long it will take to get crews out here to dig through that."

"Damn." Bermont hissed. "Those things are probably already starting to expand their numbers under there."

"I am aware, yes," the man said, sounding frustrated and more than a little frightened.

Bermont was generally part of strike teams and hadn't spent much time dealing with militias in the past, but he wasn't dense enough to miss the emotion, and he was fully aware it had to be stepped on before it spread. He put a hand on the man's shoulder and leaned in, making sure that he was speaking over the suit's localized systems and not the unit-wide frequencies.

"Listen, pal, I know this looks bad, and you know it looks bad, but if you start looking like you're expecting to be slaughtered any second now, then the men are going to freak out," he said earnestly. "This would be a bad thing, particularly since they're carrying some *very* scary weapons, right?"

The coranth nodded, his eyes widening.

"So, you and me, we're going to stand around and bitch about the brass and generally look bored as hell while still keeping a tight watch," Bermont said, his tone deathly serious.

"Because the last thing we need is a nervous Nellie opening fire with portable weapons of mass destruction. Deal?"

The man looked confused. "Uh…yes. But one question?"

Bermont nodded. "Sure."

"Nervous Nellie?"

Bermont laughed cheerfully, loud enough that everyone around could hear him, and while he kept one eye on the seismo readings as they started to come in, he explained the meaning of the expression to the commander of the militia teams.

▼

MONS SYSTEMA COMMAND CENTER

▲

▶ IN THE SYSTEM command center, Nero was growing more frustrated as things progressed. Where the news was good, it was very good, but where it was bad, it more than filled his quotient of headaches for the next century.

"No, listen to me," he growled over a commlink to one of the men in charge of city maintenance. "You will find me a team that can move that debris, or I will come down there myself and find someone who *can*!"

The man on the other side instantly started to protest. "You're talking about demolishing a sector of Mons Systema without permits!"

"That sector has already *been* demolished, you insufferable…" Nero shouted, then fought for control. "The area must be cleared. If it is not, the Drasin in the area will be able to replicate themselves beyond our ability to control the situation."

"You cannot be serious," the man blurted. "I am not taking my construction teams into a war zone!"

"If you do not, then this whole *world* becomes a war zone!" Nero began, only to stare in shock as the signal went dead.

He punched in a query and stared a little longer as the response came back.

"That little imbecile disconnected the comm," he said with wonder in his tone. Nero left the command pit and walked to where Tanner was directing orbital defenses.

"Rael, we have an issue."

"Can you handle it?" Rael Tanner asked, looking tired and more than a little ragged. Nero knew the smaller man hadn't left the command center since the initial reports came through over a day earlier, and he looked it. "I think we have a new cipher sequence that should permit our orbital systems to discriminate incoming Drasin from other debris and increase our detection threshold significantly—we're running tests now."

Nero started to reply but a young woman strode up beside him, looking purposeful.

"Orders cut from Central, Commander," the young ithan said, handing him a data chip.

Nero frowned, but slid the chip into his portable relay system. His eyes got very wide before he glanced back at the ithan. "This came from Central?"

"Yes, Commander." She nodded. "Direct from the Council's priority line—triple-checked. The orders are authentic."

"Thank you, Ithan." He turned to Rael. "Actually, I believe that I can handle this situation without you or the Council's intervention."

"Excellent, Nero," Tanner replied, looking distracted as he focused on the code gliding past his screens.

Nero permitted himself a dark and predatory smile as he stepped back down into his domain and immediately summoned over the coranth of the deck. "Tera."

"Yes, Commander?" the slim woman asked as she stepped over.

"Take over the defense integration command," he ordered. "I have business to deal with."

"Sir?" She looked confused.

"Orders from Central," he said. "You'll do fine. Just keep them from shooting each other or the civilians."

"Yes, Commander."

He nodded to her, then pivoted on his heel and stalked out of the command center. As he left the main chamber, Nero waved to one of the security personnel that were posted outside.

"Summon your relief," he ordered. "You and your team are with me."

They stared just a moment too long, and he gave them a fiery glare.

"Yes, Commander!" the coranth in charge stammered out, immediately sending one of his men to call for a relief team. While they were waiting, he nervously eyed the big Colonial commander. "What are we doing, then, Commander?"

"We're going to go inform some civilians about the facts of life and what happens when you refuse to provide needed support during a critical military crisis," Nero said, his teeth showing just a little too much.

The coranth fell back a step, involuntarily putting some distance between himself and what he perceived viscerally as a threat to his life.

The relief crew arrived quickly. Then Nero hustled the team out and into the public transport tubes that interconnected the entire massive metropolis. They commandeered a car for themselves, waving a few civilians and even what looked like a councilman back while Nero called out the destination.

He and the security team were both shocked to find that their path had been precleared and priority routed. They shunted aside several other cars in the few seconds of high-speed travel that brought them from the center of the system's command and control base to the city's industrial sector. While the transport tubes were extremely fast, it normally took several minutes to cross the city center due to the regular pauses in motion while cars higher in the queue were directed to their destination.

We were jumped to the top of the queue. How? I didn't even bother requesting it. It would have taken longer to get that clearance than to simply deal with the delays.

Nero didn't have time to think on it just then, however, as the car came to a rest near their destination and they disembarked into the lobby room of that section of the Mons Systema central pyramid and walked the short distance through the corridors to where the Office of Municipal Maintenance was located.

"Commander?" Coranth Sinu spoke up, clearly confused. "Why are we here?"

"I need to speak with a *man*," Nero said, twisting the word dryly, "about his duty to our home. Do as I say, otherwise remain silent and stern in the background. Understood?"

"Y...yes, Commander."

It was times like this that Nero disliked the smoothly melting doors that existed within the city proper of Mons Systema. On the outer colony he had been raised on, they had doors that swung open on flexi-spines. *You could kick those open when you wanted to make a point.*

The door melted away as he stepped up to it, and he focused on glaring intimidatingly at anyone that crossed his line of sight. Those who did quickly found other places to be as the unusually large and apparently quite angry man stomped through the offices.

"Manager Lithsa," he growled once as he located the source of his current mood, "I would like to have a word."

"C...commander," the short, noticeably pudgy man stammered out.

"I have need of your crews."

"I already told you, I won't take my crews out into a war zone!" Lithsa rallied from his shock.

"And you will not be turned from that decision?"

"I will not."

"Arrest him," Nero growled, waving his men forward.

"What?"

The security men stared in shock.

"Commander...Are you certain?"

"I have here orders from Central to move those crews into place"—Nero held up his display—"and authority to get them there by any means necessary. Lithsa, if you will not move your crews out, I will find someone here who will."

The security men stared in shock between the men for a moment, the situation completely beyond their expectations. They weren't authorized to arrest or detain citizens, at least not normally, but if anyone or anything on the planet could change that, it would be Central.

Nero knew that he was on thin ice, at least so far as his traditional authority extended. For various reasons, military authority within Mons Systems was extremely curtailed outside of direct action. However, with the writ provided by Central, he could at least exert some real-world pressure on the situation. If he had time, Nero was confident that he even could have had the man prosecuted in open court. Time, however, was not on his side in this case, so he was going to push harder and faster than would normally be advisable, and when it was done, they could have his rank if that was the consequence.

Lithsa, however, was having none of it. The smaller man was an alarming shade of red as he shook his fist in the air.

"You can't do this! I know where your authority stops, and you've overstepped by so far you'd need an orbital satellite to relay the distance!" he yelled, growing redder and redder as he bulked up his reactor mass.

Nero was about to order his arrest again when someone else cut in.

"I'll do it."

Everyone fell silent, looking over to where a man was walking out of the back of the offices.

"What?" Lithsa blurted.

"I'll lead a team in," the man said calmly. "Volunteers only. I won't let you press-gang anyone into this."

"That's fine. Get your team together, gather your gear, and make it fast," Nero rumbled in return, the two of them completely ignoring Manager Lithsa as he started to get even redder.

"Micra! You don't have the authority to—"

His blustering came to an abrupt end when Nero stepped forward and clamped a big meaty hand on his shoulder, then almost literally threw him at one of the military security people he'd brought.

"Detain him until the current crisis is over," Nero ordered. "If that fool slows us down, we could lose the entire city."

"Yes, Commander..." The man hesitated. "Are you certain, though?"

"On my personal authority." Nero nodded. "I will deal with the consequences."

The man nodded, this time with less hesitancy. "Yes, Commander, it will be done."

"It is done," Nero answered. "Secure him in his own rooms, but put a guard in place."

"Understood."

"Go now."

"Yes, Commander!" the guard said, before dragging the still-protesting man along with him.

Nero turned to the man who had spoken up. "Micra, is it?"

"Yes, Commander." The younger man nodded.

"I will not lie, this is not to be a safe operation," Nero said. "The Drasin collapsed several buildings on their own position during their...*infiltration* of the area. We have teams in place to deal with them, but with all that material, my people are unable to get to them."

"I understand, Commander," Micra replied, hesitating. "What of rescue operations?"

Nero looked grim. "If you can pull anyone out alive, I expect you to do so, but I do not expect that you will find many. The impact was...energetic."

"I understand. Still, we must try."

"Then we understand one another," Nero confirmed. "Gather your team. We have work ahead of us."

▼

RANQUIL, BRAVO AO

▲

▶ "THIS IS LOOKING bad," Sean Bermont confided over the private battle network, speaking with the major while the two of them looked over shared data compiled from the seismographic sensors. He'd seen bad before, but this was really bad. Sean was starting to wish he were back home with his bike and a few hundred klicks of open road.

"Agreed. Can you do anything?"

"Not at present," the Canadian admitted tiredly. "We don't have enough demo gear here to clear this mess, so we're waiting on locals. The honcho here says that the big cheese in charge of the militia was taking a personal hand in it, but he doesn't have anything new yet."

"Right. Well, if Commander Jehan said it'll be handled, it'll be handled, is my impression of the man," Brinks replied. "What I'm concerned about is the timeline. The readings are getting stronger."

"Aye," Sean said, disgusted by the situation. "Any chance you could detail Burke and Savoy over here to maybe drop some deep-penetration munitions on them?"

"I could, but without getting a clean idea of the impact cavern and what they've dug out, we couldn't be sure of getting everything," Brinks said. "Try and get some more seismographs into place while I requisition a couple thumpers to try and map that area out."

"Roger that. Wilco," Sean confirmed. "We'll get things in place."

"Good luck, Lieutenant," Brinks said from his position on the overwatch shuttle, orbiting the multiple impact points.

"Thanks, Major." Sean paused, cocking his head as an alert popped up on his HUD. "Hold one. Major, we have trouble brewing here."

"Confirmed. Details?"

"I think they're coming out of their hole."

"Pull back, Lieutenant!" Major Brinks ordered. "Don't get caught in the middle of that mess!"

"Roger. Wilco!" Sean Bermont confirmed, already moving and sending orders over the waypoint system. "Time for us to earn our pay here, Major."

"Good luck, Lieutenant."

The major signed off while Sean was already in motion, running toward the local militia group leader who was helping put another seismo kit into place.

"Time to move!" he called over the open comm, his voice echoing from the wreckage all around them. "We have company coming!"

The coranth looked up, sharply and with confusion clearly on his face. "Company? Who?"

"The unfriendly kind!" Sean snarled, pointing at the ground.

It took several seconds for the young officer to make the connection, as he was not used to thinking of threats, but to his credit, as soon as he realized what Sean was talking about, he started giving orders that matched those Sean had already issued to his own men.

"Everyone, move back! The Drasin are coming to the surface!"

Hesitation kills in combat, and Coranth Gemma learned that the hard way when his own people stared at him for a second longer than they had. Explosions of dirt and dust erupted up from around their feet, and three of them were pulled down into the newly filled holes beneath them. They had time to scream, but little else before their lives were strangled off along with the sound of their shock and dismay.

Sean didn't hesitate. He grabbed Gemma and the closest militiaman beside him and leapt up and into the debris of the buildings around them. Behind him, the ground they had stood on exploded into dust and debris, and Drasin drone soldiers the size of large dogs erupted out and swarmed the ground.

"Off the dirt, boys!" he called in midair, crushing the breath out of his "recuees." "Grab the locals if you can, but don't be around when they come for you."

There was no round of acknowledgments from his men— not vocally, at least. Their icons lit up across his HUD as they toggled the simple "acknowledged" option and leapt into action. Around them, the ground was riddled with puffs of dirt and debris as the Drasin exploded out, often right on their heels as they ran just one step ahead of their pursuers.

"They're coming right up through the concrete," Sean muttered, pretty shocked by that turn of events. He hadn't really thought that they were in serious danger, at least not in such an immediate fashion.

"Concrete?" the coranth asked in confusion while he was gasping for breath beside Sean.

They and the ithan he had grabbed were perched about twenty meters up on the horizontal remains of what passed for a local skyscraper. Not that it didn't, in fact, scrape the sky, in his opinion, it was just that Sean wasn't used to seeing buildings quite so large. He was also a little put out by the fact that it was still almost intact despite the fact that it was lying on its side in the middle of an orbital impact zone.

"Yeah, the surface material."

"I am not sure what concrete is," the coranth admitted, "but that is three-foot-thick ceramic composite. The Drasin must have used explosives to broach the surface."

"Not unless they have some really kick-ass-shaped charges." Bermont shook his head. "The back blast would have fried them. They're tough, but we know they can be taken out by overpressure."

"Then I do not know, but it takes an industrial laser to slice through that material."

"Well, one thing about those things"—Sean shrugged— "we know that they have lasers on par with your own military models."

"Lasers would have cut through and burned through us as well!"

"Well, they've got *something* that turns the ceramic stuff of yours into freaking dust," Sean said, trying to analyze the situation. Before he could say anything else, however, three of his team's icons went red.

Sean froze, half turning, then looked back. "Stay put."

He didn't wait for a response before he jumped clear, dropping the twenty meters to the ground, even while unslinging his rifle. He landed hard, letting his suit absorb the energy as it was designed, then used that same energy to power his next move. The leap flung him more forward than up, straight toward where the three red icons were still angrily flashing on his HUD.

He dove through the debris of the fallen buildings, spotting the place where his men had been just as he began the downward arc. Sean toggled into their chatter, using his command codes to force open the mics in their armor, and almost instantly regretted it. Screams filled his ears as his armor picked up the distinctive detonations of explosive rounds cooking off from their guns.

He hit the ground in a slide, throwing his arm out and thrusting down into the powdered mess that had been a solid ceramic mass. He grasped blindly, trying to find either of his missing soldiers. His hand closed around a familiar form, and he shifted his grip quickly to grab the hook on the man's shoulder before rolling clear and pulling with all the enhanced strength he had.

The man pulled free. Then there was a sudden pull of extra weight, and Sean grunted under the strain. He clawed about, finding another section of pulverized ceramic, and dug his fingers into the edge as leverage before pulling again with even more force.

The weight began to give, and first one soldier's helm appeared and then his upper torso. Sean kept pulling and quickly saw the reason for the extra weight as the soldier he was pulling on had a death grip on his fellow.

Literally, unfortunately, Sean realized as he pulled them both free of the hole. The first man's lower body had been sheared off, well beyond even the advanced armor's ability to maintain any sort of medical treatment.

"Damn," he hissed, keying straight into the second man's armor. "God damn it, Simon, you alive in there?"

A moan was all he got, but it was enough for him to redouble his efforts, even while patching over to a wideband channel.

"Command, Bravo Actual!"

"Go for Command, Bravo Actual," Major Brinks came back instantly, all business.

"I am declaring Trojan Horse!"

"Say again, Bravo Actual."

"Trojan Horse," Sean confirmed, pulling Cpl. Simon Bell clear of the pit and rolling over him to unload his pistol magazine into the dust pit the Drasin had dug out. Air support and medevac would be on the way.

Hopefully not in that order.

▼

TERRAN COMMAND AND CONTROL

▲

▶ COLONEL REED SWORE at the tactical display, unable to do much else and unwilling to do nothing.

"What does this mean, Trojan Horse?" Ithan Chans asked, confused.

"Trojan Horse is a code phrase. It means that the unit has been overrun," he answered. "Enemy units mixed in with friendlies. We can't engage with artillery strikes without hitting our own men. Bermont has called in close air support and medical evac as well as any reinforcements we can spare."

"This is bad, then?" she asked, her tone making it clearly rhetorical.

He answered her, anyway.

"Extremely. Bermont has basically said that, if he can't reestablish control of his AO soon, we'll have to take the area out while he and his men are on-site."

"Why would he do that?"

"Because he's a soldier, Ithan," Reed answered, then shrugged, "and because he knows that if he can't get control of the area, everyone dies."

He reached forward, keying open a command channel. "Shuttle Three, I have a tasking for you."

"Roger, Command. Three is standing by."

"Proceed to Bravo AO, code Zulu. Deploy your ground teams and proceed to provide close air support. Copy."

"Copy code Zulu, Bravo AO. Wilco."

"What do we do now?" Milla asked.

"Nothing. We wait. Until something changes, that's all we can do. It's up to the men on the ground now."

That had been true all through history, though proponents of air superiority might argue it. In the end, there were some things that just had to be decided in the mud.

NACS ODYSSEY, UNCHARTED DYSON CONSTRUCT

▲

▶ WITH THE CAPTAIN off the bridge, hopefully sound asleep and getting the rest he was going to need in order to handle what was coming, command was left to Roberts to keep an eye on things as they continued to sling around the star hidden in the center of the Dyson swarm.

"Commander, we have a problem."

Commander Roberts turned to look at the woman manning the advanced sensors in the place of Lieutenant Winger and glared for a moment. "I presume you mean beyond the fact that we're currently surrounded by probably more enemy ships than the entire population of Earth?"

"Uh…yes, Commander," Lamont muttered.

"You may as well lay it on me, then." He sighed, walking over. Honestly, he didn't know why he was feeling any surprise at all. *Two missions out, two completely insane situations. Either we're cursed or we're blessed. I guess I'll know which if I live long enough to retire.*

"It's our course, sir. We're on a collision trajectory with one of the plates."

Waters half twisted, objecting instantly. "That's impossible, sir. I triple-checked that course when we slung around the star. It was clean."

"The inner and outer plates have altered their orbits," Lamont countered. "I don't know why…I don't even know how, but we're aiming right dead center for one of the inner plates, now."

"Damn." Roberts leaned over her to check the calculations, but quickly confirmed them as accurate. "Lieutenant Waters, recheck our course, and start plotting alternate burns to adjust."

"Aye, sir."

Roberts shook his head, crossing back from the sensors station to the command station of the *Odyssey*. The captain was sleeping at the moment, taking advantage of the fact that even if they were spotted, it would be hours before anything could happen, but now he had to consider whether to wake him. No, he decided, there was nothing the captain could do yet.

Until they had the new course alterations and predictions, the captain could rest a while longer. With the new information, Roberts was thinking that they would need the man at his station fresh and alert more now than before. No matter what, firing their retrothrusters now would almost certainly warn someone of their presence within the swarm.

Once that happens, we'll have all hell on our tail and probably a good piece of it sitting right in front of us, too. Briefly, he wished that they'd just turned tail and ran for it before they entered the godforsaken swarm, but Roberts knew enough about physics to know that the odds would have been even worse then.

To reverse course would have required full CM and a lot of time, given their initial starting velocity. Building delta-v to escape would have taken so much time that any response from the swarm would have had more than enough time to catch them.

Now, at least, they had momentum going in the right direction. The downside, of course, was that they were *inside* the swarm and may be forced to fight their way out through any response that was mustered to intercept them.

The passing intercept will be shorter, though, than if we tried to run on the way in. We'll already have considerable velocity, and they'll have to build from a zero-zero start rather than us having to kill momentum before we could pull away.

He wasn't convinced that the velocity advantage would quite make up for the fact that they were as deep inside enemy territory as they were, but that wasn't his call.

"Commander," Daniels spoke up hesitantly, "I think we have a problem."

"Another one?" Roberts just shook his head and walked over that way. "What do you have to drop on the fire?"

"At a guess, sir? About twenty-five terawatt laser cannons and more fighters than I can count."

Roberts lost his casual demeanor in an instant. "Talk fast."

"The plate we're heading toward, we're starting to get imagery back from it," Daniels explained. "I'm counting twenty of the Drasin cruisers docked at it, and five of those unknown-class ships. If they spot us, we're going to see some action on the way out."

"If they spot us, son." Roberts shook his head. "What makes you think they haven't already?"

"Sir?"

"Never mind." So much for anyone getting any rest. Roberts walked back to the command station, where he keyed it open to the stewards' channel.

"Commander?" the man's voice came through questioningly.

"Wake the captain."

There was a pause and a long yawn before the man responded, "Aye, sir."

Cursed, it is, Roberts decided tiredly.

RANQUIL, EN ROUTE TO BRAVO AO

▶ "SUIT UP, CROWLEY!"

"You got it, Master Chief," Jackson Crowley replied, ignoring the fact that he was technically the superior officer on board as he started unstrapping from his bolster and grabbing the rails above the armor unit strapped in beside him. "What's the sitch?"

"Trojan Horse at Bravo's AO."

"Oh shit," Crowley muttered as he swung himself into the armor.

"Oh shit is right, boy!" the master chief called. "We've got squad casualties and a whole shitload of enemy combatants mixed in with friendlies on the ground. Medevac drones are being dropped ahead of our insertion, but we're going to have to get that area pacified, otherwise the shit is going to hit the fan in a big way."

Crowley pulled the hatch on the armor shut behind him, cutting the master chief off for a moment as the suit booted up. From a cold boot, the armor took seven seconds to bring basic systems online, another ten to warm up all the advanced sensors and other similar gear. By the time his external camera came online, the master chief had moved on to the other guys in the shuttle.

"Aerial units show two dozen enemy targets and counting," he was saying. "They're coming up out of the ground, so we don't have exact numbers. That means, once we drop, we'll be in a Trojan Horse ourselves until we can get the wounded and any civilians out of the area. The buildings the impact strike brought down make aerial strikes less than effective, so the enemy has cover from our heavy weapons."

"What's the plan, Master Chief?"

"We'll be carrying the heavy weapons in with us," the master chief said. "If we get a chance, we're to access the enemy infrastructure and blow it to hell."

"Infrastructure?" Crowley blinked. "What infrastructure?"

"The little bastards are like ants, Lieutenant," the chief said. "They dig tunnels. Find a way in, get some explosives deep enough, and we'll collapse the whole system on them. They're tough, but we know that they aren't impervious to overpressure."

"Right. Roger that, Chief." Crowley shunted power to his weapons systems.

"Good! Drop in twenty seconds!"

The droplight turned yellow as the men all got to their feet and prepared for what came next.

BRAVO AO

▶ BERMONT GLANCED UP as the shuttle swept in against the blue-green sky. He could see the jump doors opening in its belly from where he was, the drones dropping first. They were a lot like the para-packs used for infiltration jumps, but more so in many ways. They were designed to provide emergency response in a pinch, to pick up wounded, or to supply additional air surveillance as needed. He immediately signaled for a priority medevac and dragged Simon Bell farther up onto the fallen building, above the debris of the battleground, to where the drones could more easily get to them.

"Hold on a little longer, Corporal. We've got reinforcements arriving. I've called for a medevac."

"I guess I get out of this mess first, then, huh, Lieutenant?"

"Yup. Check out the nurses for me, will you?" Sean asked with a smile. "I'll probably wind up in the bed next to yours before this is over."

"You're too lucky, Lieutenant."

"I'm lucky? Didn't I just have to ask you to check out the nurses for me?" Sean snorted. "I think you and me need to have a little chat about what luck really is."

The medevac drone dropped into range, and Sean grabbed the hook it lowered. He clamped it onto Bell's armor and signaled it to lift clear. Bell flashed him a thumbs-up as he was pulled up by the CM-powered drone.

"We'll do that, Lieutenant," he said. "Just nail those bastards."

"Can do, Corporal."

The drone reversed its thrust and pulled clear of the building, drawing the wounded man along with it. Now that he wasn't carrying Bell around, he brought his rifle forward again and started looking around for targets.

The shuttle was finished spewing drones, most of them already in low orbital positions over his location, so he didn't waste any time signing into the battle network they had established. Knowing what they were up against, the techs on the *Odyssey* had spent some time recoding the drones' software to look for heat sources above human norms. Armor IFF designated the *Odyssey* troops as friendlies in blue on his HUD, near-human normal temperatures were shown in green, and anything hotter than that was designated as hostile red.

A glance at the latest data crawling across his HUD told him that the situation wasn't getting any better. The computer tally on hostiles had topped to three dozen now and was still climbing as more of the Drasin poured out of their tunnels.

Jesus. How fast do they reproduce, anyway? They make rabbits look like monks.

Bermont snarled as he popped up over his cover and leveled the rifle down at a grouping of red dots his HUD had steered him toward. The Drasin were a little larger than big dogs, which he actually found a lot creepier than the big horse-sized versions they'd fought the last time around.

Spiders shouldn't be bigger than I can squash with my boot.

He flipped over to full autofire and toggled the smart rounds to thermal tracking, then simply opened fire.

The big battle rifle roared, unloading the entire magazine in just seconds. He didn't wait for the results, knowing that the Drasin had effective ranged weapons. Once he was back in cover, he simply requested a live feed from the overhead drones to view the results of his handiwork.

The heat sources were still there, but several were a lot fuzzier than before and had stopped moving. *Being spread across the ground will do that to you.*

"Bravo Actual, be advised Shuttle Three is dropping reinforcements in five seconds."

"Roger, Shuttle Three. Bravo squad," he called his remaining team members, "cavalry inbound. Cover their landing."

"Huah, Lieutenant!" they called back.

Sean cat-crawled a short distance to where the local militia were huddled and found the coranth in charge. "All right, we've got to get this area secure, or things are going to get real ugly for the city. Your boys up to it?"

"We will hold our part, Lieutenant," the coranth promised as he gripped his weapon, probably too tightly.

"Good. Here comes some help." Sean nodded upward.

They looked up as the shuttle swept overhead, men pouring from the belly of the bird and dropping to the shattered terrain around them. Just when they thought the last man had dropped, a hulking figure appeared in the hold and threw itself clear.

"What is *that?*"

Sean was glad that his helmet hid his expression as he rolled his eyes. "Combat mech prototype."

The mech hit the ground with enough force to send tremors to their positions, weapons opening fire as it cleared a 360-degree circle around it.

"It is very well armed."

"Put a gun on a turd and it would be well armed, too," Sean muttered.

"What is a turd?" the coranth asked, the translator completely missing the word.

"Never mind. The turd has the area cleared for the moment," Sean replied, amused with himself. "We're going to have to do some definitive search and destroy. We can't let any of those things get loose."

"You are correct. I will rally my men."

Bermont nodded and followed, electing to stay close to the militia in his role as liaison. Nothing sucked more than a blue-on-blue incident between fresh allies.

▶ ▶ ▶

The Drasin were well used to having their own way on the various worlds they visited, though admittedly few of the species would think of things in those terms. It wasn't that they didn't incur losses—most of the inhabitants of any world they landed on were understandably perturbed to be hosting what amounted to the *ultimate* invasive species of the universe. Resistance was normal; however, it was generally futile as well.

Being capable of extremely quick reproduction and immune to most forms of natural threat they might encounter, a Drasin force generally accomplished its assigned task and died happily in the process.

This world, however, had already survived one incursion and the mind that guided the alien drones could already detect signs that things were not going well at all.

The local weapons had changed; no longer were they encountering the light energy beams they had been engineered to use as alternate energy sources. Now every opposing unit they faced appeared to use kinetic-strike weapons that were far more difficult to defend against.

The mind was well aware that no world changed so completely in such little time. This could only be caused by an outside force, but the Drasin were already committed, and the remainder of the Drasin forces were too far away to warn.

Its forces would continue until they succeeded, or until mobility functions ended. That was their way.

▶▶▶

Lt. Jackson Crowley was grinning with such rigor that had anyone seen the expression on his face, they would almost certainly have recoiled in horror. He circled the powerful mech he was sitting in, weapons extended in opposite directions, while the computer kept a running tally of the kills he'd been racking up.

When the area was clear, he paused for a moment and took stock of the situation, noting that, while he had indeed landed in a relatively clear space as he'd intended when he jumped, he'd managed to get himself blockaded in by the debris scattered all around him.

Well, time to prove this suit's worth on a real battlefield, he thought as an eager charge ran through him.

He wasn't deaf, nor was he immune to the slings and arrows sent his way when his comrades saw the EXO-12 for the first time. He even understood it, given the relatively poor showing most walking robots had displayed over the last century or so. Even the very best autonomous designs couldn't hope to navigate a battlefield in anything resembling a reasonable time, and interface solutions that put a human in command were often worse.

That was until the NICS interface had been designed. It took years to make it work for a system as potentially complex as human ranges of motion, but once that had been done, the sheer precision the system allowed for was staggering.

Jackson evaluated the situation briefly, then let go of the weapon control handles. When they designed the EXO-12, there had been two options debated by the designers. The first had been to integrate the weapons into the armor's arms, but that had been discarded due to a lack of flexibility and mobility caused by the required feeds for ammo, energy, and cooling.

Instead, his tri-barrel autogun and laser cannon were mounted on gimbal articulating arms that retracted into the back of the armor. In effect, the weapons stored themselves when the armor-shod fists of the EXO-12 let their handles drop.

That left his hands free to grasp out and climb clear of the debris, Jackson taking a moment while on top to quickly scout the immediate area before contacting his team and Bravo squad.

"Bravo, Gamma, Gamma Actual."

"We're online, Actual," his team answered instantly.

"Bravo Actual, here. Bravo is linked into the network."

"Confirmed," Jackson said, checking the nearby icons. "The debris here is not conducive to a clean operation, Bravo. Suggest we fall back and contain the area until we can get some serious demo in here."

"Negative. They've had less than an hour, and they damned near overwhelmed our forces. If we leave them any more time, these bastards will rip the planet out from under our feet."

Yes, well, there was that. Jackson felt a shiver run down his spine. He'd been briefed on that before he shipped out, but it was a sort of abstract concept unless you were standing on the planet in question.

All right. Fine, so falling back isn't an option.

"Confirmed. Gamma Team, deploy and support Bravo. Bravo Actual, suggestions?"

"How much are you packing in that Tinkertoy?" Bermont came back quickly.

"More than your squad started with."

There was a pause over the comm for a moment; then Crowley noticed tags going up on his HUD. Bermont was labeling areas on the fly, so Crowley left him to it while he jumped down from the debris he was on and stomped over to a section he was reading a human heat source from.

The EXO-12 was a combat chassis, but the engineers saw no reason to skimp on raw power in terms of lifting strength. So when he determined that the person was trapped under the debris, Jackson shouldered into the section of building and dug titanium-shod fingers into the section of wall and lifted. It gave slowly at first, then with a smooth acceleration as his hydraulic pumps whirred into action, and a few seconds later, he'd cleared the fallen chunk of wall.

"If you can move, get the hell out of my AO," he told the person lying under the rubble, hoping the translator got the point across. "You're in the way."

It was a man, lying shocked there for a moment before scrambling across the ground away from the EXO-12. Jackson sighed, rolled his eyes, and grabbed the panicked guy by the leg. This didn't reduce his panic in the slightest, as he was dragged back to where Jackson lifted him up to look him in the face.

"Wrong direction." He pointed with his free hand. "That way."

He let the guy go, and this time, he thankfully scrambled away from the enemy's positions.

"Gamma Actual, Bravo Actual."

"Go for Gamma," Jackson said.

"I think we've got a plan."

"I'm listening."

▶▶▶

A hundred kilometers away, at the first impact site, Savoy looked over the mess they'd made, one eye on the seismo readings as he glanced over to where the battered Navy SEAL was slouched on the ground.

"I think we've got the last of them," he said finally.

"Hoorah," Wilson muttered, completely unenthused. "I figured that out when they stopped trying to kill us."

"There were fifteen of the bastards left then, Chief," Savoy countered, "We nailed them with pocket TBs, remember?"

"That was twenty minutes ago."

"You have any idea how hard it is to clean up the noise from these seismos when we have heavy fighting going on in the same zip code?" Savoy shrugged. "The major dropped a shit ton of ordnance just a hundred klicks from here. We're still picking up echoes from some of it."

"Hoorah." Wilson pulled himself to his feet and rested the gravity impeller on his shoulder as he turned around. "So, we're clear?"

"Looks like it. We'll need to leave the sensors and keep some of the militia boys here to stand watch," Savoy said, "but this site looks secure."

"Glad to hear it, Lieutenant."

Both men started when Colonel Reed's voice injected itself into the circuit.

"Sir!"

"We've got a problem brewing at Bravo squad's AO," Reed said, not bothering to acknowledge the startled soldiers. "Leave a trip wire team and haul ass to Bravo's location."

"Roger that, sir. Uh…We're going to need a lift," Savoy answered.

"Shuttles are all tied up. I've wrangled you a seat on a Priminae orbiter."

"Great," Savoy replied dryly. "It won't melt if we hit rain, will it?"

Reed ignored the question and, in fact, simply signed off, leaving Savoy hanging. The lieutenant groaned.

"Man, I really don't trust those things. Who builds a ship that can melt, anyway?"

"In World War Two, there was a serious plan to build aircraft carriers out of ice," Master Chief Wilson answered as he got to his feet. "It was only canceled because the war ended. So I suppose the answer to your question is we're all a little crazy. Probably has to do with the uniform cutting blood off to the head."

Savoy rolled his eyes. *A Navy master chief with a sense of humor. Great, now I know the world is ending.*

Of course, the moment he thought that, Savoy remembered the consequences of leaving even a single one of the Drasin drones intact. A cold shudder passed through his body at the thought, and he firmly pushed that entire line of thinking well away.

Some things just weren't funny no matter what angle you looked at them from.

▶▶▶

Crowley gnashed his teeth as he had to drop his laser cutter, letting the articulated arm pull the weapon back into its slot along the back of his armor, so he could grab a chunk of debris and loft it clear of his road. The hardened construction material flipped end over end through the air and came down on a small grouping of Drasin soldier drones with a crash that shook the ground.

He guided the EXO-12 armor through the gap he'd made, leading with the tri-barrel cannon already spinning up. As the combat network reported, there were a dozen of the dog-sized drones waiting for him—well, they *thought* they were waiting for him.

What they were really waiting for was the hundred-round burst from his tri-barrel. The explosive shells tore them apart, splattering molten silicon across the terrain in the process.

The energy cost these things have to have, just to stay mobile, is insane.

Crowley was something of a thinker, one of the reasons he'd volunteered for the experimental testing of gear like the EXO-12. He loved getting his hands on things no one else had seen before and discovering all the little things that made them special, both for good and for ill. The Drasin cued that part of his mind every time he saw a new bit of intel on the species.

The molten silicon they used for blood, or what passed for blood, intrigued him to no end. Certainly, the high heat was a boon in many ways to the creatures. It let them be mobile, for one, since silicon was rather solid at temperatures normally encountered on life-bearing worlds.

Well, human life-bearing worlds, at any rate.

No, what made it so damned *weird* in his book was the fact that there were so many other ways they could have gone. Silicon based or not, they could have—no, they *should have*—developed in some saner way. The high heat that the Drasin exhibited simply *had* to be enormously energy intensive. In order to maintain it for any length of time, it was clear that they had to *eat* or somehow take in energy very nearly constantly.

On its own, that wasn't entirely unheard of, there were many simpler species on Earth that did the same thing. What made it completely bizarre, however, was the fact that these things ate and reproduced on a level that could literally consume *planets*.

And that, right there, was when Crowley's intelligent, curious, and downright insatiable mind shut down and said it had had enough for the day, come back tomorrow, if you please.

The word *impossible* wasn't something that he liked to throw around, particularly when it concerned something that clearly *wasn't*, but the Drasin were so completely impossible that if he'd encountered them in one of the many science fiction novels he loved to read, he would have instantly screamed foul and called the author an idiot.

And yet, here I am, the man thought wryly as the gentle vibration shook him through the massively insulated system, proving how very powerful the tri-barrel autocannon really was.

A pair of stray Drasin tried to flank him, but with the compressed imagery in his HUD, he spotted them easily and reached back to pull his laser cannon back into play. The powerful laser mounted on his armor was a smaller, much smaller, version of the *Odyssey*'s primary array. Designed using trillions of nano-scale light-emitting diodes, the cannon emitted just under a gigawatt of narrow frequency energy.

Compared to the multi-terawatt beams tossed around by the Drasin, it wasn't a lot; however, the other trick it could do made up for it. The beam also acted as part of a targeting and diagnostic system completed by hyperspectral scanners in his armor. They analyzed the composition of the surface being targeted, then adjusted the frequency of the laser to the precise degree that would be most completely absorbed. With near 100 percent efficiency, the beam was lethal beyond its measure as it vaporized almost any material it was aimed at.

So when he swung the laser out and triggered a pulse into the nearest Drasin, the vaporized material expanded into gaseous state so fast that the Drasin was blown back by the jet of exhaust gasses and then exploded into shards. The second followed less than two seconds after the fist.

"Gamma, Bravo, Gamma Actual," he said calmly as he looked around the killing ground he was centered in. "Sector cleared. Moving on."

"Roger. We're reading more activity below the fallen buildings, copy," Bermont responded, his voice tense.

"Copy that," he responded, his own tone matching the other lieutenant's.

As powerful as the EXO-12 was, he couldn't move that much debris on his own, and there was no way in hell that the standard power suits could shift even the smaller pieces of the toppled buildings.

They couldn't do the job with what they had. There was just no way.

He toggled into the command channel, copying Bermont as well. "Sir, we can't clear this area. We do not have the assets."

"I concur," Bermont said. "We need combat engineers, pronto."

There was a pause while the system compressed the messages, pulsed them out, and then waited for Colonel Brinks to receive the data and respond. In the meantime, both lieutenants went about their duties and continued to attempt the impossible and clear the area.

"Roger that, Gamma, Bravo," Reed answered a short while later. "Stand by for reinforcement from Savoy's team."

"Thank god, how far out are they?" Bermont asked.

The channel was now live, so Reed responded quickly. "One hundred klicks, waiting on a lift from a local bird."

"ETA?"

"Fifteen minutes."

Bermont swore, making Crowley cringe. Generally, it was a bad idea to start swearing at a full-bird colonel, even one who'd spent most of his career in the field the way an SF man would have.

"That's how long it'll take to shake the nearest bird loose," Reed said, thankfully ignoring the profanities. "No can do any sooner."

Bermont sighed audibly. "Roger that, sir. With that kind of time, however, we have an issue. These things make rabbits look like cloistered monks, Colonel. Even minutes count here, trust me. Talk to Savoy, he's seen the inside of their burrows."

"Copy that. I can't change the speed of the universe, boys, but I'll do what I can. In the meantime, hold the line."

"Copy that," Bermont answered dully.

"Copy," Crowley signed off the command channel, leaving the team leader tac channel open. "You've been here before, what do you think?"

"I think we're going to get overrun," Bermont answered frankly. "They've already got way more drones than I thought possible, and it won't be getting any better."

"Roger that."

One problem with powered armor and suits in general was the fact that you really couldn't do simple things like scratch an itch or wipe away sweat. Right at that moment, there was nothing Crowley wanted to do more than wipe the sweat from his face. It was the one part of his body that wasn't covered in a wicking material that both pulled moisture away from his skin and gave him a little friction to scratch against.

Unfortunately, the face had to be left clear so he could access and control all the HUD-based systems, so all he could do was turn down the temperature and have some air blown through to clear the fog.

That done, Crowley accessed the overhead intel from the drones. He spotted the closest section of heavy resistance and tagged it for immediate response.

"Gamma Team, Gamma Actual. Friendly fire inbound."

He waited a beat for his team to answer in the affirmative, then fired his thrusters as he jumped straight up. His armor had the power to kick itself twenty meters into the air in a jump; with thruster power and a mild CM hit, he could do a lot better than that. His leap arched just under forty meters, clearing the debris with a high enough angle to come down right in the center of the hostile grouping.

Men threw themselves down as he roared in, landing in a crouch to absorb the impact, and extended his weapons out in opposite directions. The rotary cannon spun up quickly, then began roaring in thunderous counterpoint to the near-silent operation of the laser firing from the other side.

He swiveled, turning in full circles as his armor computer tagged the drones and took over the firing sequence for him. Gapping the fire so it would hit the enemy while simultaneously *not* hitting his teammates was a problem beyond human reflexes at the speed the engagement was progressing. IFF fire control, however, was capable of making decisions in literal nanoseconds, so while Crowley maintained control over the absolute fire/hold decision, he passed the timing of the decision over to the computer.

The roar of the cannon never even stuttered audibly, his pass moving so fast that the deliberate breaks in fire were so quick that they couldn't be noted by human hearing alone. Three full circles later, the area around him was motionless, and Crowley too slowed to a stop.

"Everyone all right?" he asked across the team channel.

Men slowly stirred, looking up to make sure that there weren't any more bullets or beams flying overhead.

"LT," one of them muttered as he climbed to his head, "most people don't consider *themselves* to be incoming *artillery!*"

"Was I wrong?" Crowley grinned.

"I know I'm never going to look at that hunk of junk the same way again."

Crowley walked over to the man, literally towering over the normal-powered armor the corporal was wearing, and looked down at him. "If you want, me and this 'hunk of junk' can just sit the fight out from here on through."

"Uh...No, sir, that won't be necessary. It's a nice shiny hunk of junk and all," the corporal offered, probably grinning like a loon under the helm.

Crowley rolled his eyes. "Right. All right, on your feet, boys. Work isn't done yet."

The squad got to their feet and assembled behind Crowley and the EXO-12 as he looked up the next segment of hot spots showing on the overhead map of the area.

"Cleanup on aisle three, let's move out."

▶▶▶

The entity known to the Priminae as "Central" wondered briefly if what it was experiencing would qualify as pain. The Drasin were carving out chunks of the earth at various points around the city of Mons Systema, destroying whatever they touched and somehow even managing to disrupt the local electromagnetic field. The effect was something the entity had only previously experienced when dealing with the Drasin attack thwarted previously by the Terran forces.

How can they be doing this? The entity had no idea. It had never encountered anything that could apparently destroy the resonance of the planetary magnetic field in the way these *things* did.

The only thing the ancient being could be certain of, the one thing that it *knew*, was that they had to be *stopped*.

While this time his own people were reacting with more effectiveness and power, he recognized that, once more, it would not be them who decided the outcome of this battle.

This must not continue. The Priminae must stand on their own. Central was firm on that decision. *There are no consequences worse than extinction.*

▶▶▶

Bermont was a few hundred meters from where Crowley was forming up with his team, ducking under a burst of plasma that was clearly aimed to take his head off. They had been moving through a clockwise sweep of the sector when the Drasin swarmed up out of the ground, almost overrunning their position before they could react.

The split second of forewarning provided by their helmets' thermal response and the overwatch from the drones was just enough to allow them to jump back by the numbers and take cover. They returned fire from cover, hunkering down behind the debris, bullets, and plasma blasts crossing wildly between the two groups.

"Grenade!" Bermont called out, palming a cylinder from his gear.

He flung the weapon into the open zone, arming it in the air from his suit HUD. It exploded three feet from the ground, in the center of the target group. The shock wave from the explosive was easily visible in the squad's HUD, shattering the Drasin and slamming their remains into the debris along the sides.

"Move out!"

They jumped the cover, advancing with weapons firing on the few remaining drone soldiers. A plasma burst exploded past Bermont, slapping one of his men down. He flinched, but didn't turn to look until they'd finished off the threat.

"Man down!" he called, turning back then.

The plasma had vaporized the armor plate when it struck, the explosive force enough to throw the man back several feet, but he seemed intact.

"I'm alive," the man groaned, rolling over.

Bermont forced him back, checking the damage. "Inner trauma plate is intact. You got lucky."

"Lucky? Hell, I feel like I just got hit by a truck."

"Yeah, that plasma may not weigh anything, but it sure packs a nice punch when it reacts with your armor, huh?" Bermont said with forced cheer as he noted that the man's armor was basically shot to hell, computer response was patchy, and if the lack of power hadn't automatically activated the armor's passive external speakers, he wouldn't even be able to talk with him.

"Yeah."

"OK, you're done for the day, Jeff," Bermont said, signaling a medevac drone.

"I can still move!" The man, Jeff Styles, started to get up again.

"Yeah, but you can't keep up. You're done," Bermont said, patting the guy on the shoulder. "Grab some chow when you get back to base. If we don't get things under control here, you'll have enough work soon enough, anyway."

The medevac drone dropped into their midst, so Bermont quickly grabbed the cable from the drone and slapped it onto the eyebolts in the downed man's armor. The drone took up the slack as soon as it was cleared and pulled the man clear.

Bermont casually cradled his rifle as he remained crouched with his squad around him. "All right. We've got another sector cleared. We'll move on to the next."

"Where the hell are they all coming from, Boss? The damned thing only hit here a couple hours ago now!" one of the men complained.

"These things put bunnies to shame, boys. Give them just a few weeks at most and they'll eat a planet out from under you," Bermont reminded them. "Since they break down entirely when killed and become completely inert, we haven't been able to figure out how they do what they do, or how fast."

He sighed. "Mil intel thinks that it's some sort of nano-tech, and if they're right, then we could easily be looking at a geometric progression. One dozen now, five dozen in an hour, five hundred dozen in a day. We have to hammer them back now and keep hammering until the boss can get Savoy's combat engineers over here to clear this chaff from our AO. Good to go?"

"Good to go!"

"All right, move out!"

They continued the clockwise patrol, circling toward the next group of hostile contacts on the overwatch map. Bermont knew he'd talked a good game, but also was aware that unless they got the chaff cleared away so that they could get into the impact zone, they'd have no shot at containing the problem before it became an irreversible threat. All they were doing at this point was pissing into the wind, and that wind was rapidly turning into a hurricane.

If we don't get this crap cleared in a hurry, this windstorm is going to huff and puff our little house right down.

▲

▶ERIC GLARED AT the screens, wishing they'd show anything but what they were showing. He felt both better and worse after having some rest, since he was now awake, but then he found himself staring at *this* and his stomach felt like it had dropped down into his ankles. *Have I gotten us all killed?*

"So that's it, then," he said finally.

"Yes, sir," Roberts said quietly from his side. "We backtracked the orbits. They moved those plates after we slung around the sun. They're tracking us, no doubt in my mind."

"How?" Eric couldn't understand it.

It wasn't that he had faith in the cam-plate settings that hid them; it was that Eric *knew* that they were basically perfect camouflage for the *Odyssey*. Without active beams, which the *Odyssey* would certainly detect, there was practically no chance of her being detected at stellar ranges. At the very worst, the ship would appear as a miniscule black dot on the very best sensor arrays, and even then only if they passed in front of a contrasting surface. Granted, Eric knew that they were in a worst-case scenario for being detected at the moment. The plates of the Dyson construct were lit by the sun they orbited around, giving sensor arrays something to contrast the *Odyssey* against. In theory, at least. In practice, however, physics were impossibly against that happening at the distances involved.

No, it would take active scans to pick up the *Odyssey* at these ranges.

Active scans that they would have detected.

"Best guess, sir? Gravity detection." Roberts shrugged.

"You're talking about equipment on a scale I can barely even imagine. The array that would take would be..." Eric trailed off, his eyes on the massive plates that currently surrounded the *Odyssey*. "The size of a...solar system."

"Yeah," Roberts said dryly. "That was my reaction too when it dawned on me."

"Well, crap," Eric muttered. "We're flying through a massive gravity detection array...And we thought we were being sneaky."

"Well, sir, I expect it's actually used primarily to track any mass that might impact the plates."

"Not much comfort, not when we're facing down a small fleet at the end of this orbit." Eric sighed, shaking his head. "Maybe I should have turned and ran at the start. They would have had more time to overtake us, but they wouldn't have had time to gather a fleet, either."

"Doesn't matter now, sir." Roberts shrugged. "What matters is...How do we handle things?"

"If they're tracking us by gravity, they can't know who we are," Eric said. "They know what we mass, but without a profile to compare it to, they can't possibly know anything more about us than that."

"I'm not sure what that gives us," Roberts admitted after a moment's thought.

"If they know we're a ship, they have to be assuming that we're a Priminae vessel," Eric said. "That means they'll have developed their response protocols according to Priminae ships. Think about it, even if they've heard about the *Odyssey* already...They can't be expecting us here."

"Priminae vessels are faster, better armed, and generally all around more powerful than us, sir. The fact that they're expecting a Prim isn't making me feel any better," Roberts told him dryly.

"Tell that to the Drasin ships we've splashed in our last three encounters." Eric smiled nastily. "If they're expecting a single Priminae vessel, we'll tear them a whole bunch of new ones before they take us out."

"That still leaves us as expanding gasses inside this god-damned sphere, sir."

"I know that, Commander," Eric said, "which is why that's my GOTH plan."

"Thanks for letting me in on that, sir, but I'd really like to hear Plan A now, if you don't mind."

Eric smiled. "Here's what we're going to do..."

He leaned forward, and the two started to chart out the *Odyssey*'s strategy for the contact coming in just a few hours.

At least they had time to plan. For that, he was grateful.

RANQUIL, TERRAN COMMAND AND CONTROL BUNKER

▼

▲

▶ LIEUTENANT SAVOY WAS on the line to Reed, and Reed could almost hear the impatient tapping of his foot as he spoke.

"Sir, where's the Primmy bird?" He sounded annoyed. "My team is sitting here on a pile of demo that we'd like to get to where we can put it to use."

"What?" Colonel Reed said, surprised. "You should have been in the air five minutes ago."

"We're as grounded as Commander Stevens after he's annoyed the captain one too many times in a day," Savoy responded. "Check with the Prims, sir, 'cause we're going nowhere fast."

"Roger that. Hold tight."

"Nothing else we can do here."

Colonel Reed signed off and turned to the liaison officer. "Ithan, where is the shuttle I asked to pick up Lieutenant Savoy and his team?"

"It should have arrived," she said, looking genuinely confused.

"It hasn't."

"I will check."

Reed didn't take the curt manner personally, nor did he worry overly about the way the liaison seemed to dismiss him. Keeping his cool was a prerequisite in his career choice; as a Green Beret trainer, you didn't often get to work with the most polite folks around, so a thick skin was not just a good thing, it was a requirement.

When Milla came back, however, his patience was sorely tested.

"All shuttles are in use," she told him, clearly nervous as she tried to avoid looking directly at him.

Through it all, however, Reed kept his cool and even managed not to yell, scream, or snarl at the woman.

"We need those men in the air ASAP," he said calmly.

"Ay sap?"

All right, now I'm starting to lose my patience. "As soon as possible."

"I was told that the shuttle will be redirected as soon as it is available," she offered, clearly knowing that her words weren't going to be taken well.

"Damn it, woman!" Reed growled. "If we don't get that demo team into place thirty minutes ago, my men and yours are going to be in a world of pain, son."

Now she just stared blankly, clearly confused by the statement.

Reed just continued to railroad over the befuddled woman. There was, after all, a time and place for cultural sensitivity, but the morning before Armageddon wasn't either.

"What I'm saying is shake one of those birds loose *now.*" He leaned in to the liaison, practically snarling at her.

"I am sorry, Colonel, but there are none free," she said, grimacing.

"You had nothing *but* free birds just ten minutes ago!"

"A priority request came directly from Commander Nero, Colonel."

Reed pushed his hair back, letting out a sigh of exasperation. "Can you please inform him that we have urgent need of an orbiter, immediately."

"I already did so," Milla told him.

"And…?"

"And he said that the orbiters would be free soon."

"How soon?"

She shrugged helplessly, hands spreading uncertainly. "He said soon."

Reed fell back to his "professional" demeanor as best he could. It was obvious that he wasn't going to get any further through intimidation. He'd seen it before, but almost never in any place he was sent to train men. Normally, this sort of bureaucratic bullshit was something he only saw in developed nations like the United States.

Usually, a country without a strong military would have had its politicians strung up by their entrails long before they managed to create quite this much red tape.

BRAVO AO

▶ "WHAT DO YOU *mean* the demo team has been delayed?" Bermont snarled as he pressed back into some cover, plasma bursts sizzling overhead. Fighting in the Priminae city was touchy at best, but things were rapidly getting out of hand. "Things are getting a little hot down here, sir!"

The colonel's announcement wasn't sitting well with the teams on the ground, unsurprisingly. Bermont was the one howling over the comms, but the rest of the teams knew what it meant just as well as he did.

The enemy they were dealing with was like nothing any of them had ever imagined. It had gone from a relatively low number, possibly as little as one, to what seemed an endless flood in just a few short hours. Bermont's troops were just grunts for the most part, but none of them were particularly stupid. They knew that, without the fallen buildings cleared out of the road, all they could do was fight off the enemy's disposable forces until eventually they were eliminated by the effect of attrition alone.

The Drasin were unreal—impossible, even. They knew there was no way that more than a small handful of viable enemies could have possibly been intact after an impact of the nature they'd seen. Yet they'd already killed dozens of the dog-sized drone soldiers, and overwatch heat sensors were showing dozens more while the planted seismographic gear was showing rumblings of potentially hundreds more under the ground on which they stood. The last time he'd encountered them, the Drasin had engaged with armored units the size of large animals. Horses, maybe; elephants, more realistically. Bermont wondered if this time they were specifically limiting their size so as to increase their reproduction rate.

In the end, it hardly mattered in the short term. If he lived, he'd ask the question and hope someone from the geek squads could answer it. For the moment, however, he had bigger concerns.

"Listen, sir, we're being overrun!" Bermont growled, emerging from cover to put another burst downrange. He didn't bother to aim, his computer was tied into the overwatch system, and the smart rounds would handle the rest, which limited his exposure to enemy fire. "We nail a couple dozen of them for every one of us taken out of the fight, but they're still *winning*!"

"How is that possible, Lieutenant? They can't have those kinds of forces on-site, they just can't," Colonel Reed responded.

"You've read the reports, Colonel. They make more of themselves out of locally available materials."

"Do you have any idea how much sheer energy it must take to create that many enemy drones this fast?"

"Well, maybe that's why they're only dog-sized this time around, sir. I don't know, talk to the eggheads about it, but do it later, sir!" Bermont countered. "We need Savoy and his engineers!"

"I'm breaking one of our own birds loose," Reed told him. "It'll take a little time. Hold the line."

"The line isn't the problem, sir. I'm worried about the big hole they're digging under our feet. Seismo is off the charts!"

"Copy that, Bravo. I'll expedite."

"You do that, sir," Bermont muttered. "We'll be right here...until we're not. Bravo out."

He killed the live comm, swapping back to the team tacnet. Bermont took a breath, getting a little control over himself. "All right. Boss man is shaking loose one of our birds to bring Savoy's team up here, but we have to hold until they get here."

"Lieutenant, from what I'm reading, we're in serious danger of having the ground collapse right under us," Corporal Matthews spoke up. "I'm getting warnings that match the signature of a sinkhole, sir."

Crap. Bermont slumped. "All right, Matt. How long do we have?"

"No way to tell, sir."

"Gamma Actual, Bravo Actual," he signaled.

"Go for Gamma," Lieutenant Crowley came back.

"We need to fall back. The ground is not...I say again, *not* stable."

"Roger that. Call the play."

"Fall back to Zulu-Zulu-Sierra," Bermont ordered. "We'll regroup there and wait for the demo team."

"Confirmed. Gamma is falling back."

"Bravo as well," Bermont said, swapping to the team channel. "All right, pull back by the numbers. We're falling back to Zulu-Zulu-Sierra."

The team acknowledged, and they broke from their position by squads, falling back while covering one another. In pairs, they dropped out of the firefight, giving ground as they fell back under fire. The exchanged bursts of plasma, and explosive rounds split the air around them, so they kept low to the ground and as much behind cover as possible while covering each other's movements.

"They're rallying!"

"Where the hell are they coming from? We've spread dozens of them across the whole area! They can't possibly have many more!"

"Can the chatter!" Bermont cut in, shutting the group down. "I don't know where they got the numbers, either, but right now, I don't care! Just take them out!"

"We're trying, LT! But they just keep coming! Where's the demo squad?"

"They're delayed," Bermont growled, feeling like the whole conversation had an air of déjà vu in it.

"Delayed? Why? By what?"

"If I knew that, Matt, I'd tell the colonel to shoot whoever delayed them and they wouldn't be delayed any longer. Now, shut up and fight, damn you!" Bermont snarled, opening the local channel to Gamma Team. "Crowley, how are you holding up?"

About fifty meters away, Jackson Crowley was the sole member of his squad standing in the open. One problem with the EXO-12 unit, he was now noticing, was that it made taking cover somewhat more difficult, given the fact that it was just over twelve *feet* high. Thankfully, the armor itself was commensurately tougher, so the plasma bolts off the smaller dog-sized enemy did only a little worse than scorch the surface.

The vibration dampeners in the suit were getting a solid workout; he hadn't let up on the tri-barrel in so long he was actually starting to worry about munitions. By comparison, the steady *tick-tick-tick* of the laser's capacitor discharging was completely lost in the chaos of the situation.

"We have casualties over here, Bravo," he answered Bermont's call when he had a moment. "But the fire is too thick to risk evac. Any word on reinforcements?"

"Negative. They're 'delayed.' Unknown cause."

Crowley just grunted in response. Honestly, he wanted to whine about where the backup units were, but he just didn't have the time. Unlike simulations, he had men bleeding around him, and they weren't going to be able to fall back any farther.

"This far," he said on the open tactical net. "No farther."

"Sir?"

"Hold line!" he ordered, stepping forward. "We can't fall back with our wounded, we can't medevac them in this mess, and we sure as *hell* can't leave them behind. This far! No farther!"

A short distance away, Bermont rallied his squad. "You heard Gamma, boys. They're pinned down worse than we are. So here's what we're going to do. Let's plot a breakout. We'll punch through the north flank and circle down to Gamma's location and hook up with them. That's where we'll make our stand. Got it?"

The men acknowledged, most of them now too simultaneously tired and hyped up to do more than ping the "acknowleged" icon on their HUD.

Bermont slung his rifle and pulled a matched set of grenades from his kit, keying both to his armor computer before chucking them underhanded toward the north flack of the Drasin offensive.

The twin thunderous explosions were the signal the team needed; they broke cover with rifles chattering. The normal sonic booms of the weapons were completely lost in the general melee. Bermont took up the rear as he shoved one of his men along when things were going a little too slow.

His rifle locked on an empty chamber, but he'd been expecting as much, and so he just slung it back and pulled his sidearm in the same motion. The standard-issue hand cannon didn't have the power the 112 rifle had, but it was respectable enough in the close quarters of the debris-strewn battlefield they were fighting in.

"LT!"

"What is, Matt?" Bermont growled, his pistol barking twice.

"You have a location on any of the militia types?"

That stumped him briefly. The last time he'd see one of them had been a while back. "Come to think of it..."

"I don't see any on my HUD, either. Where the hell did they get to? Did they bug out on us?"

That didn't make sense to Bermont. The guys he'd worked with seemed good enough sorts as a rule. Granted, he was almost as happy that they weren't around, as he would be able to have a few extra guns, but that was because they weren't trained in close quarters fighting like this and he didn't feel like being shot in the back by a gravity-propelled diamond. More to the point, they knew the stakes here as well as he did, so while some of them might have panicked and ran, he didn't buy it that they *all* had.

"Keep moving. We'll figure it out when we have some breathing room!" he decided finally.

"Right."

Navigating the fallen buildings and debris was oddly like playing an old-school video game from over a century earlier. They could see themselves on the overwatch network, moving through the mazelike mass of fallen debris, with red glaring hotspots showing the enemy units that were moving to cut them off.

All we need is a powerup so we can munch those bastards' ghosts before they munch us.

"Bravo, Bravo, Gamma."

"Go for Bravo, Gamma," Bermont said quietly as the team weaved through the debris.

"I see you coming in from our south flank, confirm."

"Confirmed, Gamma."

"Intend to hook up?"

"Like prom night, Gamma."

"Roger that. I spent mine at home studying."

Bermont rolled his eyes. "Somehow that doesn't surprise me, Crowley."

"Yeah, yeah, and yet I'm the guy driving a tank and you're not. Who wins?" Crowley told him wryly. "We're adjusting our flank. Take up the slack on the south and east."

"Roger that, Gamma. Wilco." Bermont chuckled. "We're light on munitions. Call for resupply?"

"Can do. Secure the perimeter. We'll have some bullets and bombs dropped."

"Just make sure they drop each on the right targets, Gamma."

"Yeah, sure. Which is which again?"

"Smartass," Bermont growled, dropping back to the team comm. "All right, we're taking up the slack in Gamma's south and east flank. Move into positions and secure the perimeter while we call for resupply."

The team acknowledged the order and spread into position as they arrived at Gamma Team's perimeter.

"Control, Bravo Actual," Bermont signaled.

"Go for Control, Bravo."

"Bravo has hooked up with Gamma, established new perimeter. Request resupply, ASAP."

"Roger Bravo. Medevac possible?"

"Negative. Fire is too thick."

"Roger. Resupply dispatched."

"Thanks, Command. Any word on the demo team?" he asked as hopefully as he looked about it. The battlefield was getting a bit messy, and he would be really quite grateful for anyone who could clear the way. *Nothing quite clears the way like high explosives.*

"We shook a shuttle loose. Demo will be on-site in ten minutes."

"About time, thanks. One thing, Command…" Bermont hesitated for a moment.

"What is it, Bravo?"

"We're missing our militia."

"Excuse me? Say again."

"Bravo and Gamma both lost track of local militia, Command."

"KIA?"

"Negative, or no sign of that on overwatch, but we don't have time to backtrack, either. Suggest you look into it."

"Right. Wilco. Hold the line, we'll get you some backup ASAP, Bravo."

"Roger. Wilco," Bermont signed off the command channel and returned his focus to the fight at hand.

Something was wrong—well, something beyond the obvious, that was—he could feel it. The militia guys wouldn't have run out, not all of them, that was for certain. They knew the risks here, what was at stake. Some of them might have panicked, but Bermont didn't believe for an instant that they all would.

So where the hell are they?

COMMAND AND CONTROL BUNKER

▶ "WHERE THE HELL are they?" Colonel Reed demanded, glaring openly at the overwatch maps that were playing out on the secondary repeater displays.

When Bermont had tipped him to the absence of the militia in their area, he'd immediately set his gear to back-tracking the battle. The overwatch system maintained a complete recording of everything it saw, tracking anything moving inside the battlespace and correlating it with IFF signals to keep track of soldiers and engagements. This time they were able to track the militia as well, since while they didn't have IFF transponders, they did exhibit human heat signatures and the enemy didn't.

That made a digital search easy enough; tracking the movements of any non-IFF human was an easy tag to run through the system. What he found was that they'd been separated early on, likely due to the capability and mobility of the armored units, then at some point were clearly ordered to withdraw from the area.

What the hell is going on here? Reed scowled, turning from his screens to head over to where his liaison was standing.

"Ithan Chans, what's going on?"

She frowned at him, puzzled. "Excuse me?"

"I know something is up. All your orbiters go missing, and now the militia in the active AO vanish?" He glowered. "Don't take me for a fool, Milla. I know your military is up to something, and I don't like being kept in the dark. I have men in the middle of this. What the hell is going on?"

As a member of the Special Forces, and as an SF trainer, specifically, Reed knew how to read people. He had to cultivate this talent. It was a necessity born of literal life-and-death crucibles, particularly when an "ally" was lying to him. Usually that happened right before someone tried to put a bullet in his back, often the very same ally.

Ithan Chans, however, was pretty easy to read, and she was mostly just as confused as he was. She seemed genuinely puzzled by the situation, which gave him some hope that there wasn't another aide waiting in the wings to put a bullet in the back of his head.

Unless she just doesn't understand a word I'm saying because this damned translation software is screwing up again.

"Look," he sighed, softening his tone, "call your command and control, find out what the hell is going on. We've got a major problem here, and we really need to communicate better, or we're all going to lose."

She nodded jerkily. "Yes. I understand. I will call."

"Thank you."

BRAVO AO

▶ "THIS SUCKS, LT!"

Jackson couldn't agree more, but he didn't have time to say anything about it. His tri-barrel was dry, now parked back in its clamps since there were few things in the world more useless than an empty gun. The ticking sound of the laser capacitors firing, inaudible to him within the armored shell of the EXO-12, was counting down the depletion of his reactor pile as well.

When that went, he'd be locked down and able to move only on battery power, which wouldn't last long enough to get him very far with the Drasin soldier drones crawling all over his back.

"Just grab some bullets from the resupply crates and get back on the line, Davis," he ordered. "We've got five minutes before the demo team arrives, and then the real work kicks off."

"How much longer can that tin can of yours fight, Boss?" PFC Davis asked. "'Cause my armor is under 20 percent."

"Powerpacks are in the crates, too, so stop asking questions and move!"

"Should I grab you one?"

"Not compatible, Davis. Just get," he snapped, waving with his free hand in a manner that looked frighteningly natural on the immense robot form.

The EXO-12 used a fission pile. What he needed was a half hour of downtime to recharge his capacitors to full strength, but he wasn't going to get that anytime soon. Once his men and those of Bravo Team were restocked, however, Jackson would reload his tri-barrel ammo from the resupply and at least be able to cut back on laser expenditures. The power-intensive beam weapon was currently the highest-single draw on his power system, taking more than 80 percent of his total power alone.

It wouldn't make any difference, however, if they didn't find a way to shift the tide of battle soon. The long game played out in the Drasin's favor, no matter how he cut the cards. The absolutely impossible way they reproduced meant that letting up on them for even an hour was probably fatal.

We really need to figure out how the hell they do this, because it's like nothing I've ever seen before. He'd spent most of his military career around various top-secret projects, working with things that made bleeding-edge technology seem quaint by times, but none of that had prepared him for anything resembling this. If it weren't happening, he would have sworn that their reproduction speed alone violated the laws of thermodynamics—or at least common decency.

The only thing that came to mind when he looked for something to compare it to was the old "gray goo" scenario from the early days of nanotech. Obviously, these things weren't nano-sized—and Crowley paused for a moment to thank the fates for that—but that was what they most resembled.

Come to think of it, he thought as he opened fire again with his laser, *why* aren't *they nano-sized? Wouldn't that be a more cost-effective payload?*

Of course, if they had actually evolved like this, he supposed that might account for it. Crowley really didn't want to see the kind of environment that would cause a species to naturally select for *this* insanity, though.

"We're locked, LT!"

"Take up the slack while I reload," he ordered.

"Roger. Wilco."

Crowley fell back from the point he'd been holding, finally able to let up on the laser discharges, and stomped over to the resupply crate and pulled a one-meter-long box magazine from it. He ejected the spent mag, the heavy metal case hitting the ground with a thud that registered on the local seismographs, then reached up over his armor's helm piece so she could drop it into place and drive it home.

As his weapon cycled the rounds into place, he watched the computer display shift from red to yellow as it checked the munitions supply. When it finally flashed green, Crowley pulled the tri-barrel forward again and flipped the safety cap up to start the weapon spinning.

He turned and stomped back to the line. "How's it looking?"

"I don't know."

Jackson frowned. "Pardon?"

It was then that he looked around and realized that the entire line was quiet, suddenly, causing him to widen his scan to the entire overwatch network. The fighting had dropped off across the entire line. "What the hell is going on?"

"Worry later!" Bermont cut into the line. "Evac the wounded now while we can!"

Crowley shook himself, then instantly nodded. "Right! Gather the wounded in the center of the perimeter. Command! Send every medevac drone available. We have a lull in the fighting!"

"Roger, medevac units dropping in."

Overhead, the circling drones stopped circling, dropping out of the sky like stones as they zeroed in on the center of the perimeter. When they landed, the squad members not on the line of fire scrambled, hooking up as many people as they could, as fast as possible. The whole operation took only seconds before the drones started lifting off again, with men draped below them.

"Wounded clear!"

"Good timing," Bermont growled. "Seismo readings are getting weird here."

"Define *weird?*" Crowley asked, toggling into the seismo readings.

"They went quiet a couple minutes ago. Now I'm seeing movement—a lot of movement." Bermont said. "Command, Bravo Actual."

"Go for Command, Bravo."

"ETA on shuttle with demo team?"

"Three minutes."

"Not enough time. Request priority dust off. I say again, request priority dust off," Bermont snapped out fast, calm, yet with an undercurrent of the tension that was growing.

"Roger, dust off dispatched. What is the situation?"

"I think we're about to be overrun."

"Understood. Time frame?"

"Imminent."

"Understood. Hold tight, we're coming."

"Roger," Bermont said, eyes on the seismographic signals. "Be aware, I think everything to this point was just to keep us busy."

"Understood. We're watching the seismographic readings now. Concur with your assessment. Advise you withdraw immediately."

Bermont checked the topography of the area, considering withdrawal routes. "Crowley, how well can that thing of yours navigate this mess?"

"Almost as effectively as your armor," Jackson responded. "I can hang, Sean."

"Understood," Bermont said, already mapping out an egress path. "We're hauling ass in thirty seconds, people! Check your HUDs for new waypoint data!"

They fell back from the fixed positions, grabbing more ammo and gear from the resupply crate. They loaded up what they could carry, then left the rest as they jumped clear of the perimeter and began a fast egress from the area.

"Command, Bravo Actual."

"Roger, Bravo, go for Command."

"Bravo and Gamma Teams are withdrawing from AO now."

"Roger that."

The men jumped clear by teams, with Crowley taking up the rear. He kept the seismographic sensors on his HUD, and his eyes widened as the teams were almost clear.

"Move! Move! Move!" he ordered, jumping straight up as the ground under his feet began to explode in pockets of dust and debris.

Jackson swung his tri-barrel downward, spinning the weapon up as he fired his jump thrusters. A ripping sound filled the air as he fired off a long burst, tearing into the drones as they burst through the ground. His thrusters carried him to the top of a debris field just west of the teams' retreat path, and he landed on the precarious perch in a low crouch with the armor's free hand holding tightly to the debris as a stabilizer while he fired off another long burst.

"Is everyone clear?" he called, still firing.

"All accounted for. Good call, Crowley," Bermont replied from ahead. "They must have noticed us pulling out."

"I'll cover your withdrawal," Crowley announced. "I'm in a good position—have 90 percent ammo on my tri-barrel and my reactor is slowly recovering from red status."

"Are you sure it'll hold?"

"As long as I don't waste power on the laser," he said, "I should be good."

"All right, roger that. Don't get dead."

"That's high on my list of priorities. Just get my team clear."

"You got it."

Jackson shifted the position of his armor, using the computer to stabilize his aim while he continued to fire into the Drasin that had dug out the teams' previous position. He still couldn't believe how many of the damned things had grown out of a single impact sight.

This is like some kind of nightmare! He wondered at the sheer number, still unable to wrap his mind around the situation he found himself in. He was still firing and boggling when the seismograph display blinked urgently, turning red in the corner of his HUD.

Crowley was about to shift over to it when he heard a loud groaning noise actually drown out the sound of combat. He froze for a second, then kicked off again on instinct. Thrusters flared as he hung over the battle space, the groaning sound growing louder until an earsplitting crack filled the air and the ground below him began to shift slowly as it fell into a sinkhole.

"Holy…" he swore, angling his thrust to carry him to the edge. "I hope you guys are getting clear!"

"Not fast enough!" Bermont came back. "We're trying to outrun an earthquake, here!"

"Damn!"

"Couldn't agree more," Bermont called, "and we're about to be too busy to talk. Good luck, Crowley."

Jackson looked for a place he could safely land, but beneath him, the entire section of the city was coming apart. He vectored for a partially stable-looking section of a building, and dropped.

▶▶▶

Forty odd meters away, Bermont was leading the remnants of the two teams as they scrambled up a rapidly steepening incline. The shattered buildings around them were crumbling further as they abandoned their rifles to their slings, leaving them to clatter against their backs as they were often reduced to scrambling on all fours as they tried to outrace the collapse.

Bermont keyed into the command channel, careful to not broadcast where the men could hear.

"Command, Bravo Actual."

"Go for Command."

"We're not making it out of here, Command. The collapse is going to beat us."

"Understood. Keep together. Hold on. We have shuttles inbound."

"Roger, Command," Bermont answered, knowing that if something didn't change soon, the shuttles wouldn't matter.

He didn't bother saying any more. Command now knew what they needed to, and he was going to need to conserve his breath. The ground was behaving in a distinctly un-ground-like way, tilting wildly as they kept trying to hop up the incline. Under them, the ground teetered wildly, causing the teams to throw themselves down and dig in where they could.

A man slipped, sliding wildly down, so Bermont just managed to snag his rifle as he slid by, swinging him around until they both wound up holding tightly to a shard of what used to be a building as the world went topsy-turvy.

"Hold on!" he yelled, hugging the only purchase he could as the ground began to slide below him.

They did just that, but each had his suit's imaging systems looking down in the direction they were sliding, where they could see the ground *crawling*.

"What the *fuck* are these things?" Corporal Matthews screamed as they began to slide down into the crawling pit.

"I *fucking* refuse to go out like this," Bermont snarled, palming one of his remaining grenades. "I will not be eaten by some bastard alien movie rip-off!"

He armed the grenade, and his HUD showed more prime, as others did the same. He knew they were thinking the same thing he was: it was one thing to die in a fight, but he wasn't going to let them turn his body and armor into more of those things.

They were tilting dangerously at over thirty degrees, the slab of concrete or ceramic or whatever it was they were on sliding its own. Sliding down, down into the pit that was crawling below them.

He closed his eyes, shutting out the HUD for a moment.

"Well, guys, it's been fun."

"Lying bastard," Matthews muttered, priming a couple of his own grenades.

"I only regret that we don't carry enough firepower to take these fuckers all to hell with us."

A few more grenades primed, all of them waited on signals from their controllers to detonate.

"This is gonna suck." Bermont sighed.

"Uh...LT..."

"What do you want, Matt?"

"You might want to look up."

Bermont opened his eyes and found himself staring at a quintet of Priminae orbiters hovering above them, and buildings were being pulled up into the air all around them. Bermont looked down and realized that they weren't sliding downward anymore; instead, they were moving up and away from the crawling mass below.

"All right, who prayed for the miracle?" he asked softly.

Three guys raised their hands.

"You're all promoted. Nice work."

"Bravo Actual, Command."

"Go for Bravo, Command."

"Stand by for extraction. We finally found out what the Priminae were doing with all their shuttles."

"Let me guess," Bermont muttered, "they were slapping tractor beams on them?"

"They call them 'excavation equipment,'" Colonel Reed replied, sounding a little peeved but a lot relieved by the turn of events. "How's the team?"

"All accounted for, save Crowley and his beast."

"I've got him on overwatch. He's hanging off the side of a building about thirty meters northwest of your position, eighty meters above you."

Bermont looked up and nodded. "Roger that. I see him, looks like one ugly Christmas decoration from here."

"You do know I'm copied into this channel, right?" Crowley asked tiredly.

"No, but I was hoping."

"All right, fun is fun, but you may want to grab some cover as soon as you can. Savoy's team is orbiting the AO now, and they're going to hit that pit with everything they've got just as soon the Priminae finish clearing the debris and give them a clear shot."

"Copy," Bermont said. "Better late than never, sir."

The slab continued to slide up and away until they were clear of the pit, and then Bermont caught the strike warning flash across their HUDs. High above them, Savoy's shuttle banked into an attack run, followed by four carnivore drones.

"Bruisers inbound," the pilot announced as the missiles launched.

An even dozen contrails roared into the ground, but before they even finished forming the hole, the world shook around them as the high-powered strikes tore through the ground and threw flames, smoke, and debris skyward.

Bermont and the others grabbed some cover until the sky finished falling, then crawled back out of their burrows.

"I can't believe we survived that," Bermont said, looking down at the grenade he was still holding.

The warning light flicked off his HUD as he deactivated it, and he glanced around the group that was standing by him. Other grenade lights dropped off as the others deactivated their explosives as well.

"So...uh," Matthews spoke up, "how do you suppose we tell this story?"

"I don't know about you"—Bermont shook his head as he began to trudge away from the battleground and toward the designated landing zone marked on his HUD—"but I'm not bragging to *anyone* that I was ready to blow my own ass up just so some dogs wouldn't get lunch."

NACS ODYSSEY

Interior, Uncharted Dyson Construct

▲

▶ "HERE THEY COME, Captain."

Eric nodded, taking a sip from his coffee mug as he considered the motion of the ships. The Drasin ships were—or rather, had—launched from the plate they had gathered at. The sight of twenty Drasin cruisers coming his way was in no way calculated to make him relax, but Eric didn't intend to show it. He could see by the plots that they were more than an hour from making contact at extreme engagement range, and there was really no sense in getting worked up just yet.

"What about the bogies?" he asked lightly.

"Bogeys One and Two have detached from the Dyson plate," Winger answered. "They do not appear to be accelerating at this time."

"Damn," Eric said softly. He'd been hoping to see them up a little closer, maybe get an idea of their capabilities while he had the chance.

He was fairly certain that these ships belonged to the fourth entities he'd been speculating on since he'd seen what the Drasin did to Port Feuilles and the other systems they'd torn to shreds. The Drasin didn't make sense to him as a species: everything from their "life cycle" to how very well they seemed to be adapted to taking on the Priminae just screamed "weapon" to him. The appearance of these bogies within a clearly Drasin-controlled area like this just confirmed it in his eyes.

What both intrigued and terrified him, however, was the profile and silhouettes they had gathered on the new entries into this little drama. They both seemed very familiar to Eric and his bridge crew, and that familiarity was something he had to get his ship out of here to report.

"All right, sound general quarters."

"Aye, sir," Roberts said. "General quarters!"

"Sounding general quarters!"

The alarms went off, calling the men and women of the *Odyssey* to their stations as the ship was rigged and prepared for war.

"Armor settings, sir?"

"Maintain full stealth. It's not time to let them know we see them coming just yet," Eric replied.

"Aye, sir. Full stealth."

They were still almost four light-minutes apart—highly unlikely that the enemy would open fire at that range—so he felt pretty confident that they could act fat and dumb for a little longer with minimal risk. With twenty Drasin ships, however, he knew that the *Odyssey* wasn't getting out of this one with armor modifications and guns blazing.

Since each ship almost certainly had a different laser frequency, all it would take would be for two or more of them to bracket the *Odyssey* and it would be game over. Even the *Odyssey*'s best general armor setting wouldn't stand against a laser burst from one of the insanely overpowered laser mounts on the enemy ships.

No, this is one fight we can't win.

Unfortunately, almost all the aces were sitting squarely in the enemy's hands this time around. In fact, the only cards Eric was holding that he could play were the fact that the enemy really didn't know who they were tracking or that the *Odyssey* had realized that they were being watched.

"Movement on the bogies, Captain."

"Heading?"

"They're bringing up the rear of the enemy formation, but they're coming this way as well."

Eric smiled slowly. *Well now, I guess I get a close-up look at you guys, after all. Thank you for that.*

Two more ships didn't change the odds all that much, as far as he was concerned; the *Odyssey* was already so badly out-gunned it was almost ridiculous. What the new addition did do, in his eyes, was give them the chance to get a closer look at the bogies.

Eric licked his lips, now feeling a little nervous as he mentally began replotting his maneuvers. Getting intelligence was what had gotten them into this mess in the first place, but getting that same intel was possibly the most important thing any of them could ever do. The Drasin were beyond a threat to the Priminae, in his opinion; they were a menace to every living thing in the galaxy, as far as he was concerned. As was any species that had anything to do with them. There was simply no excuse to use the singular degree of force they employed, not against worlds that had no real way of resisting and certainly not as a standard operating procedure.

On Earth, the biggest weapon had always been nuclear. Long before the end of the twentieth century, in fact, Terran nations had built and emplaced more than enough nuclear weapons to annihilate all human life from the face of the planet several times over.

For all that, however, nuclear weapons had been used in combat precisely twice.

Originally, they had been used specifically to force an end to World War II. Since that time, nuclear weapons had been used exclusively as a threat, a method of preventing conflict—or at least preventing a certain scale of conflict. Strategic weapons were used to advance an overall strategy to win a war, as opposed to tactical weapons that were intended to win battles.

As violent and vicious as Terran wars were, Eric knew that people on Earth understood the difference between tactical and strategic weapons. The Drasin either employed—or in fact, *were*—strategic weapons, in his opinion. But they had deployed themselves *tactically*. The use of strategic weapons as a tactical option was the single-most insane thing Eric had ever seen, or ever hoped to see again. There were some things that just should not even be considered.

The very idea that there were people out here, in the black of the galaxy, who thought that way…It curdled his blood.

"Stand by the course," he ordered after a moment, flicking a switch to put him in contact with Engineering. "Chief, I'm going to be asking for full military power soon enough."

"Aye, sir," the chief replied. "We'll start spinning up the reactors. It'll be waiting when you call on it, Captain."

"I know it will, thank you." Eric cut the connection, then turned to where Waters was waiting. "Ensign, have the torpedo room start spinning up the tok. We're going to need them charged before this party kicks off."

"Aye, sir. They've been standing by," Waters said. "Tok is winding up now."

The ranges were closing faster now, and for Eric, it was now actually a pretty straightforward math problem.

Unfortunately, the enemy had stripped them of most of the bag of tricks in this situation. The *Odyssey* couldn't hide from them, her electronic warfare drones were worthless, so there were no fancy tricks waiting at the end of this ride. Since the enemy could track them through stealth, by their mass and its effect on space-time, the options available to them were positively archaic. Basically, their options boiled down to two: they could run, or they could fight.

Which really meant that they could run, since fighting was a dead end with capital DEAD.

With that in mind, Eric just had to figure out the best time to make their bolt, and in what direction to head when he did. When they dropped stealth and powered up the CM generators, the plus side was that the gravity array would lose track of them when the apparent mass of the *Odyssey* bled away. That would give them between two to three minutes in which they were effectively invisible—the time it took for the energy signature of the CM field to reach the closest sensors after their mass signature vanished.

Two, maybe three minutes for the rest of our lives. Eric knew that what he did with that window would decide if the *Odyssey* survived its second mission or if they died out in the middle of nowhere amid an engineering miracle.

"Stand by to the roll ship," he ordered, his eyes on the tracks.

"Aye, sir! Standing by," Daniels replied automatically.

"Make your heading niner-two-fiver-break-four-seven to the negative eighteen," he called out. "Engage new course on my mark."

"Aye, sir. New heading entered. Niner-two-fiver-break-four-seven, eighteen degrees downbubble," Daniels repeated. "Waiting final orders to engage."

"Ensign Waters, status on the pulse torpedoes?"

"All tubes armed, ready to fire."

"Stagger firing frequency to allow for a…half-degree-arc range at three light-minutes," he ordered.

"Aye, aye, Cap." Waters leaned in, tapping in a series of commands. "Firing frequency is being adapted now."

"Daniels, five seconds after we fire, I want you to bring the CM to full power and engage the new course. Don't spare the engines or the fuel."

"Understood, Captain." Daniels grinned a little. "We'll break records."

"I'm counting on it, Lieutenant."

Eric turned his attention back to the plot, watching the numbers fall with increasing speed. The enemy ships were accelerating, which meant that they were closer to the *Odyssey* than the numbers indicated, but he still had a little bit of lee-way in his calculations. Plus, if the enemy ships committed themselves to a pursuit vector now, they'd be caught all the more off balance when the *Odyssey* changed course.

He watched the projections, mentally adjusting for what he knew about the Drasin's capability.

They have a higher top end than the Odyssey, *but I've never seen them maneuver quite as sharply as we can. Let them commit, then we mess them up on the way out.*

He was reasonably certain that they could skirt the enemy ships. He couldn't avoid engaging them entirely, but it would be a passing engagement. Eric thought—no, he hoped—that they could keep the engagement short since any prolonged fight would favor the superior numbers of the enemy squadron.

We'll be showing them our flank for at least…twenty minutes. He shook his head. That was a long time to be dodging lasers, especially beams that could punch through the hull of the *Odyssey* with even a glancing strike. *Best reflection is useless, but we have one or two cards we can play.*

Eric took a deep breath and relaxed slowly into his seat. "All stations, go, no go, for maneuvering."

"Helm, go for maneuvering," Daniels answered immediately.

"Tactical, go…"

"Engineering, go."

"All stations, all departments, report go for maneuvering, Captain," Commander Roberts reported calmly, his tone merely serving to underscore the rising tension.

"Tactical," Eric said, "estimate for enemy squadron's location and fire all tubes."

"Aye, sir. Targeting estimated location…firing all tubes," Waters replied.

A full brace of pulse torpedoes erupted from the *Odyssey* in staggered launch, the extreme range of the shot making it necessary to stagger the launch so the charged-particle weapons wouldn't spread too much before they arrived on the far end of their track. After the last torpedo had left the *Odyssey*, Eric counted slowly to five.

He didn't have to say anything, as Daniels had apparently been counting as well.

"Coming about to new course, CM field forming up, engaging maximum thrust," Lieutenant Daniels said calmly as the deck of the *Odyssey* seemed to tilt under them.

The CM field was forming, but until it fully charged, they hung onto the edges of their seats as the big ship twisted in space and began to accelerate.

"Start a countdown clock for when the closest ship detects our CM field," Eric ordered.

"Aye, sir. Clock initiated."

All right, time to get lucky. If they didn't get suspicious and paint the *Odyssey* with a tacyon pulse, Eric knew that they now had a window—a window that was closing fast—but it might just be enough for them to slip past the dogs and make a run for open space. *We found what we came here to find, that and so damned much more. Now we just have to live to report back. Earth and the Priminae* need *this information. We will not fail now.*

"Velocity increasing," Daniels reported. "Engines coming up to flank speed."

"Understood," Eric replied. "Inform the engine room we're breaking records today."

"Aye, sir." Daniels smiled. "I'll let them know."

"Belay that." Eric shook his head. "I'll tell them myself."

He stood up. "Commander, you have the bridge. Call the relief watch and get everyone some food. We have time."

"Aye, sir." Roberts nodded. "I have the bridge until the relief arrives."

Weston nodded to the commander before striding off the bridge.

▶▶▶

"Chief of the deck?" Weston asked as he drifted through the engineering decks, gesturing for the crews to remain as they were.

"He's back with the reactors, sir," a man offered. "I'll go get him."

"Never mind, I'll head down there myself. Don't bother him." Eric shook his head. "His job is more important than mine right now."

"Uh…yes, sir…I mean, no, sir," the man stuttered. "I mean…"

Eric just kicked off and drifted past him. "I know what you mean, sailor. As you were."

"Yes, sir."

Eric glided along the rails, sticking to the safe areas that were marked off with yellow lines. He made his way to the reactor control rooms and stopped when he arrived just outside the control sector, waiting while the chief finished up what he was doing.

The man wrapped up what he was doing, triple-checking the reactor pile's temperature, then finally turned in Eric's direction.

"What brings you down to mechanic's country, Captain?"

"Had a few minutes, felt like slumming it, Sam." Weston smiled easily. He liked the slightly irascible yet generally easygoing chief who, unlike most on board, seemed to know that there was a time and place for protocol and a time and place to toss it out the airlock.

"Sure you did." Wilson chuckled. "Well, slum away, Cap."

Eric smiled. "Wanted to drop fair warning on you, Chief. We're going to be stress-testing your engines."

Wilson nodded. "Yeah, I guessed as much."

"Don't spare the fuel, OK, Chief? We're going to need to break records on this run," Eric said softly, shaking his head. "If you've got to fly this heap apart, fly it apart."

THE HEART OF MATTER • 587

"We do this, the *Odyssey* is spending the next six months at the commodore's base for complete refit, you know that, right?"

"Yeah, I know," Eric confirmed, "but we've got intel that has to get out, Chief. *Has* to get out."

Wilson nodded slowly. "I get you, sir. Me and my reactors won't be letting you down."

"Never thought you would," Eric said, "just wanted to give fair warning of what was coming."

"Fair enough," Wilson said. "Consider me warned, Cap. We're big boys down here. We've got our eyes wide open."

"Keep them that way, and open up the reactor some more while you're at it," Eric said as he drifted back from the control room. "We're going to need everything you've got down here."

"You want us to get out and push? There's one or two guys down here I could spare."

"I'll let you know if it comes to that." Eric grinned, tossing the chief an easy wave as he kicked off and began working his way back toward the front of the section. "As you were, Chief."

"We'll catch you on the other side, Cap," Wilson promised.

Eric nodded, then began pulling himself along as he headed back to the habitat decks.

Back in the habs, the corridors felt empty as he made his way to the cafeteria, though he knew that it was mostly just his imagination. After sending out all the shuttles and ground crews, along with the Archangels, Eric could have sworn the halls echoed a little deeper with his footsteps than when the ship's full complement was on board.

He would have felt better with the Angels aboard, considering the coming fight, but that was just more psychological nonsense. There wasn't a thing they could do in this one, not if he wanted to recover them when the fight was done. Even with CM, the Archangel airframe didn't have the delta-v to manage a fight and still catch up with the *Odyssey* at full burn.

No, it was better that they weren't on board. *At least if we don't make it out of here, we won't have taken everyone down with us.*

The men in line at the cafeteria made way for him as he walked up, and Eric nodded gratefully to them. Most times, he wouldn't cut in line, but he wanted to be back on the bridge before the relief watch was replaced, so he took a deep mug of coffee and snagged a slice of cake as he went by.

Eric liked to walk through the ship, particularly when tensions were bound to be raised. He remembered being stationed on the *Enterprise* during the war. Her captain of the day was an irascible old son of a bitch, but come hellfire or high water in the lower decks, he would always be found calmly wandering about the ship as if there were nothing wrong in the whole of the world.

The old man wasn't the sort Eric would ever emulate, except in that one area. He could still remember nervously waiting in the ready room, knowing his first air battle was coming, and seeing the old man walk by and stop to chat with the CAG like nothing remotely wrong was in the air.

It was the only thing he'd ever admired about the old man back in the day.

Since Eric had acquired more rank, well, he'd found a few other things he respected about the old man, but it was the effect he had when he took a walk that Eric remembered best. Sometimes seeing the old man of the ship meant more than all the speeches in the universe.

He stepped back onto the bridge while the relief watch was still there and nodded to the lieutenant commander standing watch, waving him off when he offered to hand command back over.

"As you were," Eric said. "I just want to do some quick calculations before things get fun."

The man nodded, returning to his post while Eric took a seat at his own station and checked the latest from the sensor feeds. The *Odyssey* course change had long since been detected, of course; there was no way they could hide their new direction, after all, but the enemy was precisely where he knew they would be. A few less than before they'd opened fire with the torpedoes, but right where he'd figured they would be.

There was no shock to that, however; plotting their response to his move was literally a no-brainer. If they hadn't been where he was expecting, he'd have been really shocked. Given their obvious intent to intercept the *Odyssey*, there was really only one thing they could do.

The math of space travel just didn't leave them any choice any more than it left the *Odyssey* room for any magnificent tricky maneuvers to flourish their way out of what was coming. From this point until they were actually engaged in combat, Eric knew that he could predict their every move almost to the second. Once they were joined in tactical maneuvers, of course, that certainty would fly out the window.

Eric was coding evasive protocols when Commander Roberts arrived back on the bridge and relieved the watch commander. Over the next few minutes, the rest of the first watch arrived and took over their stations, leaving them with the full watch back on duty with twenty minutes remaining to the opening shots of the initial engagement. Eric let them settle in before he spoke again, knowing that there was no hurry at all.

Finally, with ten minutes to extreme laser engagement range, he gave his first order of the coming battle.

"Sound general quarters," he said, "and bring us to battle stations, Commander."

"Aye, Captain. Battle stations, aye!"

The alarms sounded through the ship, really just making official what everyone on board already knew. The crew was already suited up for the most part, so in the outer sections of the ship, all that happened was men and women racking their helmets shut and connecting to shipboard air.

With the range closing, Eric kept the *Odyssey* on a steady course. The benefits of playing games with their maneuvering path now would be countered by the effect it would have on their escape velocity.

There's a time to be fancy and a time to just run like hell.

"Lead element is entering extreme laser range, Captain."

"Steady on."

"Aye, sir. Steady on."

As he'd proven in the past, Eric knew that timing was the key to space combat. At planetary distances, even light was a tad sluggish, and there simply were *no* weapons that moved faster than light—not within the gravity effect of a star or large planet, at least. So knowing that it was possible for the enemy to have already fired on him really only meant that Eric had to adjust his course sometime in the next twenty or thirty seconds.

He had time to consider his actions, time to plot a little, even time to pray if he wanted to.

Ten seconds later, Eric nodded. "Adjust course to evasive alpha, on your board."

"Aye, sir. Evasive alpha entered."

"Go ahead and engage."

"Course engaged."

The *Odyssey* used a drive system that allowed for thrust vectoring, a system originally designed for fighter jets over a century earlier. The design allowed it to redirect the direction of the main engines' thrust as part of the maneuvering system, allowing for better control during high-velocity maneuvering.

It wasn't a system Eric used often. Mostly, the *Odyssey* was an arrow he pointed in a direction before letting the string loose. Courses were normally calculated to take advantage of gravitational wells along the trajectory plot, running mostly ballistic courses for least time and best fuel consumption.

The designers, however, had included the much less efficient but higher performance vectored thrust system into the *Odyssey*'s design. So when the preprogrammed evasion course was entered into the shipboard computers, massive "turkey feather" deflectors were swung into place over the engine exhaust to push the high-velocity particles aside.

The *Odyssey* twisted in space, its path veering into a corkscrew pattern with about a radius of three light-seconds.

Eric doubled-checked the course, satisfying himself that they were still accelerating along their previous course with almost 93 percent of the power being aimed in the direction he needed. The remaining 7 percent was now dedicated to making the *Odyssey* devilishly hard to hit at the current range.

It didn't take long for one of their pursuers to take a shot at beating those odds, however.

"Coronal burn off a laser, Captain!"

"Analyze and adapt our armor to match."

"Aye, sir."

Adapting the armor to one ship out of twenty was hardly a great advantage, but 5 percent was better than nothing, he supposed.

*Actually, a bit better than 5 percent…*Eric noted calmly. *There are only eight enemy ships in range.*

He smiled and chuckled loud enough to garner surprised and confused looks from the others on the bridge, amused by his own thoughts.

Only eight. As if that really mattered.

Luckily, no one knew how sarcastic his inner thoughts were; they just saw the captain laughing almost literally in the face of death. Eric decided that it was better that they not know that much, at least not until they'd made it clear of the current mousetrap.

"Enemy ships still closing," Winger said quietly into the silence.

"Maintain current evasion course."

"Aye, sir," Waters said. "Maintaining course."

With the ranges still closing, the *Odyssey* continued to twist through its corkscrew path in space. They were in the closing phase of the engagement, and would be for almost twenty minutes before the *Odyssey* would begin to draw clear. Eric knew that the worst of it would be when the *Odyssey* was pulling away, not while they were closing.

Once the *Odyssey* was showing its tail to the enemy, they'd lose more and more of their maneuvering depth. Every time they dodged, they would be moving *away* from their goal, wasting velocity and distance, while their enemy gained on them. That was when they were at their worst disadvantage, and that was coming from a ship looking at the wrong side of twenty-one odds.

We have no chase armaments. They're going to rip the ever-living holy hell out of us before we can pull clear.

Eric frowned, then reached for the comm panel and flipped a switch.

"Flight Deck, here."

"Weston, here. I have a task for you."

"Sir, we don't have any birds left. You know that, you ordered them off."

"I need something else this time," Eric said. "Listen very carefully."

"Yes, sir."

A few minutes later, on the flight deck, there was only a skeleton crew left; most of the men and women normally assigned there had been sent off with the shuttles back in Ranquil. Those who remained, however, were in a flurry of motion as they raced to fill the captain's orders, just glad for the most part to have something to do that would contribute to the coming fight.

Eric, on the bridge, was just starting to relax a little as his plan began to firm up in his mind.

Then the universe exploded, the ship bucking like none of them had every felt before, throwing Eric hard into the side of his console and dropping several others to the ground.

"Laser strike!" Roberts called from where he was manning the damage control station. "Forward stations, lost contact with half the stations in the bow!"

"What the hell was that?" Eric demanded as he gripped the other side of the chair. "I've never felt that kind of impact while the CM fields were fully powered!"

"The blast vaporized a chunk of our hull right at the edge of the field!" Roberts snapped back. "Blew out like a reactor jet!"

"Helm!"

"Adjusting course to return to previous heading!"

"Belay that!" Eric snarled. "Execute bravo maneuvering!"

"Aye, sir. Bravo maneuvering!"

"Winger, what do you have on your sensors?"

"We were bracketed, sir," she responded. "Eight laser strikes, all within coronal range of the *Odyssey*. That one was just the lucky hit, and it was only a glancing shot."

Eric swore under his breath, but nodded.

All right. They didn't predict our path; they just shotgunned the space they knew we'd be in and got lucky. I can work with that.

"Damage control teams are responding, Captain," Roberts announced. "Our primary laser array is out, however."

Shit.

"Can they get it back online?" Eric demanded.

"Unknown."

"Tell Corrin to ride their ass, Commander. If we can't get that laser back, we've lost a lot of our closing armament."

"That's not the end of it, sir."

Eric winced. "What else?"

"HVM control rooms are not responding," Roberts replied. "Teams have to cut through a lot of damage to see if anyone or anything survived."

"Goddamn it," Eric swore some more. "Tell them to hurry."

"Aye, sir."

Eric blew out an annoyed breath, but had to keep his mind in the game despite the damages to his ship. "Winger."

"Yes, sir?"

"Do you have coronal IDs on all eight lasers?"

"Uh…sir?"

"You heard me."

"No, sir, I can't separate them. Not soon, anyway," she replied, befuddled.

"That's fine. I want to adapt our armor to best deflection across those *combined* frequencies," he told her. "So compile the combined frequency from all eight coronal blooms and send that over to Waters."

"Sir"—Waters twisted around—"that won't be ideal for any given laser."

"Noted, Ensign," Eric told him. "I'll take best deflection across all the enemy lasers."

"Aye, Captain."

Winger nodded. "I'll get it done."

"Expedite, Lieutenant."

"Aye, sir."

The main screen still showed the plot as the *Odyssey* and the squadron of alien ships continued to close on the oblique angles. They had another four minutes before the closest pass, and already, Eric felt like he'd been personally shot in the gut after that last strike. He'd known that they were going to take some hits, there was no way to avoid that, but he had believed that they'd be able to get a lot deeper into their escape before the enemy landed the first blow.

It would only get worse from here.

The *Odyssey* was now twisting wildly, its arc tighter and faster. That would give it less time on any given firing arc from the enemy ships, but it also limited their range depth. Once the enemy got an idea of what their new pattern was, it would be easier to bracket the *Odyssey* despite the lesser exposure their current pattern would allow.

And they'll know our new pattern in maybe three more seconds, five if they're a little slow on the uptake, Eric thought sourly, not really thinking that the enemy was slow in any meaning of the word.

"Daniels, load up pattern Epsilon."

"Loading now, sir," Daniels replied as he tapped in the commands.

"Stand by to execute."

"Aye, sir. Standing by."

"Coronal blooms!" Winger announced. "Tracking our old course. We're well clear."

Eric nodded, having expected nothing else.

The lasers took several seconds to cross the space between the ships at this point, just as those ships were targeting areas of space where they *expected* the ship to be, given what they knew from even farther back. By changing his pattern after the strike, Eric had drastically changed the position his ship was in compared to where it would have been. The enemy couldn't adapt fast enough to catch him—not yet.

That would change quickly, though, as they hit their closest passing point. The *Odyssey* would be within two light-seconds of the enemy at the closest point, well within the effective range of a laser weapon the likes of which the Drasin fielded. At that range, there was a four-second delay between targeting data and laser strike. Four seconds was an almost insignificant delay for modern targeting computers. There was almost no pattern he could fly that would let him evade fire from eight ships at that range.

Eric turned to Roberts. "I need a status report on the HVM and pulse torpedo control rooms."

"Aye, sir." Roberts keyed into the damage control channels. "Corrin, we need those rooms open and operating."

▶ ▶ ▶

Rachel Corrin was in the mother of all bad moods when the commander's call came through. She and her team were crawling through the carbon-scored remains of what had once been an access corridor for the primary laser array.

"Commander, I'm standing in hard vacuum with a really *lovely* view of the inside of this extra-large beach ball we're flying through," she spoke sarcastically. "We've got about another five tons of shit to move before we can even access the control rooms."

"In two minutes, we're going to be crossing swords with eight very motivated bandits, Chief. It would be nice if we, you know, had a *sword* to swing when that happened."

"Goddamn it, Commander, there's no way!" she growled. "We're completely cut off from all the forward stations!"

"Get it done, Chief."

Corrin cut the channel and started swearing like the sailor she'd been her entire life, causing several of her crew to back off from her for fear of being caught in the splatter of her ire. Finally, after wasting more than fifteen seconds, she sliced her hand through the vacuum she was standing in and called a halt to the work.

"What's going on, Chief?"

"We don't have time to clear this chaff. We need those rooms back online," she growled. "Captain needs the weapons."

"Chief, there might be no one alive to run anything up there…"

"We'll have to take that chance," she said. "Run the patch line. Get the computers connected to the rooms. We'll clear the chaff after."

"If you say so, Chief."

"I do."

HIGH OVER RANQUIL

▶ "ARCHANGEL ZERO ONE, drop to Angels ten to get eyes on the AO below you."

"Roger that," Stephanos said as he banked his fighter into a dive that quickly brought him down through the thickening atmosphere, curling into an easy orbit of the operational area marked on his HUD.

With the cessation of bombardment from orbit and beyond, there had been little more the Angels could do with the current load out, so he was glad of the task, as it was getting dull and very tiresome sitting around waiting for the world to blow up under him. At ten thousand feet, he dipped his right wing into a steeper bank and took a look down through the augmentation of his fighter's instruments.

He didn't technically have to bank the fighter, really—it just felt more natural to turn his head and look out through the canopy at the site rather than look down through the fuselage using his HUD. The computer automatically filled in what was there to be seen in either case, his way just felt cooler.

"Control, Zero One," he called a moment later.

"Go for Control."

He took another few seconds to examine the site from above before speaking. "Looks like Priminae shuttles have moved into the AO and are clearing away the debris. I'm seeing signs that there's still fighting going on. Check my telemetry for details."

"Roger. Thanks, Zero One," Control said. "We needed the overhead view. Our drones crapped out when the Priminae started blanketing the area with CM field generators."

Steph winced. *Well, that's not good.* "Roger that. Will remain on station," he said in return.

"Confirmed, Zero One. Stay at Angels ten," Control ordered. "We still don't know exactly why the drones went dead."

"Wilco."

No worries there, Steph thought grimly. He didn't want to dig his bird into the turf after the fighting was all but over.

"Be advised," Control came back, "reports from the ground indicate that Drasin resistance is falling off. We may have won this one."

"Good news, Control," Steph said, more than a little relieved. Hundreds of billions of civilians notwithstanding, he had no wish to die slowly in space while his air ran out just because the planet was gone and he had nowhere left to land. "Zero One out."

NACS *ODYSSEY*, UNCHARTED DYSON CONSTRUCT

▶ THE *ODYSSEY* SHIFTED course, angling slightly away from the pursuing ships. Eric knew that they had just pulled away from the enemy ships a little more, but in exchange, they'd also extended the time they'd be exposing their rear end to the enemy lasers. He would have preferred to close sharper and make them scramble to catch them when they blew past, but that would expose the *Odyssey* to fire from the entire squadron of ships instead of the eight currently close enough to be a threat.

"One minute to our closest pass!"

"Understood, Lieutenant. Commander!" Eric called.

"Chief Corrin," Roberts growled, "we're running out of time."

A few more seconds passed before Roberts looked up sharply. "Lines are patched to the control rooms, Ensign Waters. Are they showing on your screens?"

"I've got them!" the ensign called. "Hold one."

He tapped furiously on his controls, then spoke in his earpiece in quiet tones. Finally, Waters half turned and nodded.

"HVN and pulse torpedo rooms are both manned and online, sir," he said, then flushed. "However, the torpedoes are not charged. Containment was shot, so they flushed the system."

Eric winced, but nodded. As much as he wished to have the powerful pulse weapons on tap, it was better not to have them than to be missing the entire forward section of the *Odyssey*. "Understood. Have containment restored and charge the banks."

"Aye, Captain."

"HVM launchers are to stand by for target assignment," Eric went on. "We'll fire as we pass."

"Yes, sir. Launchers to stand by."

The range fell with increasing speed as they got closer and closer, the enemy ships already well into their pursuit arc so they wouldn't lose too much velocity on the *Odyssey* as she passed. That actually put them out just a little ahead of the *Odyssey*'s position as Captain Weston put the firing plan into action.

The *Odyssey* tipped its bow into the enemy position, still accelerating at full power, and on her captain's orders went to rapid-fire launch on all HVM banks. The second generation of the high-velocity missiles were a marked improvement over the first-gen devices used on the *Odyssey*'s initial mission, but the basic technology had been unchanged.

The hundred-kilogram weapons were essentially chunks of steel with a rocket motor, a CM generator, and a high-powered capacitor attached. They launched on magnetic rails from the *Odyssey*, then immediately went to full power on the CM field as they left the ship's influence. The rocket motors roared into action at the same time, accelerating the weapons to better than 0.8c in just seconds.

They flashed across the intervening space, almost as fast as a laser but infinitely more massive.

The enemy ships had only seconds to react, which wasn't enough for the closest ones. The HVM devices were already locked onto targets and had precoded terminal instructions, causing the second-generation weapons to do something no one on Earth had really considered a need to do in the past. They reversed the CM field just before impact, and one hundred kilos of mass became over ten thousand for a few thousandths of a second just as they slammed into their targets.

The resulting kinetic conversion annihilated three Drasin ships before the rest began firing back, lasers vaporizing the weapons before they could go terminal. Two more made it through the wall of light that attempted to defend the squadron, and two more Drasin ships vanished in a fury of energy that blinded everyone in range for several more seconds.

The *Odyssey* ceased fire when the first explosions effectively destroyed their targeting capability, twisting back onto their escape path, and now began to power away from the pursuit ships for the first time. Behind them, the remaining ships of the pursuing squadron emerged from the fires they'd just flown through, no hesitation evident in their pursuit, no break in their determination.

On board the *Odyssey*, Eric knew that now it was a race. They *Odyssey* had the velocity advantage—they'd been building delta-v all along—while the enemy squadron had initially been accelerating *into* the gravity well as they closed on the *Odyssey*. Now the *Odyssey*'s path would cause them to pull slowly away from the pursuing ships, but for all that, it wouldn't be a speedy or painless process.

Eric opened a channel to the flight deck. "Flight Deck, Bridge."

"Flight Deck, here, Captain. We're ready with the first two."

"Launch when ready."

"Aye, sir. Launching."

Winger was the first person on the bridge to notice. "Sir…
Two objects were just launched from the rear hangars."

"I know, Lieutenant. My orders."

"Uh…yes, sir."

"Helm, make our evasion pattern Lima Bravo."

"Lima Bravo, aye, sir."

Lima Bravo put the *Odyssey* into a skewed swerve, flattening her trajectory and presenting a tighter profile to the pursuing forces. Eric could see Roberts shooting him a confused
glance from where he was still handling damage control, but
didn't have time to fill in his second just then.

"Holy!" Winger swore. "Those two objects just exploded
behind us, sir."

"Helm, straight-line max acceleration!" he ordered. "Run
for the border, Daniels!"

"Aye, sir!"

The *Odyssey* stopped its dodging, putting its full power
into escaping the pursuers and the star that lay behind
them.

"Laser bloom!" Winger called, sounding surprised.
"Directly astern, Captain."

Roberts chuckled, shaking his head. "Chaff, sir?"

"Got it in one, Commander."

"Nice." Roberts nodded in appreciation.

Eric considered the benefit to be derived from the tactic, figuring that he may have another ten seconds of defense
from the field of chaff he'd arranged for the flight crews to
scatter behind them. It was an expensive loss of a drone, but it
was the only way to steer the debris into place before blowing
it across their path.

The chaff itself consisted of laser reflective foam, foil, scrap metal—basically whatever the crews could cram into and onto a carnivore drone. Detonated in the *Odyssey*'s wake, it would create an ablative shield to absorb laser fire, at least for a short time. Given the power of the enemy weapons, Eric had little doubt that the time would be very short, indeed, but he would take every second he could buy.

Even if it did cost him a multimillion-dollar drone.

Or two.

"Helm, change back to Epsilon pattern, Delta variation."

"Epsilon Delta, aye, sir."

The *Odyssey* once more skewed off course, corkscrewing into a wide pattern as pursuing ships caught up to the chaff field and burned through it.

Everything is timing.

Eric smiled at the thought, leaning forward almost eagerly. If it weren't for the fact that he'd already lost some of his crew, and would almost certainly lose more even if their escape were successful, he knew that he would be truly enjoying the game.

It was a classic ship-handling problem, from even before spaceflight. Evading a pursuing force while under fire, a particularly nasty variation given that he couldn't effectively fire back without sacrificing at least some of his acceleration in the process.

Chase guns. We need chase guns.

The problem was, of course, to outguess your enemy while they were, in turn, trying to outguess you. They needed to shoot where you would be, and you needed to avoid being where they were shooting. As the chase continued, the odds would slowly swing in favor of the pursued, since the time elapsed between a shot being fired and it arriving on target would slowly increase.

In fact, for a chase on this scale, it wasn't such a slow increase. It was almost exponential, in fact, given the fact that it took an equal amount of time to gain targeting data as it did for the weapon to traverse the distance, doubling the delay. Of course, that only held true as long as the enemy wasn't using FTL sensors, which Eric was frankly expecting anytime…

"Captain, we've been painted. Tacyon burst."

Like, say, now.

He sighed, but wasn't remotely surprised. It was as predictable as their course changes, something the enemy essentially *had* to do. Timing had been a bit of a question, but really only within a few seconds. As soon as the targeting delay became a significant factor, Eric knew they'd paint the *Odyssey*. There was no point being sneaky anymore; after all, it was pretty clear that both sides were pretty much in the open.

It did have one upside, though, Eric supposed as he looked through the new data they were getting from the tacyon sensors. The *Odyssey* now had a pretty good lock on the enemy, as well as a real-time view of the Dyson plates up ahead. Active pulses were like that—anyone with the gear to detect them would be able to use them.

He mentally adjusted a couple of his strategies now that he saw the real-time formation of the ships behind the *Odyssey*, but mostly it just confirmed what he'd already known.

This will be a long chase, Eric thought distastefully. *Or a very, very short one.*

"Status on pulse torpedoes."

"Tok is still charging. We'll have the banks charged in thirty minutes," Waters replied.

"HVM stores?"

"Moving munitions from the magazines to the firing tubes now, Captain. We can fire another round in three minutes."

"Thank you, Ensign," Eric said. "Helm…Eridani pattern."

"Eridani Prime, aye, Captain."

"Coronal bloom!" Winger called as the ship shuddered.

"Where did we take it?" Eric grimaced, reflecting that at least this time he hadn't been thrown around.

"Hold one, Captain. Data is unclear," Roberts said. "Aft section, certainly, but we're not showing any red lights."

That was surprising, given the power of the enemy weapons, Eric reflected. *Maybe the compromise adaptations to the armor did some good.*

"Sir, I'm showing some serious degradation in our maneuvering controls," Daniels spoke up warily.

Or maybe we just took the hits somewhere we don't have many sensors to report back. Eric grimaced. "Commander, get someone to eyeball the vectored thrust system."

"Aye, sir."

That took only a few moments to come back, and the news wasn't great.

"You called it, sir." Roberts sighed. "Burned up a quarter of the vectoring deflectors. No way to repair them while under way."

"Understand and concur," Eric said, mostly for the recorders to catch. "Lieutenant Daniels, you'll have to compensate for the loss with the maneuvering thrusters."

"Aye, sir. It won't be as fast."

"I am aware of that. Do what you can."

"Aye, aye."

The loss of the thrust vectoring assemblies, more commonly known as "turkey feathers," wasn't a significant loss to the top speed of the *Odyssey*, but it certainly had a massive impact on her high-speed maneuvering capabilities.

They could compensate with the maneuvering thrusters to a degree, but Eric knew that they had just lost a lot of their fluidity of motion. He ordered another pattern change and proceeded to hang on to his seat to try to look like he wasn't merely along for the ride.

The chase proceeded along those lines, settling into a routine that would have been boring if it hadn't been terrifying. The *Odyssey* ran and dodged while the pursuers chased and fired, generally missing as the range continued to open slowly and the light-speed delay continued to favor the *Odyssey* more and more.

The HVM banks were reloaded, but Eric didn't dare flip the ship to bring them to bear on the enemy, as he would lose precious minutes of acceleration while shooting back.

"Flight Deck to Bridge."

Eric flipped open the comm. "Go."

"We have two more birds loaded, Captain."

"Launch when ready."

"Aye, sir."

Eric called for a new evasion pattern while opening up a note program on his screens and adding the words *chaff launcher* to the list he was keeping there.

Granted, it wouldn't be incredibly useful in most situations, but when you had fire coming from a known vector, it would be a great comfort being able to put an additional defense between you and your attacker.

I hope that, next time, I compile a list of "suggestions" for the boys in the shipyards it isn't due to quite so pressing a set of circumstances, however.

"ETA to inner Dyson swarm?" he asked, looking up at the plot.

"We're eight light-seconds away, at current speed and acceleration"—Daniels glanced down briefly—"just over ten seconds."

Eric felt his blood chill. He honestly hadn't realized how fast they were going. The relatavisitic effects were going to play holy havoc with the *Odyssey*'s instrumentation, and he honestly didn't have the foggiest notion what they would do, if anything, to her crew.

He shook away the worry—he didn't have time for it—and looked over to the sensor station. "Lieutenant Winger, keep a close eye on the swarm. They may have had time to prepare a reception."

"Aye, sir. I've been keeping watch," she admitted, "but so far, nothing other than an attempt to shift the plate to block us. I passed that along to the helm."

"No problem avoiding it, sir," Daniels picked up the thread, "they can't move those things on a whim. The risks of collision are too high."

"Good. Once we're through the plates, maneuver to put them between us and our pursuers," Eric ordered, "if you can do it without slamming us into the outer swarm."

"Aye, sir."

The *Odyssey* exploded through the gap between the plates at better than 0.8c, well above her best-rated cruising speed and dangerously fast to be going in what was now a very crowded section of space. Daniels's precoded maneuvering set had them turning even before they cleared the thousand-kilometer-thick plates, angling both to put some defenses between them and the enemy and to hit the gaps in the outer swarm.

By the time the proximity and collision alarms were silenced, the *Odyssey* was already almost a full astronomical unit away from the inner swarm.

"God*damn* it, Lieutenant!" Eric swore. "How close was that?"

Daniels was sporting an ear-to-ear grin that seemed half adrenaline response and half rigor mortis. "No idea, sir."

"Winger?"

Eric looked over to where Michelle Winger was clutching at her console, pale as death itself, and suddenly wondered if he really wanted to know.

"I don't know."

Her whispered voice barely carried, but Eric heard her and was surprised.

"You don't know?" he asked. "How is that possible?"

"At that relative speed, my gear only has a resolution of one hundred meters square," she admitted, shaking. "All my instruments say that we *collided* with the plate, Captain."

Eric cringed, knowing that meant they had been well within the error margin of the sensing gear.

"Lieutenant Daniels," he said softly.

"Yes, sir?" Daniels hunched a little, ducking his head.

"I swear to god, son, you scratch the paint and it's coming out of your salary."

"Yes, sir."

Eric took a breath, glared at the back of his helmsman's head for a moment, and then returned to work.

"Stand by to flip the ship," he ordered.

Daniels stiffened in surprise, looking back in shock. "Sir? We don't have much maneuvering room. Less than one minute to the outer swarm."

"I know, let's clear some of our pursuers from our trail, though. Can you do it without crashing us, Lieutenant?"

"Aye, sir." He nodded seriously.

"Then stand by to do it," Eric repeated. "Waters, status on the pulse toropedoes?"

"Armed and standing by, Captain."

"Kill forward thrust," Eric ordered. "Bring our bow about."

"Aye, sir! Coming about!" Daniels echoed.

The *Odyssey*'s forward thrusters burned hard, bringing her bow around as she flashed through the space between the Dyson swarms. Eric kept one eye on the plot while calculating the targeting solution for the torpedoes. He finished it quickly and shot it over to where Waters was waiting.

"Fire as we bear, all tubes, full spread," Eric ordered.

"Aye, sir, all tubes, full spread. Firing as we bear," Waters called back.

The *Odyssey* swept about, her pulse tubes discharging in rapid-fire as they swept past the target vector, then continued around in a flat spin until they retrothrusted. The *Odyssey* swerved in the plot as its main engines roared back to life, then continued hell-bent for open space.

Behind the retreating ship, the antimatter-based pulse torpedoes flew cleanly away, their formation spreading as the charged-particle weapons repelled one another in flight. As the captain of the *Odyssey* had been known to say on occasion, timing was everything. The salvo of torpedoes roared into the target zone just as the lead element of the pursuing ships broke through the gap, none of them cutting the corner quite so close as the *Odyssey*, and slammed explosively into their formation.

The *Odyssey* was already accelerating away, however, and less than twenty seconds from the outer swarm.

"Ships dead ahead!" Winger called out. "They just came out of the shadow of the swarm, Captain! They were waiting for us!"

"Calmly, Lieutenant," Eric said, his face tense.

Michelle took a deep breath. "Sorry, sir."

"Intercept in ten seconds."

"Well," Eric muttered, "at least we know that they're only going to get one shot at us. Lock onto the ships with the HVM banks!"

"Targets locked!"

"Weapons free!" Eric called as they bore down on the small squadron, almost as fast as their HVMs were capable of traveling. *Either our missiles hit them or we do, but no matter what, it's going to be one hell of a show.* "Fire! Rapid-fire, all banks!"

"Fire! Fire! Rapid-fire on all banks!" Waters repeated as the orders went out.

The *Odyssey* trembled as the HVMs erupted from the launchers, racing on ahead of the big ship while alarms began to blare.

"Sound collision!" Eric called, even though he knew that if they hit anything at that relative closing speed, they were all dead. "Seal all blast doors!"

Alarms were drowning out the sound of other alarms. The bridge felt like the center of a tornado as the HVMs slammed into the first element ahead of them. The first three ships were split like rotted fruit by the impact, but the *Odyssey* blew past them before the explosions even began to show.

"Laser bloom!" Winger called, too late to actually warn them, of course, as the *Odyssey* bucked and twisted in space.

The lights dimmed, half their panels dropping offline before backups brought everything back. Lieutenant Daniels was hunched over his controls, swearing in what Eric thought was a language he was unfamiliar with, but the entire scene had taken on a dreamlike quality, and he supposed that he just wasn't hearing right at the time.

"Transition room!" Eric yelled over the alarms. "Stand by for emergency engagement of transition drive! Daniels! Daniels! Plot course for Ranquil!"

The lieutenant didn't even looked up as the *Odyssey* wove through the narrow gap between the plates, somehow avoiding the exploding ships that were currently populating the area. As they blasted clear into the black of deep space, he didn't even want to know what kind of odds they'd just beaten, and the navigator started to calm down enough to hear his captain yelling at him.

"Daniels!" Eric Weston pulled himself out of his command station, staggering over to the helm and put a hand on the young man's shoulder. "Ranquil! Send the coordinates to the transition control room!"

Daniels shook himself, nodding hurriedly. "Yes, sir."

Eric stumbled back to his station as the ship twisted underfoot; he could hear Winger screaming about a laser strike but didn't have time to worry about it. They weren't dead yet, and he really wanted to keep it that way.

"Transition drive!" he called. "Engage!"

PLANET RANQUIL

▶ *CLEAN UP ON this is going to be a bitch. Glad it's not my job.*

Maj. Wilhelm Brinks was looking down at the glassy crater they'd blown in a large section of the outskirts of Mons Systema. Between the damage done by the Drasin and then the strike and follow-up hits by both Earth and Priminae military, he figured it would be a long damned time before anyone was building in that spot again.

The plus side of it all was that they were reasonably sure they had accounted for every last drone sent against the planet. Brinks was just happy that most of them had been intercepted in space or the atmosphere by the orbital defenses and the Archangels. The few that had reached the surface turned into major pains in the ass in short order, with the one landing in Mons Systema being by far the worst.

That had to be intentional.

"Major."

"Lieutenant." He nodded as Savoy stepped up beside him. "Just admiring your handiwork."

"Oh, hell, sir, I just made the hole a bit bigger. The nice glassy sections are from the Primmies' orbital bombardment."

"Quiet," Brinks said dryly before he sighed. "You see the reports?"

Savoy nodded. "Yes, sir. Casualties were pretty stiff."

"Compared to what?" Brinks shrugged fatalistically.

"Point." Savoy nodded. "Still, this was one hell of a firefight."

"No question about that," Brinks agreed. "Looks like even the big-ass mech suit did OK."

"Yeah? I haven't had time to check the telemetry."

"Yeah, Crowley kicked ass in that thing. Rough terrain, too," Brinks said. "I expect that they'll OK the suit for general use."

Savoy snorted. "Captain and the Angels are going to be a little pissed over that, I'll bet."

"I look like a sucker to you?" Brinks snorted. "Anyway, different pool of recruits, to be honest. Hell, I may even get myself tested out on NICS."

"I'll deal with my standard-issue armor, sir."

Brinks expected that Savoy wouldn't be the only person to think that, but he'd been honestly impressed with the way Crowley's unit held up under heavy fire. If it was typical of what they could expect, he figured that they were seeing the future of ground combat. Big enough to pack some serious weapons, but small enough to negotiate pretty tight terrain.

He was about to say more when his comm chimed.

"Brinks, here."

"This is Reed. Figured I'd let you know. Long-range detection just picked up the *Odyssey* heading in-system."

Brinks sighed. "Thank god."

"Yeah, well, it'll be a while before she's in orbit, I'm afraid."

"Why?"

"Ship looks beat to hell, is moving almost point-seven of light, and apparently they're out of fuel," Reed said. "Priminae ships are moving to intercept and tow her in."

"Damn. There's got to be a story there."

"I'll wait for the movie," Reed replied sourly. "I'm up to my ears in training plans and raw recruits. Just figured I'd let you know that the ambassador is looking for you."

"Roger. I'll head back in. See you soon."

▶▶▶

It took several days to get the *Odyssey* parked in Ranquil orbit, and by then, her own crews were swarming over the hull and making repairs. Even to an untrained eye, it was clear at a glance that the big ship had taken one hell of beating in their last encounter with the Drasin, but many of the crew was unprepared for the extent of the damage that greeted them when they reboarded the vessel.

Admiral Tanner of the Priminae Navy was aboard at the captain's invitation, along with the ambassador and a few others, to see just what the *Odyssey* had learned in exchange for the damage she'd taken.

For most of them, the sight of the swarm construct was staggering enough, but the evidence that showed how short a time it had evidently been built in was worse. Even then, however, it was an almost unreal bit of knowledge, and most couldn't really wrap their minds around the reality and what it meant.

The combat records were something else, however, and Eric Weston had spent days poring over the details he hadn't had time to see during the battle itself. Now he had some hard questions for Tanner and the Priminae.

"As you can see, during both torpedo engagements"—Eric pointed to the screens that showed a replay of the events in split screens—"when we fired on the enemy squadron, Drasin cruisers *intentionally* shielded the unknown contacts. Whoever they are, they're calling the shots."

He stared evenly at Tanner for a few seconds. "What bothers me, Admiral, is that these unknown contacts…*match* Priminae combat vessel configurations almost perfectly."

Rael Tanner shifted uncomfortably as everyone turned to stare at him as well.

"In fact, the only thing that marks them as unusual by your standards, Admiral," Eric said, "is that their ships are composed of metallic alloys, while you use ceramic. Other than that, it looks like they copped your design. I don't suppose you have any ideas about that?"

Tanner slowly shook his head. "No. I do not."

"Yeah. Somehow I figured you'd say that," Eric said before he walked across the room and took a seat.

"What are your opinions, Captain?" Ambassador LaFontaine asked, her face a neutral mask.

Eric was silent for a moment; then he finally shrugged. "Someone out here is playing a dangerous game. I don't know if they're Priminae or not, but it's pretty clear that they know the Priminae playbook forward and backward. These ships have me worried, Ambassador, simply because I can't imagine any reason for them to build them from a strategic or tactical point of view. They can't pretend to be a Priminae ship— they're made of metal, a blind sensor tech could spot it. So I have to conclude that this is one of their standard designs."

LaFontaine nodded solemnly, then looked over at Tanner. "Admiral, where did you get the designs for your combat ships?"

"From the archives maintained by Central."

Of all the people in the room, only the ambassador noticed the sudden tension evident in the captain's face and body. She eyed him for a moment as he made a visible effort to relax, then turned back to the admiral.

"Do any other worlds have access to those designs or archives?"

"All the central worlds, several outlying colonies," Tanner admitted after some thought. "The archives are not...How is it you explained it, Captain? Classified?"

"You don't classify military ship designs?"

"Who could build them?" Tanner shrugged.

"Who could tame the Drasin?" Eric countered, a little harshly. "Two very big questions that have the same answer, I suspect."

"This is getting us nowhere, Captain," LaFontaine cut in. "For now, the mission is unchanged. When the *Odyssey* is repaired, I want you to head home and report to the NAC what you've learned."

Eric nodded. "Yes, ma'am."

"In the meantime, Colonel Reed and myself will continue with our missions here on Ranquil," she said. "But, Admiral, I do suggest that you investigate just where your enemy got those designs. The captain is right, the answer to that question may well be the most important piece of information you and your world ever uncover."

Tanner nodded slightly, but didn't comment.

Eric rose again. "I'll escort you both back to the planet."

"That won't be necessary, Captain."

"Please, Ambassador. It'll be days before the *Odyssey* is spaceworthy...I need something to do," he said with a wooden smile.

LaFontaine eyed him for a long moment, wondering just what the man was up to. She knew it was something, but didn't know what. Finally, however, she elected to merely nod.

"Thank you, then, Captain."

"Yes," Tanner said as he, too, got up. "I thank you for the information you have brought us. We will do as you suggest and try to devise the most we can from it."

Eric nodded. "Of course."

He escorted them out of the room, smiling and chatting. When they had their escorts, Weston promised to join them shortly and returned to the briefing room and looked around at his officers, the Ambassador, and others still sitting there.

"I assume that you have something else, Captain?" LaFontaine asked calmly.

He gestured to the screens on the far wall, "During the last bolt from the Dyson construct the enemy ships were splashing active scans all over the system."

"That was in the report, yes."

"What we left out, to this point," Eric said, "Is what we picked up from the scans on our own systems. We couldn't decode it while engaged, but since we transitioned out people have been poring over that data. We think we know why they built the construct in the first place, Ambassador. The Drasin drones have shown to be pretty good replicators, but they're flawed."

Everyone nodded, having read the reports based on the *Odyssey's* own examination of the long-term systems destroyed by Drasin invasion. There was an indisputable generational flaw in the drone replication, one that led them to become nearly immobile and have an extremely short lifespan. Basically, after a few generations of replicating, all they could do was eat and replicate. That hardly made them any less dangerous, unfortunately, since by that time there was nothing left to fight them on an infected world.

"We haven't seen whether the ships can replicate themselves," Eric said, nodding to the screens, "But I think we know now that they don't rely on that, not if these scans are accurate."

On the screen they saw a close up of one of the Dyson plates as the *Odyssey* passed, and inside the computer enhancement they could see the profiles of dozens, if not hundreds or thousands, of the distinctive Drasin ship profile.

"It's not a habitat," Eric said, "The construct is a shipyard."

"Oh lord," LaFontaine whispered. "There are so many."

"Yeah, and that begs another question, Ambassador..." Roberts spoke up. "If they have that many ships available... why haven't we seen them *here* yet?"

A long silence made it clear that no one in the room had a good, or any, answer to that.

Eric sighed, "We've found some answers, but all those gave us was more questions. We have a lot to do now that we know exactly what has just moved into our neighborhood. This could be the most important information we can possibly bring home. The Drasin are nothing short of a plague, and whoever is holding their leash is completely insane. We can't let them run around loose, not if we can do anything about it."

"But can we do anything?" LaFontaine asked.

"All I know for certain is that we can't do nothing," Eric said. "That'll kill us dead, guaranteed."

"What do you intend now?" she asked, curious.

"For now?" Eric shrugged. "For now, I'm going to catch up with our guests. I have business on the planet."

He dismissed his officers and excused himself from the room, looking normal and as unconcerned as possible but inwardly, Eric Weston was really only focused on one thing. He kept seeing those new ships, their profiles so very close to the Priminae ship that even now orbited Raquil just below the *Odyssey*.

Central, you and I need to have another long chat.

ABOUT THE AUTHOR

Evan has been writing most of his life in one format or another, and though his postsecondary education is in computer sciences and he has worked in the local lobster industry steadily over the last decade, writing has always been his true passion. In his own words, "It's what I do for fun and to relax. There's not much I can imagine better than being a storyteller."